COBRA COMMAND

G.I. JOE

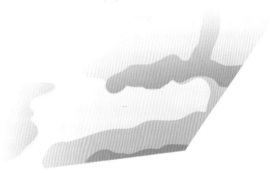

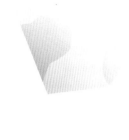

Written by **Chuck Dixon** and **Mike Costa** (Cobra #10-11)

Art by **Alex Cal** and **Beni Lobel**

Colors by **J. Brown**

Lettering by **Neil Uyetake** and **Robbie Robbins**

Series Edits by **John Barber** and **Carlos Guzman**

Cover by **Dave Wilkins**

Collection Edits by **Justin Eisinger** and **Alonzo Simon**

Collection Design by **Neil Uyetake**

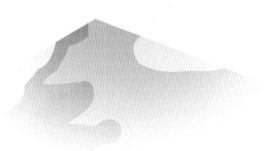

Special thanks to Hasbro's Aaron Archer, Andy Schmidt, Derryl DePriest, Joe Del Regno, Ed Lane, Joe Furfaro, Jos Huxley, and Michael Kelly for their invaluable assistance.

IDW founded by Ted Adams, Alex Garner, Kris Oprisko, and Robbie Robbins | International Rights Representative, Christine Meyer: christine@gfloystudio.com

ISBN: 978-1-61377-278-2

15 14 13 12 1 2 3 4

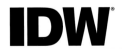

Licensed By: Hasbro

Ted Adams, CEO & Publisher
Greg Goldstein, President & COO
Robbie Robbins, EVP/Sr. Graphic Artist
Chris Ryall, Chief Creative Officer/Editor-in-Chief
Matthew Ruzicka, CPA, Chief Financial Officer
Alan Payne, VP of Sales

Become our fan on Facebook **facebook.com/idwpublishing**
Follow us on Twitter **@idwpublishing**
Check us out on YouTube **youtube.com/idwpublishing**
www.IDWPUBLISHING.com

Originally published as G.I. JOE SEASON 2 #11, SNAKE EYES Issues #10–11, and G.I. COBRA: VOL. 2 Issues #10–11.

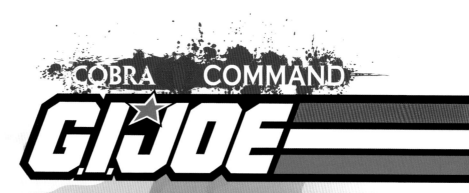

COBRA COMMAND
G.I. JOE

The new Cobra Commander has made his first move—all-out invasion of the Southeast Asian nation of Nanzhao, a center of the worldwide drug trade. As the world's eyes turn toward the attack, G.I. JOE moves in to try and stop the invasion and they soon realize Cobra's goals aren't occupation—but annihilation!

Cobra lays waste to Nanzhao's opium fields, as well as to the U.N. troops directing the civilian evacuation. While the rest of G.I. JOE tries to make sense of these tactics—and save what lives they can—Snake Eyes, Iceberg, and Helix infiltrate deeper into the country. But their presence has not gone unnoticed...

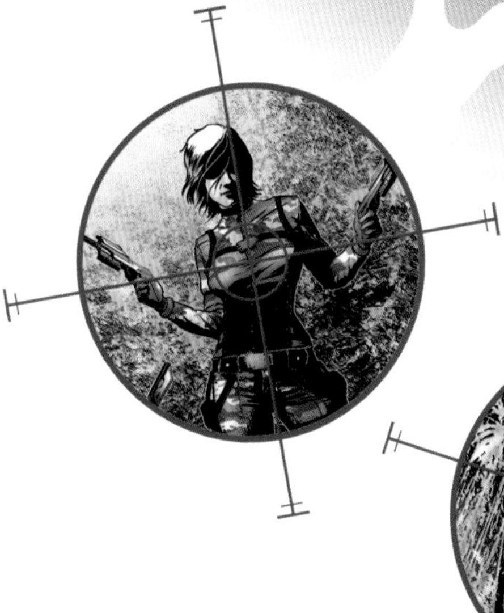

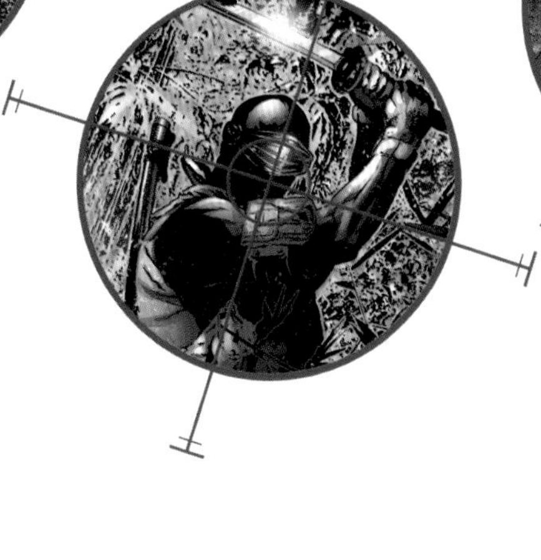

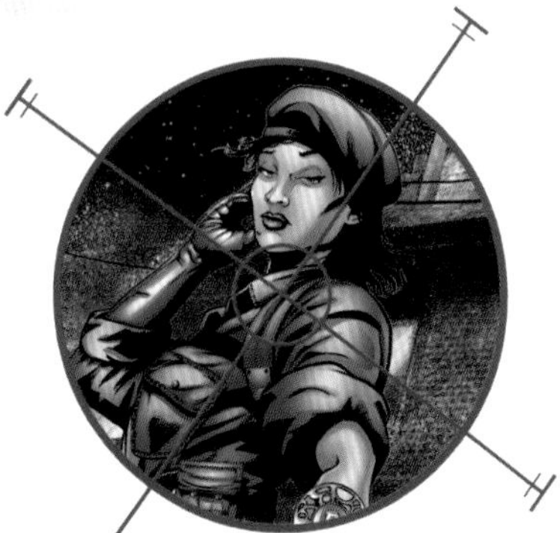

SNAKE EYES #10A by **Dave Wilkins**

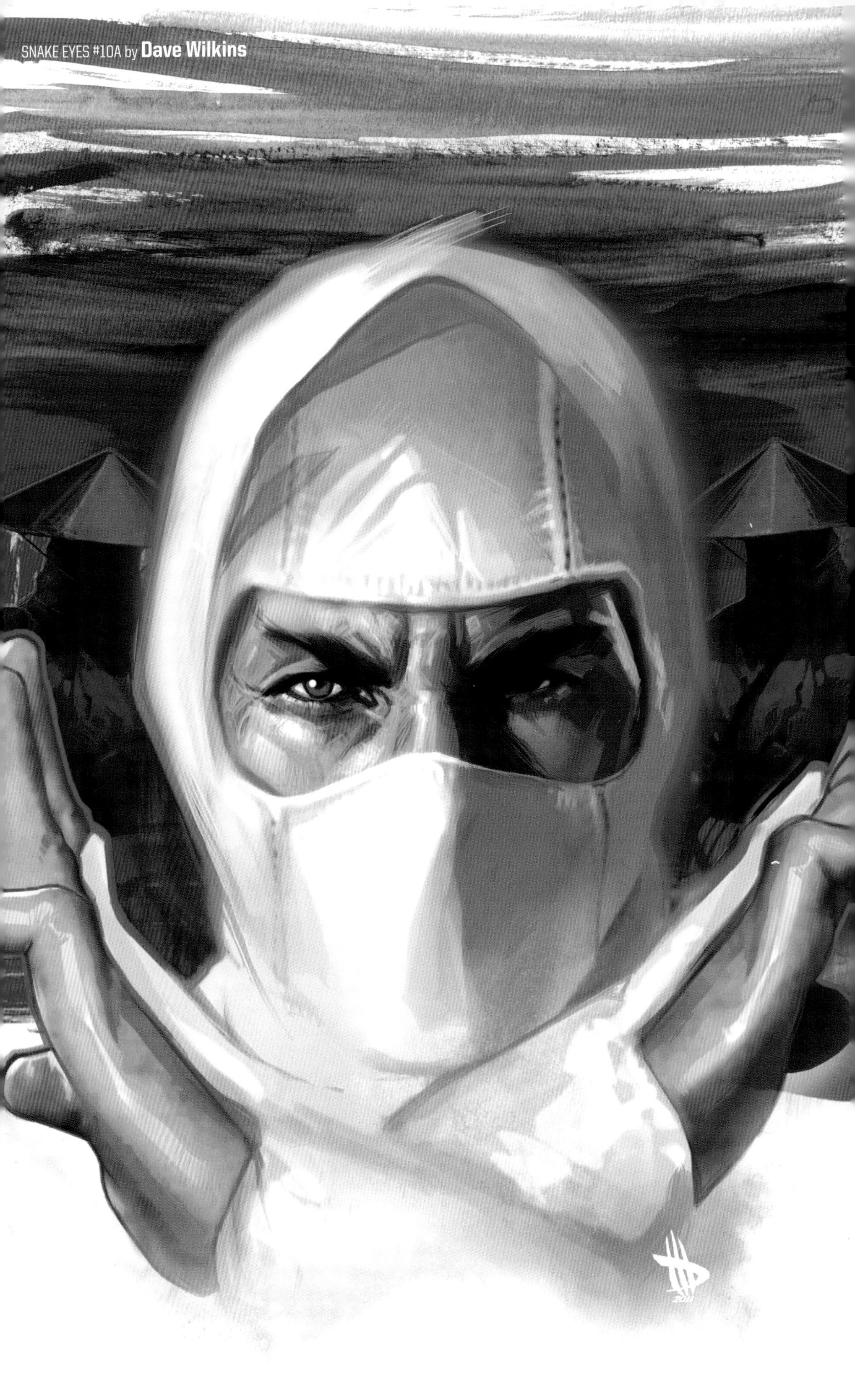

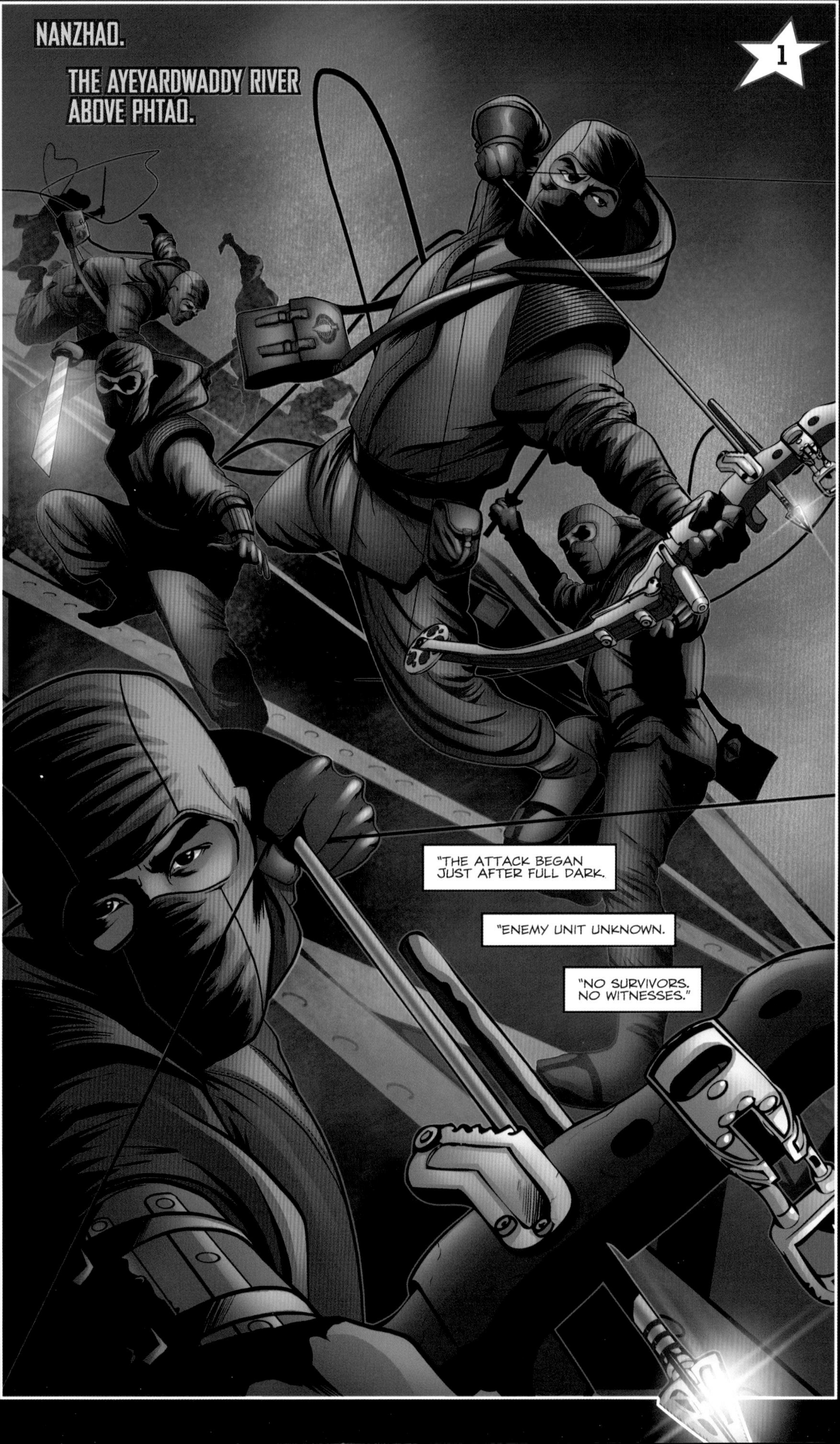
NANZHAO.
THE AYEYARDWADDY RIVER ABOVE PHTAO.
1
"THE ATTACK BEGAN JUST AFTER FULL DARK.
"ENEMY UNIT UNKNOWN.
"NO SURVIVORS. NO WITNESSES."

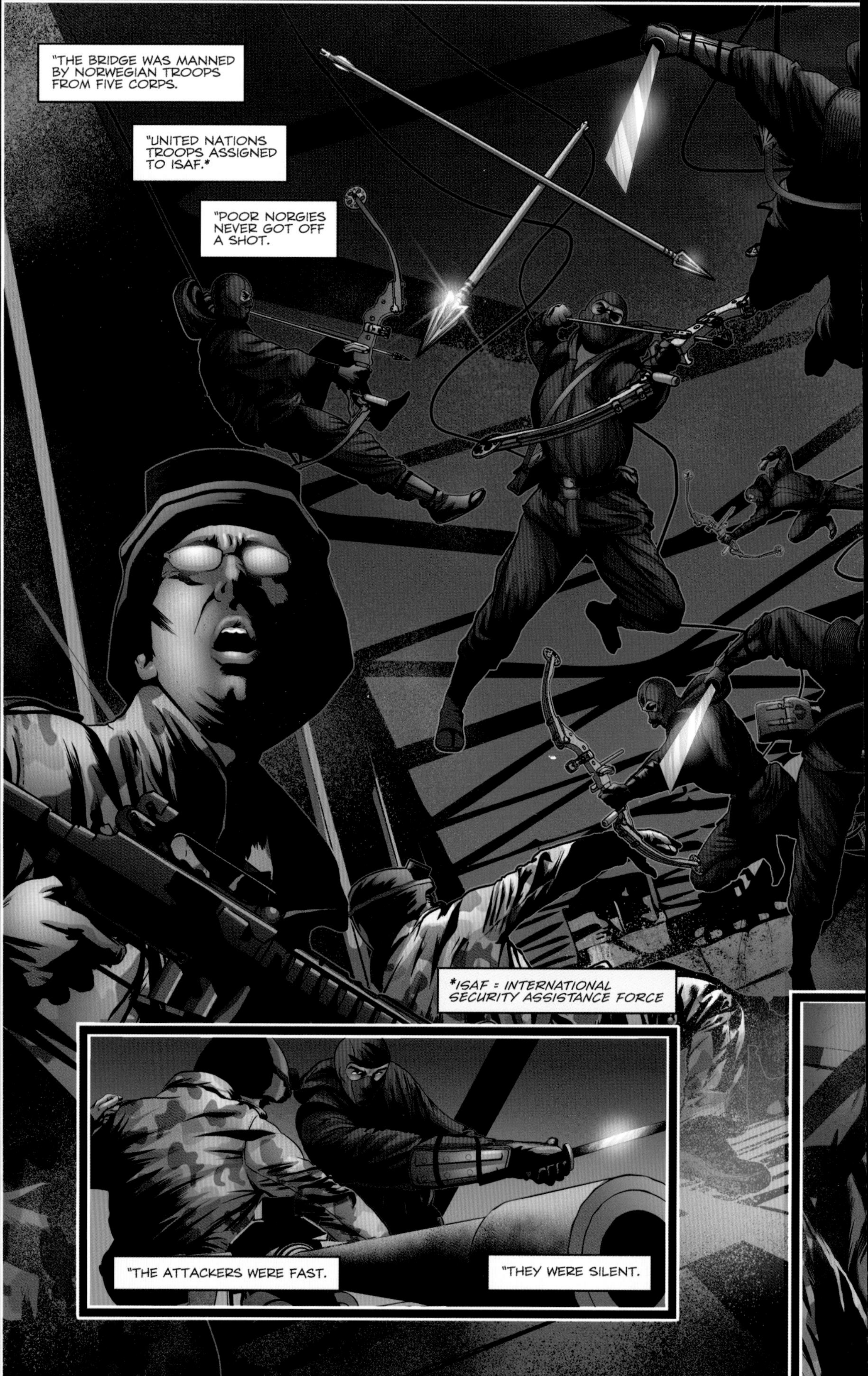
"THE BRIDGE WAS MANNED BY NORWEGIAN TROOPS FROM FIVE CORPS.
"UNITED NATIONS TROOPS ASSIGNED TO ISAF.*
"POOR NORGIES NEVER GOT OFF A SHOT.
*ISAF = INTERNATIONAL SECURITY ASSISTANCE FORCE
"THE ATTACKERS WERE FAST.
"THEY WERE SILENT.

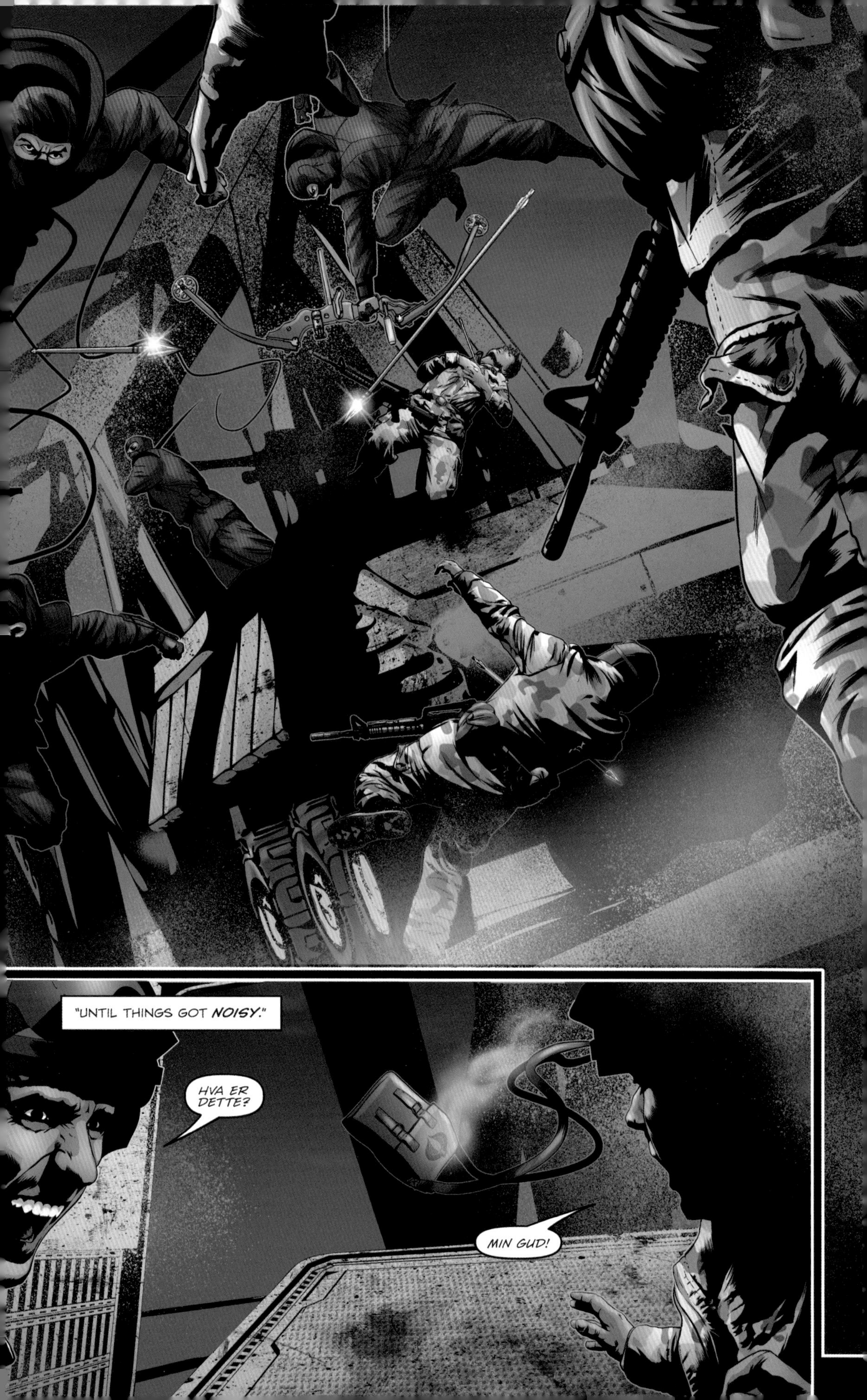
"UNTIL THINGS GOT NOISY."
HVA ER DETTE?
MIN GUD!

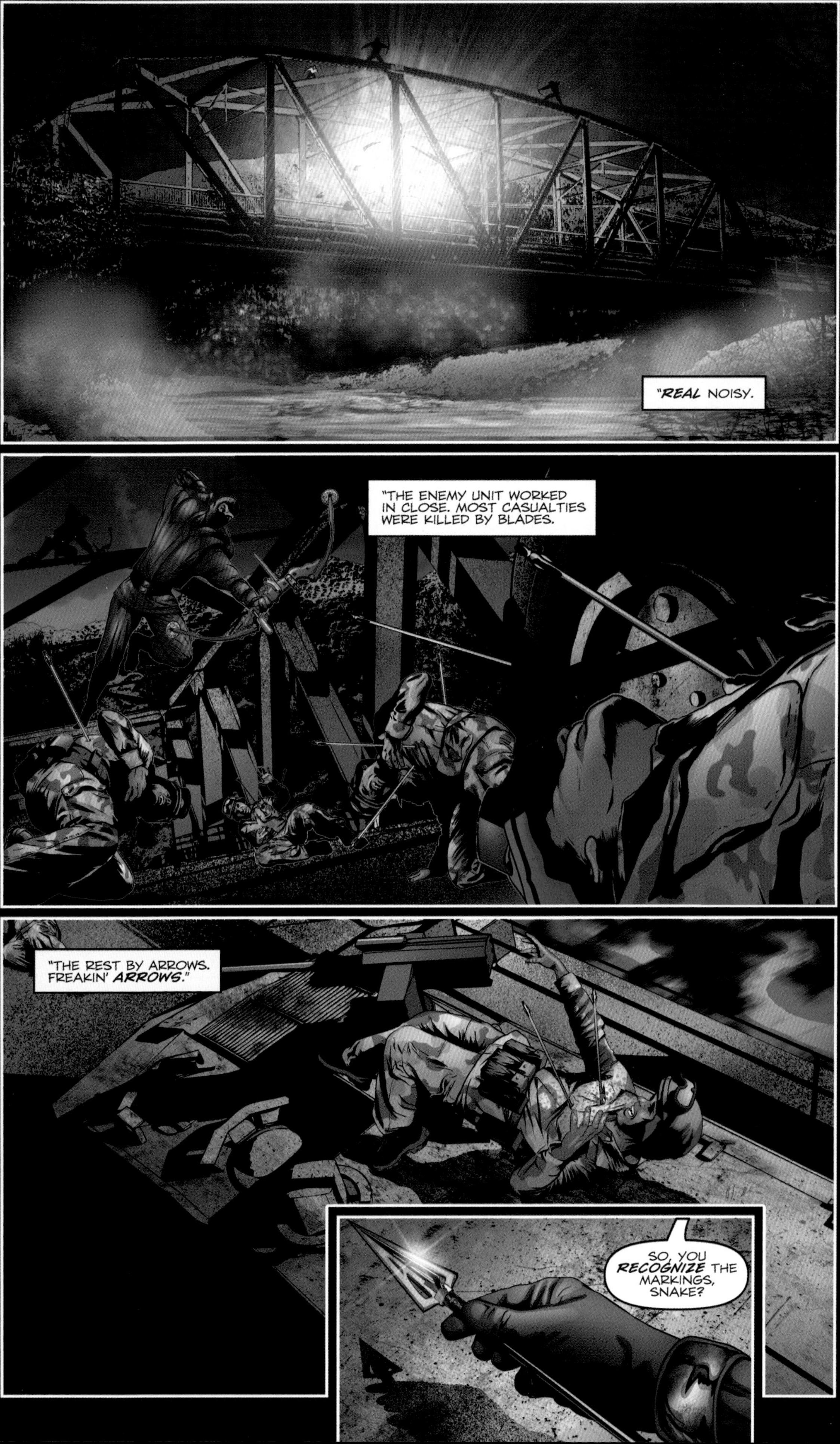
"REAL NOISY.
"THE ENEMY UNIT WORKED IN CLOSE. MOST CASUALTIES WERE KILLED BY BLADES.
"THE REST BY ARROWS. FREAKIN' ARROWS."
SO, YOU RECOGNIZE THE MARKINGS, SNAKE?

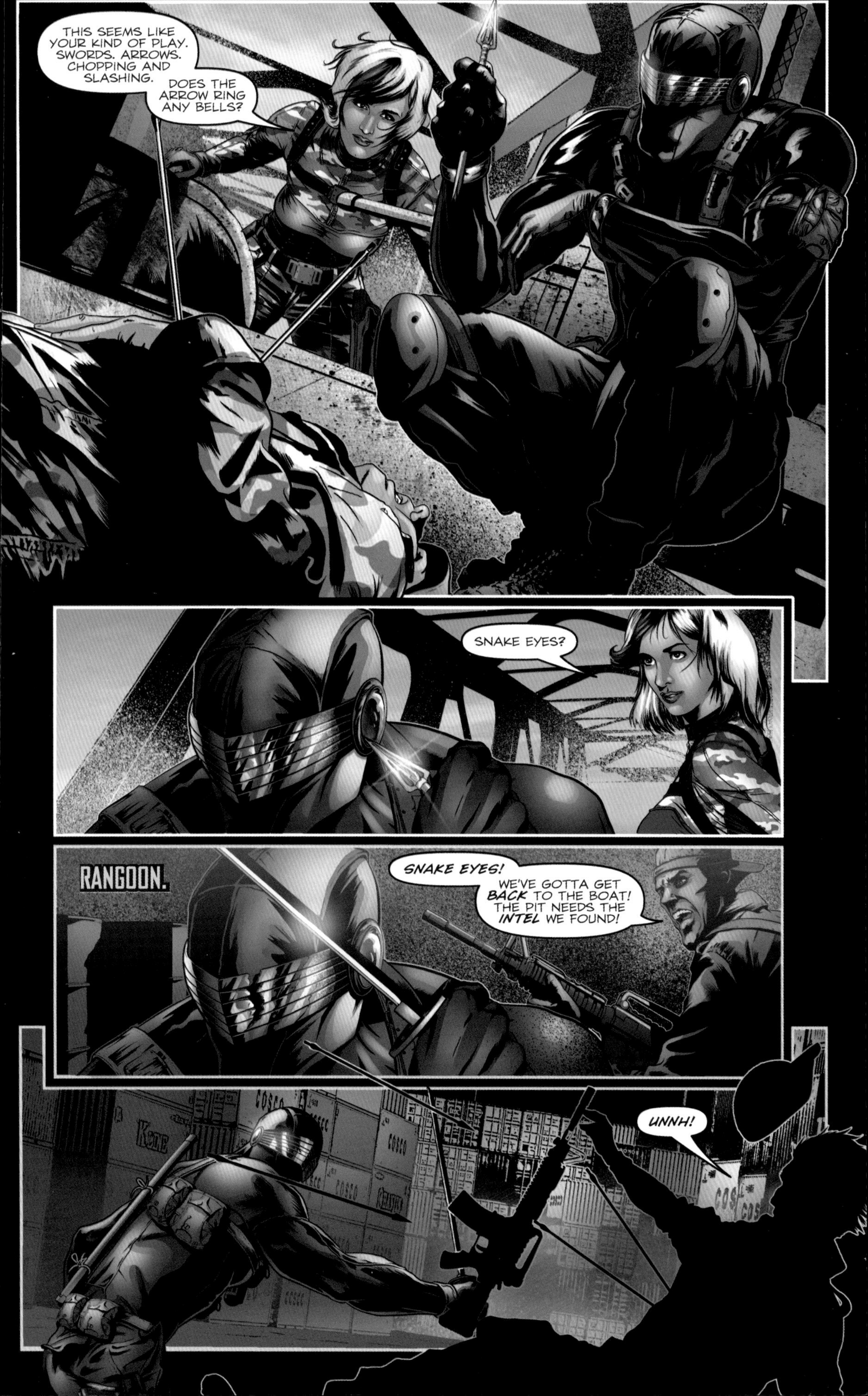
THIS SEEMS LIKE YOUR KIND OF PLAY. SWORDS. ARROWS. CHOPPING AND SLASHING.
DOES THE ARROW RING ANY BELLS?
SNAKE EYES?
RANGOON.
SNAKE EYES!
WE'VE GOTTA GET BACK TO THE BOAT! THE PIT NEEDS THE INTEL WE FOUND!
UNNH!

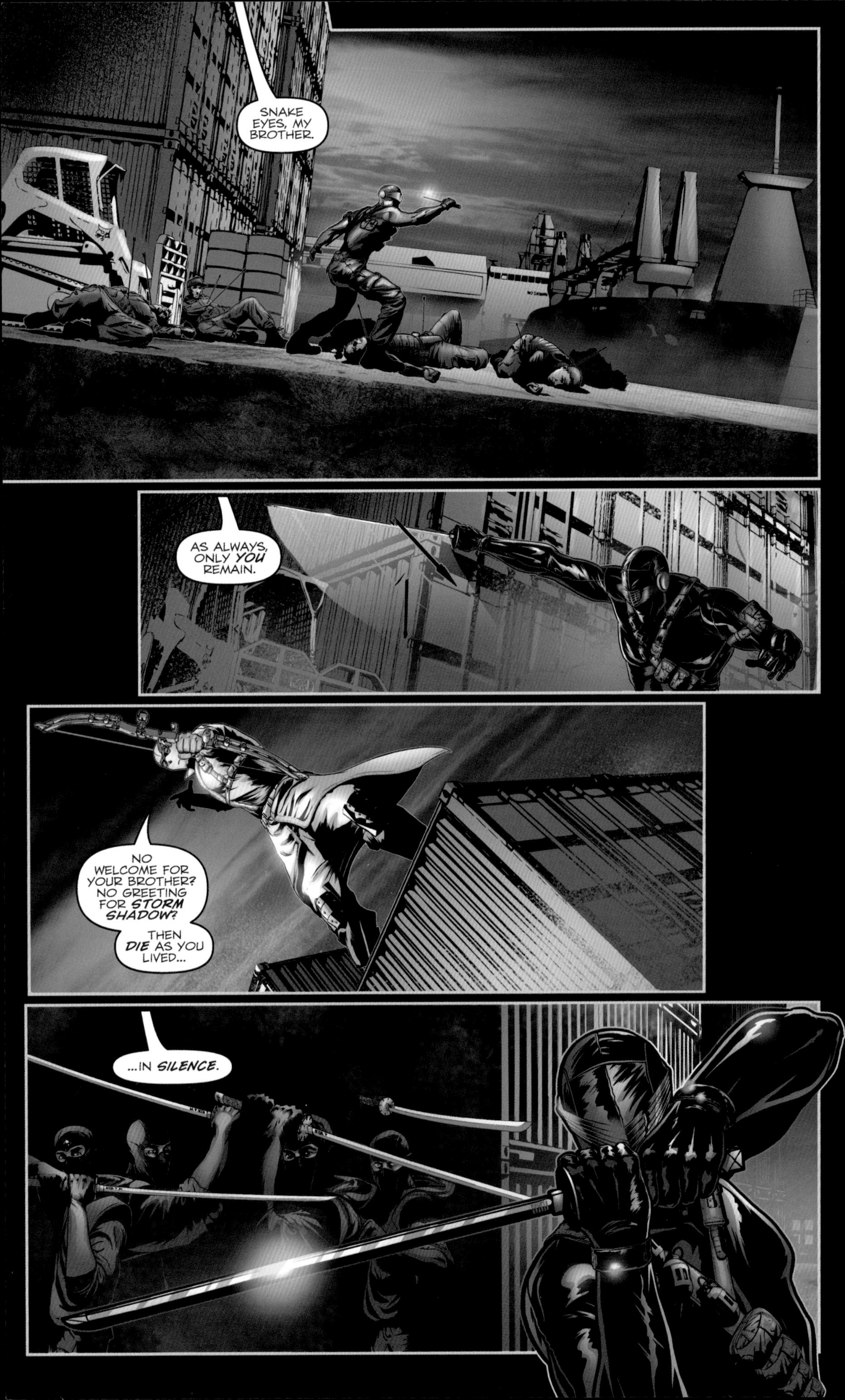
SNAKE EYES, MY BROTHER.
AS ALWAYS, ONLY YOU REMAIN.
NO WELCOME FOR YOUR BROTHER? NO GREETING FOR STORM SHADOW?
THEN DIE AS YOU LIVED...
...IN SILENCE.

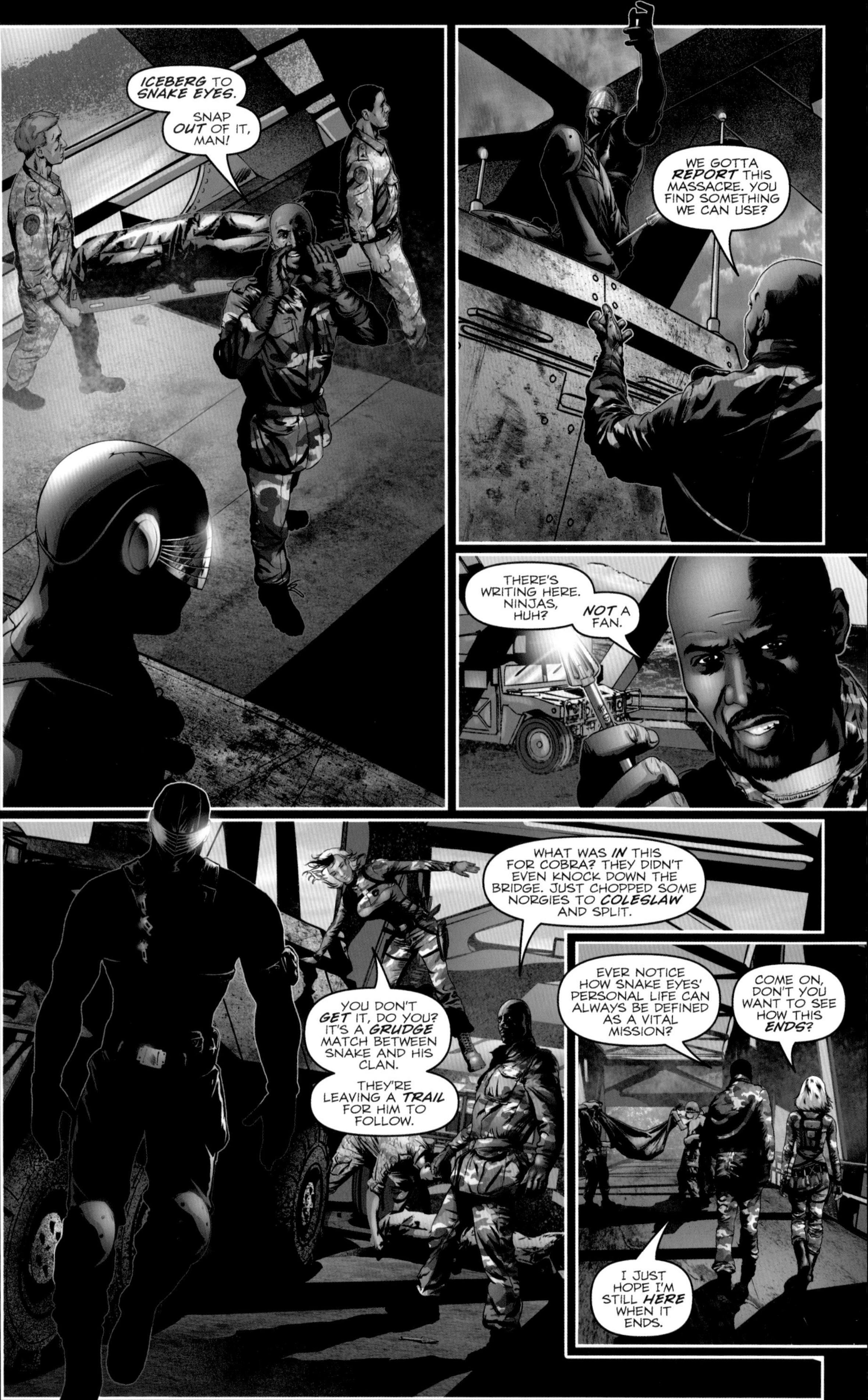
ICEBERG TO SNAKE EYES.
SNAP OUT OF IT, MAN!
WE GOTTA REPORT THIS MASSACRE. YOU FIND SOMETHING WE CAN USE?
THERE'S WRITING HERE. NINJAS, HUH?
NOT A FAN.
WHAT WAS IN THIS FOR COBRA? THEY DIDN'T EVEN KNOCK DOWN THE BRIDGE. JUST CHOPPED SOME NORGIES TO COLESLAW AND SPLIT.
YOU DON'T GET IT, DO YOU? IT'S A GRUDGE MATCH BETWEEN SNAKE AND HIS CLAN.
THEY'RE LEAVING A TRAIL FOR HIM TO FOLLOW.
EVER NOTICE HOW SNAKE EYES' PERSONAL LIFE CAN ALWAYS BE DEFINED AS A VITAL MISSION?
COME ON, DON'T YOU WANT TO SEE HOW THIS ENDS?
I JUST HOPE I'M STILL HERE WHEN IT ENDS.

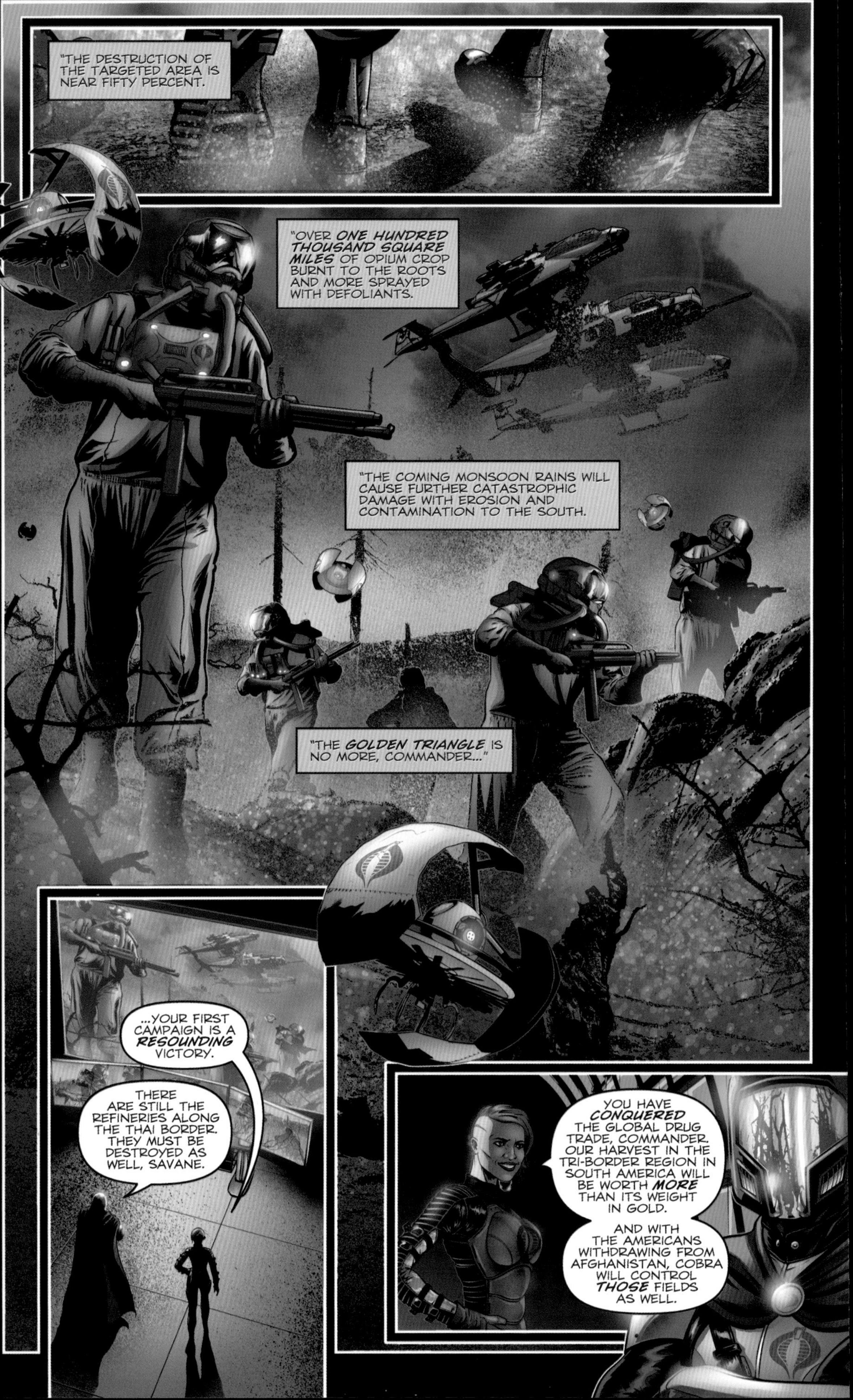
"THE DESTRUCTION OF THE TARGETED AREA IS NEAR FIFTY PERCENT.
"OVER ONE HUNDRED THOUSAND SQUARE MILES OF OPIUM CROP BURNT TO THE ROOTS AND MORE SPRAYED WITH DEFOLIANTS.
"THE COMING MONSOON RAINS WILL CAUSE FURTHER CATASTROPHIC DAMAGE WITH EROSION AND CONTAMINATION TO THE SOUTH.
"THE GOLDEN TRIANGLE IS NO MORE, COMMANDER..."
...YOUR FIRST CAMPAIGN IS A RESOUNDING VICTORY.
THERE ARE STILL THE REFINERIES ALONG THE THAI BORDER. THEY MUST BE DESTROYED AS WELL, SAVANE.
YOU HAVE CONQUERED THE GLOBAL DRUG TRADE, COMMANDER. OUR HARVEST IN THE TRI-BORDER REGION IN SOUTH AMERICA WILL BE WORTH MORE THAN ITS WEIGHT IN GOLD.
AND WITH THE AMERICANS WITHDRAWING FROM AFGHANISTAN, COBRA WILL CONTROL THOSE FIELDS AS WELL.

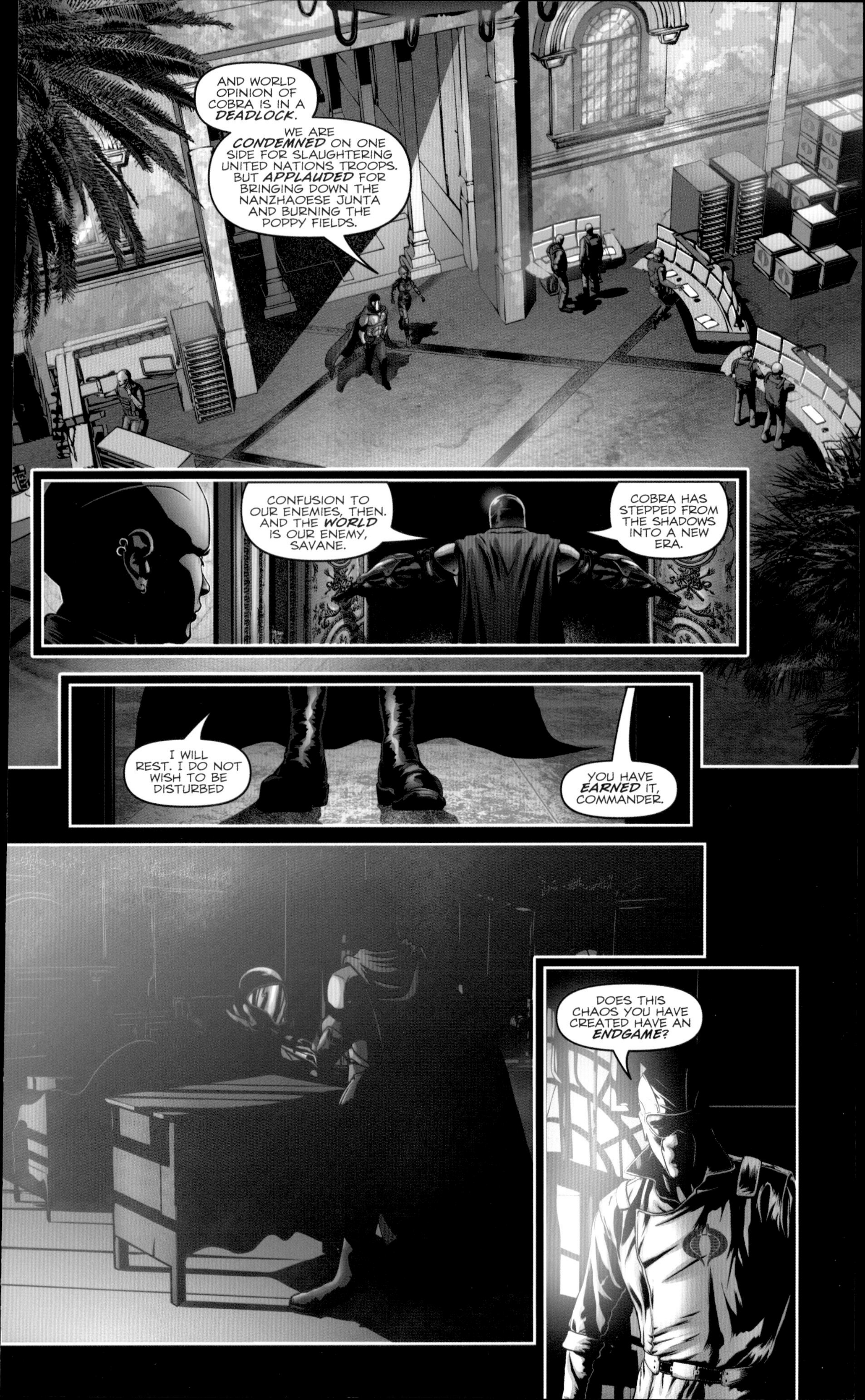
AND WORLD OPINION OF COBRA IS IN A DEADLOCK.
WE ARE CONDEMNED ON ONE SIDE FOR SLAUGHTERING UNITED NATIONS TROOPS. BUT APPLAUDED FOR BRINGING DOWN THE NANZHAOESE JUNTA AND BURNING THE POPPY FIELDS.
CONFUSION TO OUR ENEMIES, THEN. AND THE WORLD IS OUR ENEMY, SAVANE.
COBRA HAS STEPPED FROM THE SHADOWS INTO A NEW ERA.
I WILL REST. I DO NOT WISH TO BE DISTURBED
YOU HAVE EARNED IT, COMMANDER.
DOES THIS CHAOS YOU HAVE CREATED HAVE AN ENDGAME?

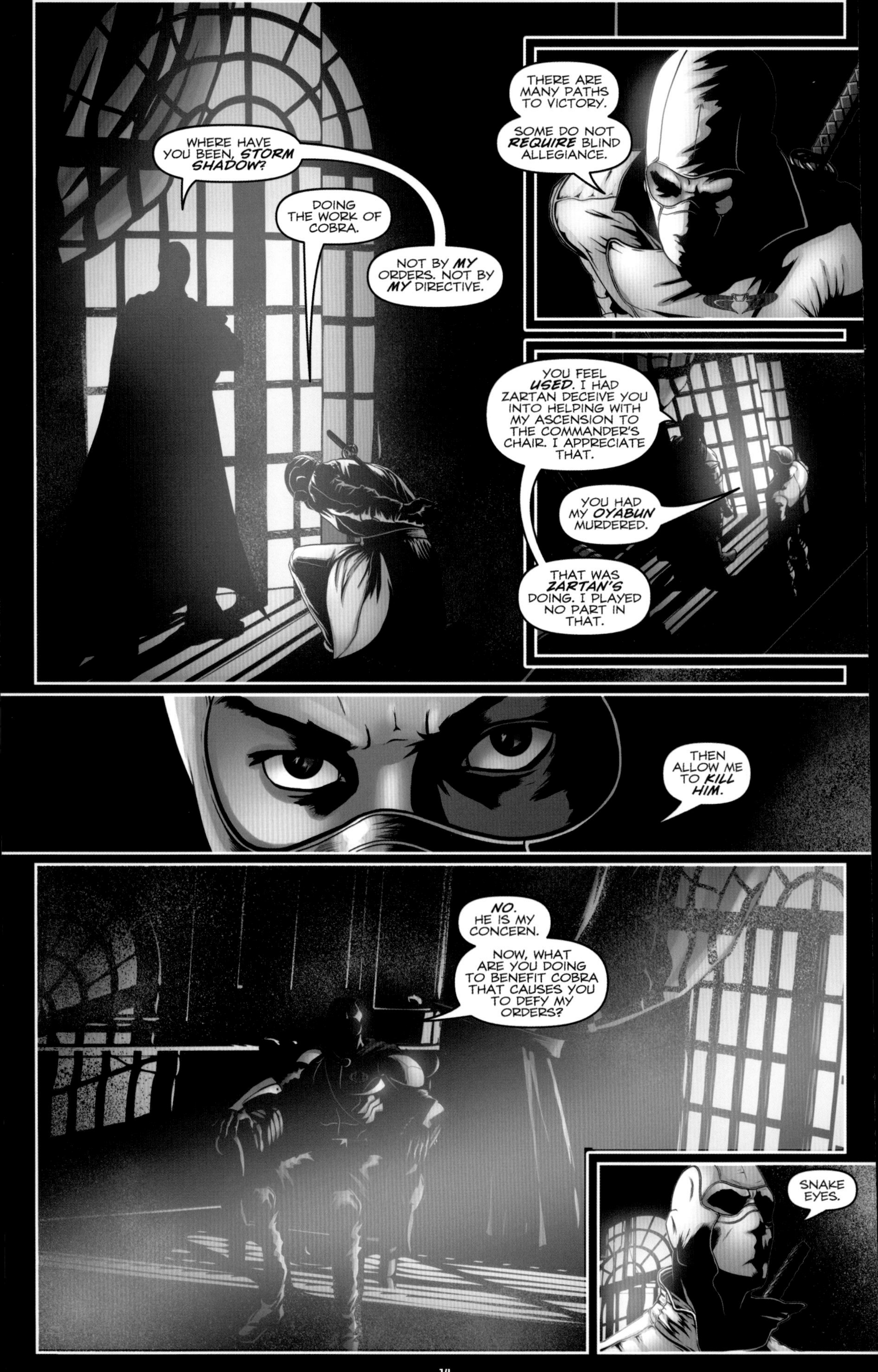
WHERE HAVE YOU BEEN, STORM SHADOW?
DOING THE WORK OF COBRA.
NOT BY MY ORDERS. NOT BY MY DIRECTIVE.
THERE ARE MANY PATHS TO VICTORY.
SOME DO NOT REQUIRE BLIND ALLEGIANCE.
YOU FEEL USED. I HAD ZARTAN DECEIVE YOU INTO HELPING WITH MY ASCENSION TO THE COMMANDER'S CHAIR. I APPRECIATE THAT.
YOU HAD MY OYABUN MURDERED.
THAT WAS ZARTAN'S DOING. I PLAYED NO PART IN THAT.
THEN ALLOW ME TO KILL HIM.
NO. HE IS MY CONCERN.
NOW, WHAT ARE YOU DOING TO BENEFIT COBRA THAT CAUSES YOU TO DEFY MY ORDERS?
SNAKE EYES.

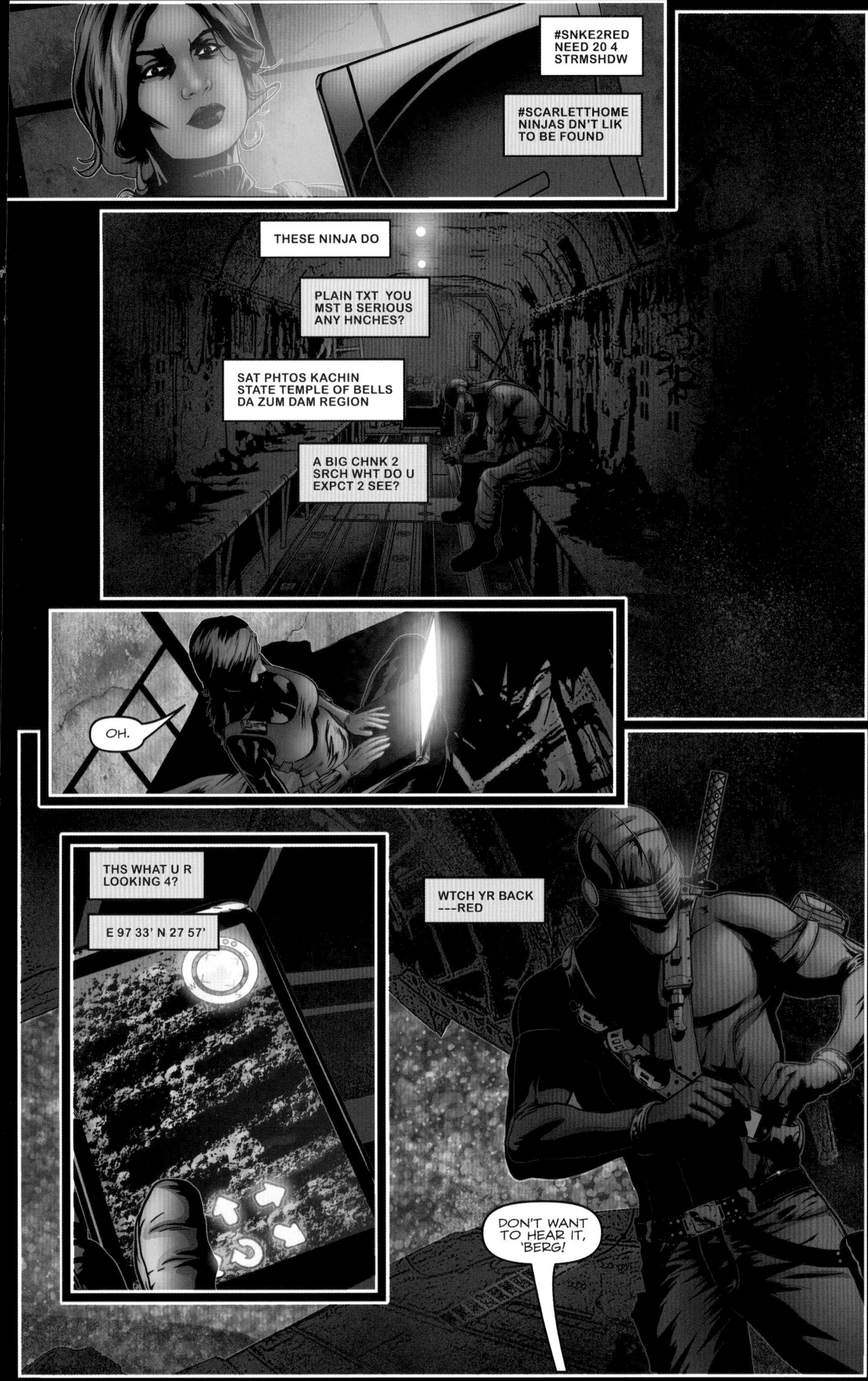
#SNKE2RED
NEED 20 4
STRMSHDW
#SCARLETTHOME
NINJAS DN'T LIK
TO BE FOUND
THESE NINJA DO
PLAIN TXT YOU
MST B SERIOUS
ANY HNCHES?
SAT PHTOS KACHIN
STATE TEMPLE OF BELLS
DA ZUM DAM REGION
A BIG CHNK 2
SRCH WHT DO U
EXPCT 2 SEE?
OH.
THS WHAT U R
LOOKING 4?
E 97 33' N 27 57'
WTCH YR BACK
---RED
DON'T WANT
TO HEAR IT,
'BERG!

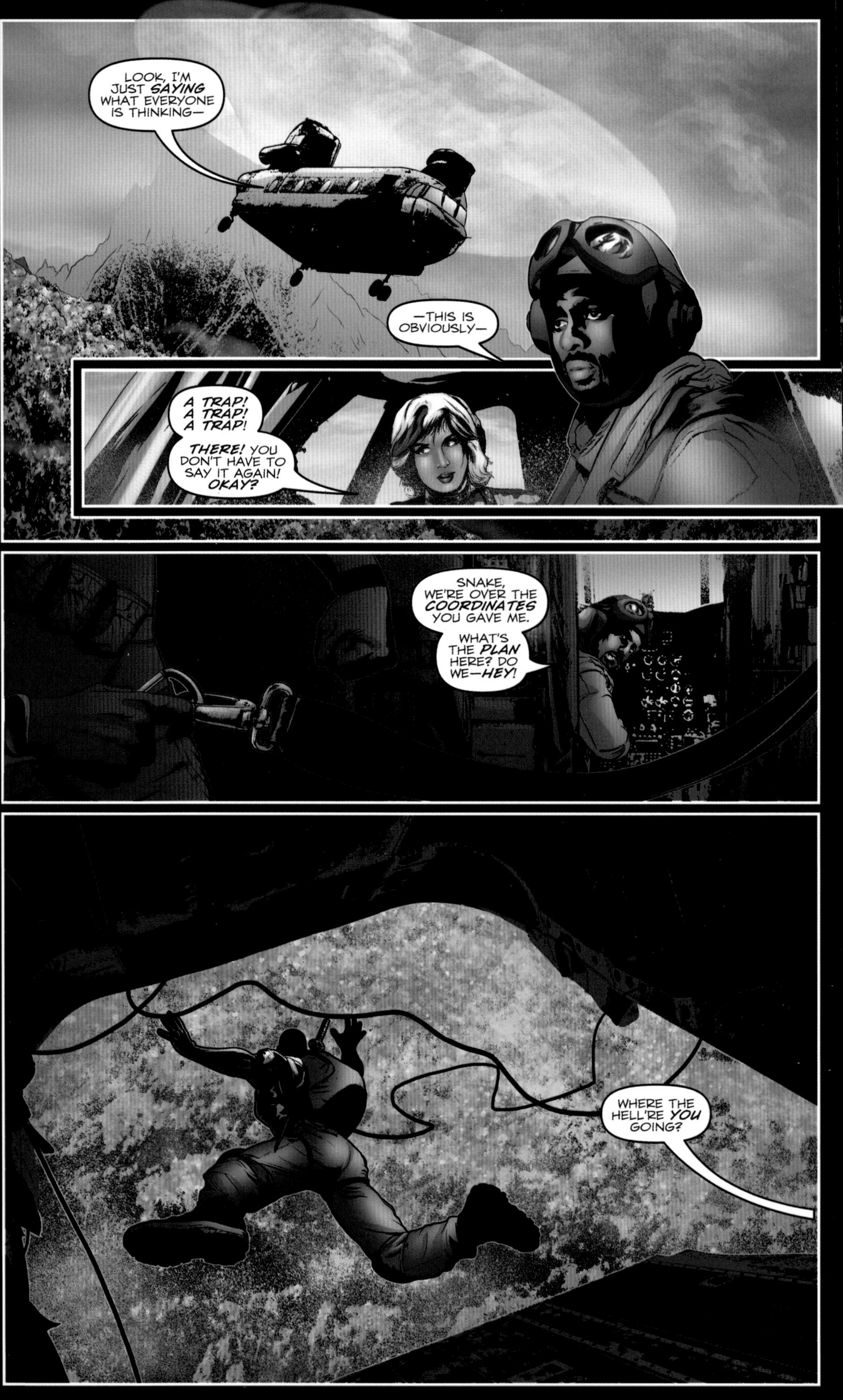
LOOK, I'M JUST SAYING WHAT EVERYONE IS THINKING—
—THIS IS OBVIOUSLY—
A TRAP! A TRAP! A TRAP!
THERE! YOU DON'T HAVE TO SAY IT AGAIN! OKAY?
SNAKE, WE'RE OVER THE COORDINATES YOU GAVE ME.
WHAT'S THE PLAN HERE? DO WE—HEY!
WHERE THE HELL'RE YOU GOING?

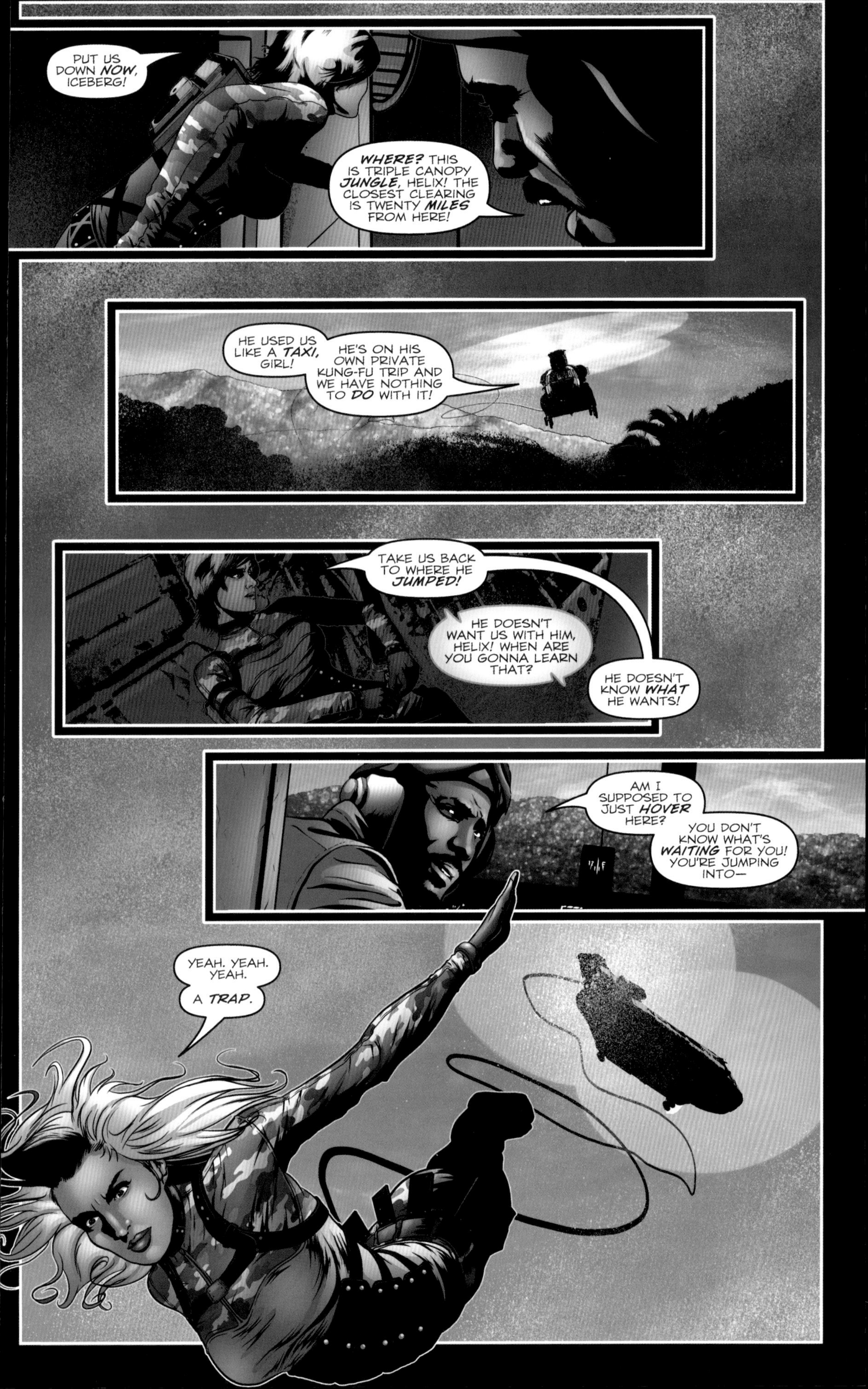

PUT US DOWN *NOW*, ICEBERG!
WHERE? THIS IS TRIPLE CANOPY *JUNGLE*, HELIX! THE CLOSEST CLEARING IS TWENTY *MILES* FROM HERE!
HE USED US LIKE A *TAXI*, GIRL!
HE'S ON HIS OWN PRIVATE KUNG-FU TRIP AND WE HAVE NOTHING TO *DO* WITH IT!
TAKE US BACK TO WHERE HE *JUMPED!*
HE DOESN'T WANT US WITH HIM, HELIX! WHEN ARE YOU GONNA LEARN THAT?
HE DOESN'T KNOW *WHAT* HE WANTS!
AM I SUPPOSED TO JUST *HOVER* HERE?
YOU DON'T KNOW WHAT'S *WAITING* FOR YOU! YOU'RE JUMPING INTO—
YEAH. YEAH. YEAH.
A *TRAP*.

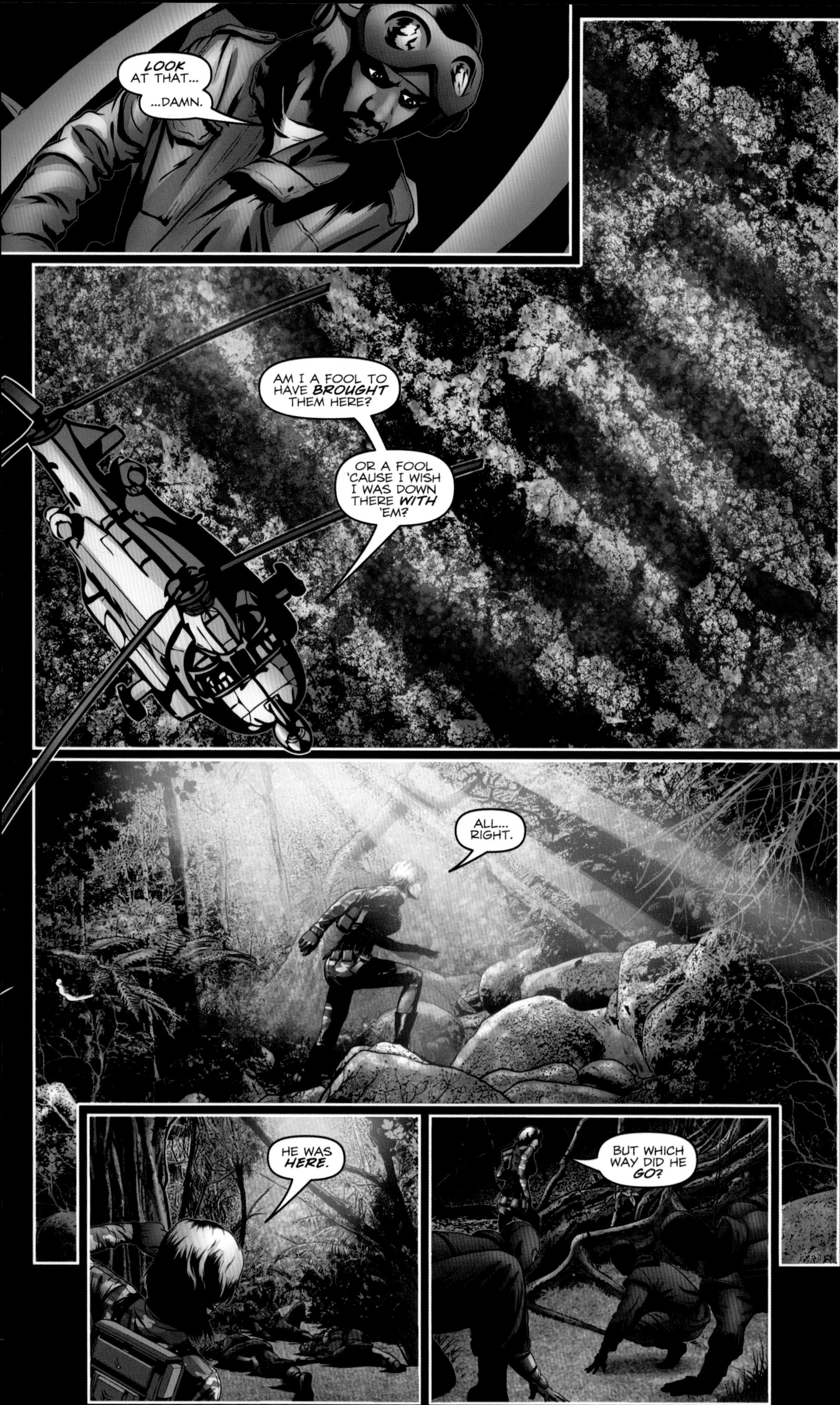
LOOK AT THAT...
...DAMN.
AM I A FOOL TO HAVE BROUGHT THEM HERE?
OR A FOOL 'CAUSE I WISH I WAS DOWN THERE WITH 'EM?
ALL... RIGHT.
HE WAS HERE.
BUT WHICH WAY DID HE GO?

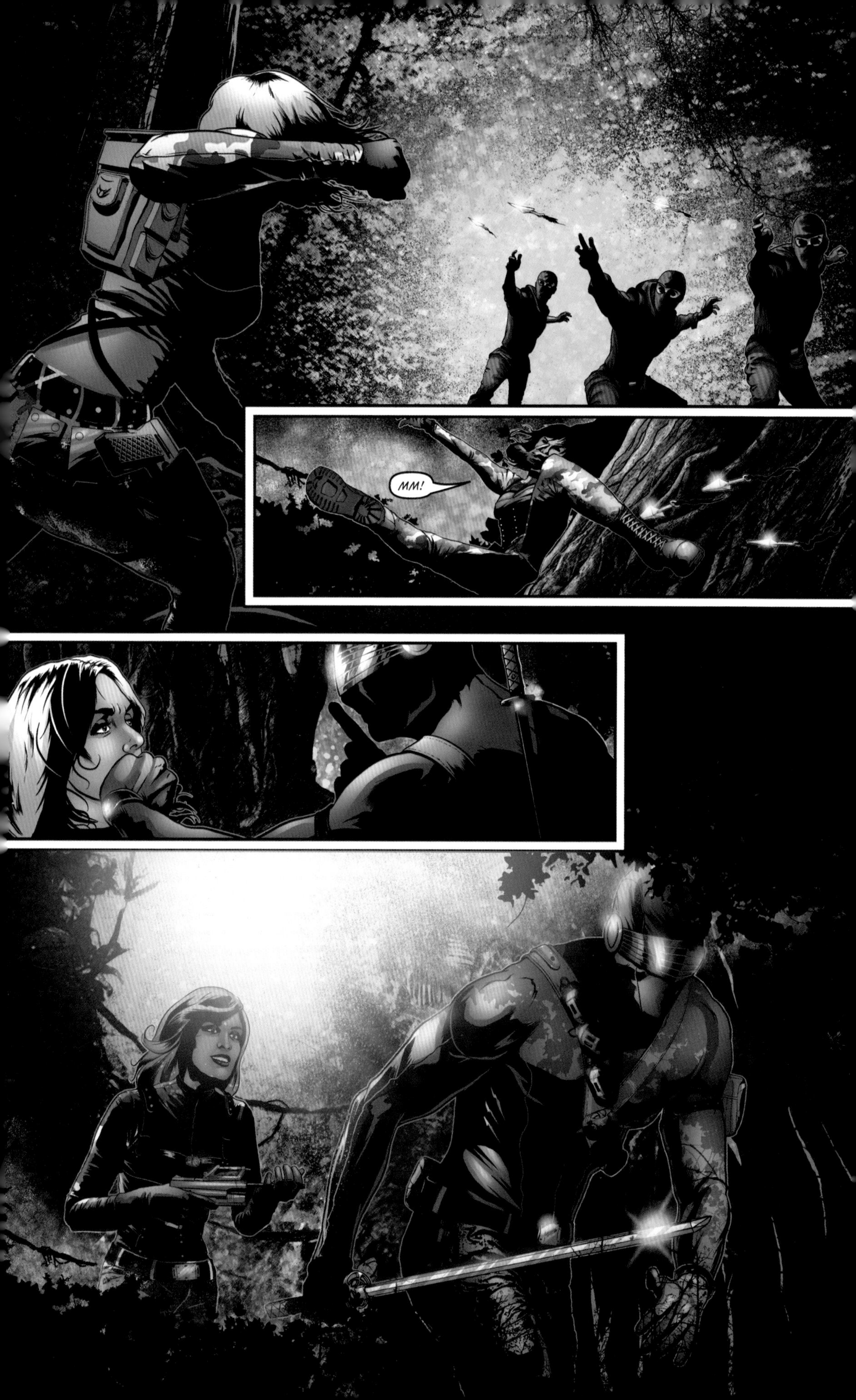
MM!

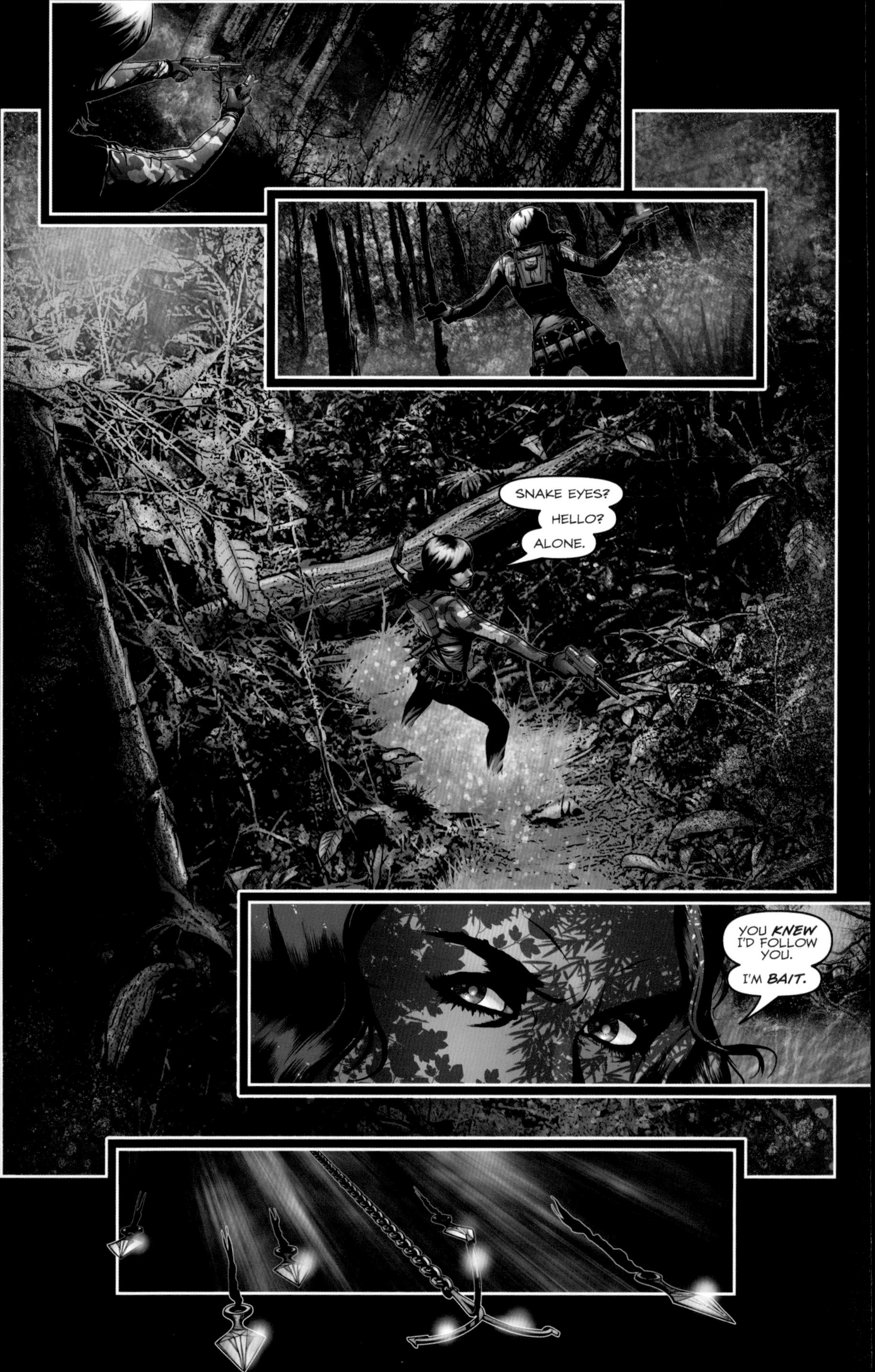
SNAKE EYES?
HELLO?
ALONE.
YOU KNEW I'D FOLLOW YOU.
I'M BAIT.

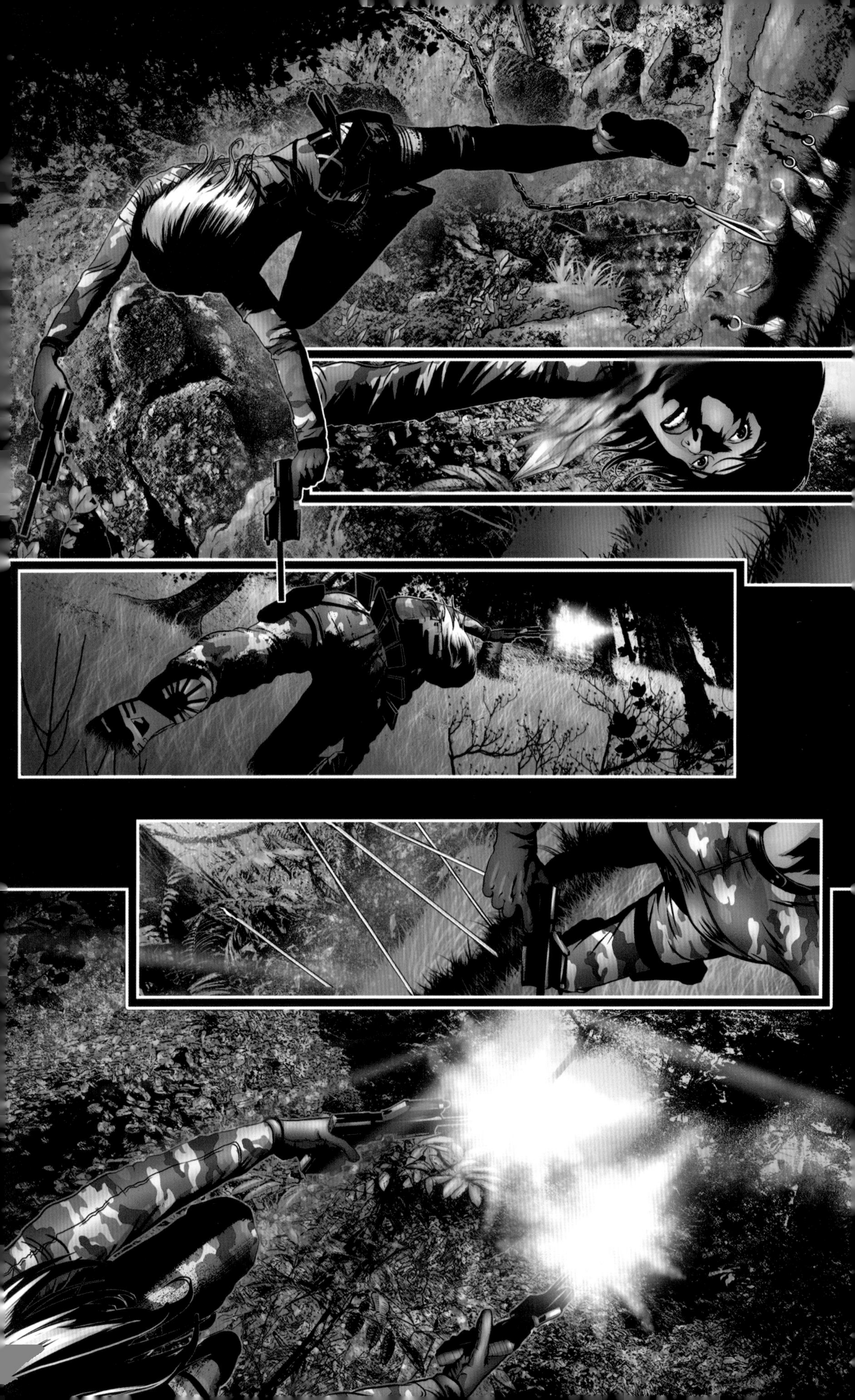

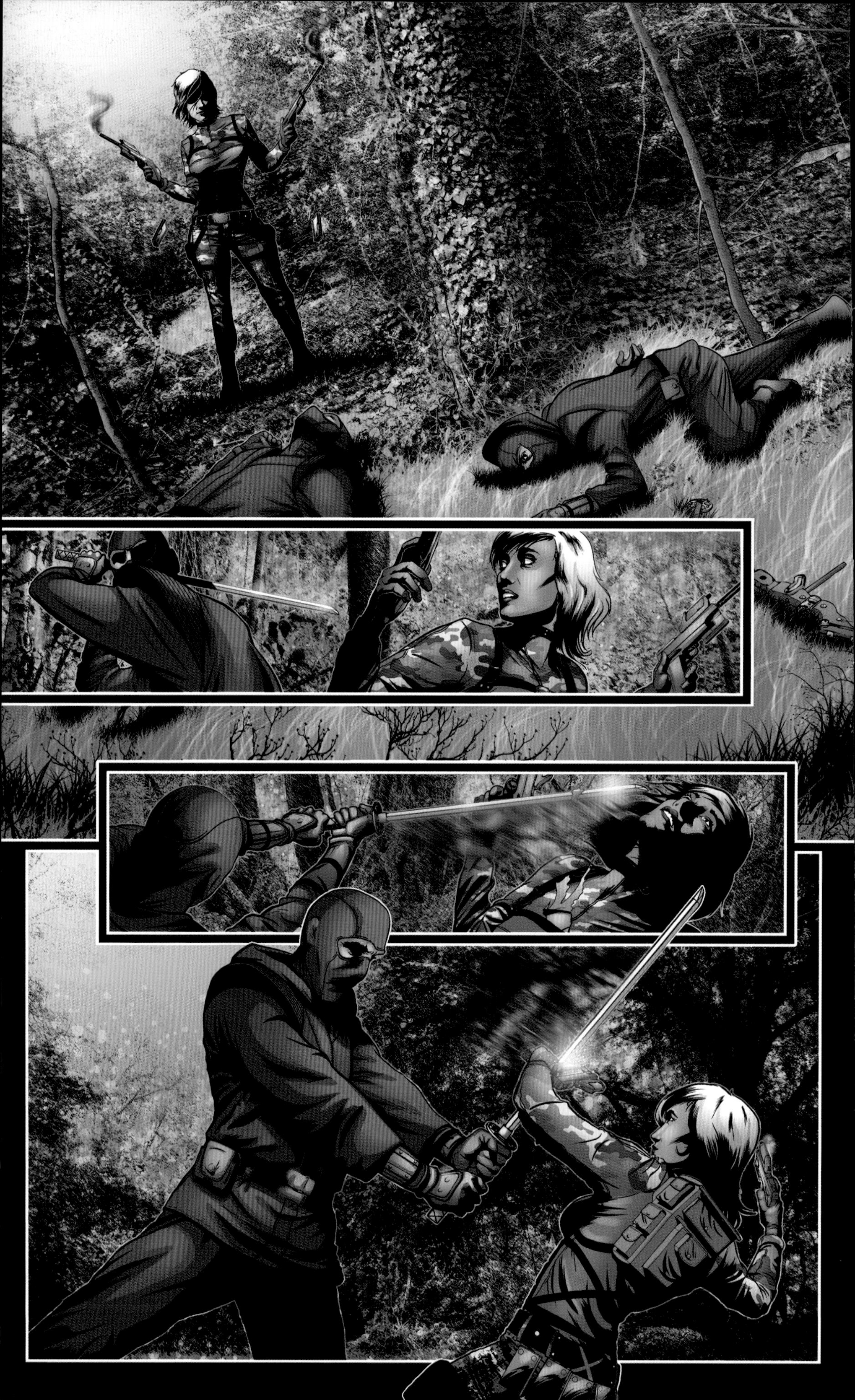

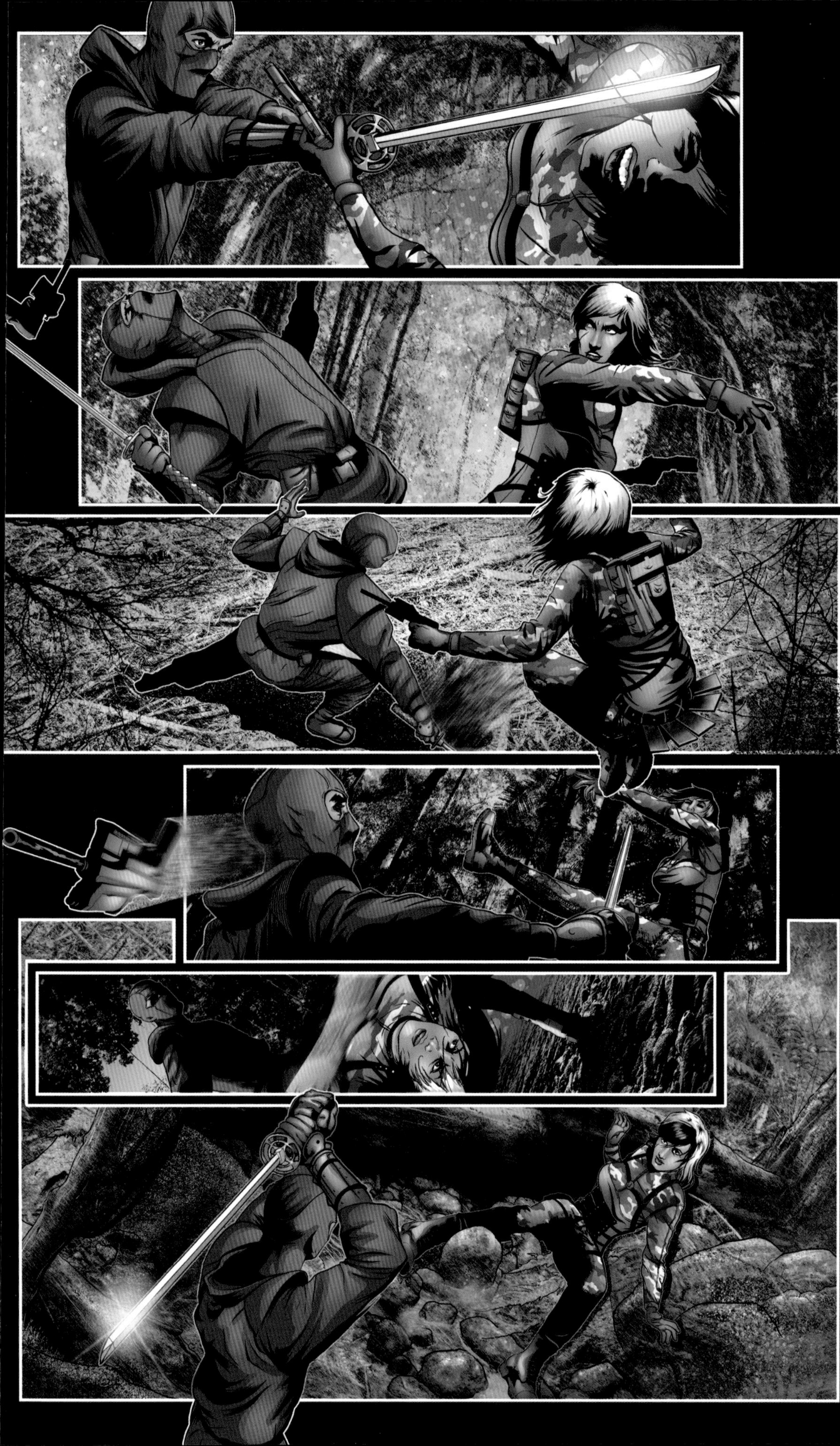

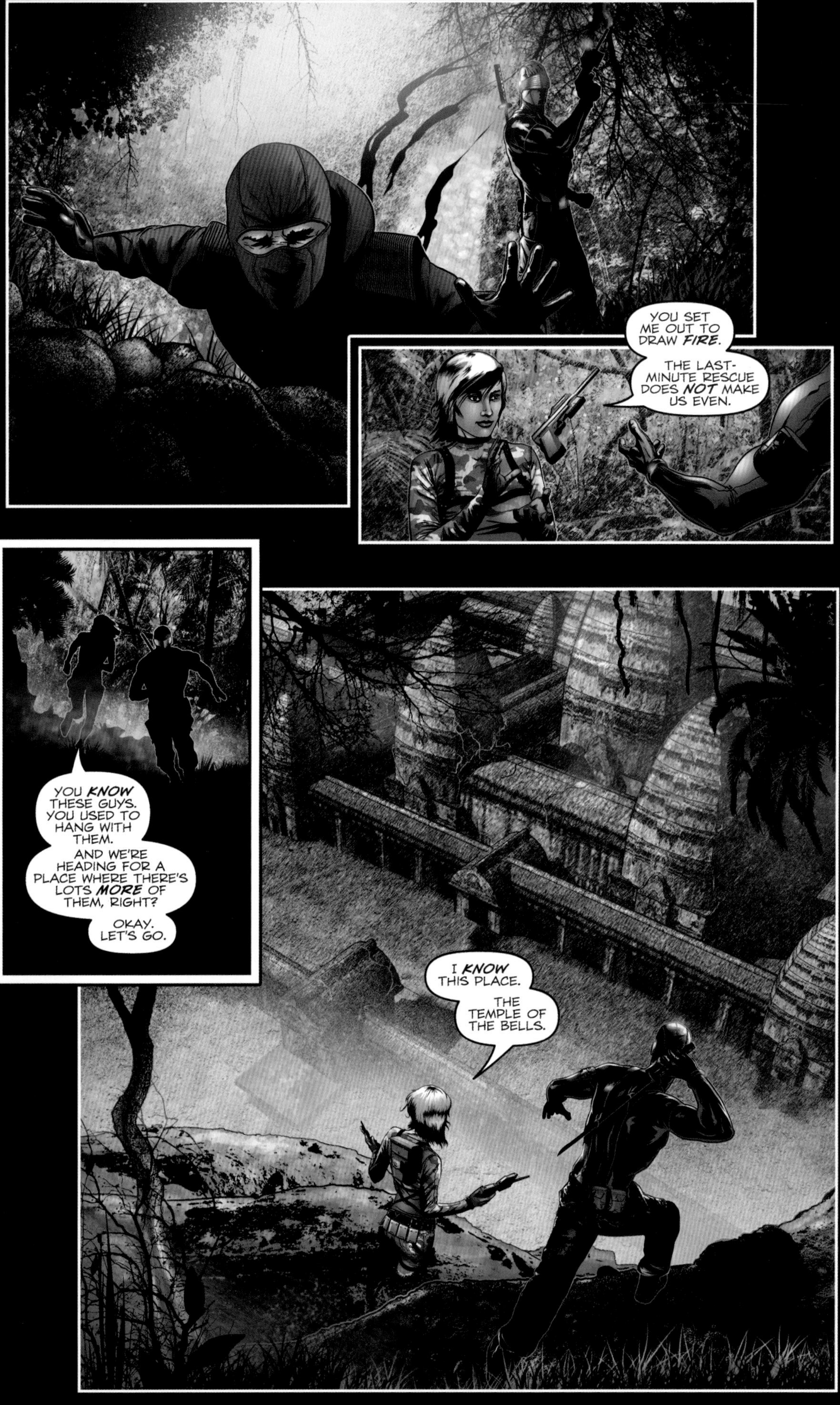
YOU SET ME OUT TO DRAW **FIRE**.
THE LAST-MINUTE RESCUE DOES **NOT** MAKE US EVEN.
YOU **KNOW** THESE GUYS. YOU USED TO HANG WITH THEM.
AND WE'RE HEADING FOR A PLACE WHERE THERE'S LOTS **MORE** OF THEM, RIGHT?
OKAY. LET'S GO.
I **KNOW** THIS PLACE.
THE TEMPLE OF THE BELLS.

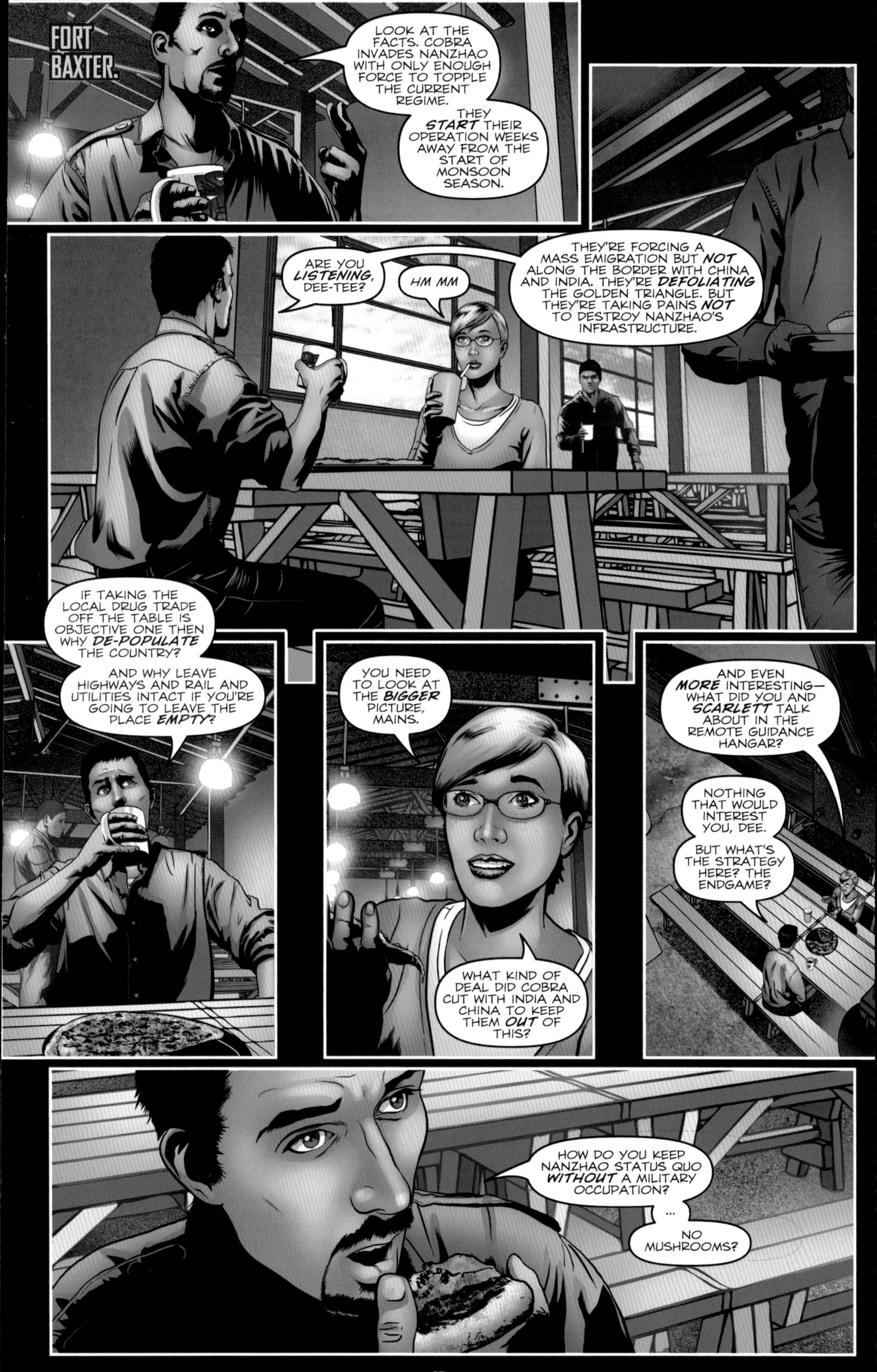
FORT BAXTER.
LOOK AT THE FACTS. COBRA INVADES NANZHAO WITH ONLY ENOUGH FORCE TO TOPPLE THE CURRENT REGIME.
THEY START THEIR OPERATION WEEKS AWAY FROM THE START OF MONSOON SEASON.
ARE YOU LISTENING, DEE-TEE?
HM MM
THEY'RE FORCING A MASS EMIGRATION BUT NOT ALONG THE BORDER WITH CHINA AND INDIA. THEY'RE DEFOLIATING THE GOLDEN TRIANGLE. BUT THEY'RE TAKING PAINS NOT TO DESTROY NANZHAO'S INFRASTRUCTURE.
IF TAKING THE LOCAL DRUG TRADE OFF THE TABLE IS OBJECTIVE ONE THEN WHY DE-POPULATE THE COUNTRY?
AND WHY LEAVE HIGHWAYS AND RAIL AND UTILITIES INTACT IF YOU'RE GOING TO LEAVE THE PLACE EMPTY?
YOU NEED TO LOOK AT THE BIGGER PICTURE, MAINS.
WHAT KIND OF DEAL DID COBRA CUT WITH INDIA AND CHINA TO KEEP THEM OUT OF THIS?
AND EVEN MORE INTERESTING— WHAT DID YOU AND SCARLETT TALK ABOUT IN THE REMOTE GUIDANCE HANGAR?
NOTHING THAT WOULD INTEREST YOU, DEE.
BUT WHAT'S THE STRATEGY HERE? THE ENDGAME?
HOW DO YOU KEEP NANZHAO STATUS QUO WITHOUT A MILITARY OCCUPATION?
...
NO MUSHROOMS?

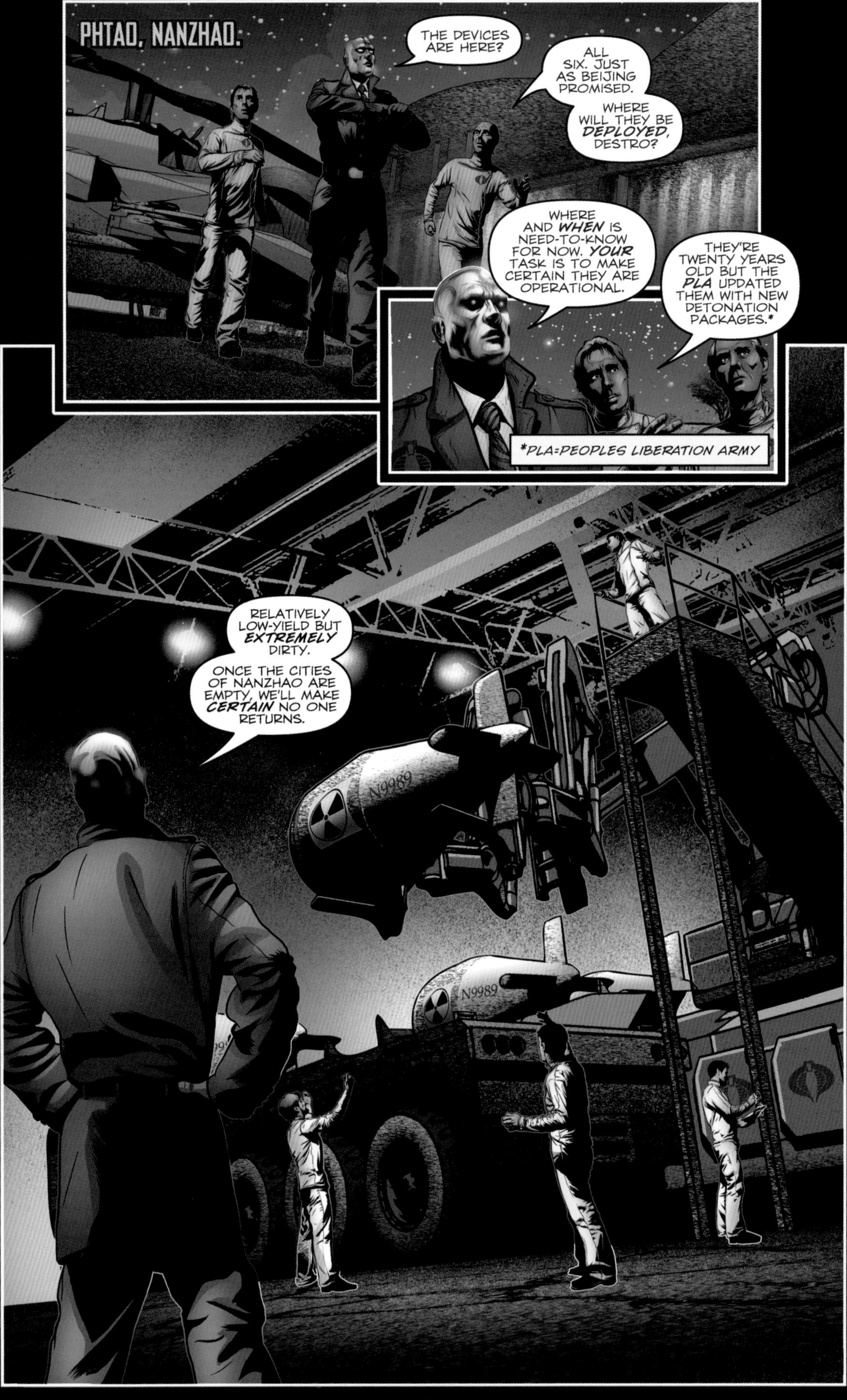
PHTAO, NANZHAO.
THE DEVICES ARE HERE?
ALL SIX. JUST AS BEIJING PROMISED.
WHERE WILL THEY BE DEPLOYED, DESTRO?
WHERE AND WHEN IS NEED-TO-KNOW FOR NOW. YOUR TASK IS TO MAKE CERTAIN THEY ARE OPERATIONAL.
THEY'RE TWENTY YEARS OLD BUT THE PLA UPDATED THEM WITH NEW DETONATION PACKAGES.*
*PLA=PEOPLES LIBERATION ARMY
RELATIVELY LOW-YIELD BUT EXTREMELY DIRTY.
ONCE THE CITIES OF NANZHAO ARE EMPTY, WE'LL MAKE CERTAIN NO ONE RETURNS.
N9989
N9982

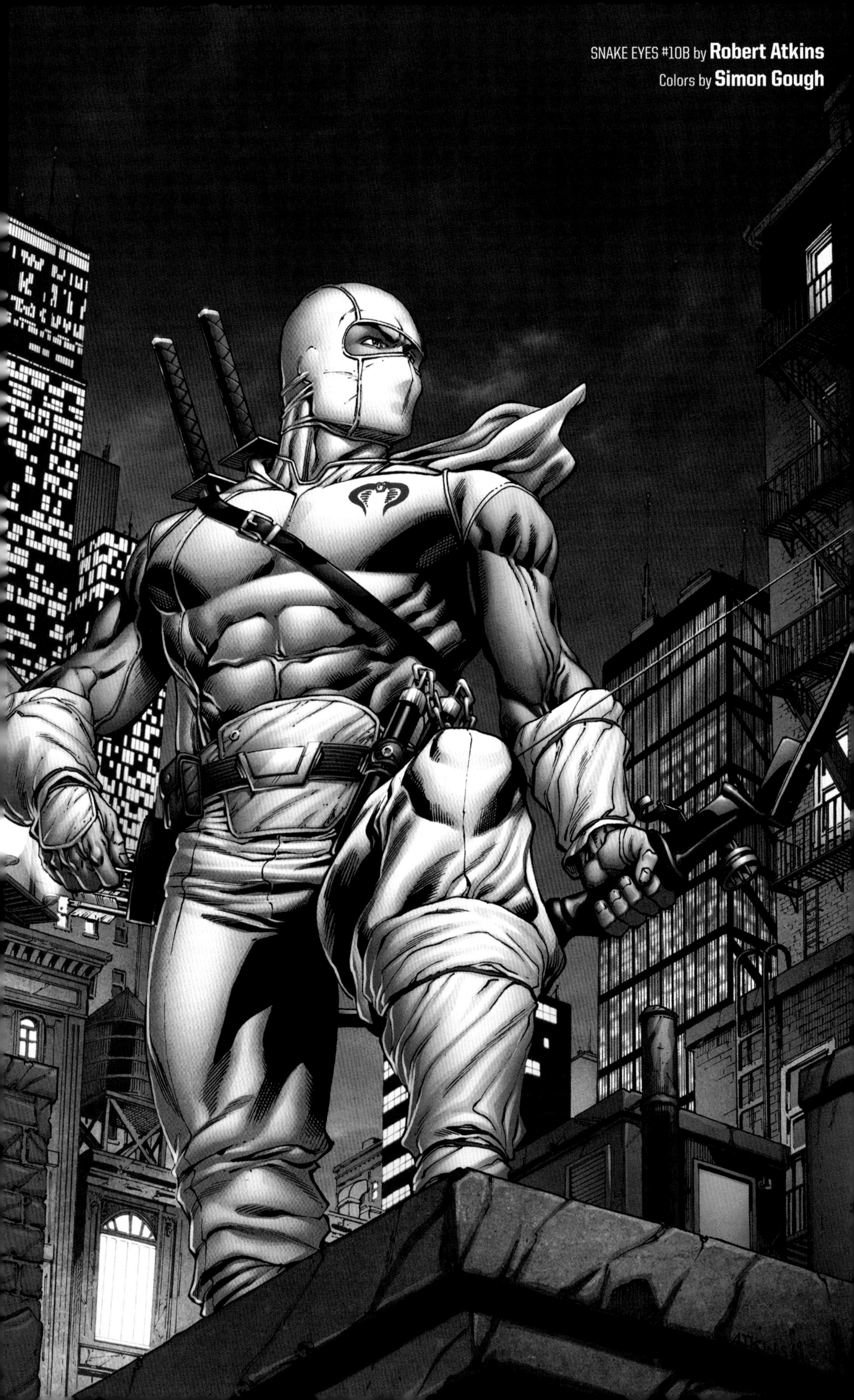

SNAKE EYES #10B by **Robert Atkins**
Colors by **Simon Gough**

COBRA #10A by **Dave Wilkins**

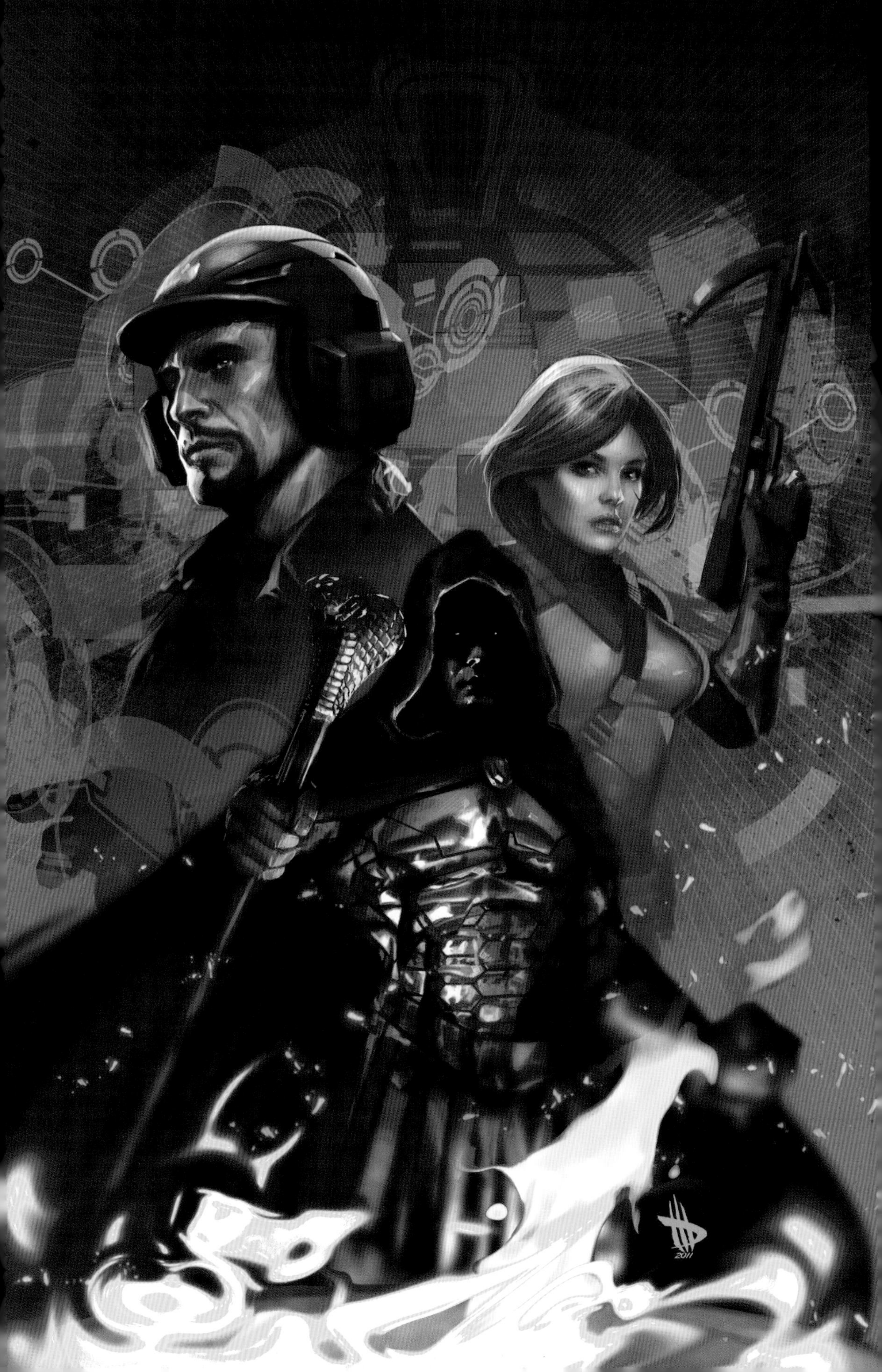

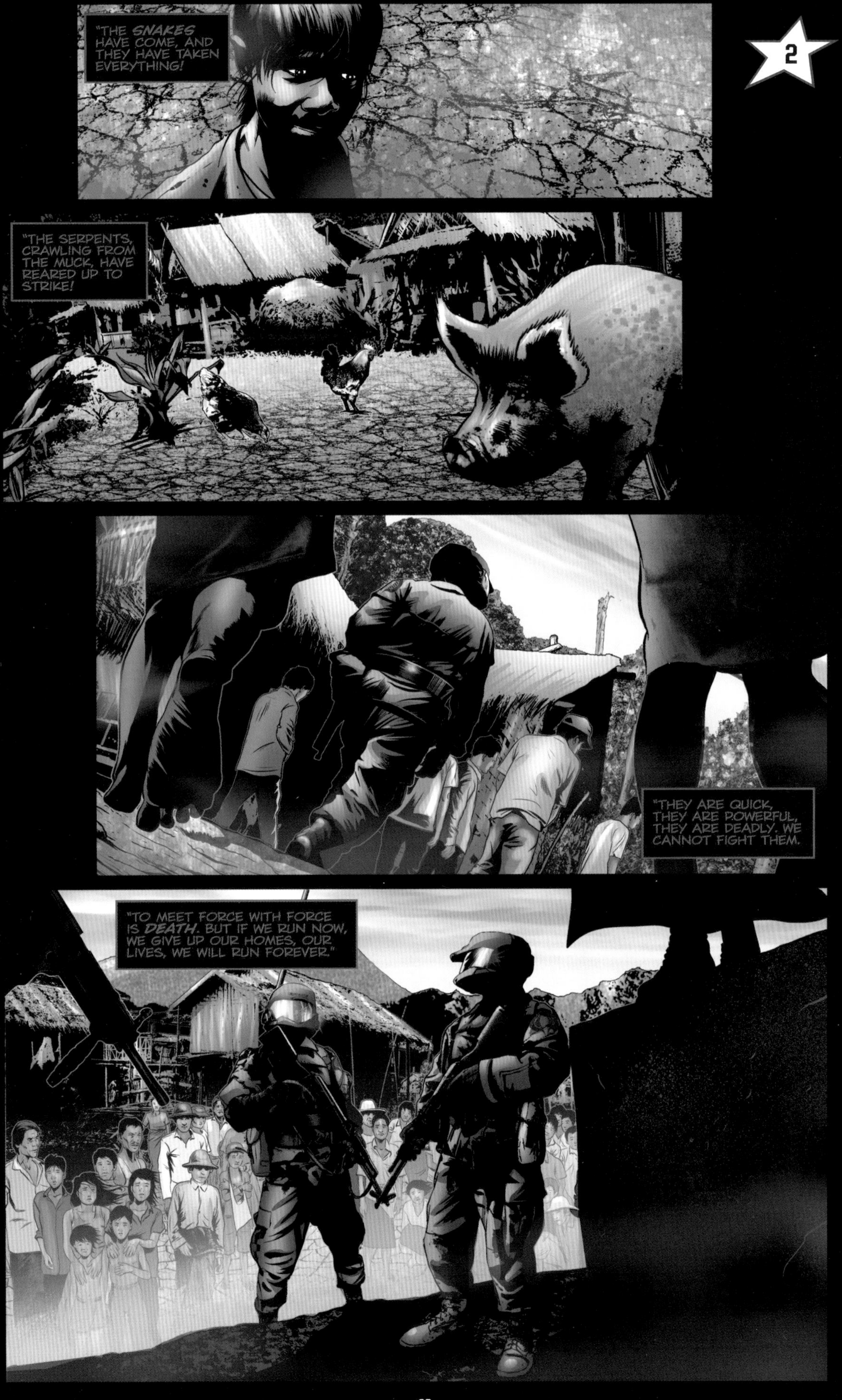
2
"THE *SNAKES* HAVE COME, AND THEY HAVE TAKEN EVERYTHING!
"THE SERPENTS, CRAWLING FROM THE MUCK, HAVE REARED UP TO STRIKE!
"THEY ARE QUICK, THEY ARE POWERFUL, THEY ARE DEADLY. WE CANNOT FIGHT THEM.
"TO MEET FORCE WITH FORCE IS *DEATH*. BUT IF WE RUN NOW, WE GIVE UP OUR HOMES, OUR LIVES, WE WILL RUN FOREVER."

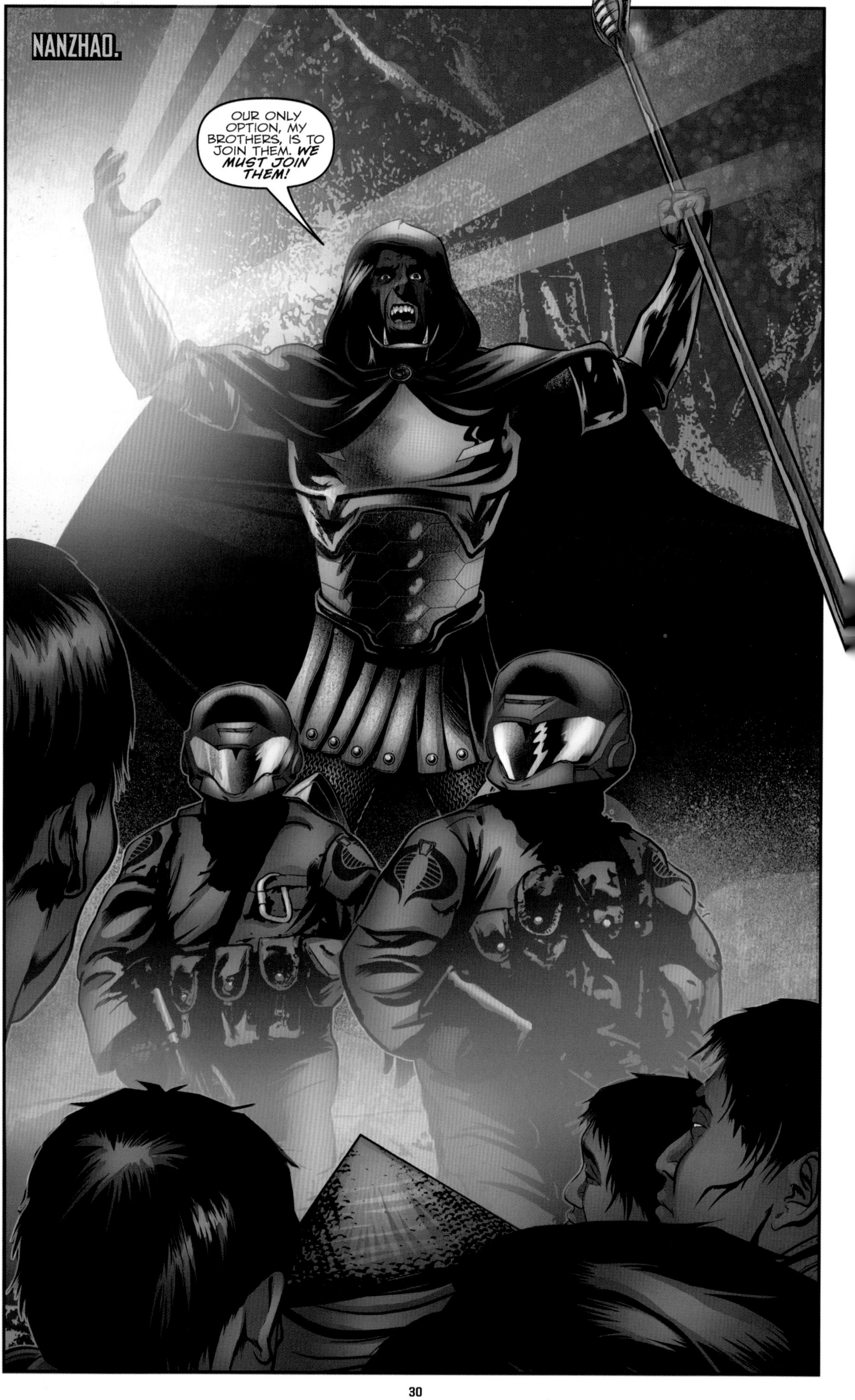
NANZHAO.
OUR ONLY OPTION, MY BROTHERS, IS TO JOIN THEM. WE MUST JOIN THEM!

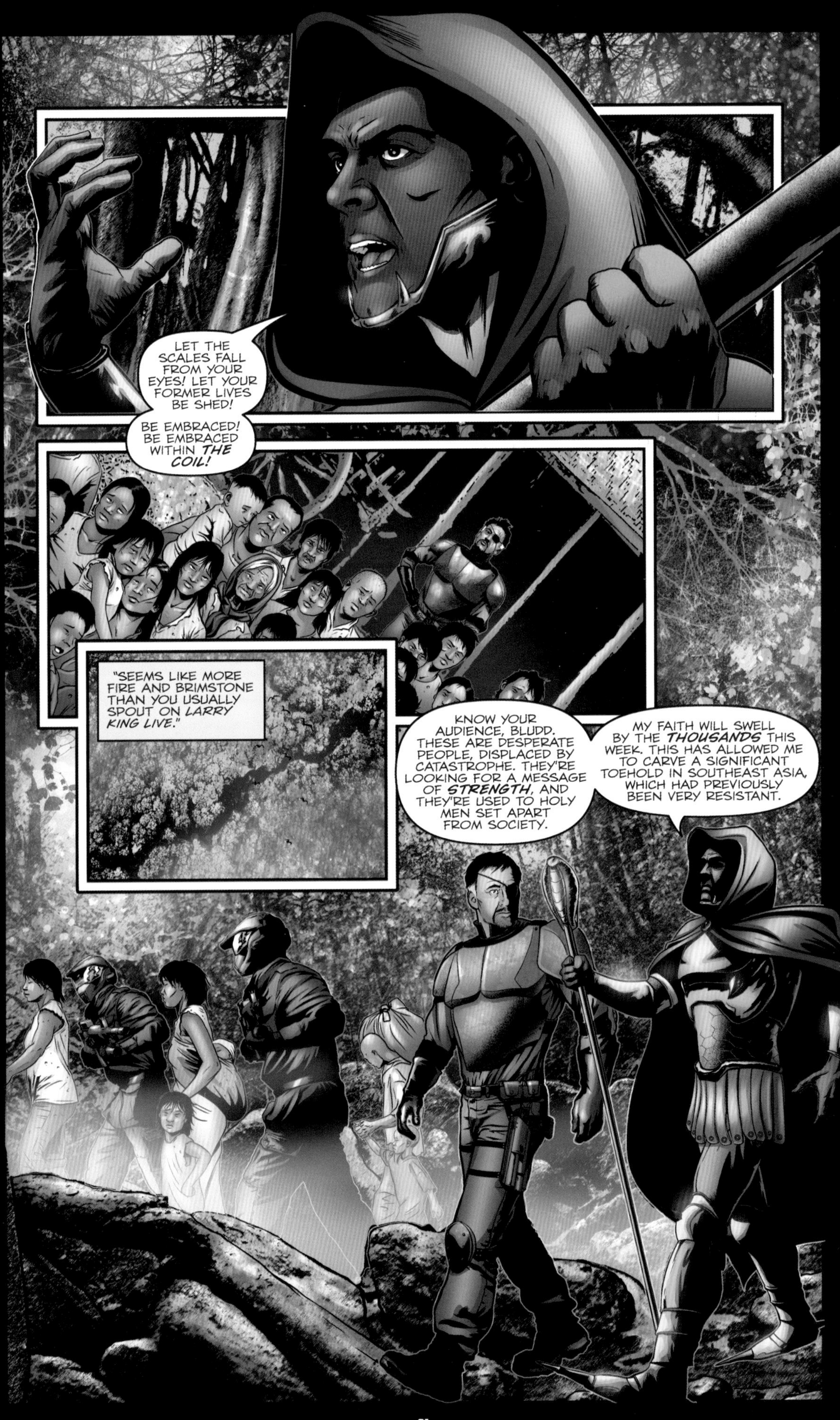
LET THE SCALES FALL FROM YOUR EYES! LET YOUR FORMER LIVES BE SHED!
BE EMBRACED! BE EMBRACED WITHIN *THE COIL!*
"SEEMS LIKE MORE FIRE AND BRIMSTONE THAN YOU USUALLY SPOUT ON *LARRY KING LIVE*."
KNOW YOUR AUDIENCE, BLUDD. THESE ARE DESPERATE PEOPLE, DISPLACED BY CATASTROPHE. THEY'RE LOOKING FOR A MESSAGE OF ***STRENGTH***, AND THEY'RE USED TO HOLY MEN SET APART FROM SOCIETY.
MY FAITH WILL SWELL BY THE ***THOUSANDS*** THIS WEEK. THIS HAS ALLOWED ME TO CARVE A SIGNIFICANT TOEHOLD IN SOUTHEAST ASIA, WHICH HAD PREVIOUSLY BEEN VERY RESISTANT.

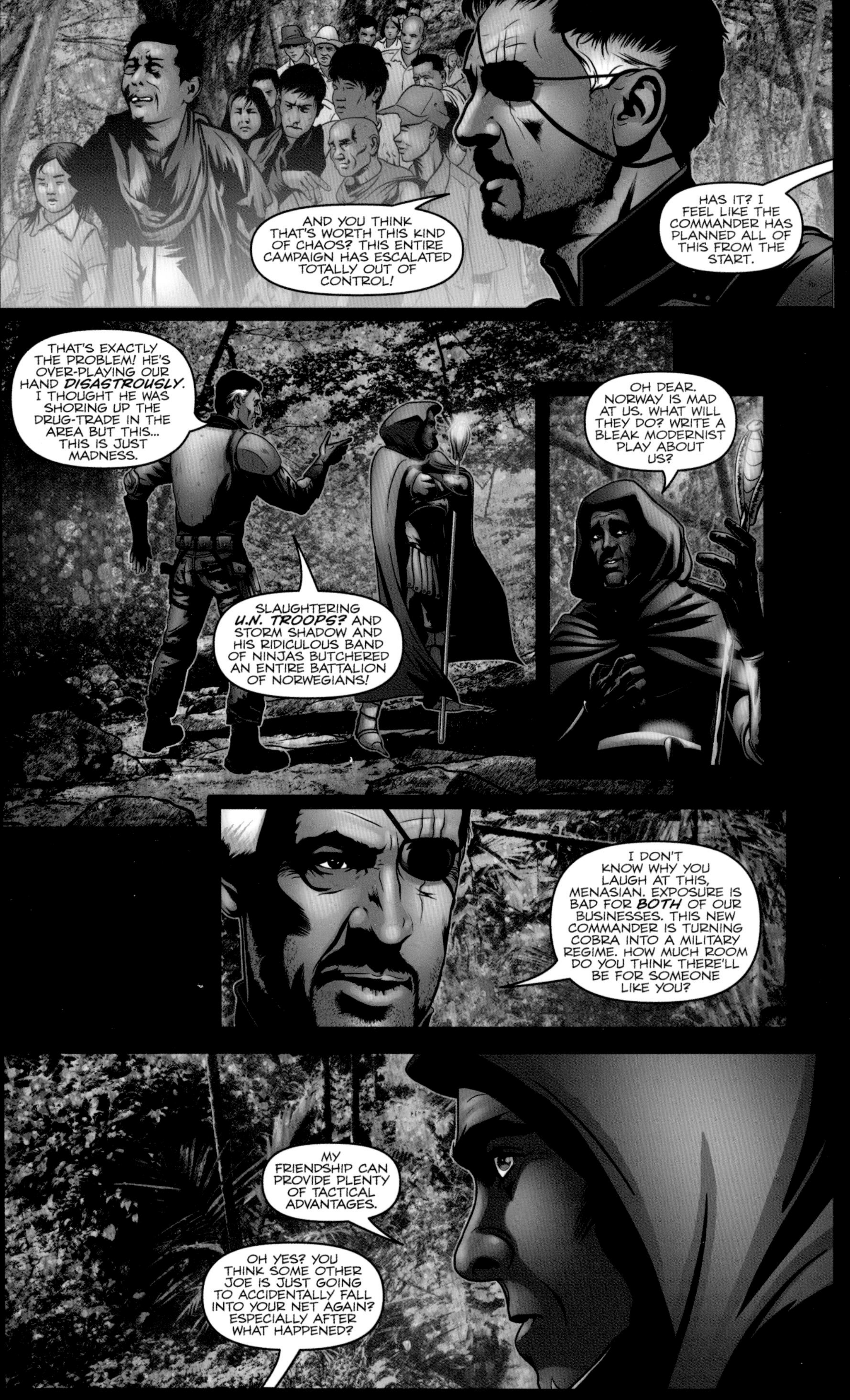
AND YOU THINK THAT'S WORTH THIS KIND OF CHAOS? THIS ENTIRE CAMPAIGN HAS ESCALATED TOTALLY OUT OF CONTROL!
HAS IT? I FEEL LIKE THE COMMANDER HAS PLANNED ALL OF THIS FROM THE START.
THAT'S EXACTLY THE PROBLEM! HE'S OVER-PLAYING OUR HAND DISASTROUSLY. I THOUGHT HE WAS SHORING UP THE DRUG-TRADE IN THE AREA BUT THIS... THIS IS JUST MADNESS.
SLAUGHTERING U.N. TROOPS? AND STORM SHADOW AND HIS RIDICULOUS BAND OF NINJAS BUTCHERED AN ENTIRE BATTALION OF NORWEGIANS!
OH DEAR. NORWAY IS MAD AT US. WHAT WILL THEY DO? WRITE A BLEAK MODERNIST PLAY ABOUT US?
I DON'T KNOW WHY YOU LAUGH AT THIS, MENASIAN. EXPOSURE IS BAD FOR BOTH OF OUR BUSINESSES. THIS NEW COMMANDER IS TURNING COBRA INTO A MILITARY REGIME. HOW MUCH ROOM DO YOU THINK THERE'LL BE FOR SOMEONE LIKE YOU?
MY FRIENDSHIP CAN PROVIDE PLENTY OF TACTICAL ADVANTAGES.
OH YES? YOU THINK SOME OTHER JOE IS JUST GOING TO ACCIDENTALLY FALL INTO YOUR NET AGAIN? ESPECIALLY AFTER WHAT HAPPENED?

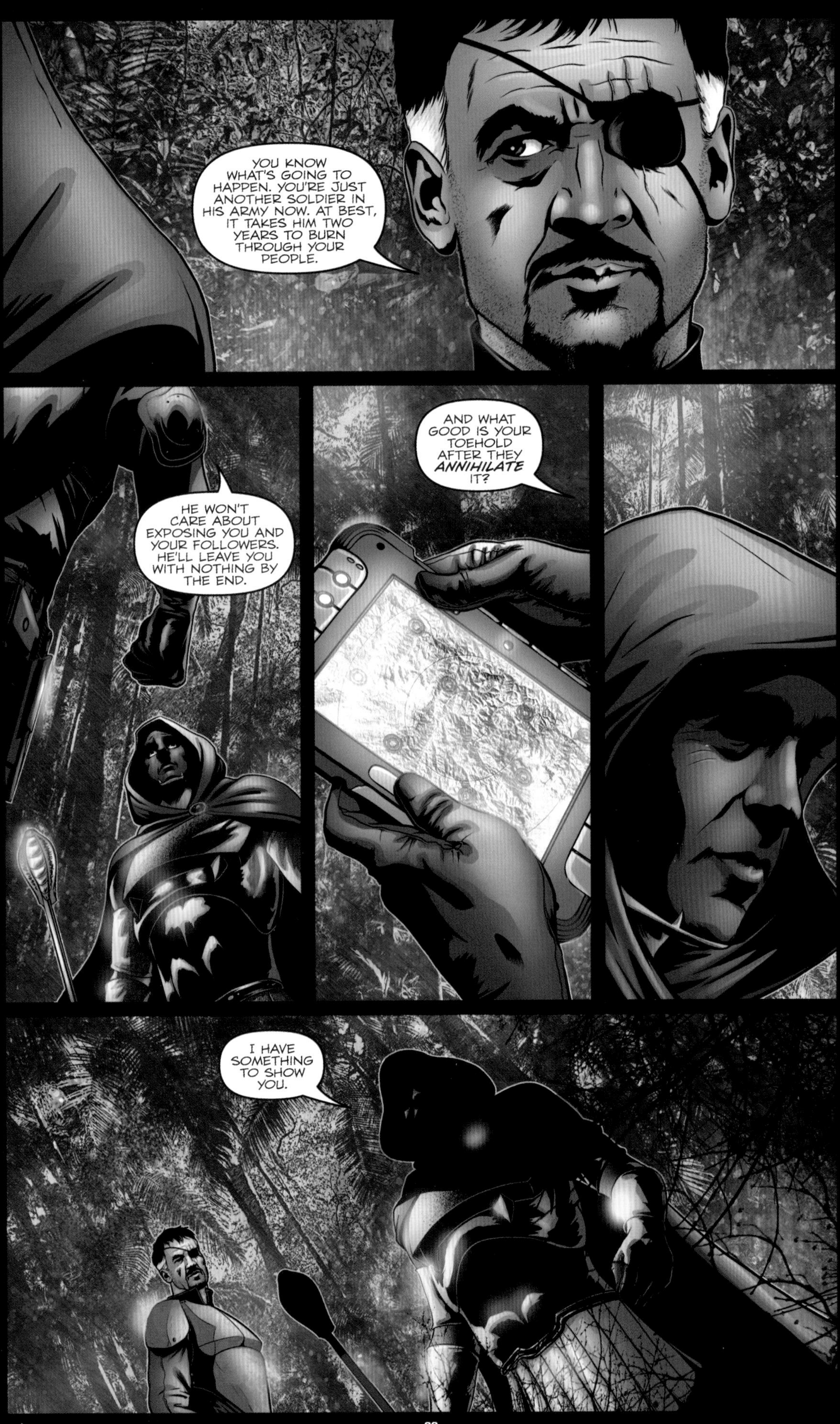
YOU KNOW WHAT'S GOING TO HAPPEN. YOU'RE JUST ANOTHER SOLDIER IN HIS ARMY NOW. AT BEST, IT TAKES HIM TWO YEARS TO BURN THROUGH YOUR PEOPLE.
HE WON'T CARE ABOUT EXPOSING YOU AND YOUR FOLLOWERS. HE'LL LEAVE YOU WITH NOTHING BY THE END.
AND WHAT GOOD IS YOUR TOEHOLD AFTER THEY ***ANNIHILATE*** IT?
I HAVE SOMETHING TO SHOW YOU.

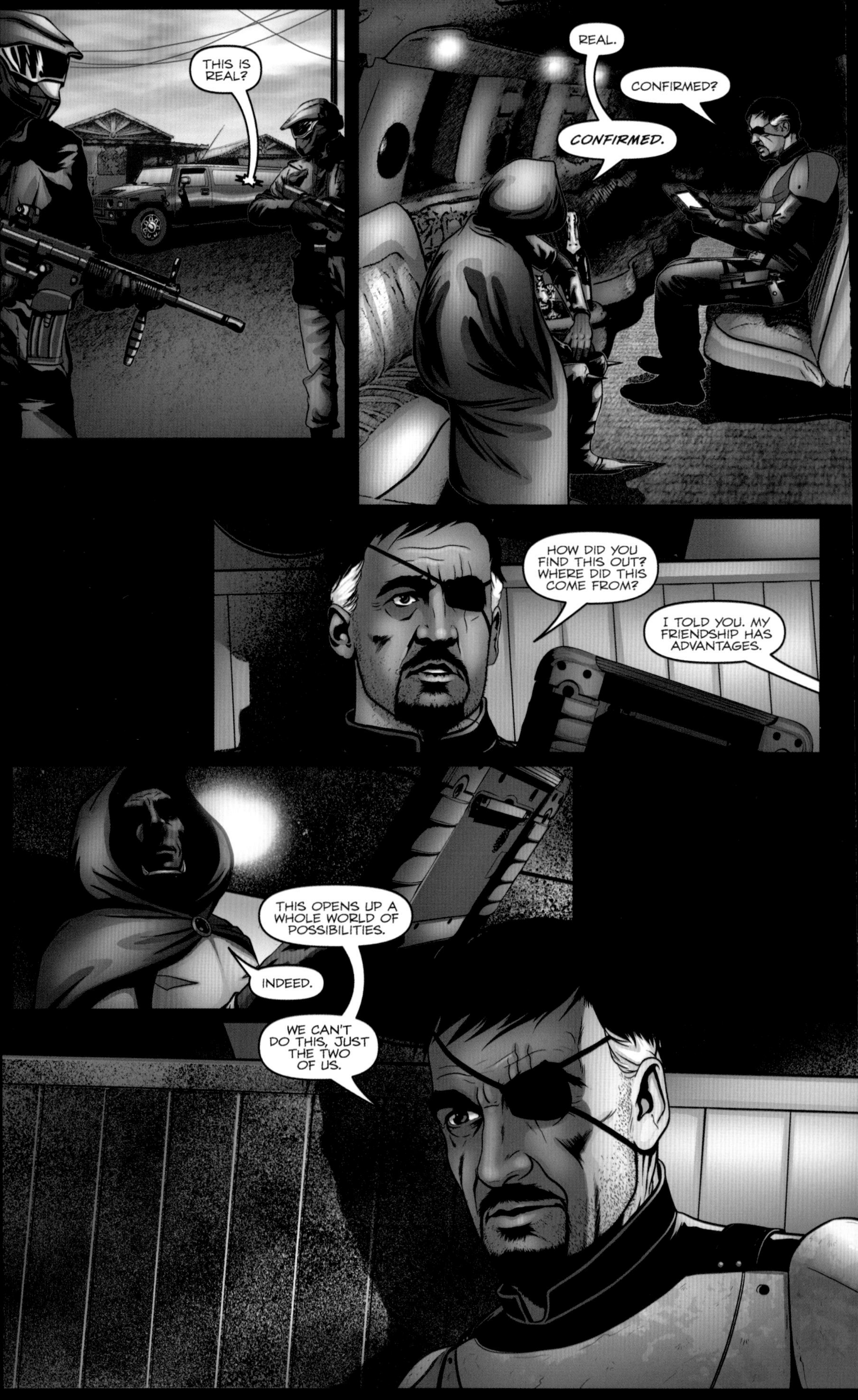

THIS IS REAL?
REAL.
CONFIRMED?
CONFIRMED.
HOW DID YOU FIND THIS OUT? WHERE DID THIS COME FROM?
I TOLD YOU. MY FRIENDSHIP HAS ADVANTAGES.
THIS OPENS UP A WHOLE WORLD OF POSSIBILITIES.
INDEED.
WE CAN'T DO THIS, JUST THE TWO OF US.

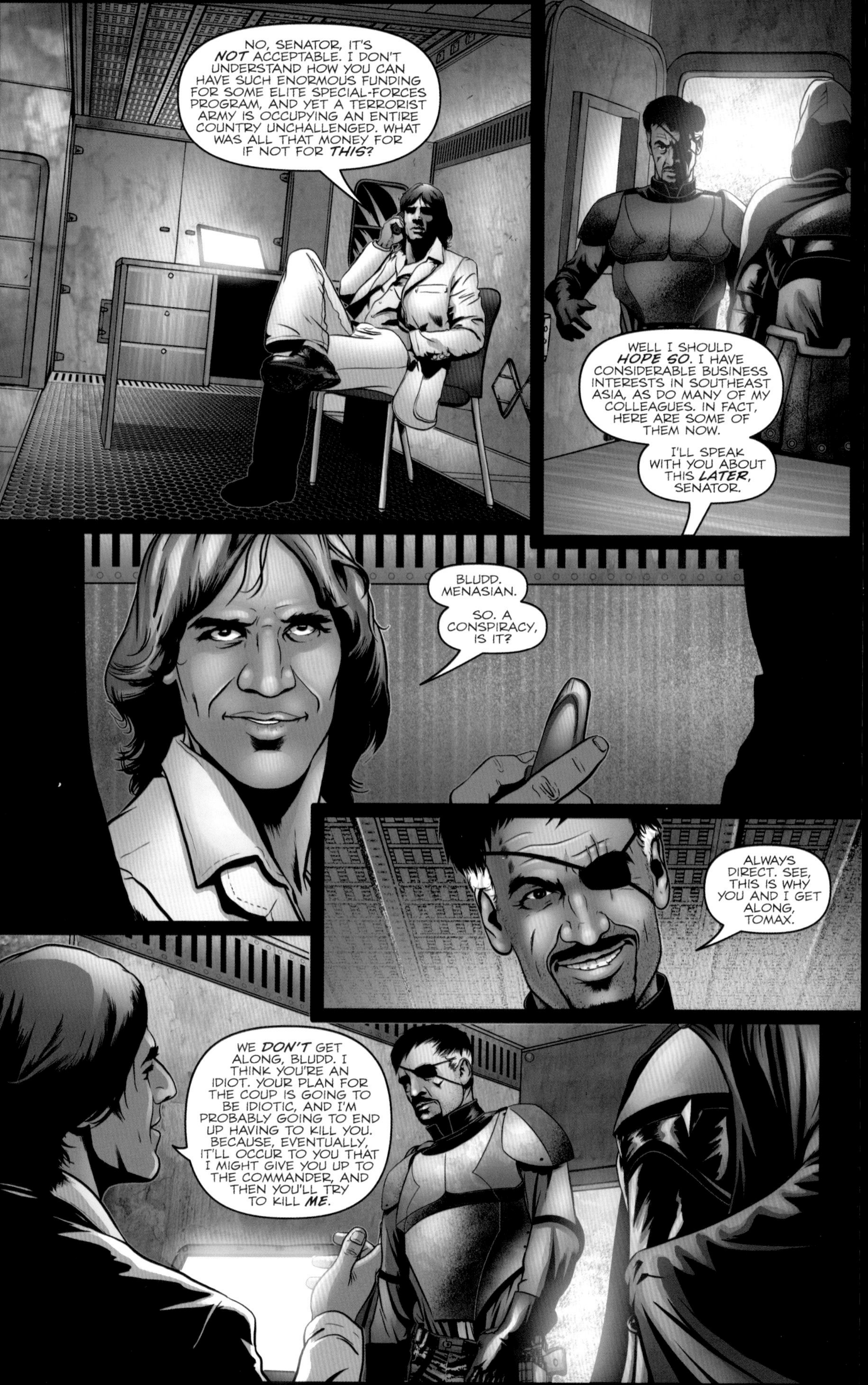

NO, SENATOR, IT'S NOT ACCEPTABLE. I DON'T UNDERSTAND HOW YOU CAN HAVE SUCH ENORMOUS FUNDING FOR SOME ELITE SPECIAL-FORCES PROGRAM, AND YET A TERRORIST ARMY IS OCCUPYING AN ENTIRE COUNTRY UNCHALLENGED. WHAT WAS ALL THAT MONEY FOR IF NOT FOR THIS?
WELL I SHOULD HOPE SO. I HAVE CONSIDERABLE BUSINESS INTERESTS IN SOUTHEAST ASIA, AS DO MANY OF MY COLLEAGUES. IN FACT, HERE ARE SOME OF THEM NOW.
I'LL SPEAK WITH YOU ABOUT THIS LATER, SENATOR.
BLUDD. MENASIAN.
SO. A CONSPIRACY, IS IT?
ALWAYS DIRECT. SEE, THIS IS WHY YOU AND I GET ALONG, TOMAX.
WE DON'T GET ALONG, BLUDD. I THINK YOU'RE AN IDIOT. YOUR PLAN FOR THE COUP IS GOING TO BE IDIOTIC, AND I'M PROBABLY GOING TO END UP HAVING TO KILL YOU. BECAUSE, EVENTUALLY, IT'LL OCCUR TO YOU THAT I MIGHT GIVE YOU UP TO THE COMMANDER, AND THEN YOU'LL TRY TO KILL ME.

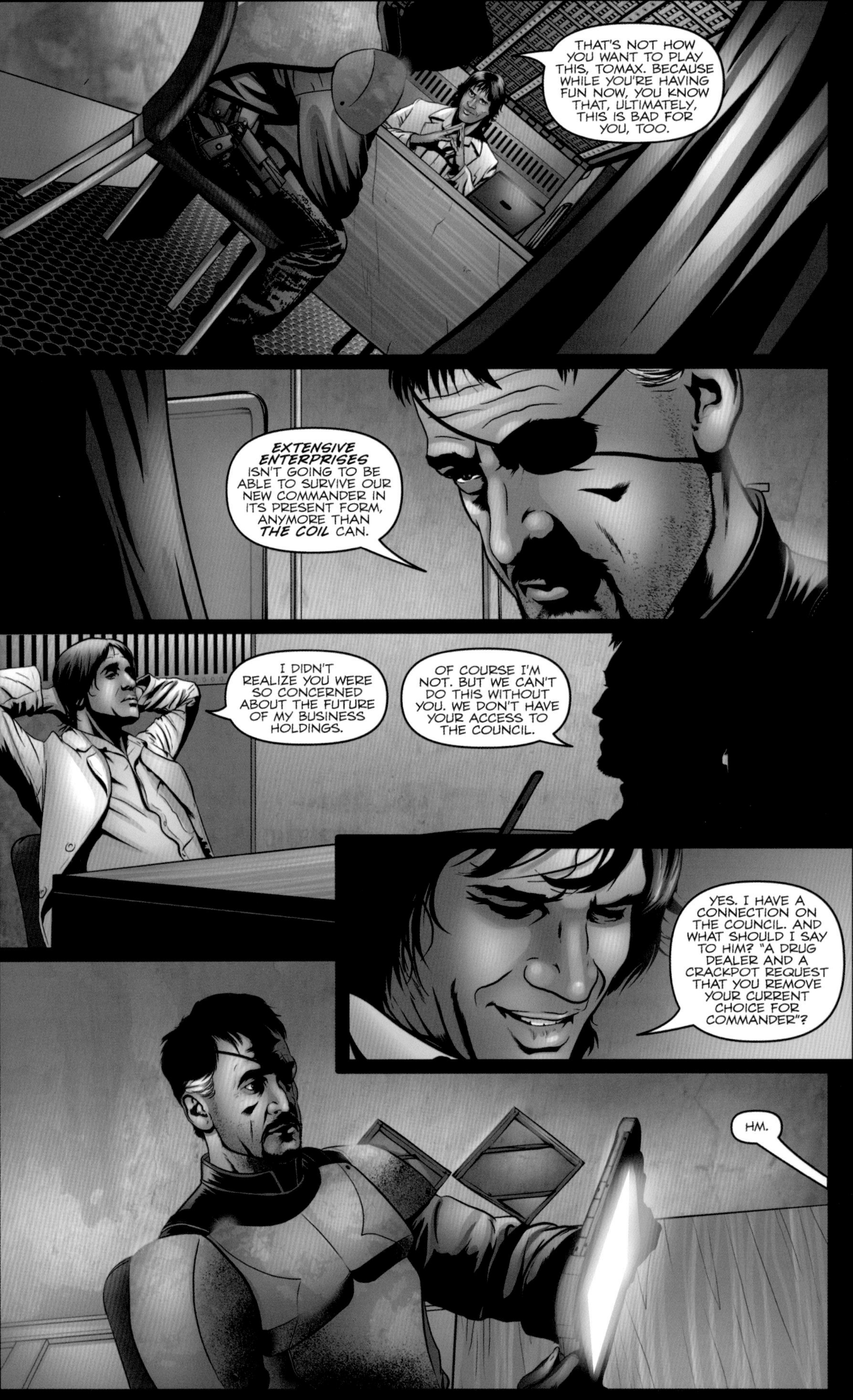
THAT'S NOT HOW YOU WANT TO PLAY THIS, TOMAX. BECAUSE WHILE YOU'RE HAVING FUN NOW, YOU KNOW THAT, ULTIMATELY, THIS IS BAD FOR YOU, TOO.
EXTENSIVE ENTERPRISES ISN'T GOING TO BE ABLE TO SURVIVE OUR NEW COMMANDER IN ITS PRESENT FORM, ANYMORE THAN THE COIL CAN.
I DIDN'T REALIZE YOU WERE SO CONCERNED ABOUT THE FUTURE OF MY BUSINESS HOLDINGS.
OF COURSE I'M NOT. BUT WE CAN'T DO THIS WITHOUT YOU. WE DON'T HAVE YOUR ACCESS TO THE COUNCIL.
YES. I HAVE A CONNECTION ON THE COUNCIL. AND WHAT SHOULD I SAY TO HIM? "A DRUG DEALER AND A CRACKPOT REQUEST THAT YOU REMOVE YOUR CURRENT CHOICE FOR COMMANDER"?
HM.

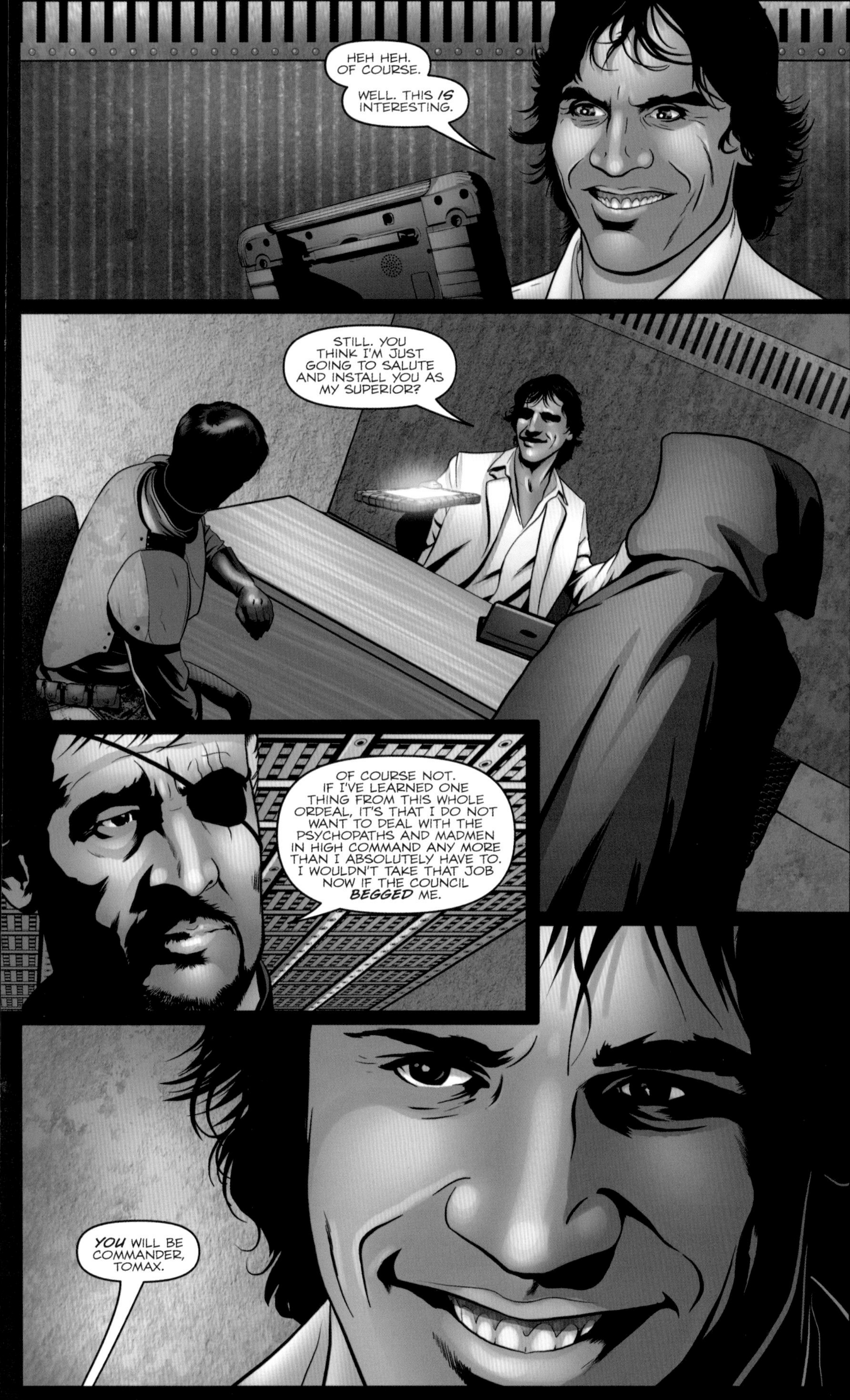
HEH HEH. OF COURSE.
WELL. THIS *IS* INTERESTING.
STILL. YOU THINK I'M JUST GOING TO SALUTE AND INSTALL YOU AS MY SUPERIOR?
OF COURSE NOT. IF I'VE LEARNED ONE THING FROM THIS WHOLE ORDEAL, IT'S THAT I DO NOT WANT TO DEAL WITH THE PSYCHOPATHS AND MADMEN IN HIGH COMMAND ANY MORE THAN I ABSOLUTELY HAVE TO. I WOULDN'T TAKE THAT JOB NOW IF THE COUNCIL ***BEGGED*** ME.
YOU WILL BE COMMANDER, TOMAX.

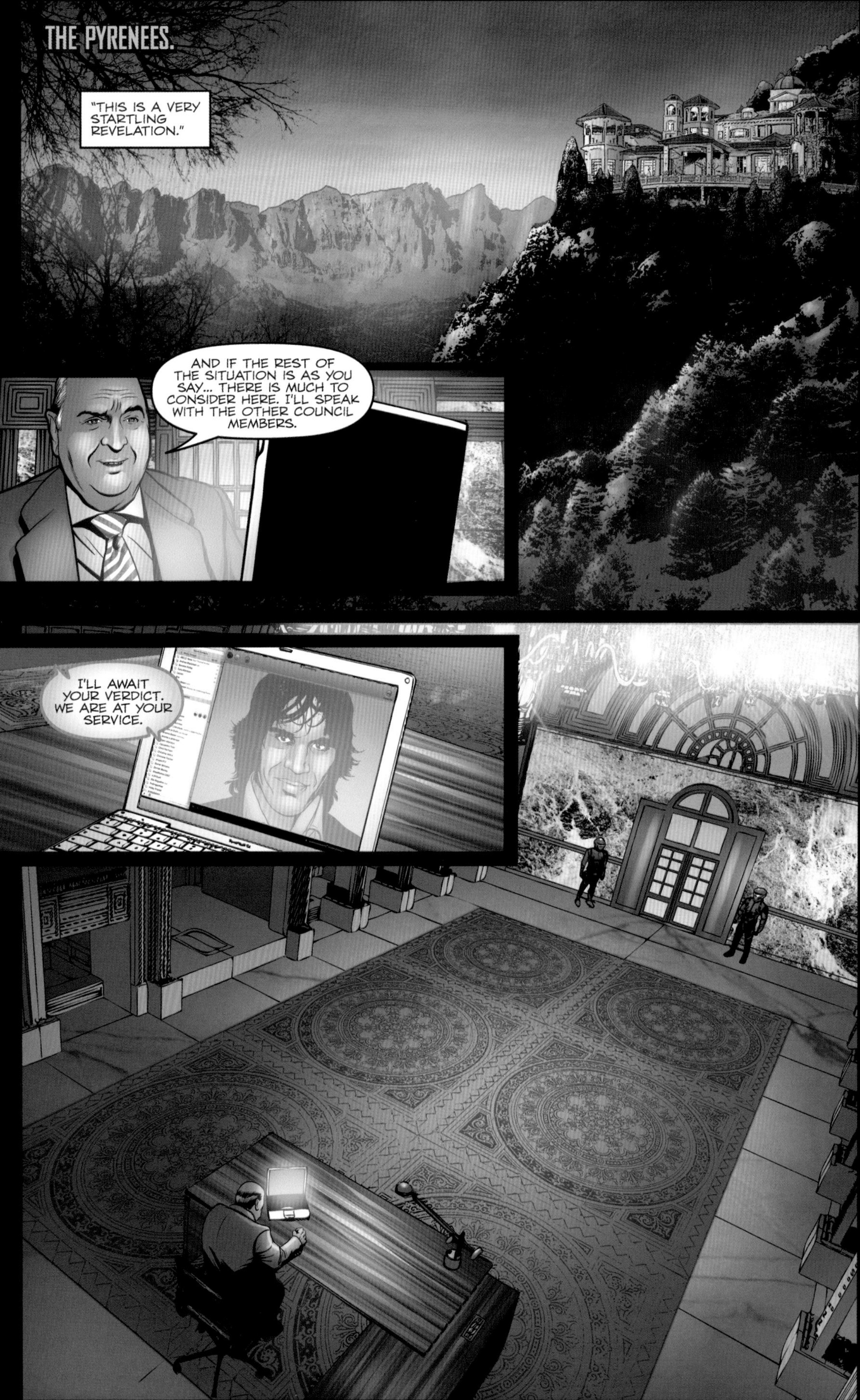
THE PYRENEES.
"THIS IS A VERY STARTLING REVELATION."
AND IF THE REST OF THE SITUATION IS AS YOU SAY... THERE IS MUCH TO CONSIDER HERE. I'LL SPEAK WITH THE OTHER COUNCIL MEMBERS.
I'LL AWAIT YOUR VERDICT. WE ARE AT YOUR SERVICE.

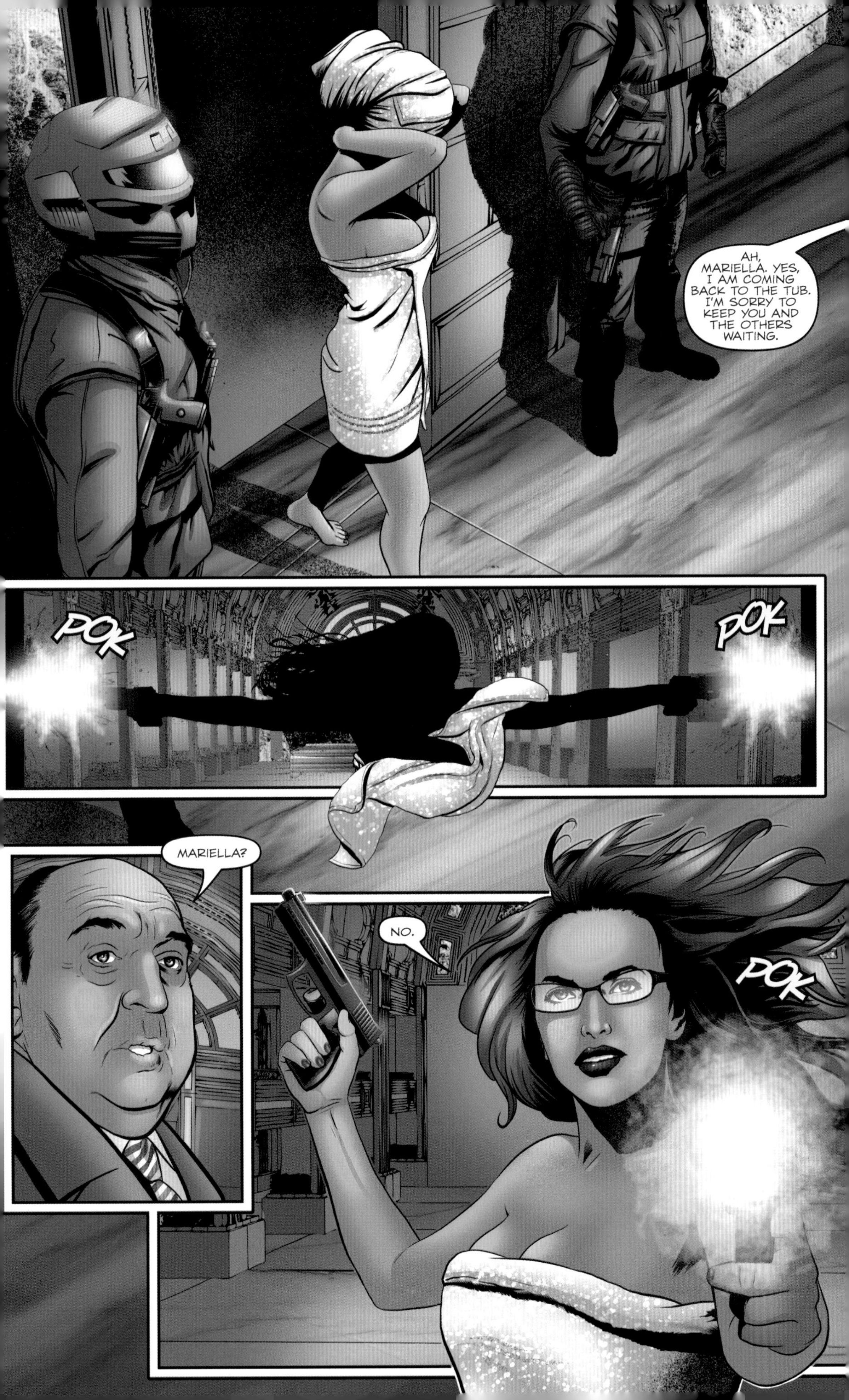
AH, MARIELLA. YES, I AM COMING BACK TO THE TUB. I'M SORRY TO KEEP YOU AND THE OTHERS WAITING.
POK
POK
MARIELLA?
NO.
POK

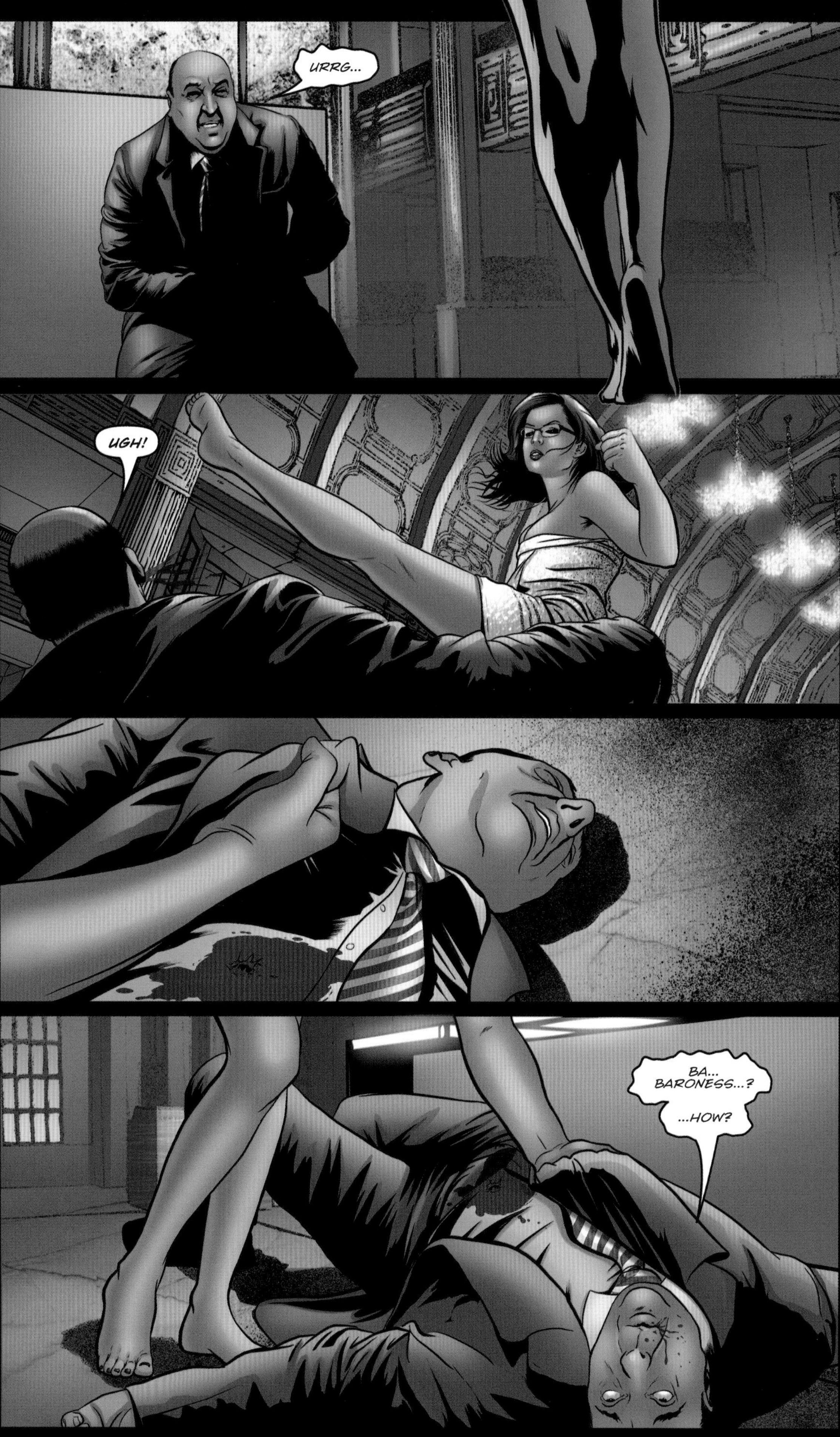
URRG...
UGH!
BA... BARONESS...?
...HOW?

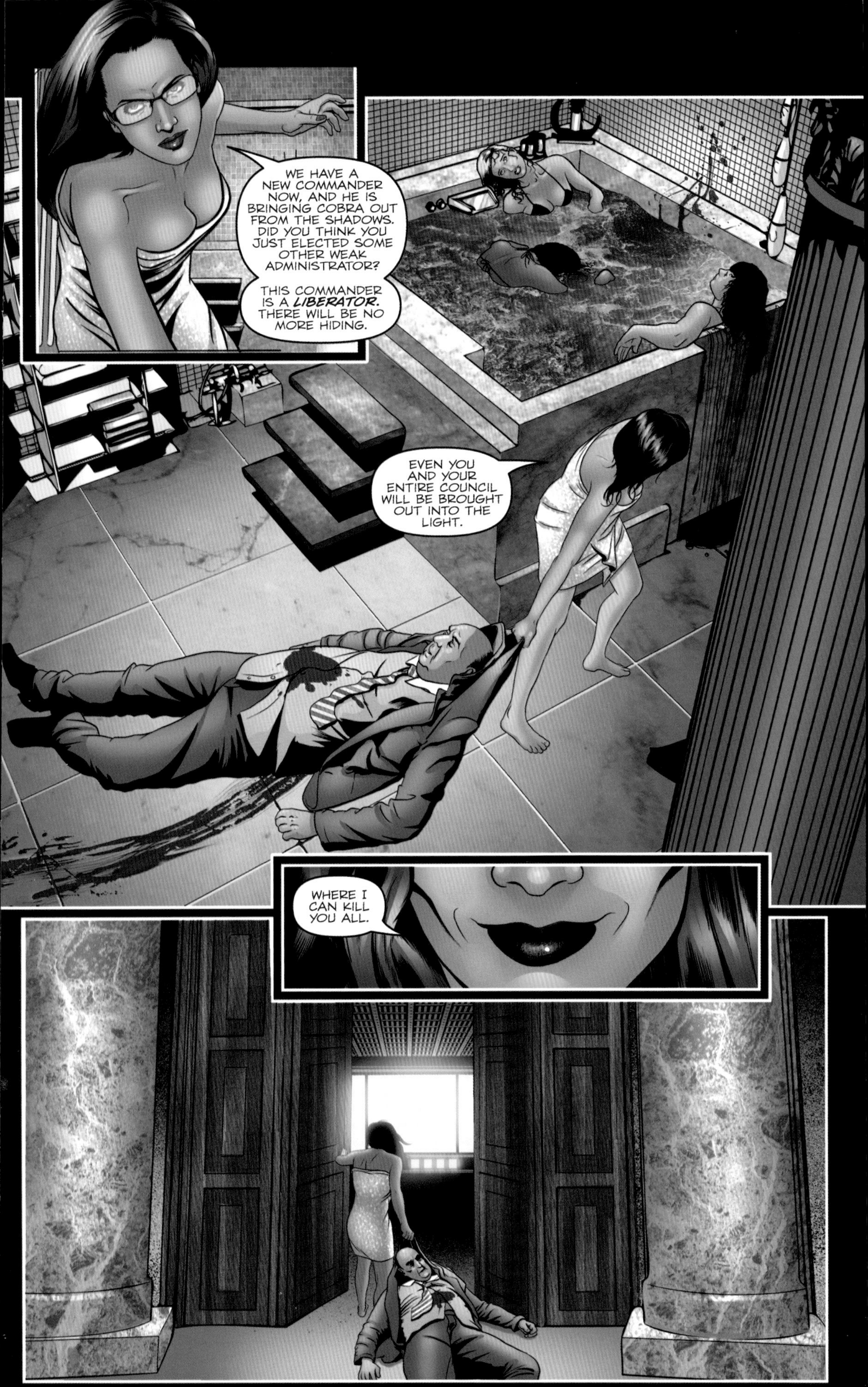
WE HAVE A NEW COMMANDER NOW, AND HE IS BRINGING COBRA OUT FROM THE SHADOWS. DID YOU THINK YOU JUST ELECTED SOME OTHER WEAK ADMINISTRATOR?
THIS COMMANDER IS A LIBERATOR. THERE WILL BE NO MORE HIDING.
EVEN YOU AND YOUR ENTIRE COUNCIL WILL BE BROUGHT OUT INTO THE LIGHT.
WHERE I CAN KILL YOU ALL.

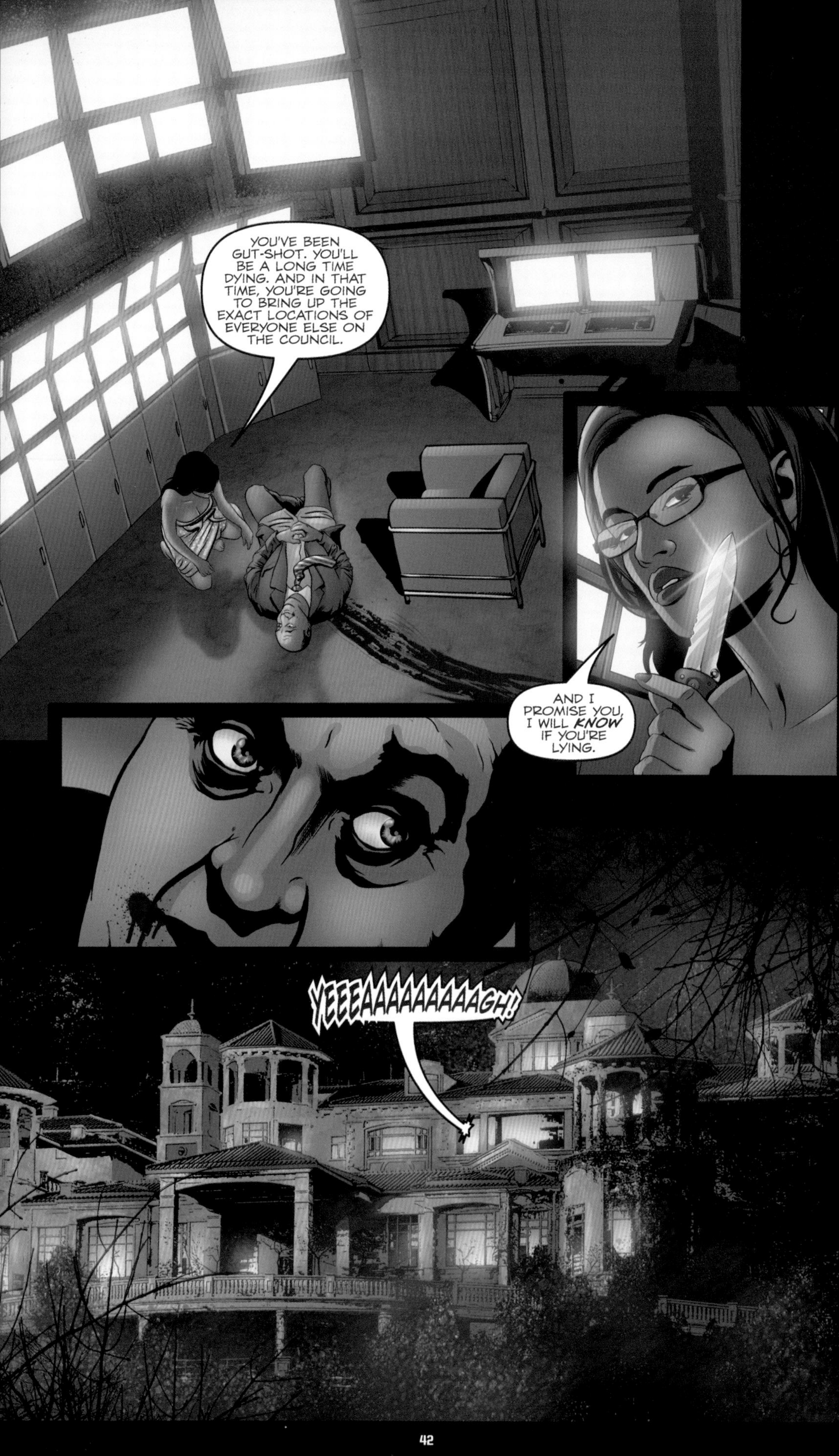

YOU'VE BEEN GUT-SHOT. YOU'LL BE A LONG TIME DYING. AND IN THAT TIME, YOU'RE GOING TO BRING UP THE EXACT LOCATIONS OF EVERYONE ELSE ON THE COUNCIL.
AND I PROMISE YOU, I WILL *KNOW* IF YOU'RE LYING.
YEEEAAAAAAAAAGH!

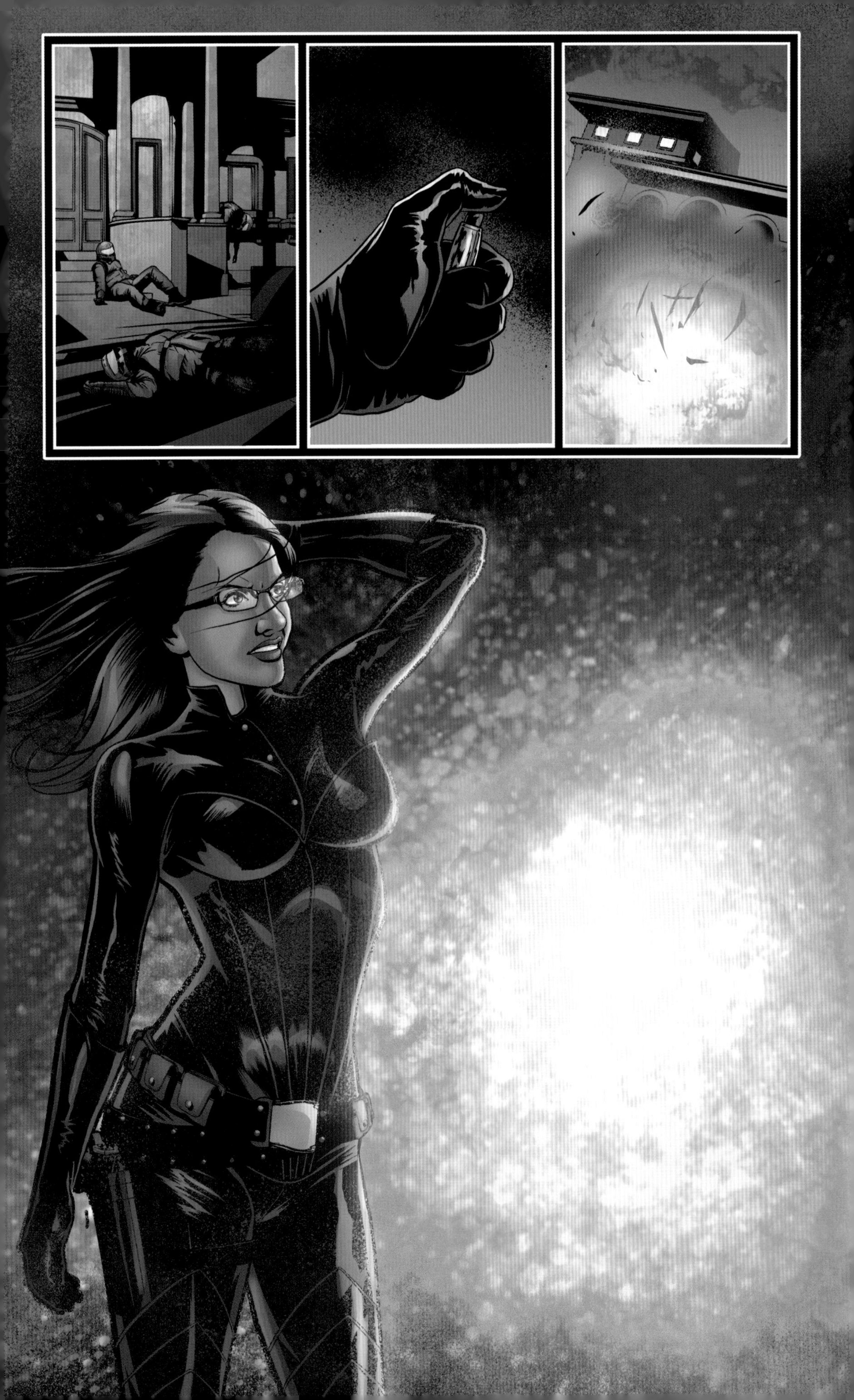

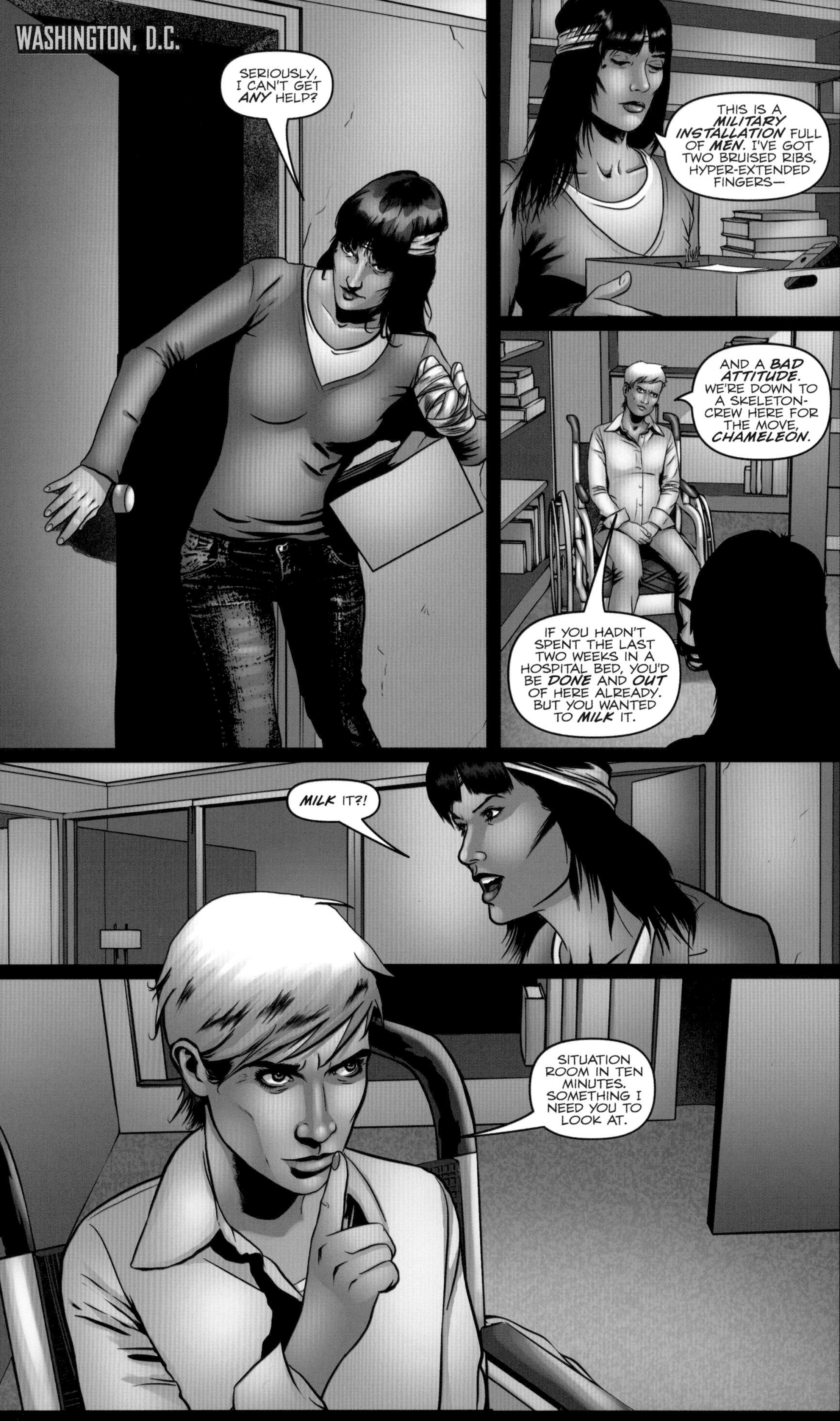
WASHINGTON, D.C.
SERIOUSLY, I CAN'T GET ANY HELP?
THIS IS A MILITARY INSTALLATION FULL OF MEN. I'VE GOT TWO BRUISED RIBS, HYPER-EXTENDED FINGERS—
AND A BAD ATTITUDE. WE'RE DOWN TO A SKELETON-CREW HERE FOR THE MOVE, CHAMELEON.
IF YOU HADN'T SPENT THE LAST TWO WEEKS IN A HOSPITAL BED, YOU'D BE DONE AND OUT OF HERE ALREADY. BUT YOU WANTED TO MILK IT.
MILK IT?!
SITUATION ROOM IN TEN MINUTES. SOMETHING I NEED YOU TO LOOK AT.

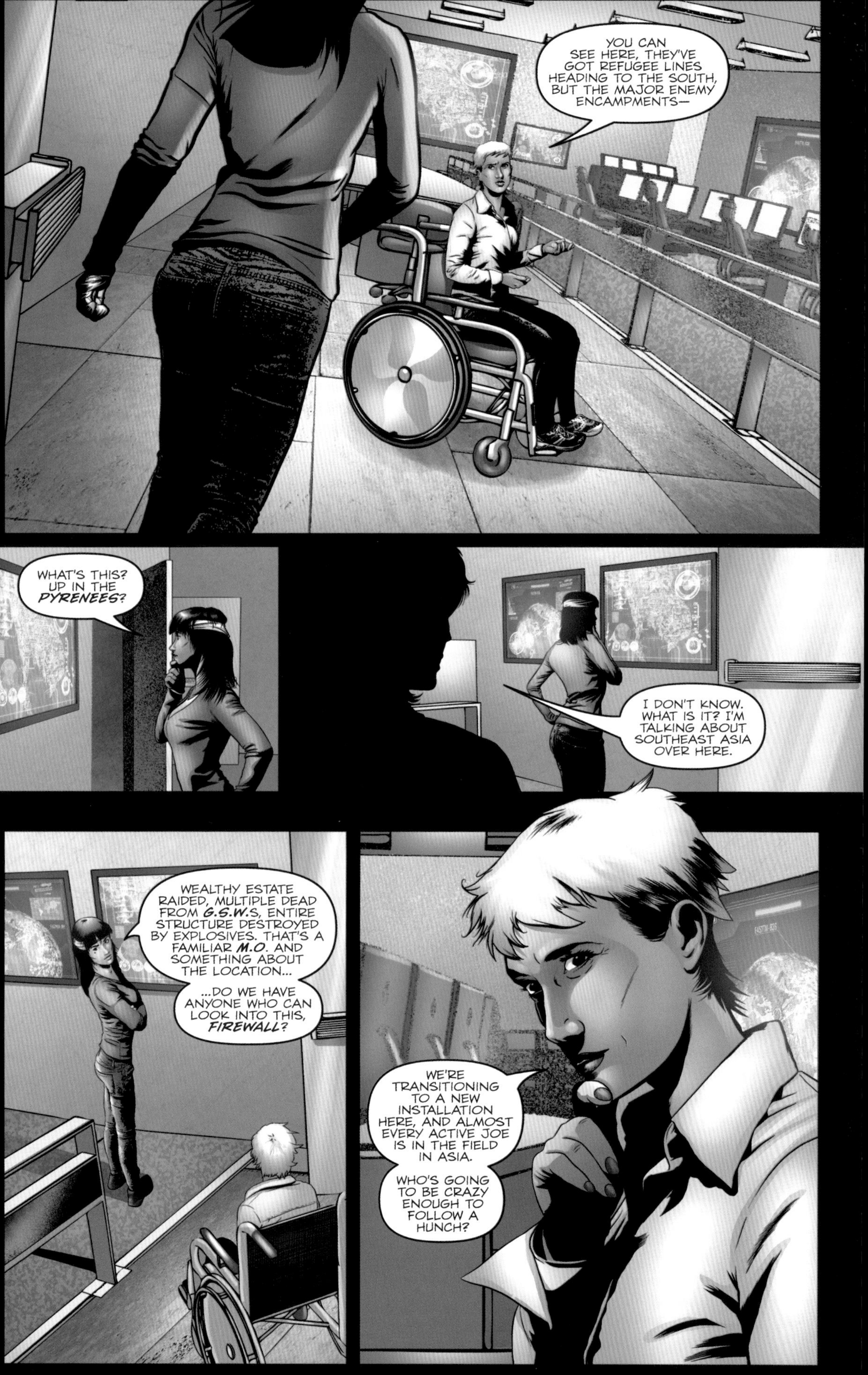
YOU CAN SEE HERE, THEY'VE GOT REFUGEE LINES HEADING TO THE SOUTH, BUT THE MAJOR ENEMY ENCAMPMENTS—
WHAT'S THIS? UP IN THE PYRENEES?
I DON'T KNOW. WHAT IS IT? I'M TALKING ABOUT SOUTHEAST ASIA OVER HERE.
WEALTHY ESTATE RAIDED, MULTIPLE DEAD FROM G.S.W.S, ENTIRE STRUCTURE DESTROYED BY EXPLOSIVES. THAT'S A FAMILIAR M.O. AND SOMETHING ABOUT THE LOCATION...
...DO WE HAVE ANYONE WHO CAN LOOK INTO THIS, FIREWALL?
WE'RE TRANSITIONING TO A NEW INSTALLATION HERE, AND ALMOST EVERY ACTIVE JOE IS IN THE FIELD IN ASIA.
WHO'S GOING TO BE CRAZY ENOUGH TO FOLLOW A HUNCH?

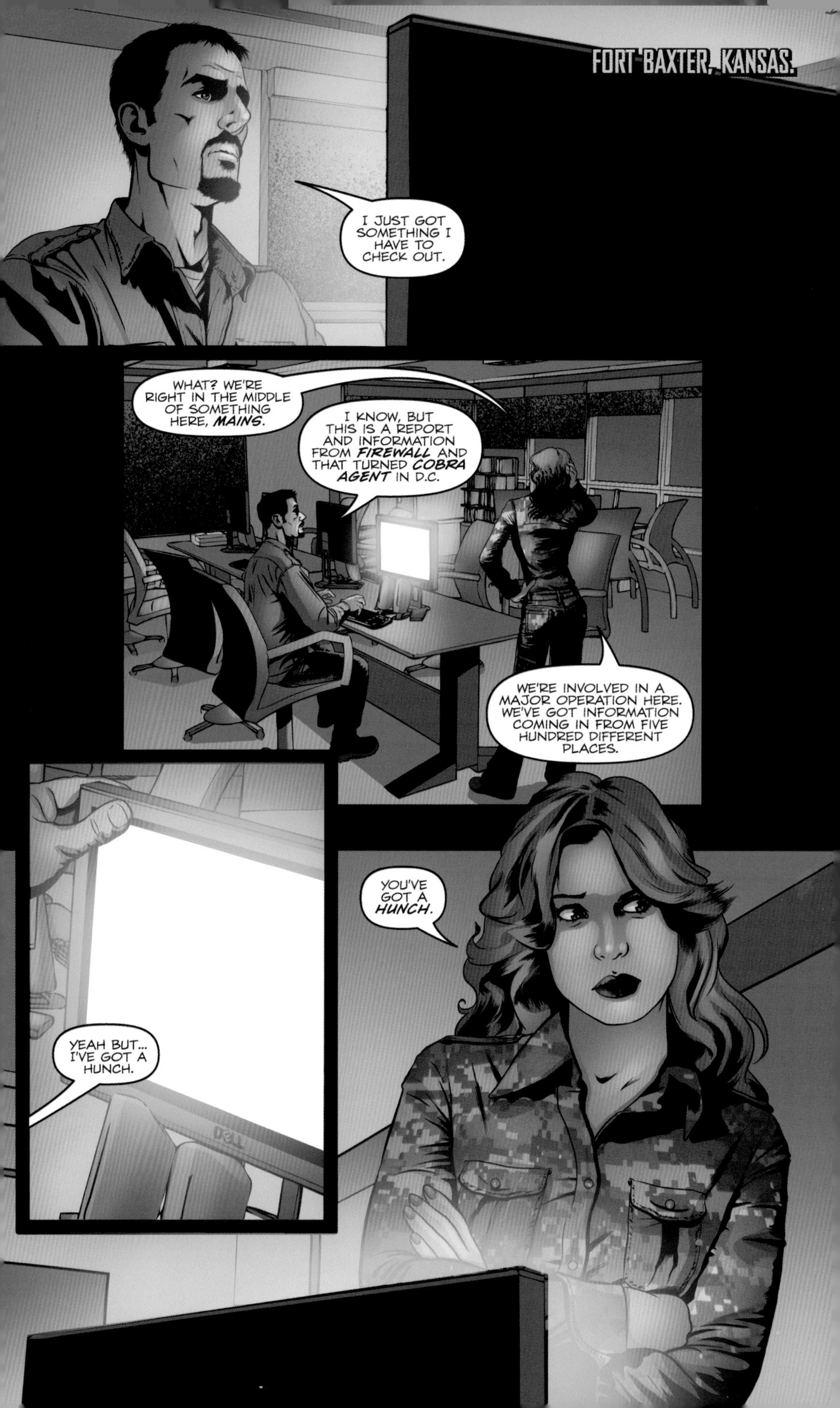
FORT BAXTER, KANSAS.
I JUST GOT SOMETHING I HAVE TO CHECK OUT.
WHAT? WE'RE RIGHT IN THE MIDDLE OF SOMETHING HERE, MAINS.
I KNOW, BUT THIS IS A REPORT AND INFORMATION FROM FIREWALL AND THAT TURNED COBRA AGENT IN D.C.
WE'RE INVOLVED IN A MAJOR OPERATION HERE. WE'VE GOT INFORMATION COMING IN FROM FIVE HUNDRED DIFFERENT PLACES.
YEAH BUT... I'VE GOT A HUNCH.
YOU'VE GOT A HUNCH.

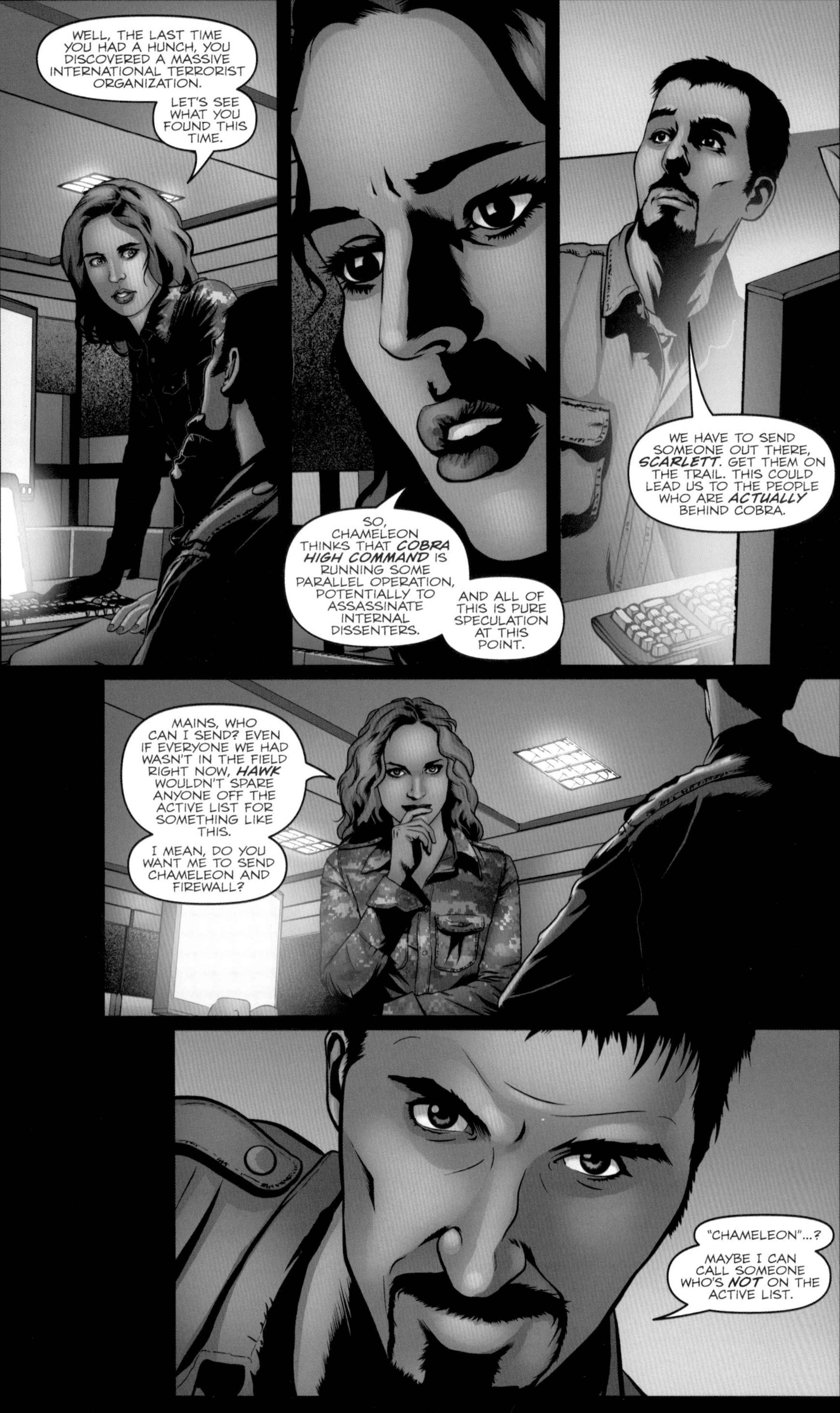
WELL, THE LAST TIME YOU HAD A HUNCH, YOU DISCOVERED A MASSIVE INTERNATIONAL TERRORIST ORGANIZATION.
LET'S SEE WHAT YOU FOUND THIS TIME.
SO, CHAMELEON THINKS THAT ***COBRA HIGH COMMAND*** IS RUNNING SOME PARALLEL OPERATION, POTENTIALLY TO ASSASSINATE INTERNAL DISSENTERS.
AND ALL OF THIS IS PURE SPECULATION AT THIS POINT.
WE HAVE TO SEND SOMEONE OUT THERE, ***SCARLETT***. GET THEM ON THE TRAIL. THIS COULD LEAD US TO THE PEOPLE WHO ARE ***ACTUALLY*** BEHIND COBRA.
MAINS, WHO CAN I SEND? EVEN IF EVERYONE WE HAD WASN'T IN THE FIELD RIGHT NOW, ***HAWK*** WOULDN'T SPARE ANYONE OFF THE ACTIVE LIST FOR SOMETHING LIKE THIS.
I MEAN, DO YOU WANT ME TO SEND CHAMELEON AND FIREWALL?
"CHAMELEON"...?
MAYBE I CAN CALL SOMEONE WHO'S ***NOT*** ON THE ACTIVE LIST.

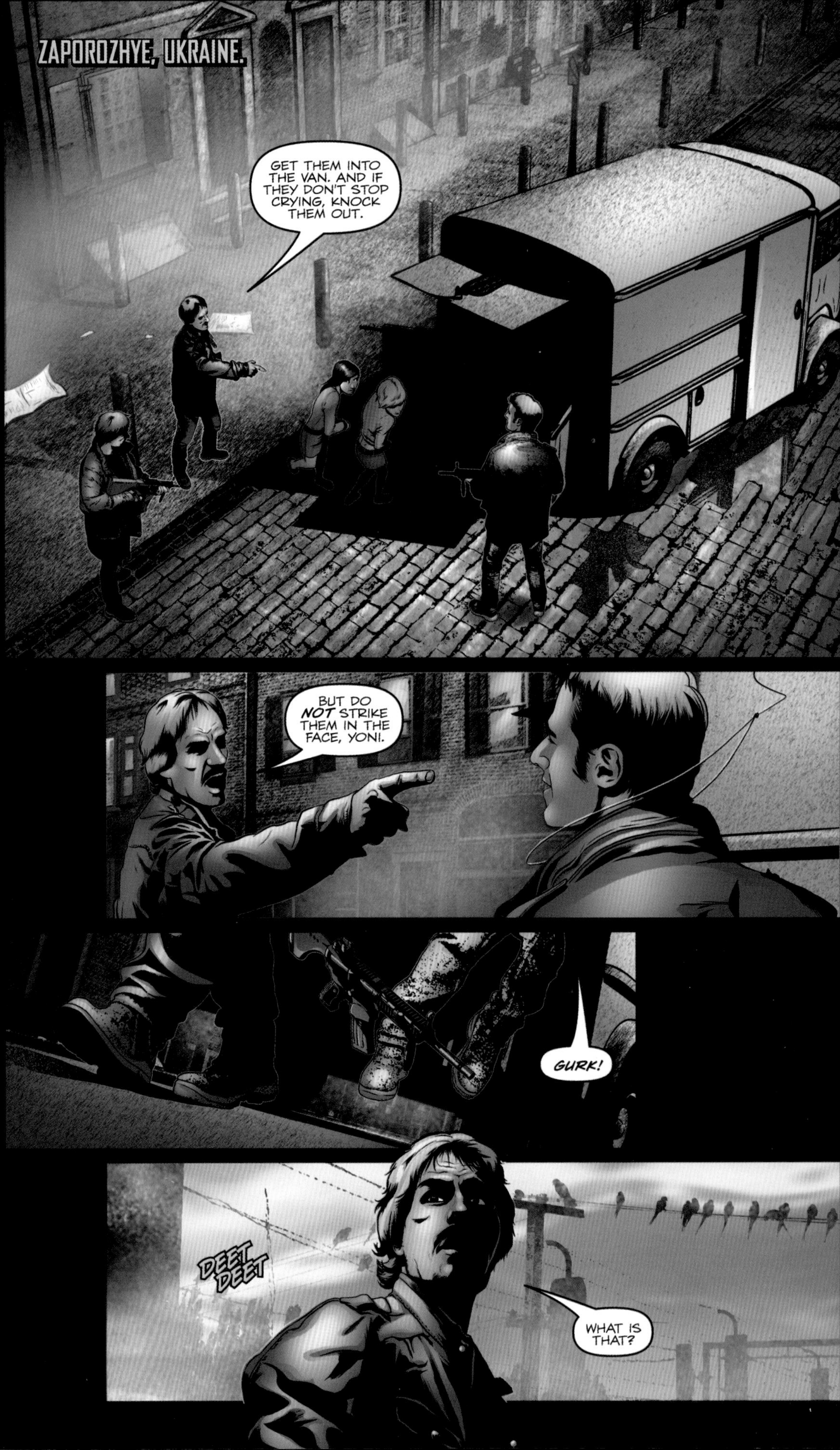
ZAPOROZHYE, UKRAINE.
GET THEM INTO THE VAN. AND IF THEY DON'T STOP CRYING, KNOCK THEM OUT.
BUT DO NOT STRIKE THEM IN THE FACE, YONI.
GURK!
DEET DEET
WHAT IS THAT?

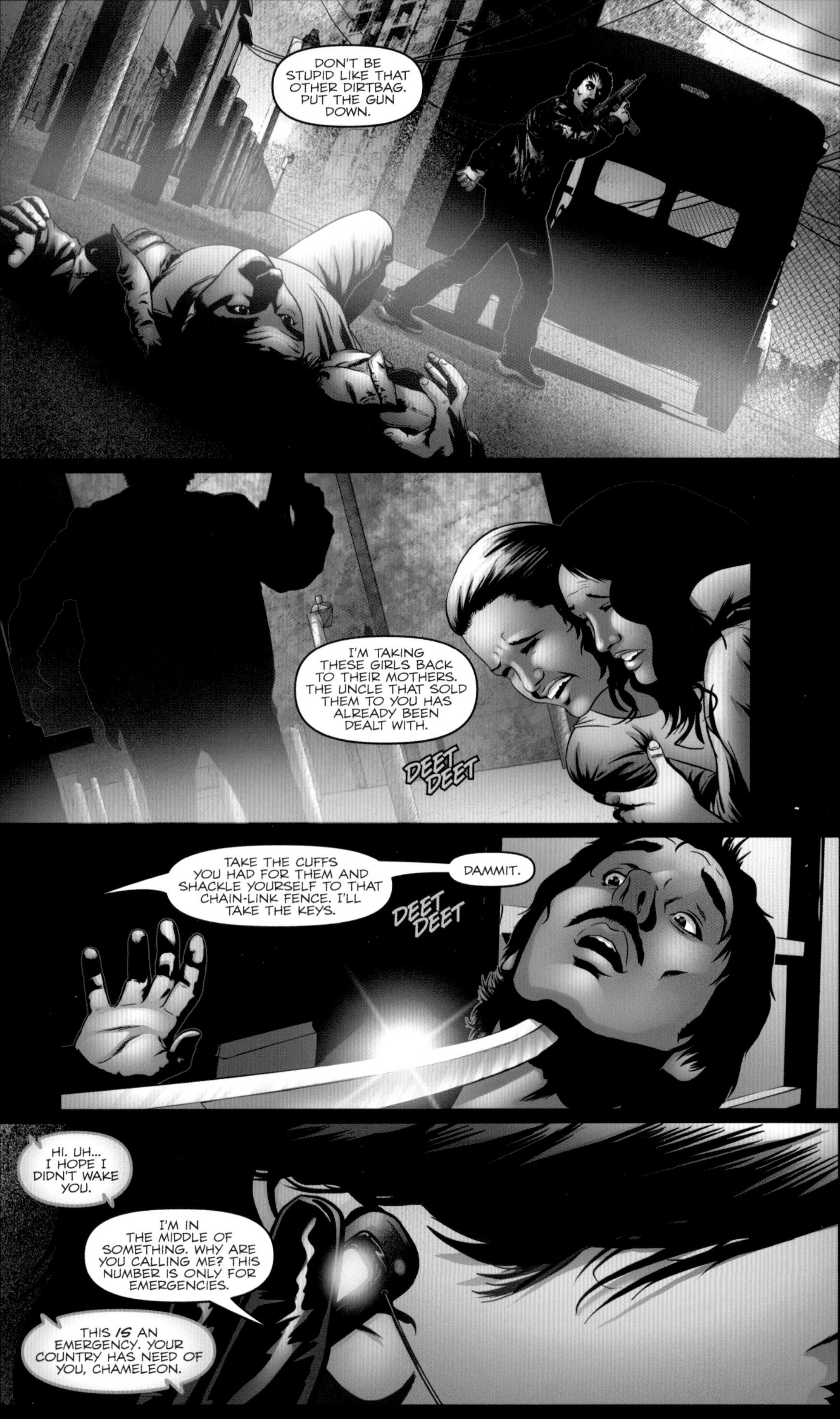

DON'T BE STUPID LIKE THAT OTHER DIRTBAG. PUT THE GUN DOWN.
I'M TAKING THESE GIRLS BACK TO THEIR MOTHERS. THE UNCLE THAT SOLD THEM TO YOU HAS ALREADY BEEN DEALT WITH.
DEET DEET
TAKE THE CUFFS YOU HAD FOR THEM AND SHACKLE YOURSELF TO THAT CHAIN-LINK FENCE. I'LL TAKE THE KEYS.
DAMMIT.
DEET DEET
HI. UH... I HOPE I DIDN'T WAKE YOU.
I'M IN THE MIDDLE OF SOMETHING. WHY ARE YOU CALLING ME? THIS NUMBER IS ONLY FOR EMERGENCIES.
THIS *IS* AN EMERGENCY. YOUR COUNTRY HAS NEED OF YOU, CHAMELEON.

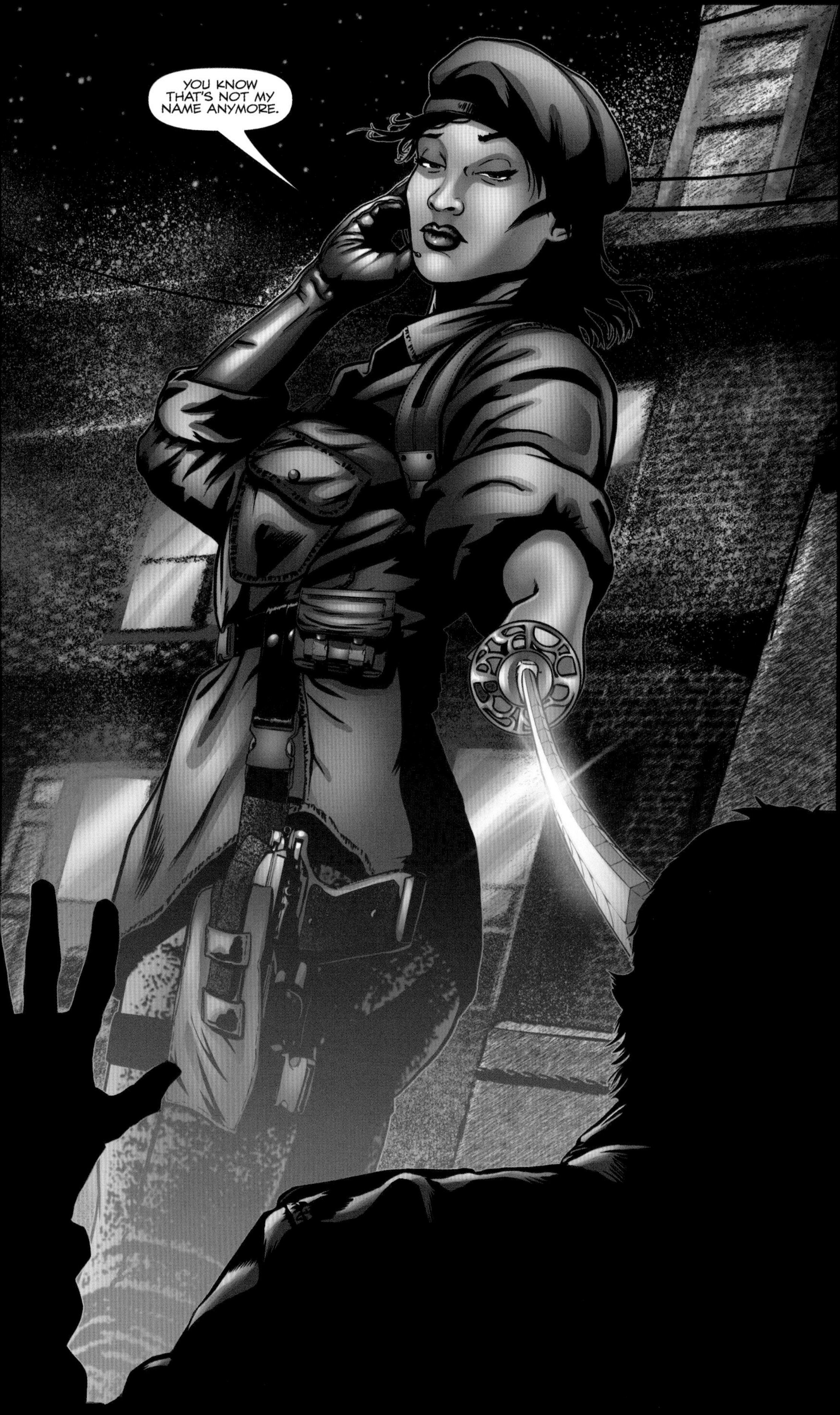
YOU KNOW THAT'S NOT MY NAME ANYMORE.

COBRA #10B by **Antonio Fuso**
Colors by **Arianna Florean**

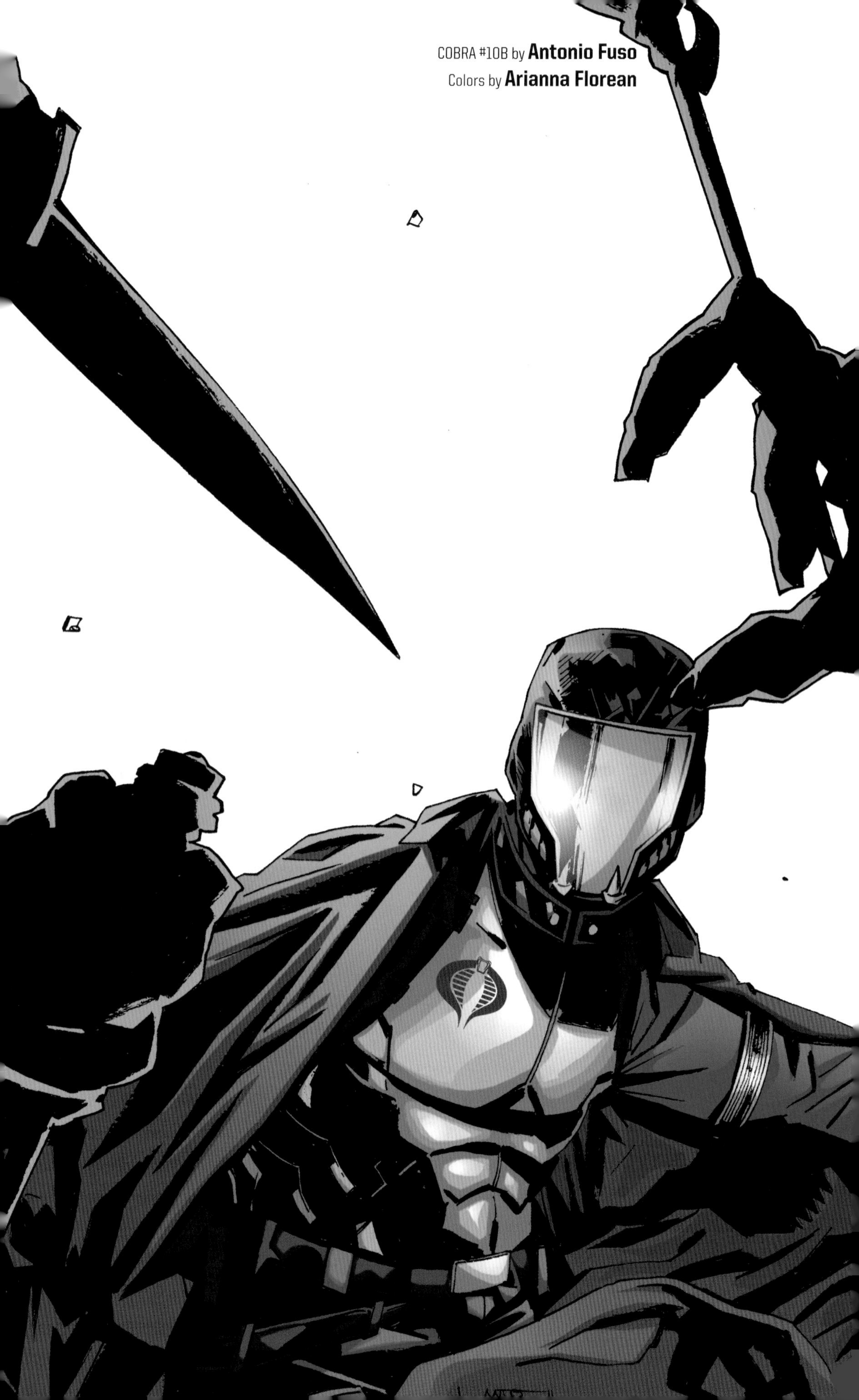

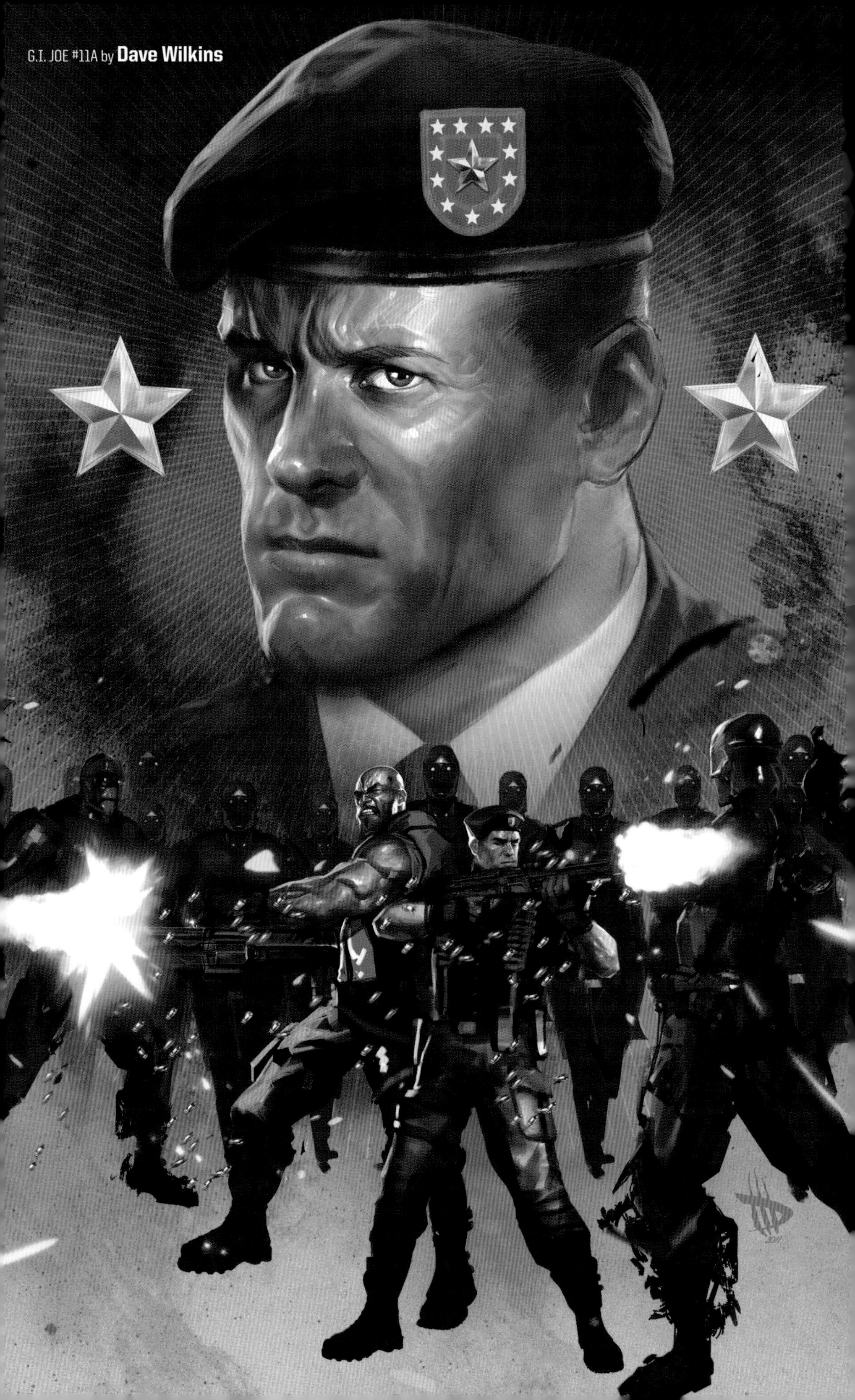

G.I. JOE #11A by **Dave Wilkins**

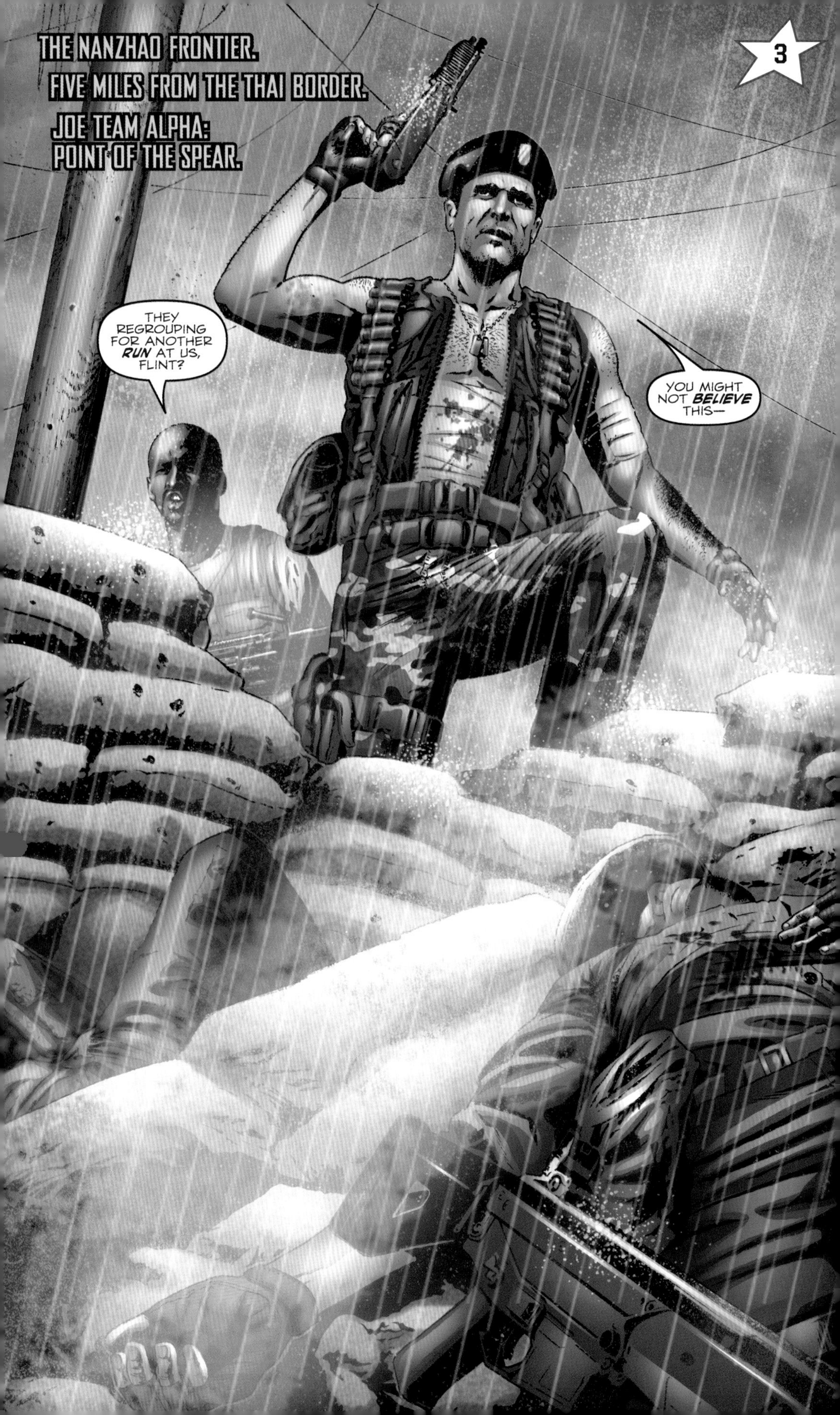
THE NANZHAO FRONTIER.
FIVE MILES FROM THE THAI BORDER.
JOE TEAM ALPHA: POINT OF THE SPEAR.
3
THEY REGROUPING FOR ANOTHER RUN AT US, FLINT?
YOU MIGHT NOT BELIEVE THIS--

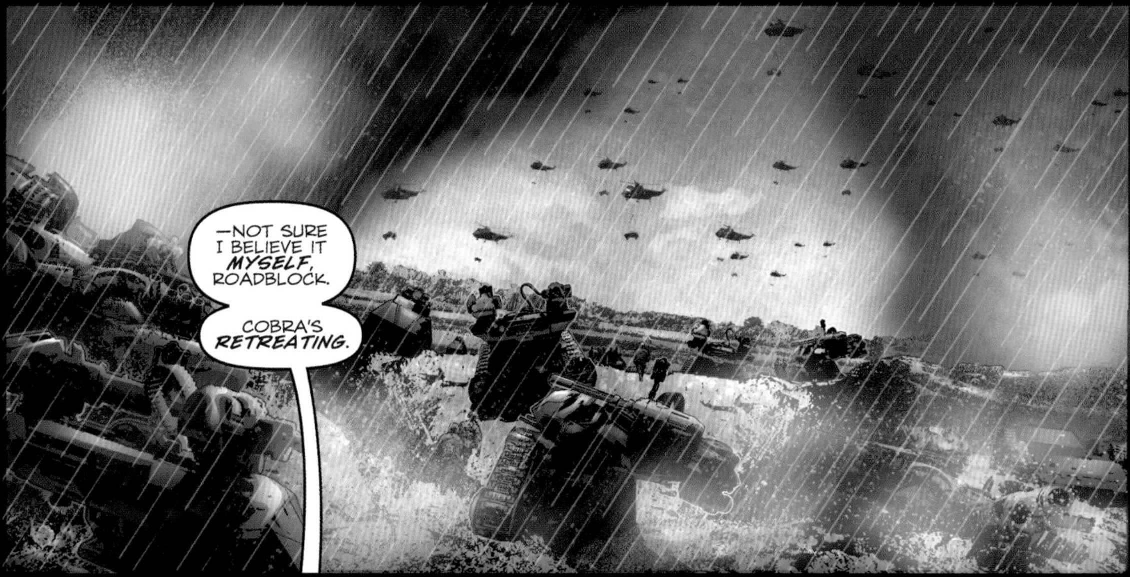
—NOT SURE I BELIEVE IT MYSELF, ROADBLOCK.
COBRA'S RETREATING.

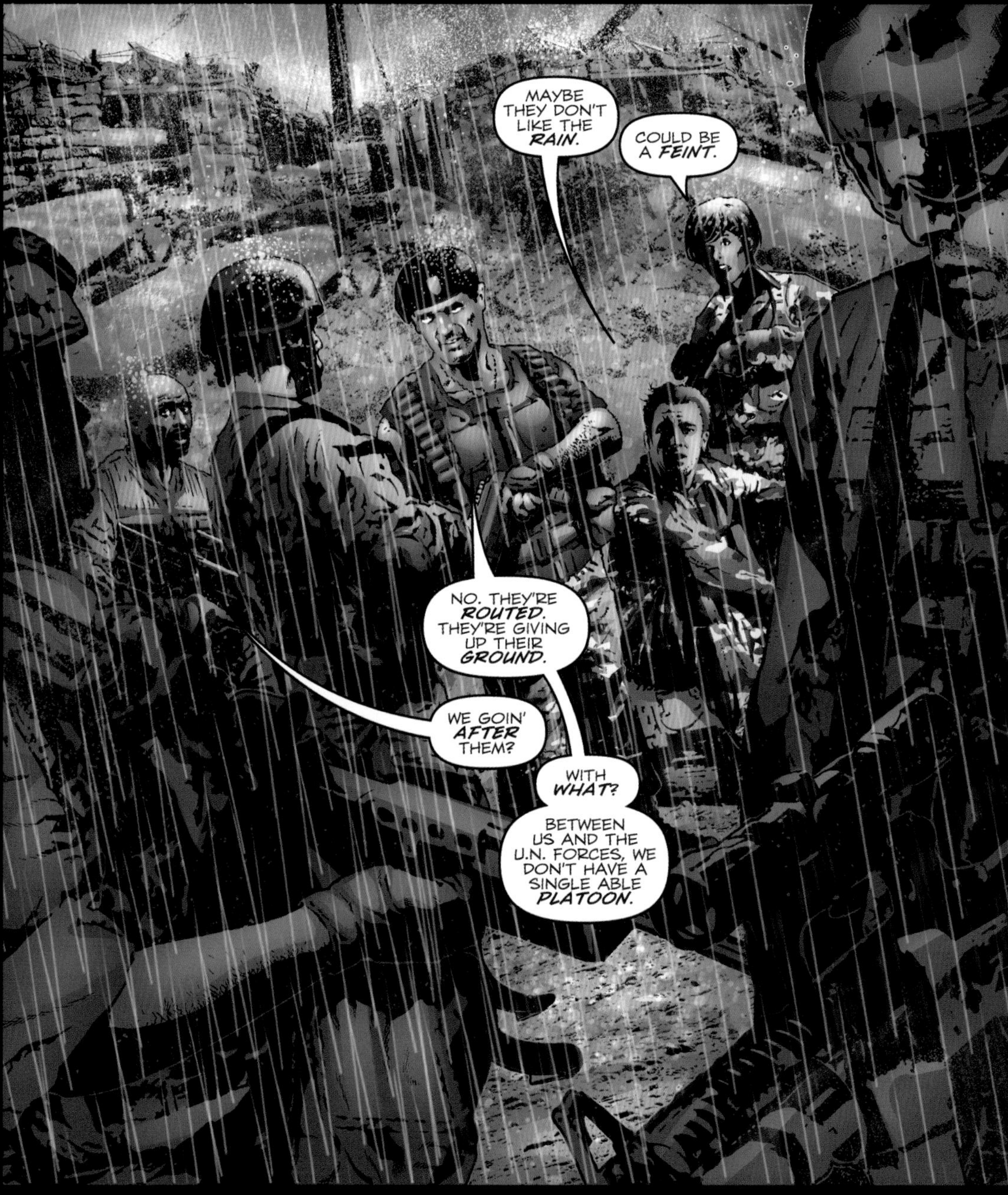
MAYBE THEY DON'T LIKE THE RAIN.
COULD BE A FEINT.
NO. THEY'RE ROUTED. THEY'RE GIVING UP THEIR GROUND.
WE GOIN' AFTER THEM?
WITH WHAT?
BETWEEN US AND THE U.N. FORCES, WE DON'T HAVE A SINGLE ABLE PLATOON.

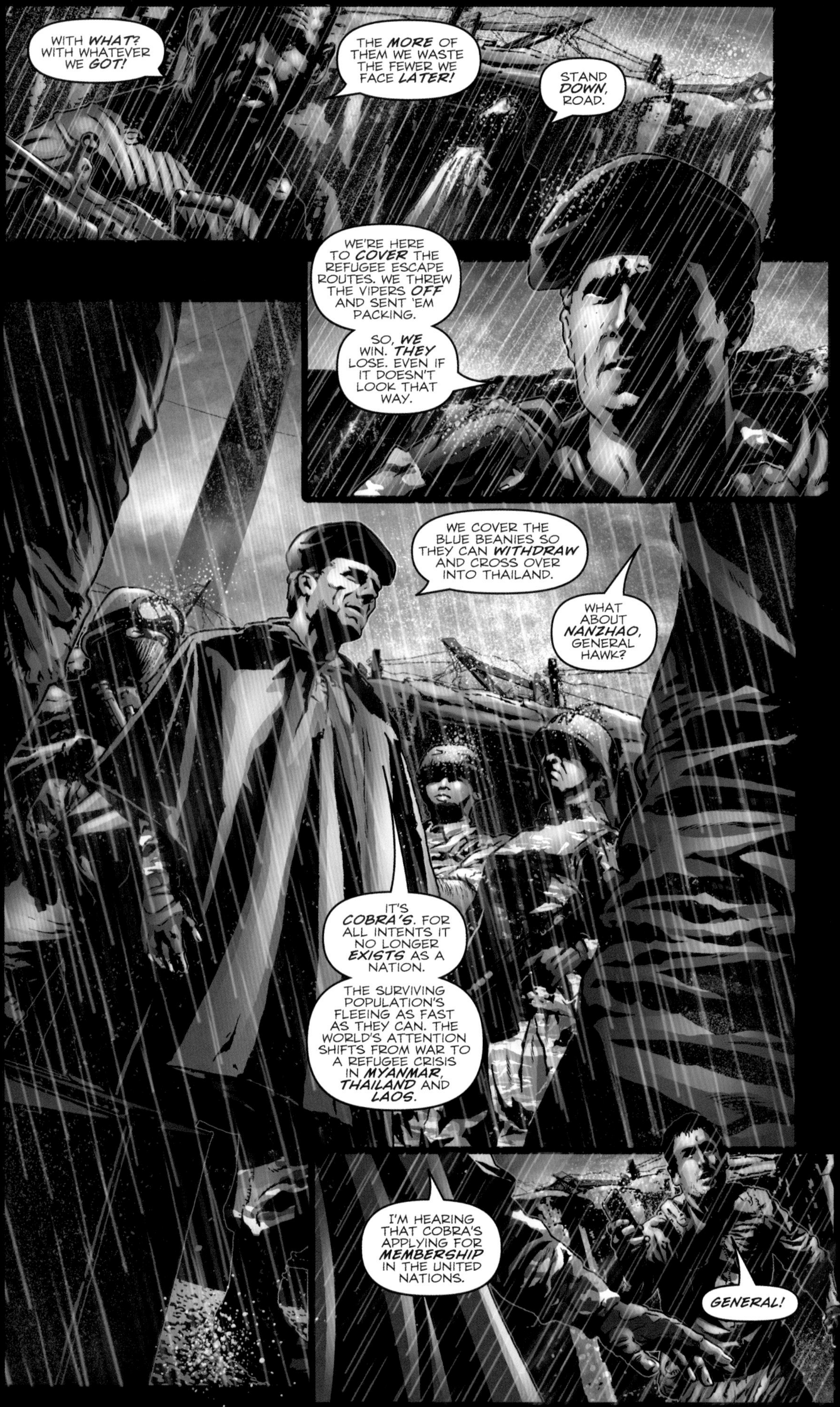
WITH WHAT? WITH WHATEVER WE GOT!
THE MORE OF THEM WE WASTE THE FEWER WE FACE LATER!
STAND DOWN, ROAD.
WE'RE HERE TO COVER THE REFUGEE ESCAPE ROUTES. WE THREW THE VIPERS OFF AND SENT 'EM PACKING.
SO, WE WIN. THEY LOSE. EVEN IF IT DOESN'T LOOK THAT WAY.
WE COVER THE BLUE BEANIES SO THEY CAN WITHDRAW AND CROSS OVER INTO THAILAND.
WHAT ABOUT NANZHAO, GENERAL HAWK?
IT'S COBRA'S. FOR ALL INTENTS IT NO LONGER EXISTS AS A NATION.
THE SURVIVING POPULATION'S FLEEING AS FAST AS THEY CAN. THE WORLD'S ATTENTION SHIFTS FROM WAR TO A REFUGEE CRISIS IN MYANMAR, THAILAND AND LAOS.
I'M HEARING THAT COBRA'S APPLYING FOR MEMBERSHIP IN THE UNITED NATIONS.
GENERAL!

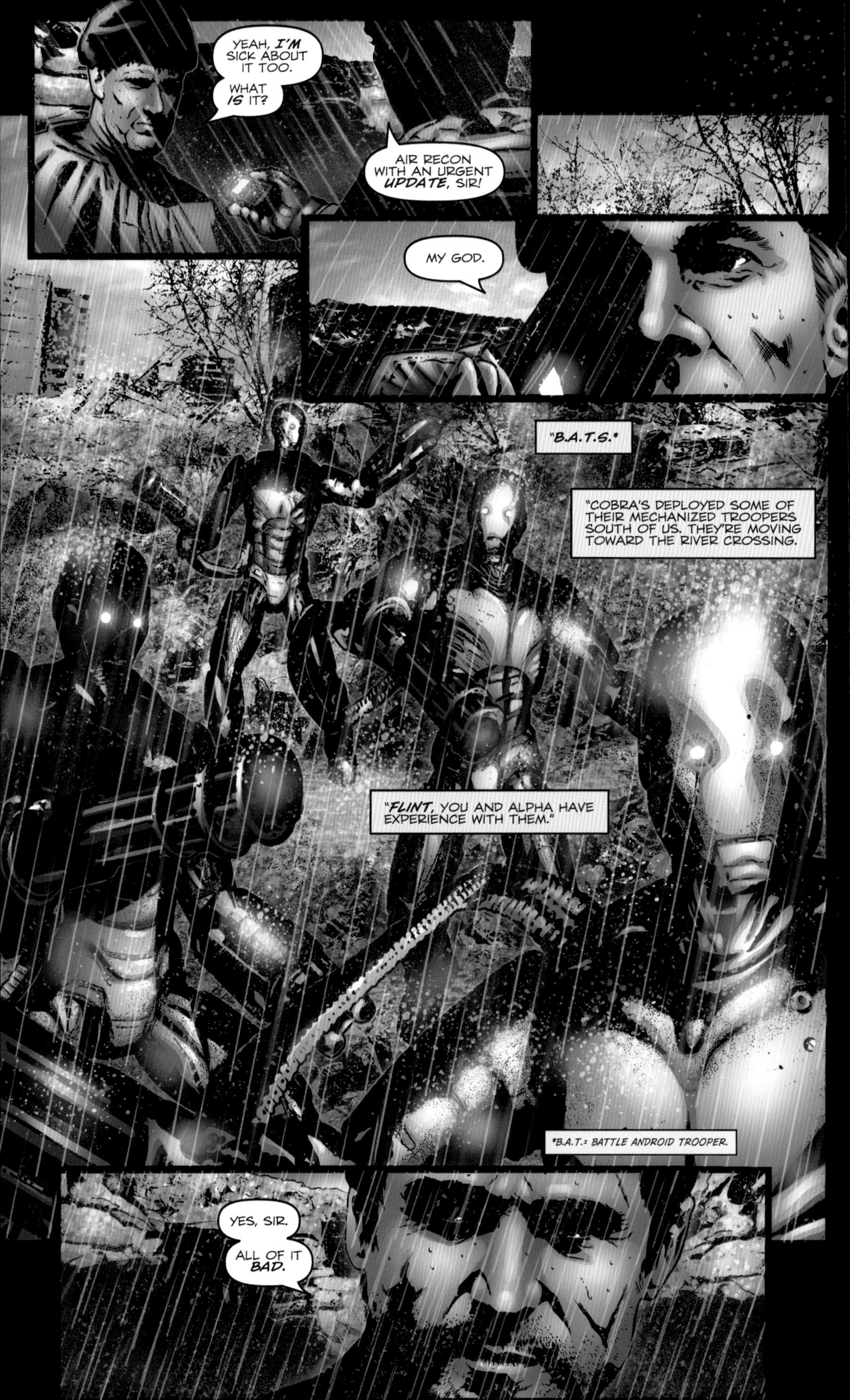
YEAH, I'M SICK ABOUT IT TOO.
WHAT IS IT?
AIR RECON WITH AN URGENT UPDATE, SIR!
MY GOD.
"B.A.T.S.*
"COBRA'S DEPLOYED SOME OF THEIR MECHANIZED TROOPERS SOUTH OF US. THEY'RE MOVING TOWARD THE RIVER CROSSING.
"FLINT, YOU AND ALPHA HAVE EXPERIENCE WITH THEM."
*B.A.T.= BATTLE ANDROID TROOPER.
YES, SIR.
ALL OF IT BAD.

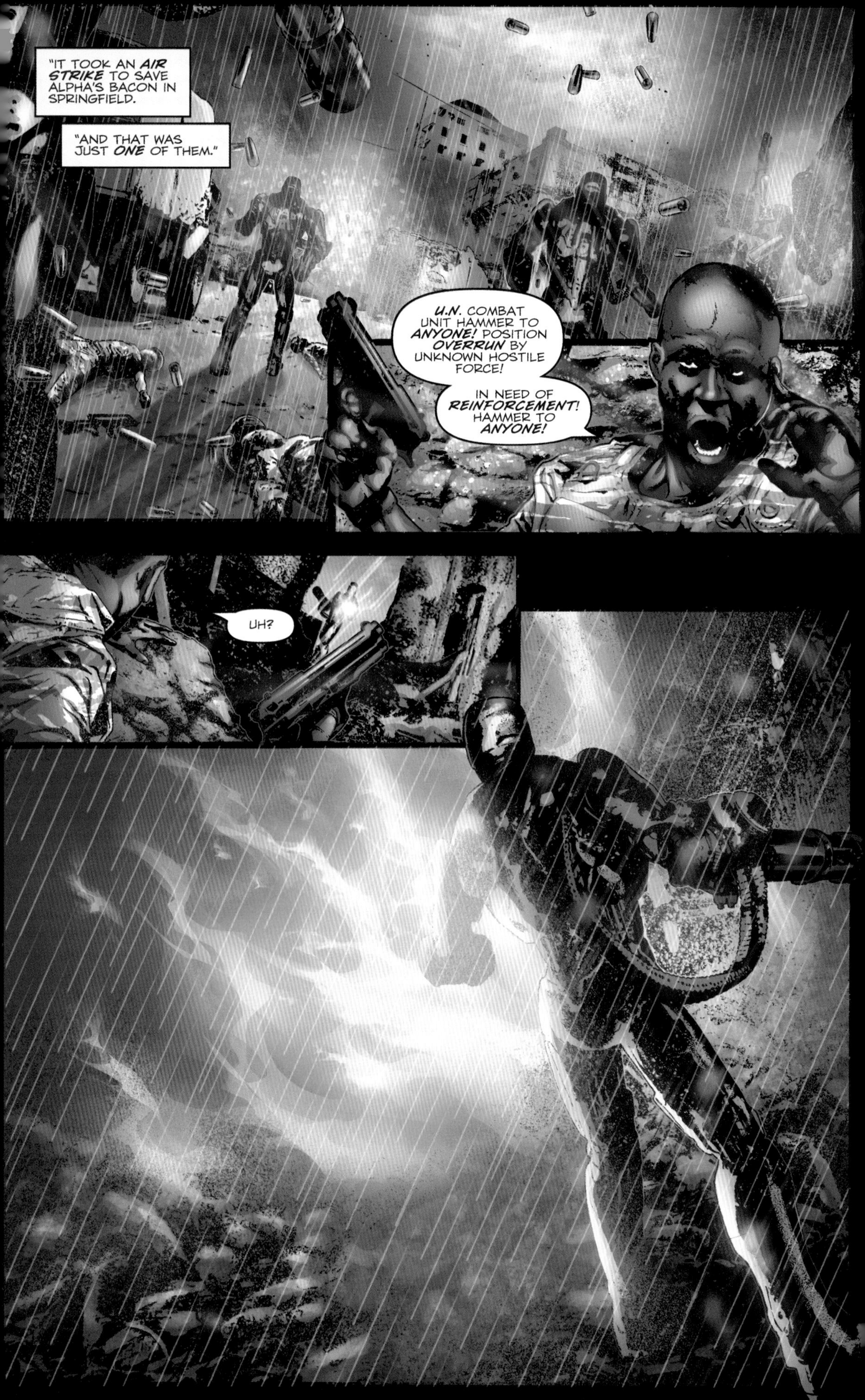
"IT TOOK AN AIR STRIKE TO SAVE ALPHA'S BACON IN SPRINGFIELD.
"AND THAT WAS JUST ONE OF THEM."
U.N. COMBAT UNIT HAMMER TO ANYONE! POSITION OVERRUN BY UNKNOWN HOSTILE FORCE!
IN NEED OF REINFORCEMENT! HAMMER TO ANYONE!
UH?

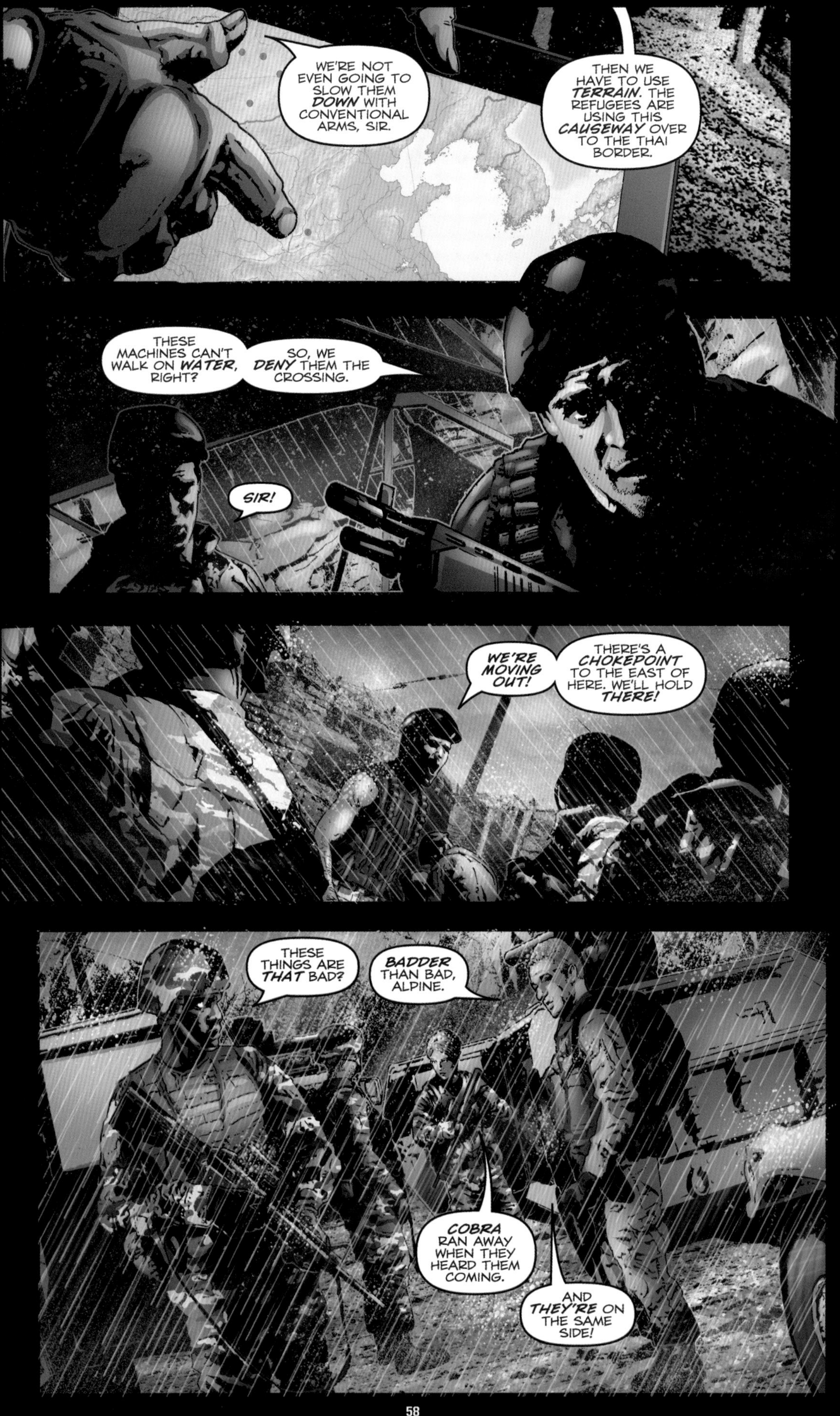
WE'RE NOT EVEN GOING TO SLOW THEM DOWN WITH CONVENTIONAL ARMS, SIR.
THEN WE HAVE TO USE TERRAIN. THE REFUGEES ARE USING THIS CAUSEWAY OVER TO THE THAI BORDER.
THESE MACHINES CAN'T WALK ON WATER, RIGHT?
SO, WE DENY THEM THE CROSSING.
SIR!
WE'RE MOVING OUT!
THERE'S A CHOKEPOINT TO THE EAST OF HERE. WE'LL HOLD THERE!
THESE THINGS ARE THAT BAD?
BADDER THAN BAD, ALPINE.
COBRA RAN AWAY WHEN THEY HEARD THEM COMING.
AND THEY'RE ON THE SAME SIDE!

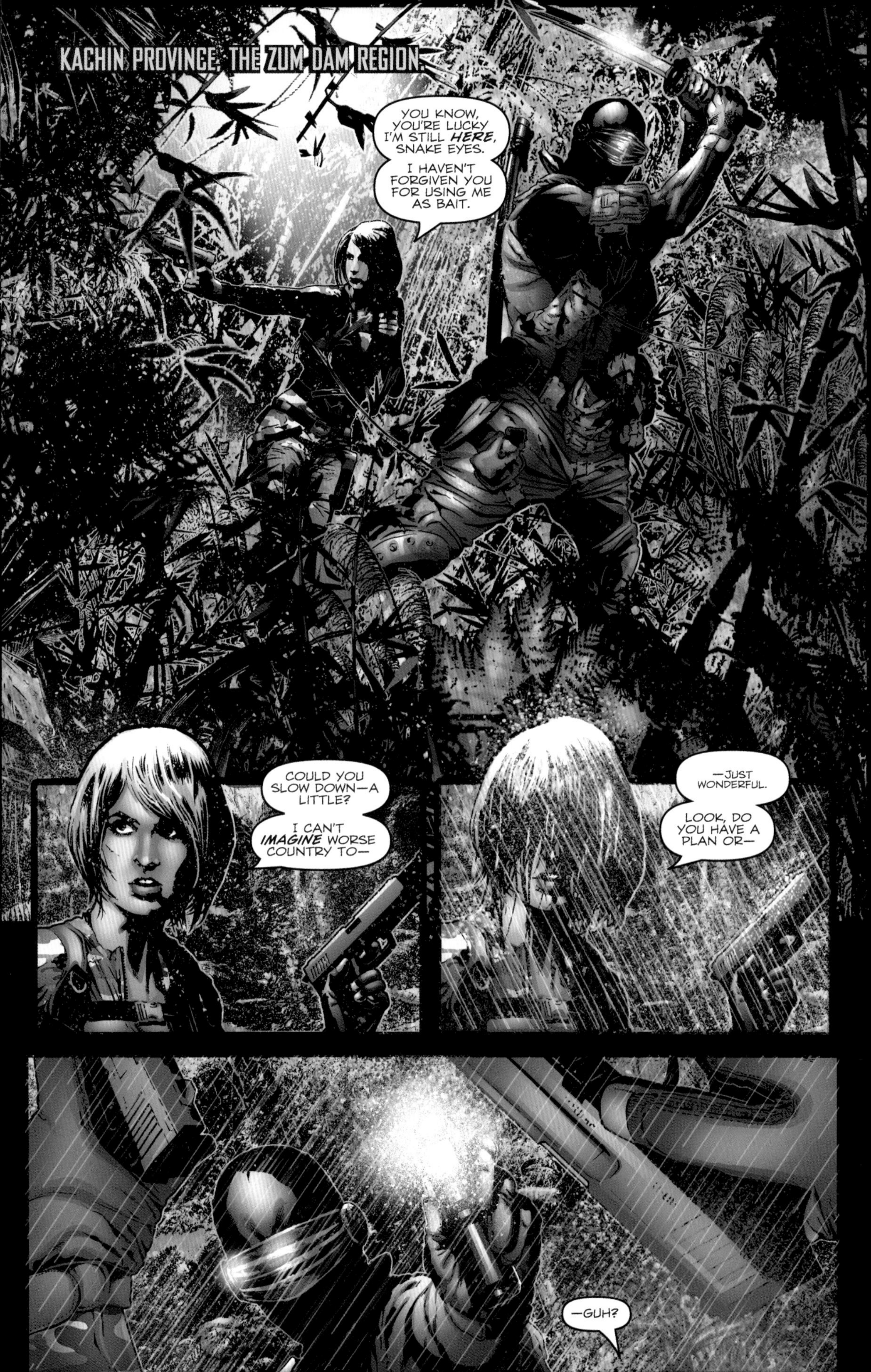
KACHIN PROVINCE, THE ZUM DAM REGION.
YOU KNOW, YOU'RE LUCKY I'M STILL *HERE*, SNAKE EYES.
I HAVEN'T FORGIVEN YOU FOR USING ME AS BAIT.
COULD YOU SLOW DOWN—A LITTLE?
I CAN'T *IMAGINE* WORSE COUNTRY TO—
—JUST WONDERFUL.
LOOK, DO YOU HAVE A PLAN OR—
—GUH?

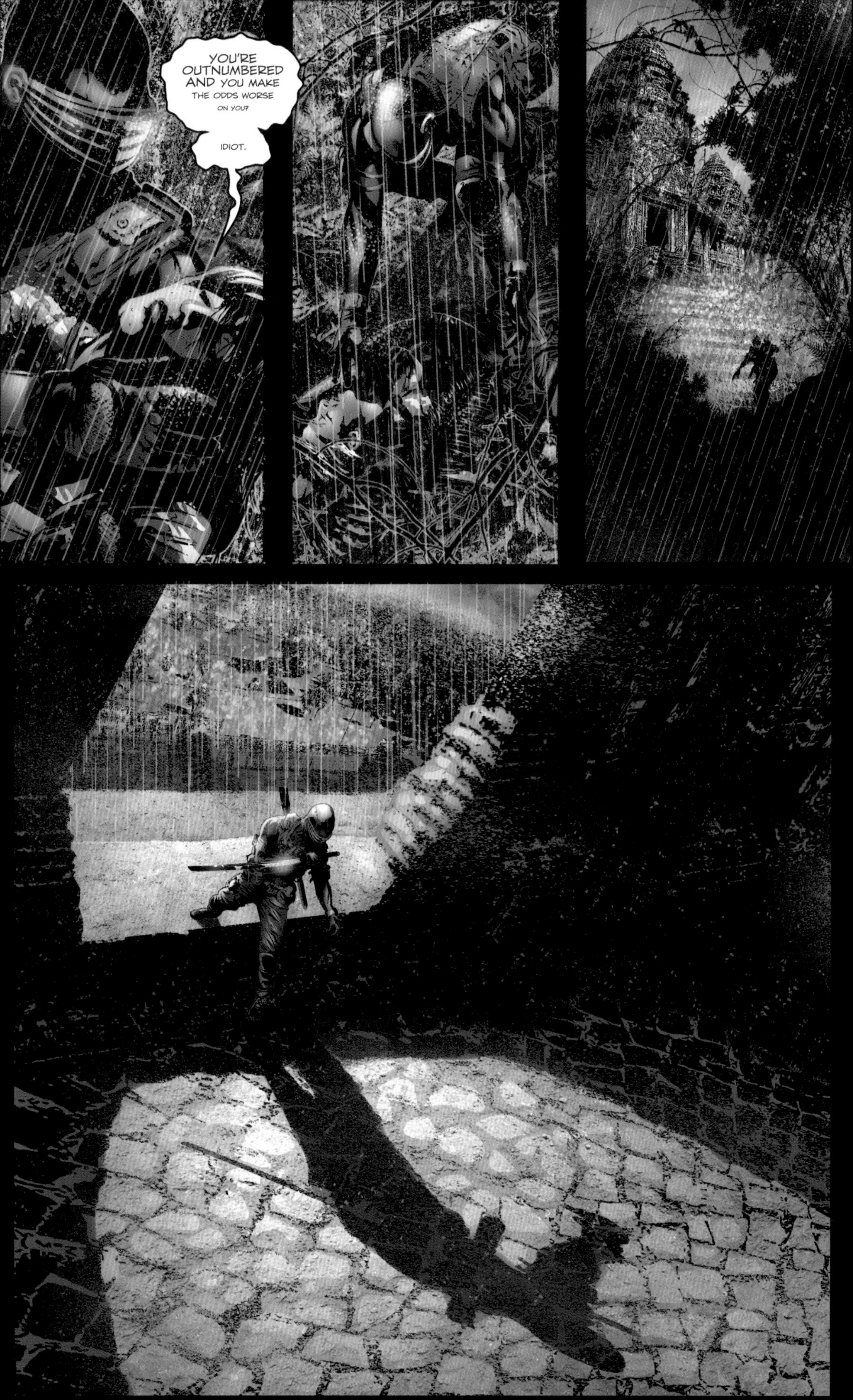
YOU'RE OUTNUMBERED AND YOU MAKE THE ODDS WORSE ON YOU?
IDIOT.

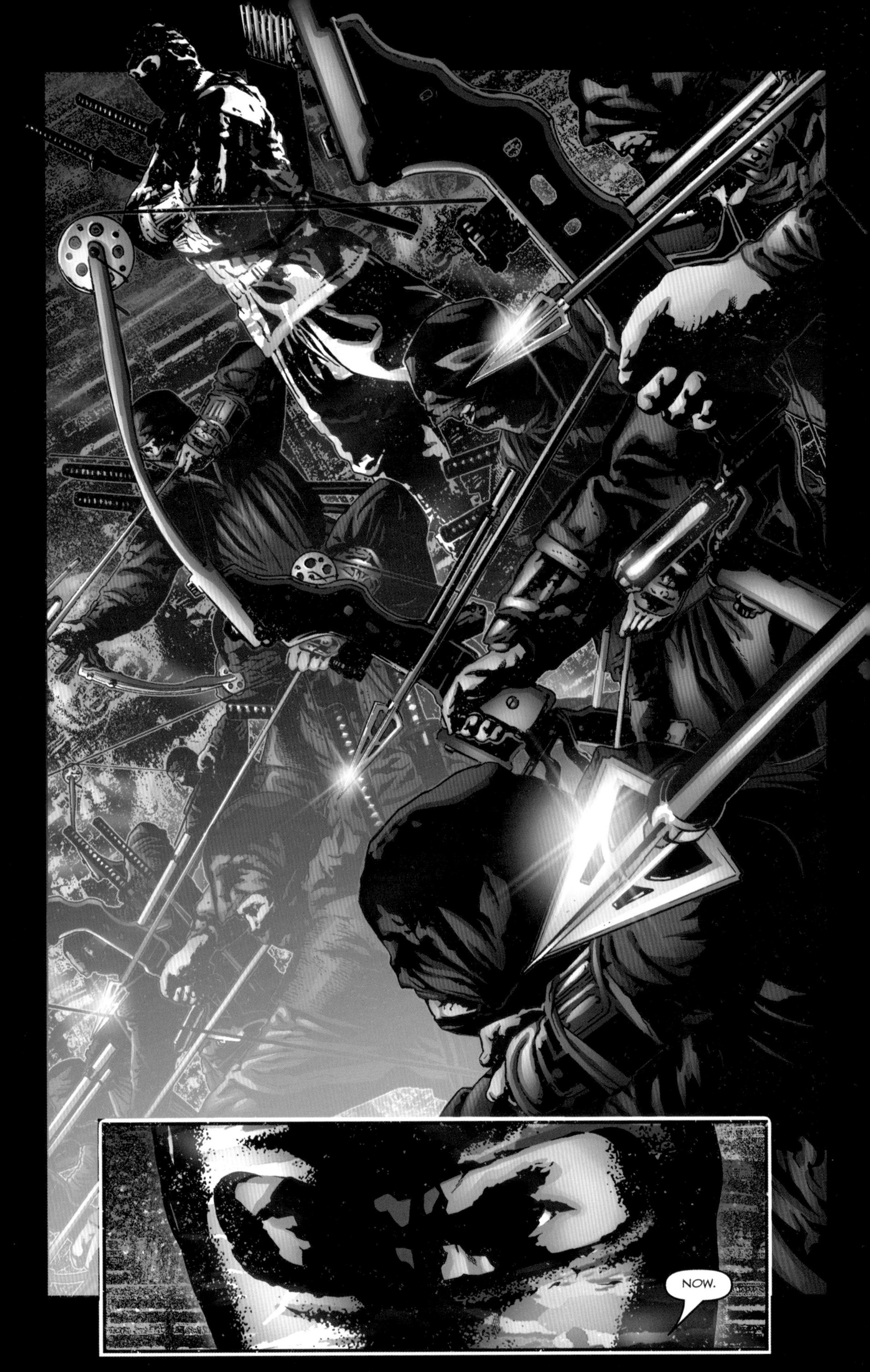
NOW.

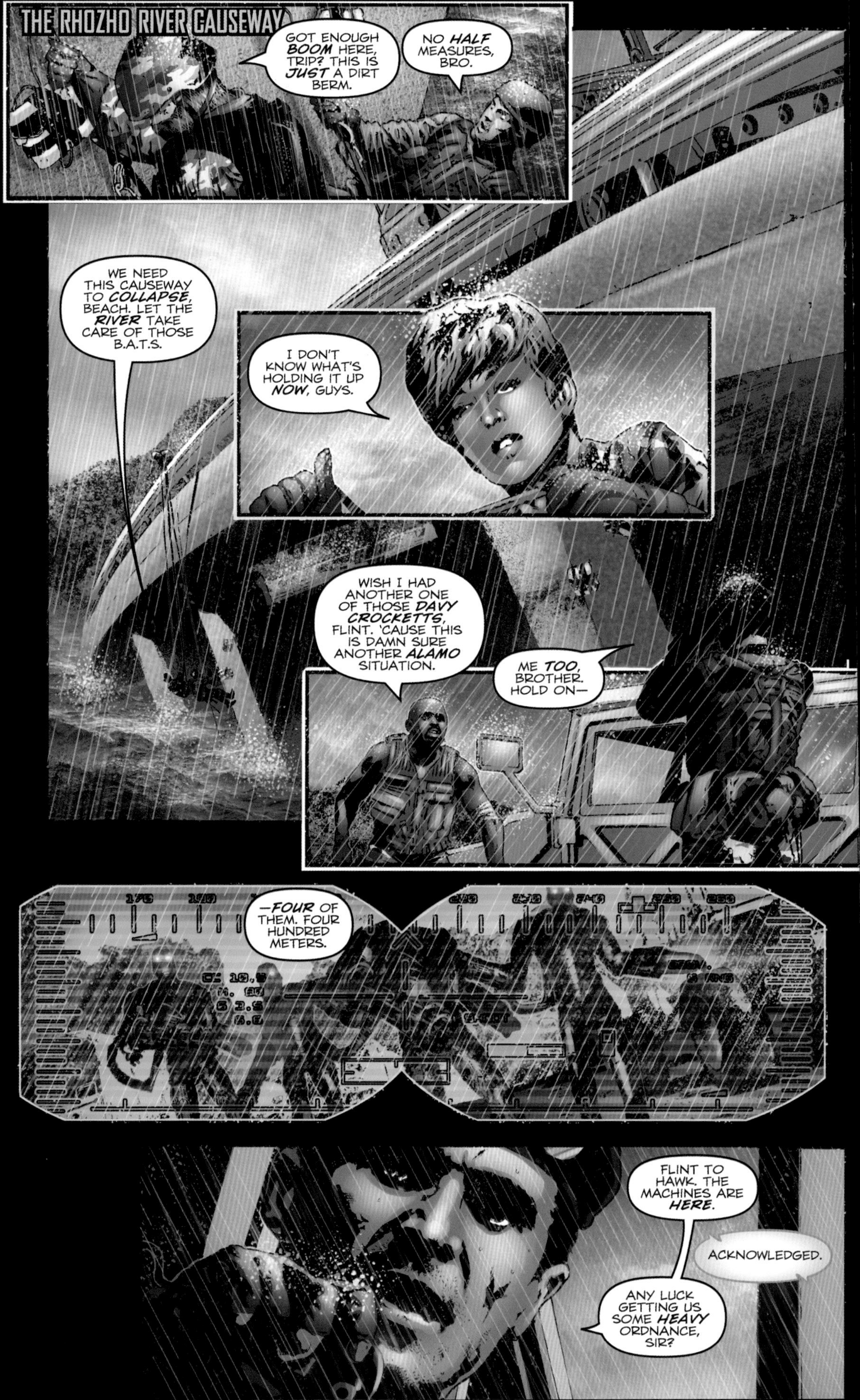
THE RHOZHO RIVER CAUSEWAY
GOT ENOUGH BOOM HERE, TRIP? THIS IS JUST A DIRT BERM.
NO HALF MEASURES, BRO.
WE NEED THIS CAUSEWAY TO COLLAPSE, BEACH. LET THE RIVER TAKE CARE OF THOSE B.A.T.S.
I DON'T KNOW WHAT'S HOLDING IT UP NOW, GUYS.
WISH I HAD ANOTHER ONE OF THOSE DAVY CROCKETTS, FLINT. 'CAUSE THIS IS DAMN SURE ANOTHER ALAMO SITUATION.
ME TOO, BROTHER. HOLD ON—
—FOUR OF THEM. FOUR HUNDRED METERS.
FLINT TO HAWK. THE MACHINES ARE HERE.
ACKNOWLEDGED.
ANY LUCK GETTING US SOME HEAVY ORDNANCE, SIR?

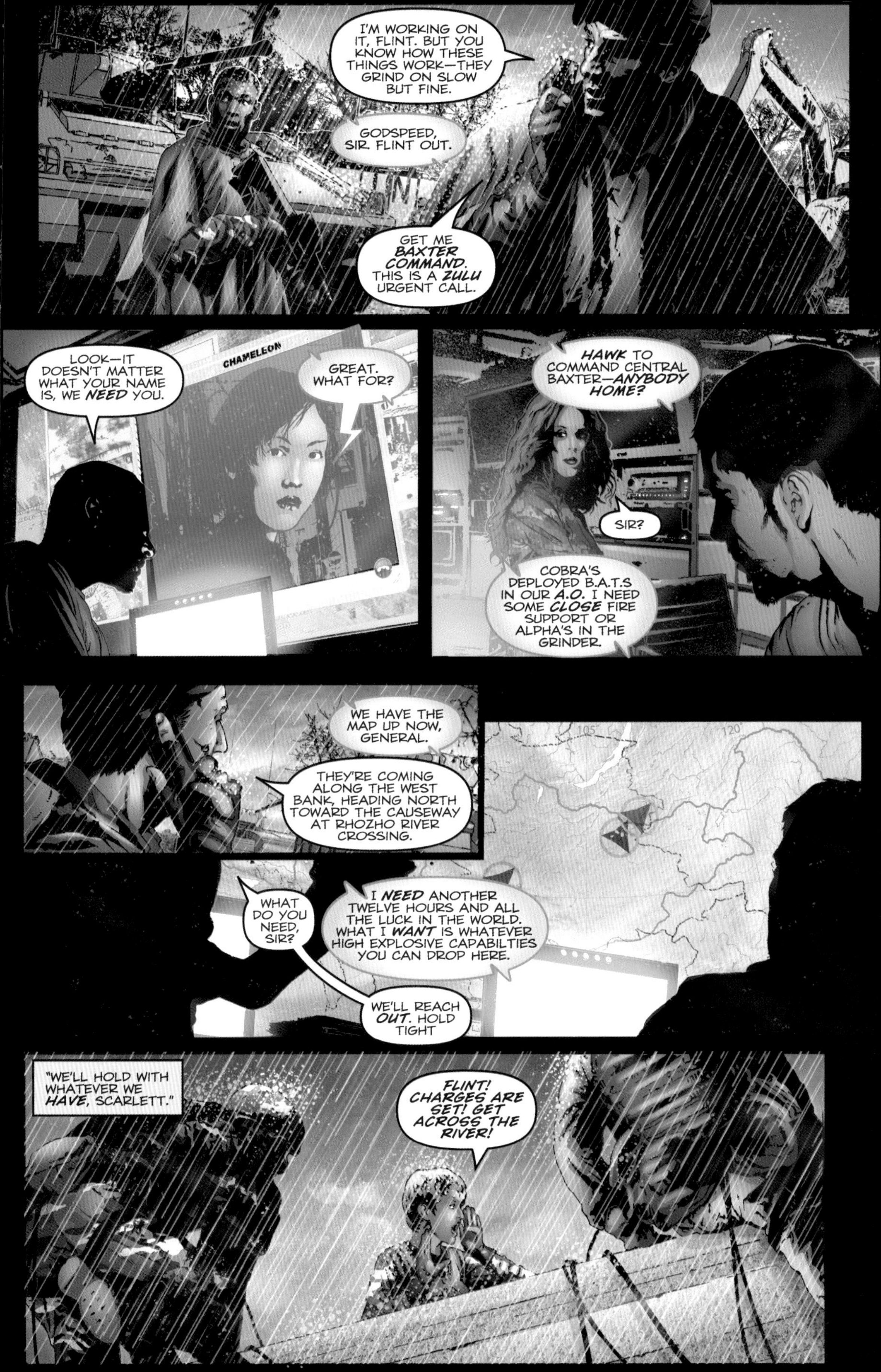
I'M WORKING ON IT, FLINT. BUT YOU KNOW HOW THESE THINGS WORK—THEY GRIND ON SLOW BUT FINE.
GODSPEED, SIR. FLINT OUT.
GET ME BAXTER COMMAND. THIS IS A ZULU URGENT CALL.
CHAMELEON
LOOK—IT DOESN'T MATTER WHAT YOUR NAME IS, WE NEED YOU.
GREAT. WHAT FOR?
HAWK TO COMMAND CENTRAL BAXTER—ANYBODY HOME?
SIR?
COBRA'S DEPLOYED B.A.T.S IN OUR A.O. I NEED SOME CLOSE FIRE SUPPORT OR ALPHA'S IN THE GRINDER.
WE HAVE THE MAP UP NOW, GENERAL.
THEY'RE COMING ALONG THE WEST BANK, HEADING NORTH TOWARD THE CAUSEWAY AT RHOZHO RIVER CROSSING.
105°
120°
WHAT DO YOU NEED, SIR?
I NEED ANOTHER TWELVE HOURS AND ALL THE LUCK IN THE WORLD. WHAT I WANT IS WHATEVER HIGH EXPLOSIVE CAPABILTIES YOU CAN DROP HERE.
WE'LL REACH OUT. HOLD TIGHT
"WE'LL HOLD WITH WHATEVER WE HAVE, SCARLETT."
FLINT! CHARGES ARE SET! GET ACROSS THE RIVER!

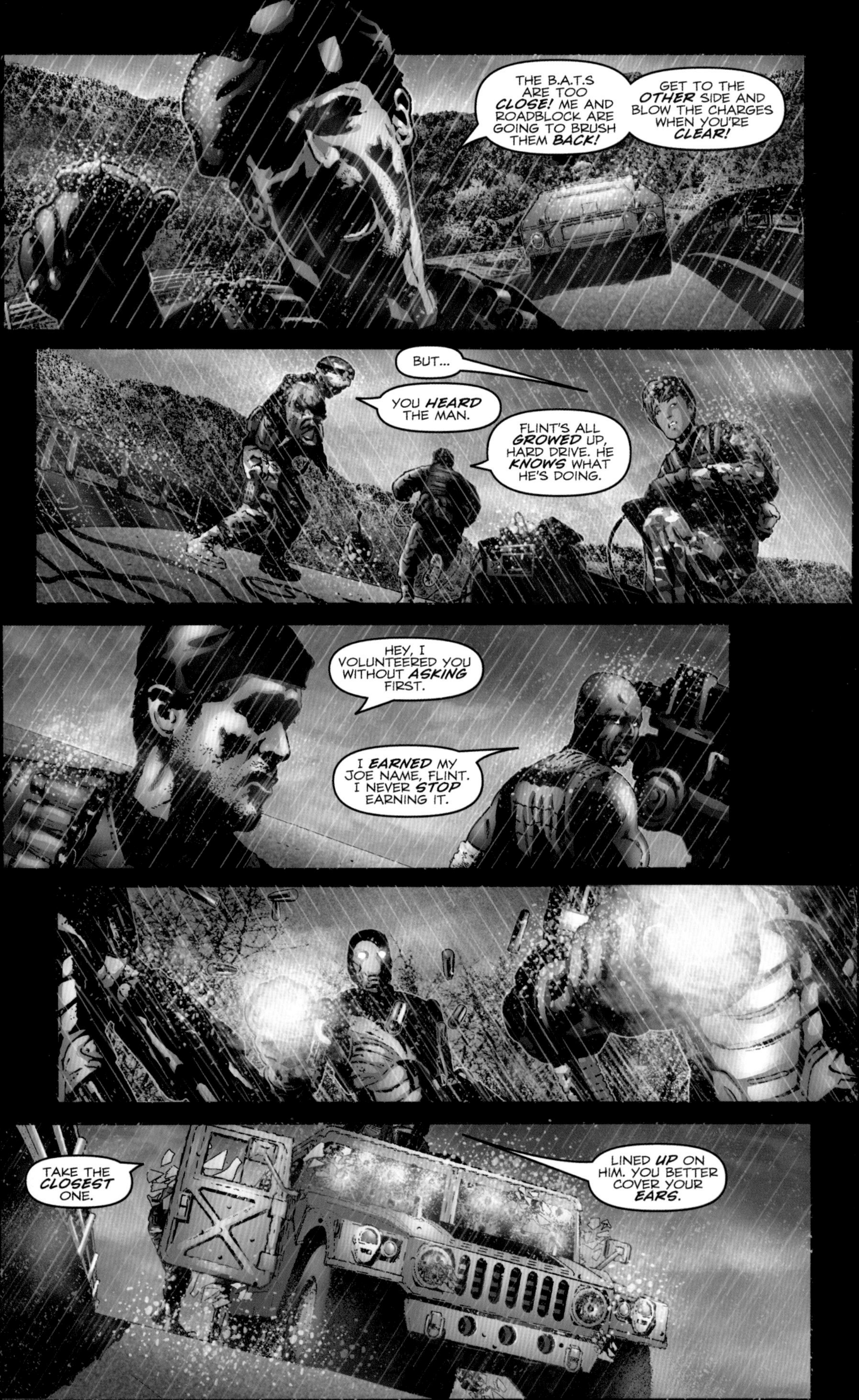
THE B.A.T.S ARE TOO CLOSE! ME AND ROADBLOCK ARE GOING TO BRUSH THEM BACK!
GET TO THE OTHER SIDE AND BLOW THE CHARGES WHEN YOU'RE CLEAR!
BUT...
YOU HEARD THE MAN.
FLINT'S ALL GROWED UP, HARD DRIVE. HE KNOWS WHAT HE'S DOING.
HEY, I VOLUNTEERED YOU WITHOUT ASKING FIRST.
I EARNED MY JOE NAME, FLINT. I NEVER STOP EARNING IT.
TAKE THE CLOSEST ONE.
LINED UP ON HIM. YOU BETTER COVER YOUR EARS.

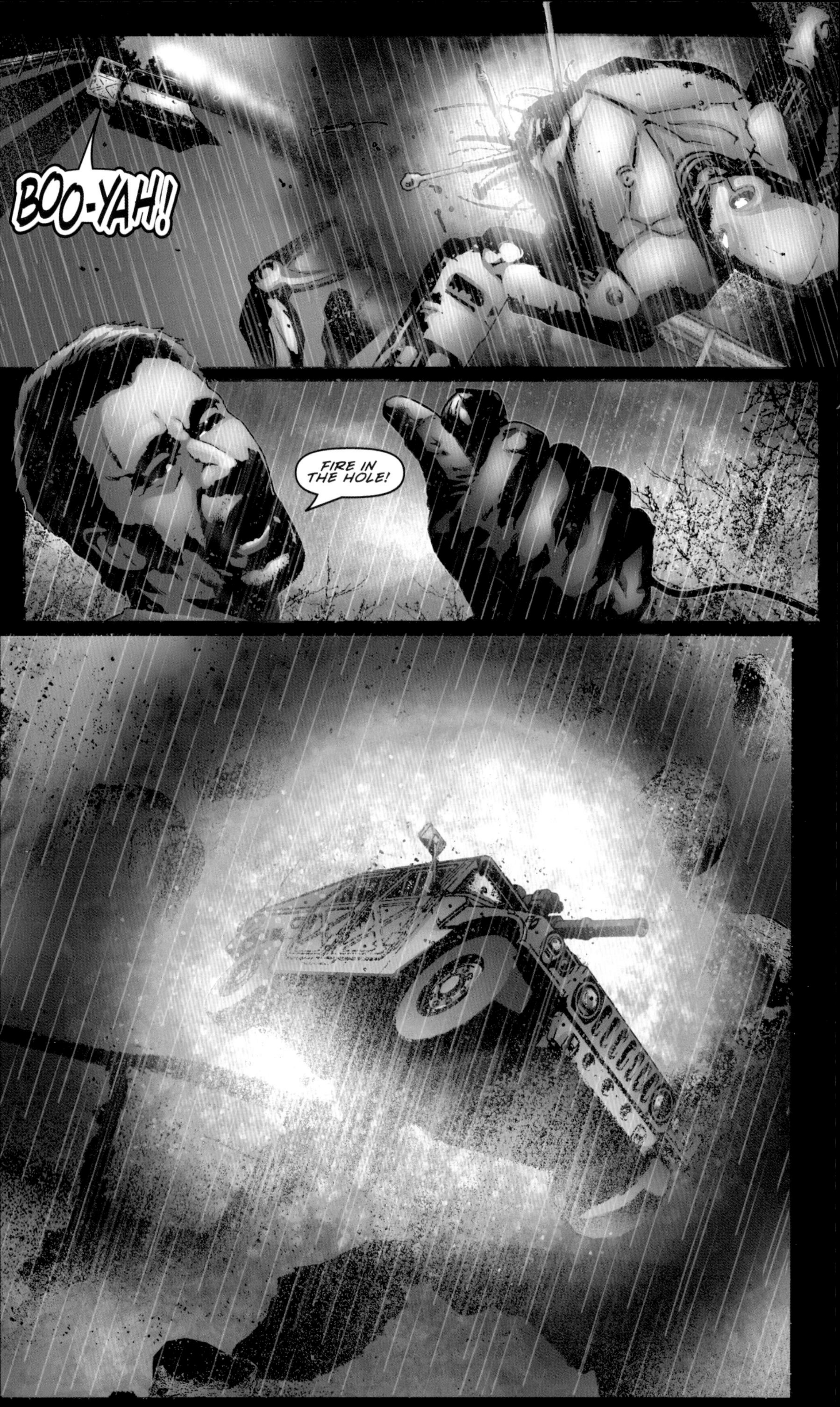
BOO-YAH!!
FIRE IN THE HOLE!

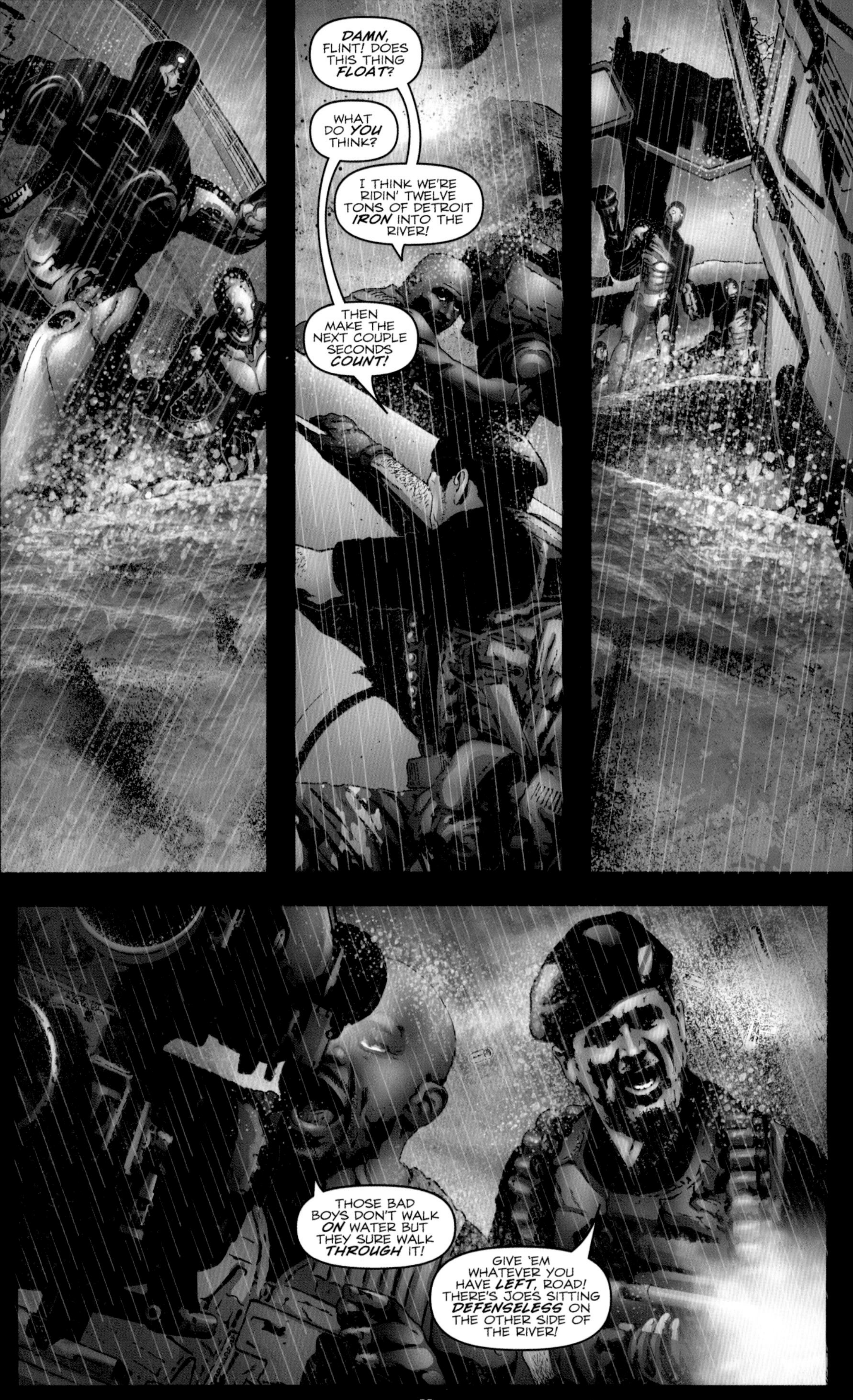

DAMN, FLINT! DOES THIS THING FLOAT?
WHAT DO YOU THINK?
I THINK WE'RE RIDIN' TWELVE TONS OF DETROIT IRON INTO THE RIVER!
THEN MAKE THE NEXT COUPLE SECONDS COUNT!
THOSE BAD BOYS DON'T WALK ON WATER BUT THEY SURE WALK THROUGH IT!
GIVE 'EM WHATEVER YOU HAVE LEFT, ROAD! THERE'S JOES SITTING DEFENSELESS ON THE OTHER SIDE OF THE RIVER!

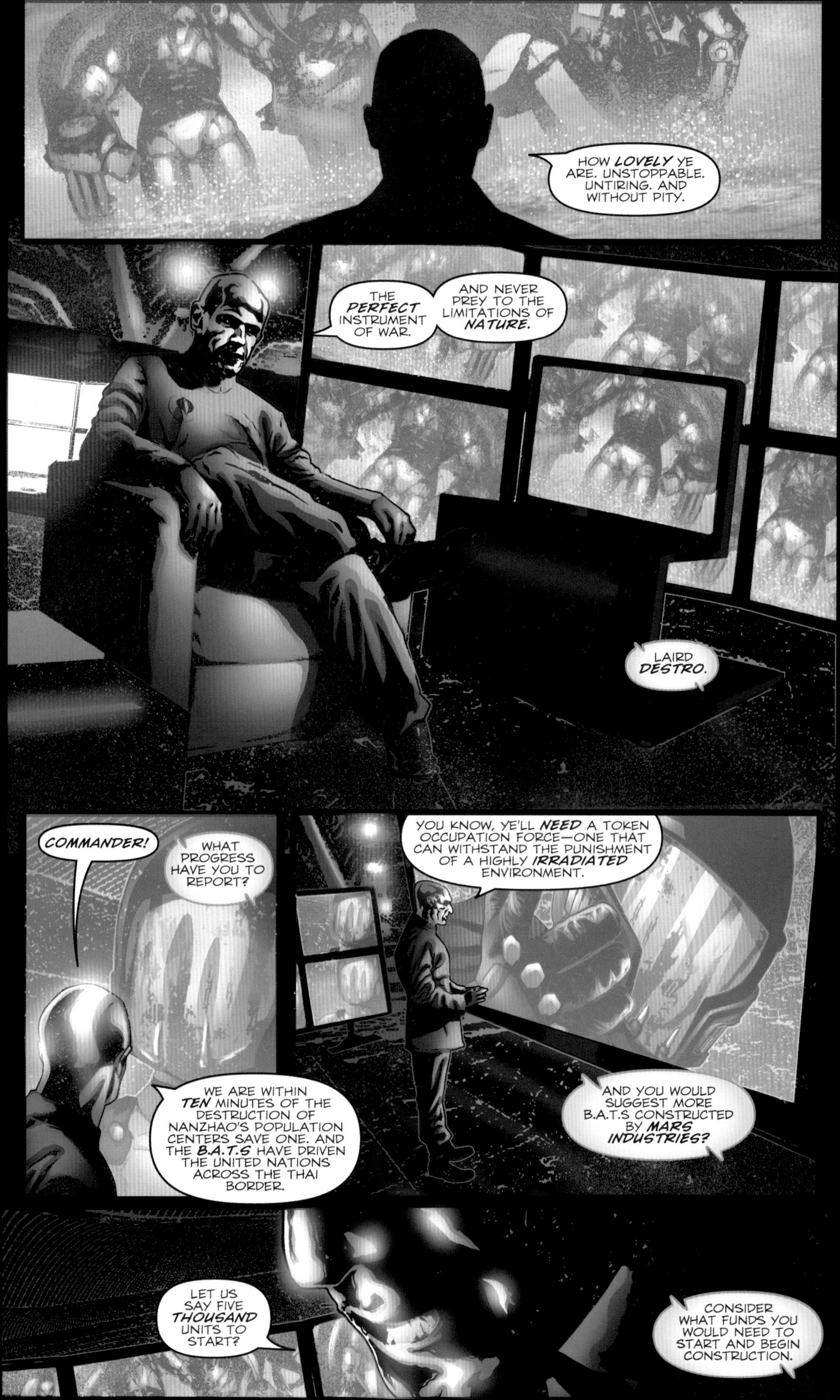
HOW LOVELY YE ARE. UNSTOPPABLE. UNTIRING. AND WITHOUT PITY.
THE PERFECT INSTRUMENT OF WAR.
AND NEVER PREY TO THE LIMITATIONS OF NATURE.
LAIRD DESTRO.
COMMANDER!
WHAT PROGRESS HAVE YOU TO REPORT?
WE ARE WITHIN TEN MINUTES OF THE DESTRUCTION OF NANZHAO'S POPULATION CENTERS SAVE ONE. AND THE B.A.T.S HAVE DRIVEN THE UNITED NATIONS ACROSS THE THAI BORDER.
YOU KNOW, YE'LL NEED A TOKEN OCCUPATION FORCE—ONE THAT CAN WITHSTAND THE PUNISHMENT OF A HIGHLY IRRADIATED ENVIRONMENT.
AND YOU WOULD SUGGEST MORE B.A.T.S CONSTRUCTED BY MARS INDUSTRIES?
LET US SAY FIVE THOUSAND UNITS TO START?
CONSIDER WHAT FUNDS YOU WOULD NEED TO START AND BEGIN CONSTRUCTION.

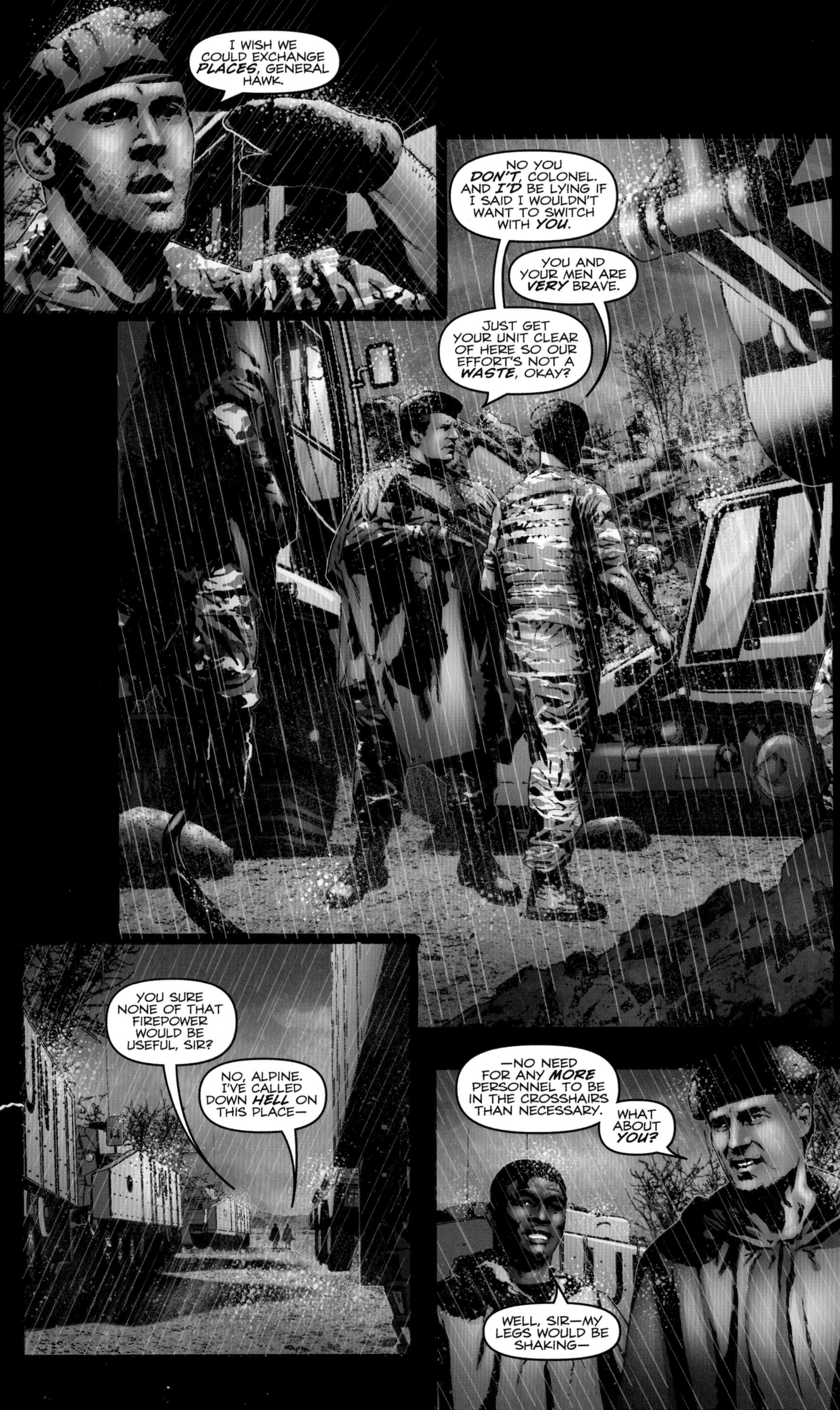
I WISH WE COULD EXCHANGE PLACES, GENERAL HAWK.
NO YOU DON'T, COLONEL. AND I'D BE LYING IF I SAID I WOULDN'T WANT TO SWITCH WITH YOU.
YOU AND YOUR MEN ARE VERY BRAVE.
JUST GET YOUR UNIT CLEAR OF HERE SO OUR EFFORT'S NOT A WASTE, OKAY?
YOU SURE NONE OF THAT FIREPOWER WOULD BE USEFUL, SIR?
NO, ALPINE. I'VE CALLED DOWN HELL ON THIS PLACE—
—NO NEED FOR ANY MORE PERSONNEL TO BE IN THE CROSSHAIRS THAN NECESSARY.
WHAT ABOUT YOU?
WELL, SIR—MY LEGS WOULD BE SHAKING—

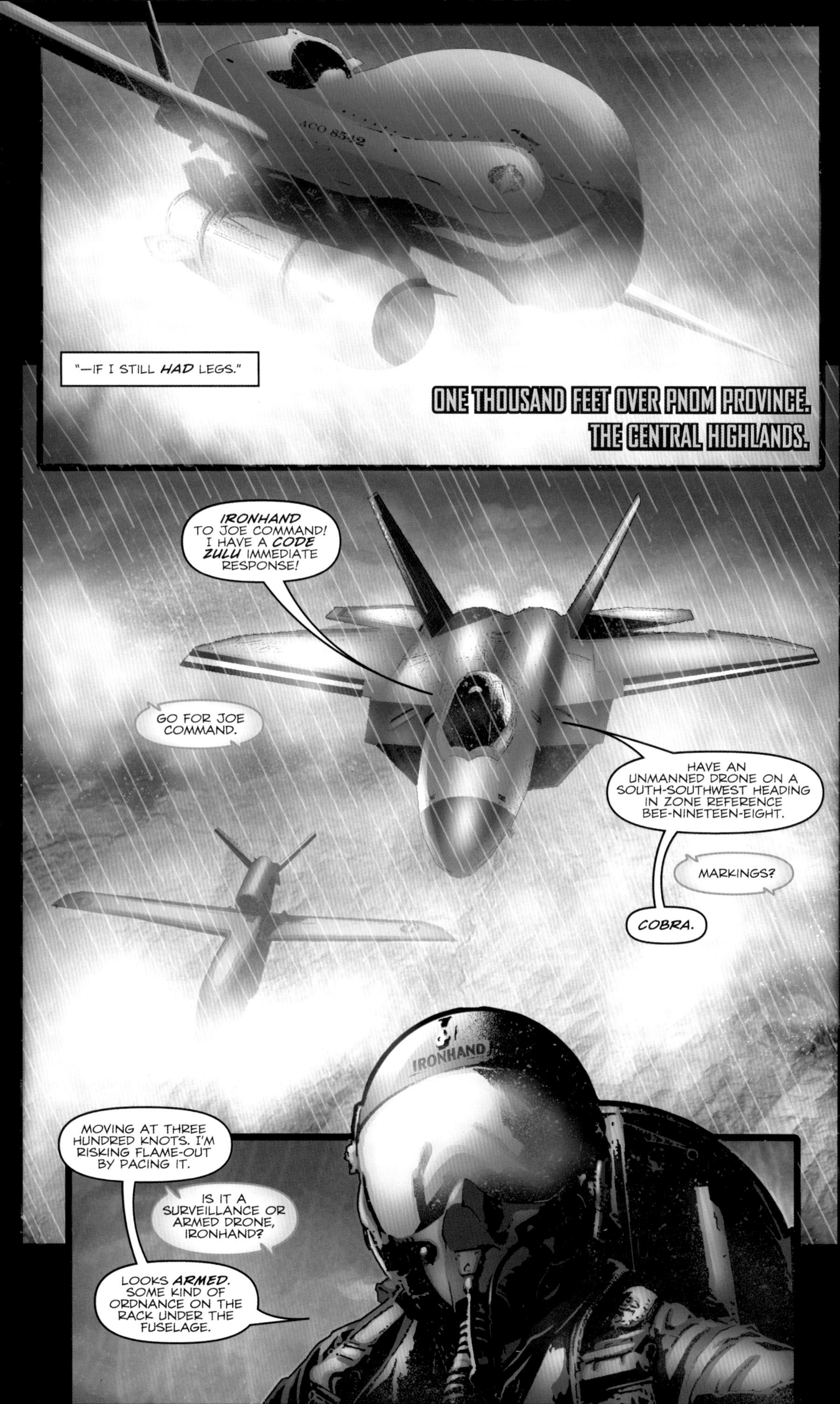

"—IF I STILL *HAD* LEGS."
ONE THOUSAND FEET OVER PNOM PROVINCE.
THE CENTRAL HIGHLANDS.
IRONHAND TO JOE COMMAND! I HAVE A *CODE ZULU* IMMEDIATE RESPONSE!
GO FOR JOE COMMAND.
HAVE AN UNMANNED DRONE ON A SOUTH-SOUTHWEST HEADING IN ZONE REFERENCE BEE-NINETEEN-EIGHT.
MARKINGS?
COBRA.
IRONHAND
MOVING AT THREE HUNDRED KNOTS. I'M RISKING FLAME-OUT BY PACING IT.
IS IT A SURVEILLANCE OR ARMED DRONE, IRONHAND?
LOOKS *ARMED*. SOME KIND OF ORDNANCE ON THE RACK UNDER THE FUSELAGE.

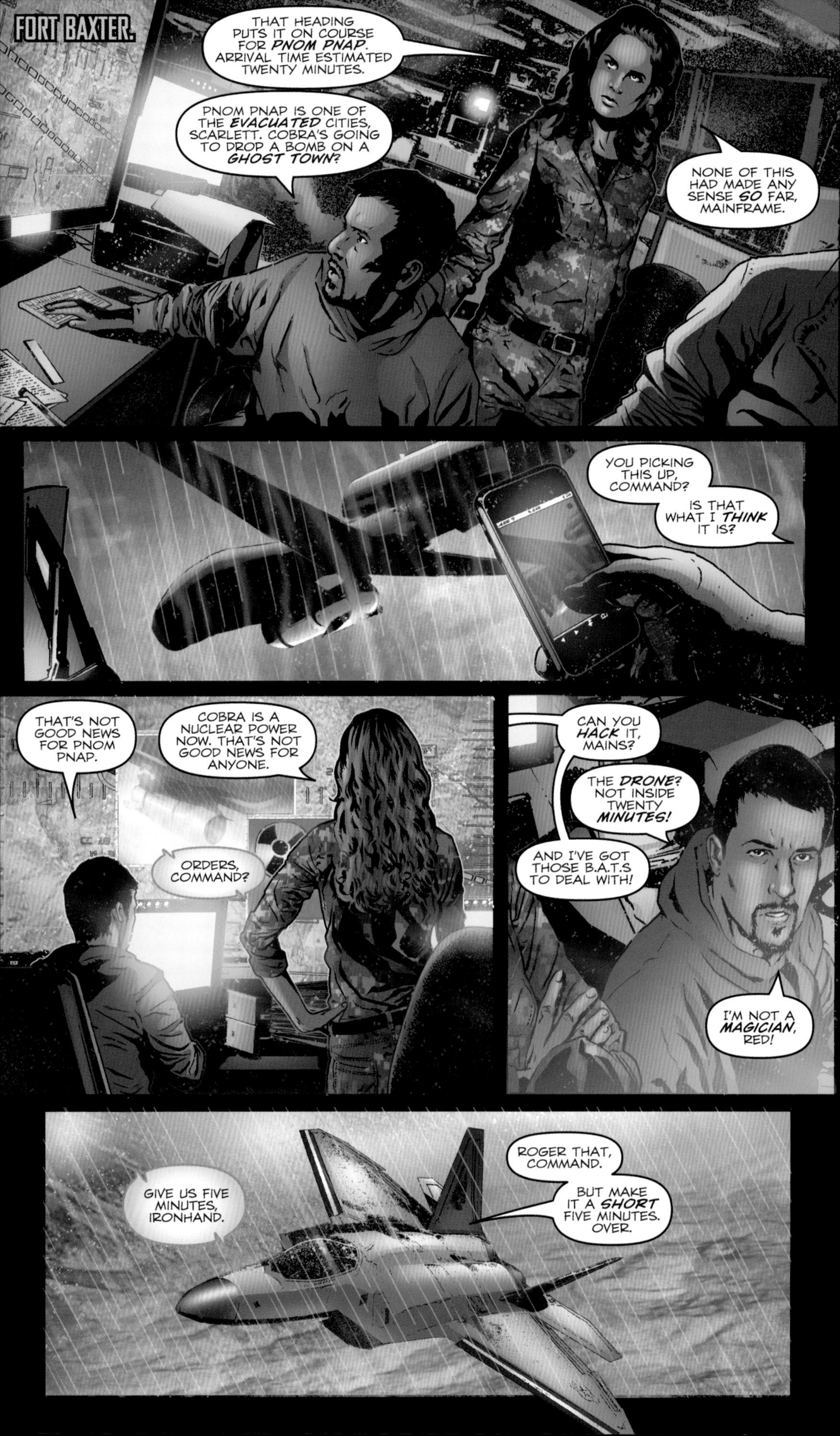
FORT BAXTER.
THAT HEADING PUTS IT ON COURSE FOR PNOM PNAP. ARRIVAL TIME ESTIMATED TWENTY MINUTES.
PNOM PNAP IS ONE OF THE EVACUATED CITIES, SCARLETT. COBRA'S GOING TO DROP A BOMB ON A GHOST TOWN?
NONE OF THIS HAD MADE ANY SENSE SO FAR, MAINFRAME.
YOU PICKING THIS UP, COMMAND?
IS THAT WHAT I THINK IT IS?
THAT'S NOT GOOD NEWS FOR PNOM PNAP.
COBRA IS A NUCLEAR POWER NOW. THAT'S NOT GOOD NEWS FOR ANYONE.
ORDERS, COMMAND?
CAN YOU HACK IT, MAINS?
THE DRONE? NOT INSIDE TWENTY MINUTES!
AND I'VE GOT THOSE B.A.T.S TO DEAL WITH!
I'M NOT A MAGICIAN, RED!
GIVE US FIVE MINUTES, IRONHAND.
ROGER THAT, COMMAND.
BUT MAKE IT A SHORT FIVE MINUTES. OVER.

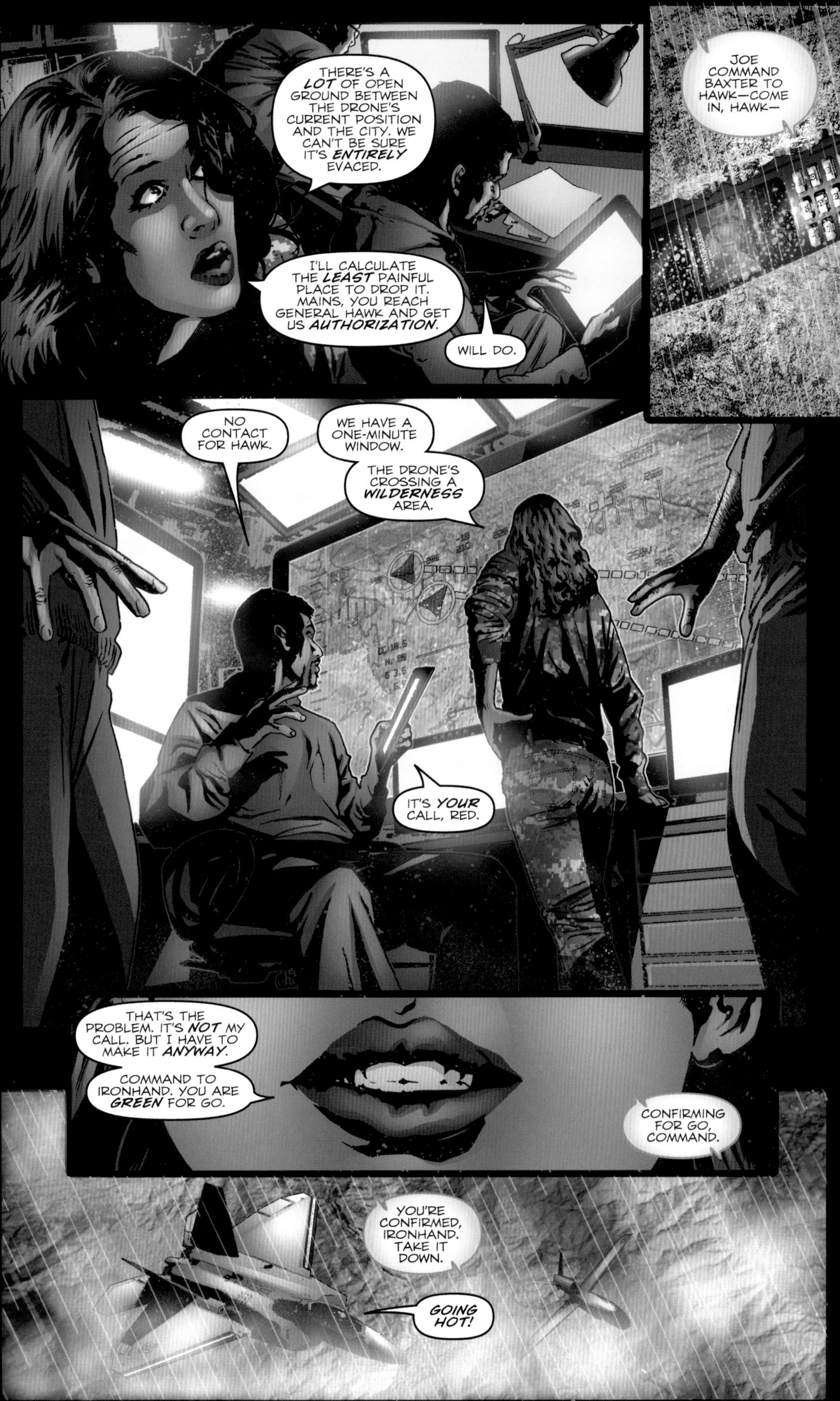
THERE'S A LOT OF OPEN GROUND BETWEEN THE DRONE'S CURRENT POSITION AND THE CITY. WE CAN'T BE SURE IT'S ENTIRELY EVACED.
I'LL CALCULATE THE LEAST PAINFUL PLACE TO DROP IT. MAINS, YOU REACH GENERAL HAWK AND GET US AUTHORIZATION.
WILL DO.
JOE COMMAND BAXTER TO HAWK—COME IN, HAWK—
NO CONTACT FOR HAWK.
WE HAVE A ONE-MINUTE WINDOW.
THE DRONE'S CROSSING A WILDERNESS AREA.
IT'S YOUR CALL, RED.
THAT'S THE PROBLEM. IT'S NOT MY CALL. BUT I HAVE TO MAKE IT ANYWAY.
COMMAND TO IRONHAND. YOU ARE GREEN FOR GO.
CONFIRMING FOR GO, COMMAND.
YOU'RE CONFIRMED, IRONHAND. TAKE IT DOWN.
GOING HOT!

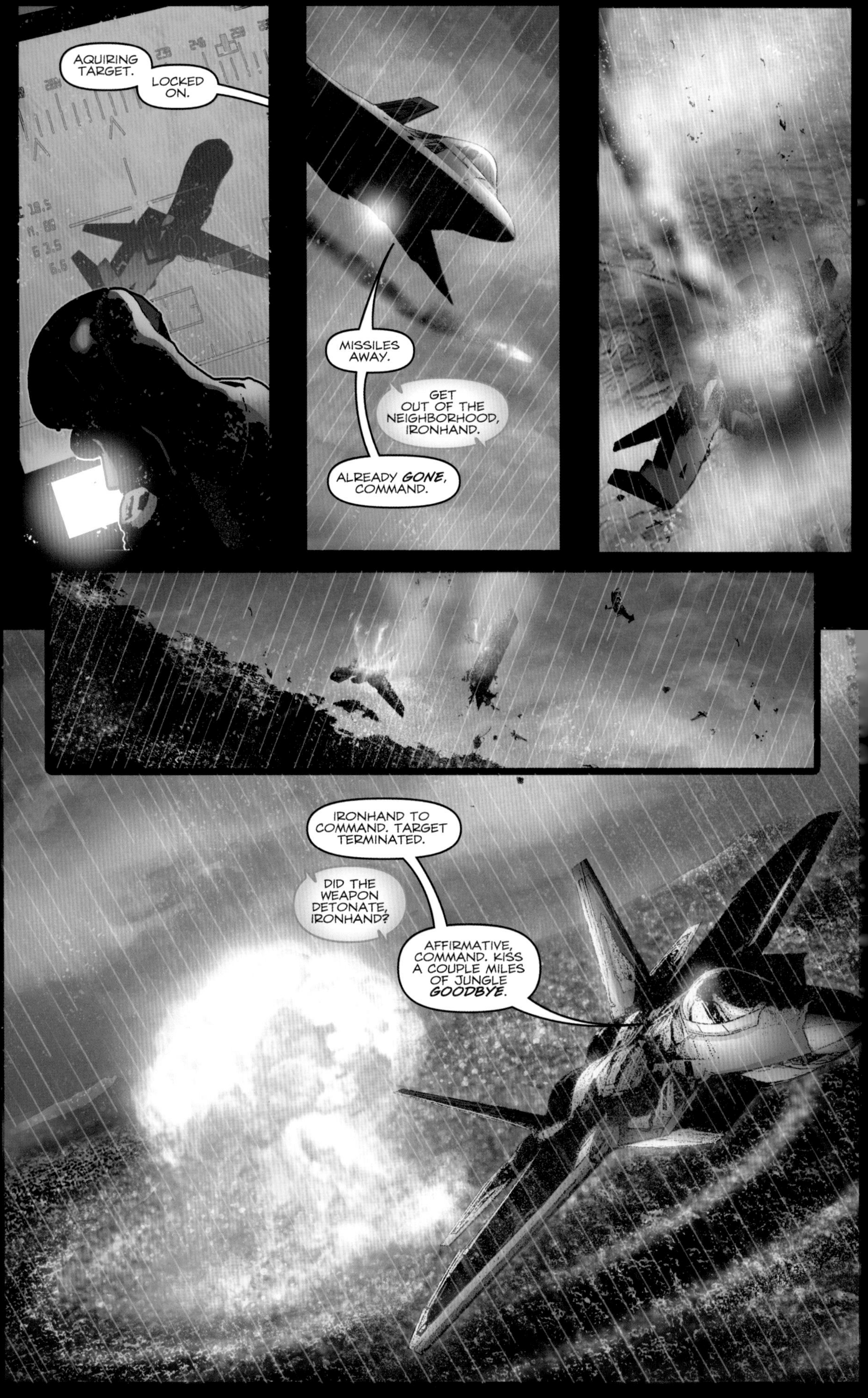
AQUIRING TARGET.
LOCKED ON.
MISSILES AWAY.
GET OUT OF THE NEIGHBORHOOD, IRONHAND.
ALREADY *GONE*, COMMAND.
IRONHAND TO COMMAND. TARGET TERMINATED.
DID THE WEAPON DETONATE, IRONHAND?
AFFIRMATIVE, COMMAND. KISS A COUPLE MILES OF JUNGLE *GOODBYE*.

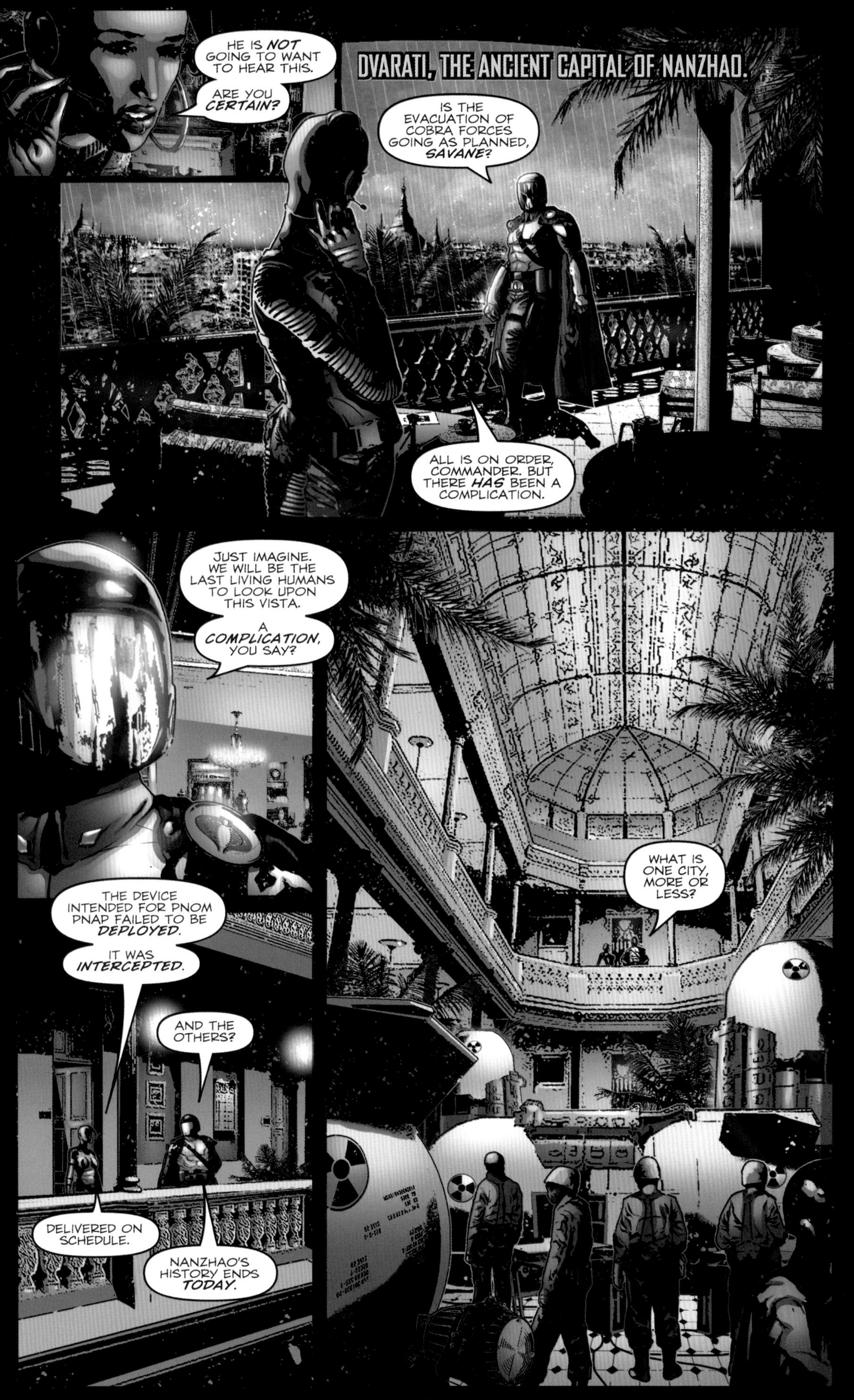
HE IS NOT GOING TO WANT TO HEAR THIS.
ARE YOU CERTAIN?
DVARATI, THE ANCIENT CAPITAL OF NANZHAO.
IS THE EVACUATION OF COBRA FORCES GOING AS PLANNED, SAVANE?
ALL IS ON ORDER, COMMANDER. BUT THERE HAS BEEN A COMPLICATION.
JUST IMAGINE. WE WILL BE THE LAST LIVING HUMANS TO LOOK UPON THIS VISTA.
A COMPLICATION, YOU SAY?
THE DEVICE INTENDED FOR PNOM PNAP FAILED TO BE DEPLOYED.
IT WAS INTERCEPTED.
AND THE OTHERS?
DELIVERED ON SCHEDULE.
NANZHAO'S HISTORY ENDS TODAY.
WHAT IS ONE CITY, MORE OR LESS?

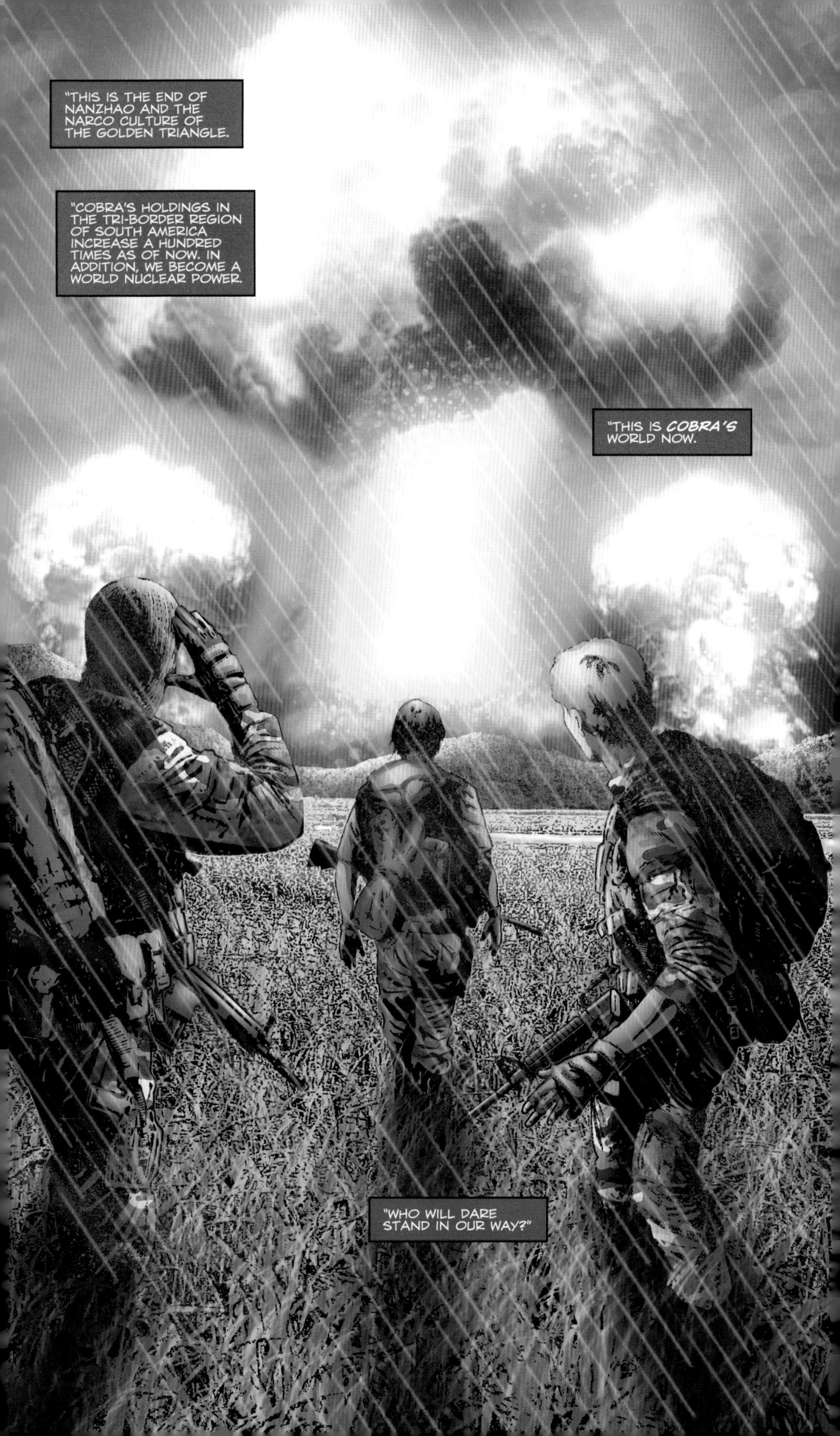
"THIS IS THE END OF NANZHAO AND THE NARCO CULTURE OF THE GOLDEN TRIANGLE.
"COBRA'S HOLDINGS IN THE TRI-BORDER REGION OF SOUTH AMERICA INCREASE A HUNDRED TIMES AS OF NOW. IN ADDITION, WE BECOME A WORLD NUCLEAR POWER.
"THIS IS COBRA'S WORLD NOW.
"WHO WILL DARE STAND IN OUR WAY?"

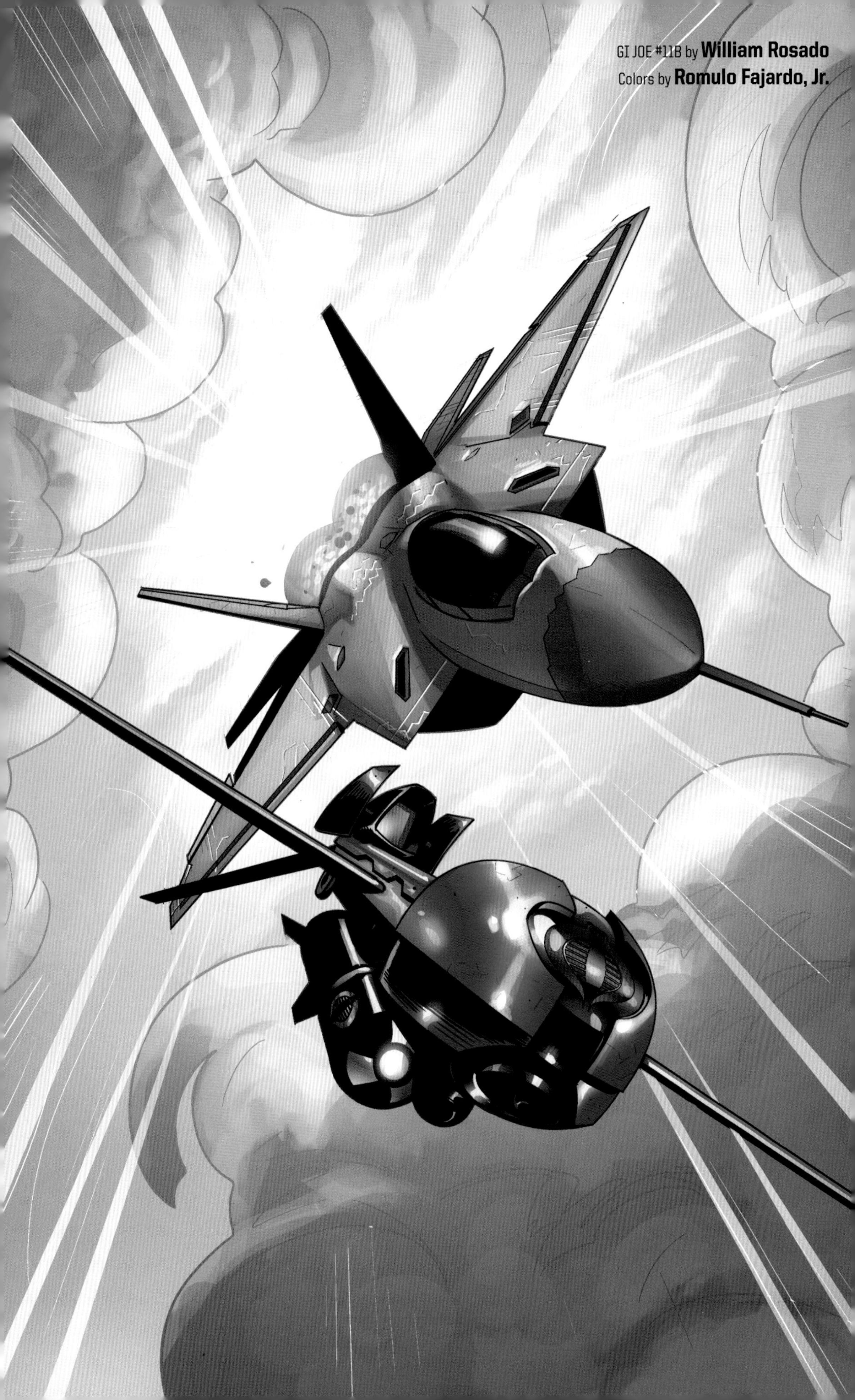

GI JOE #11B by **William Rosado**
Colors by **Romulo Fajardo, Jr.**

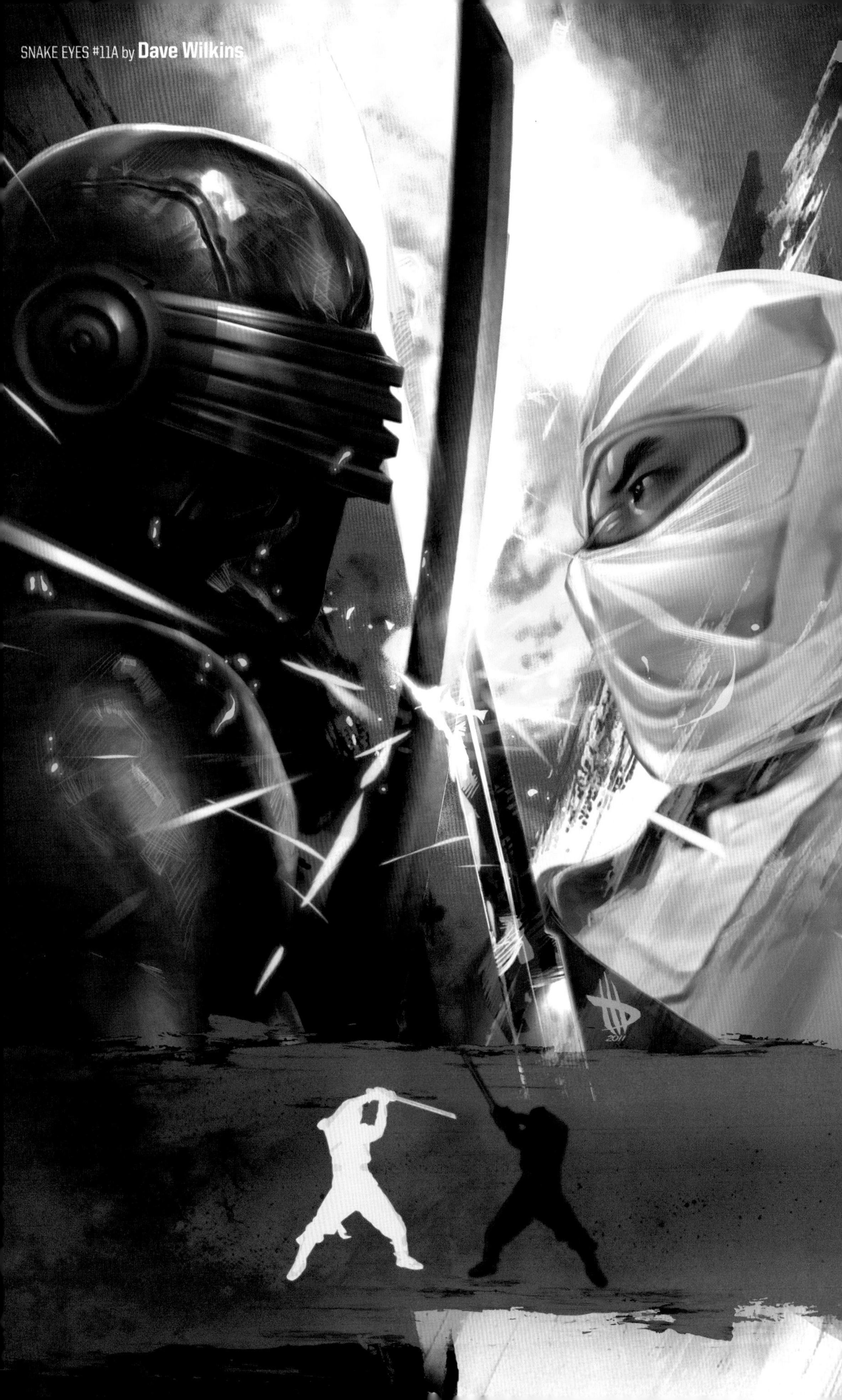

SNAKE EYES #11A by **Dave Wilkins**

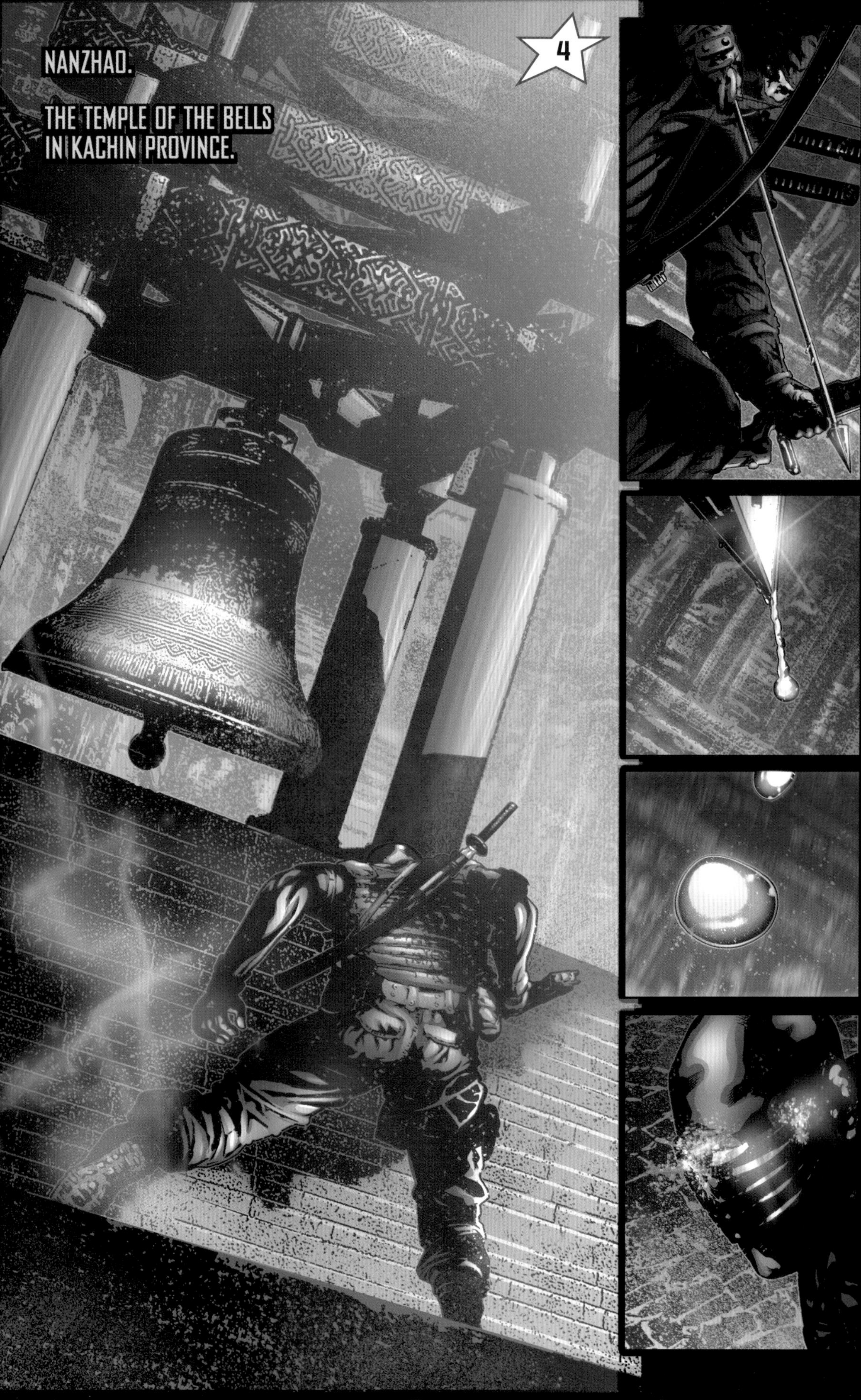
NANZHAO.
THE TEMPLE OF THE BELLS IN KACHIN PROVINCE.

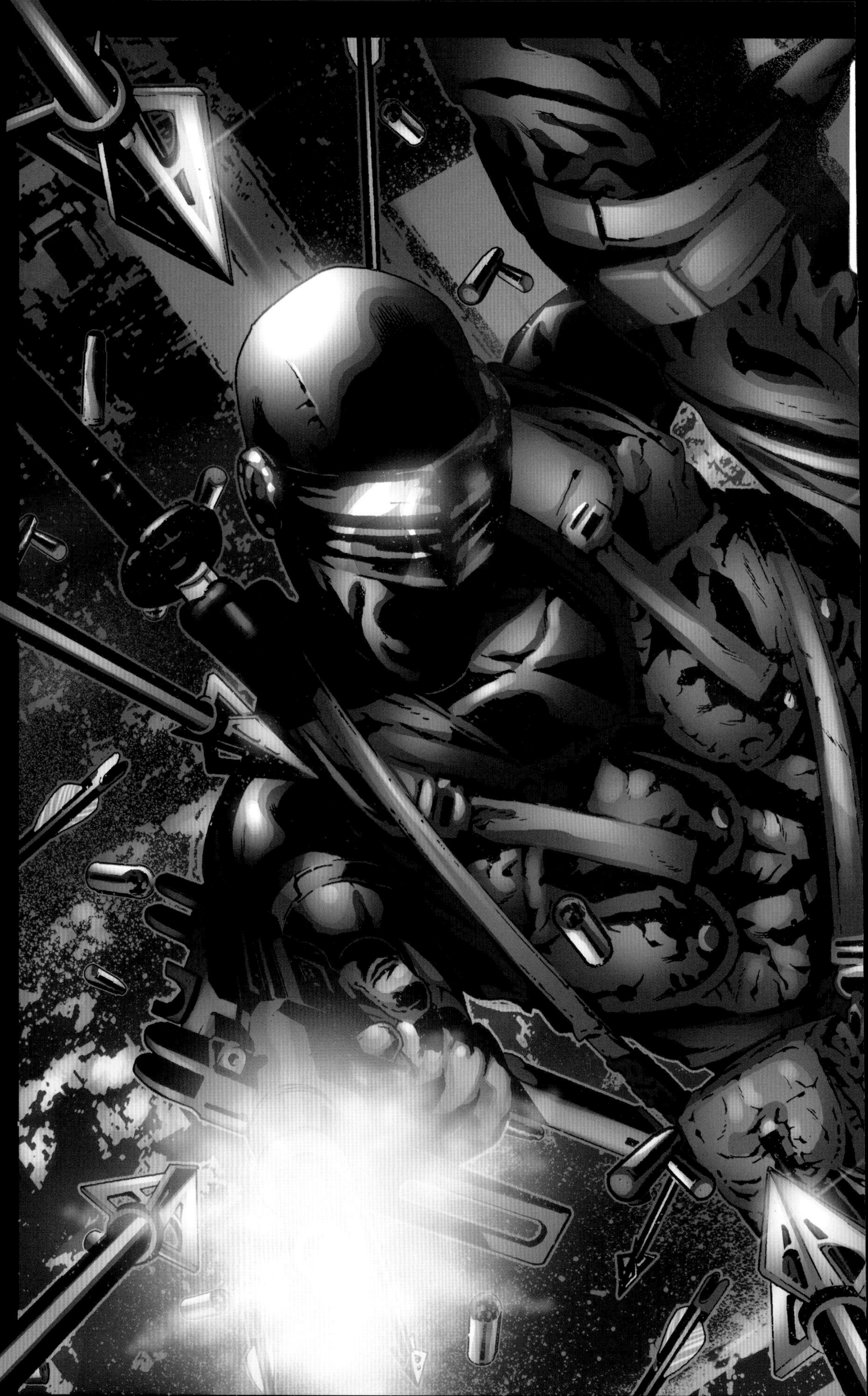

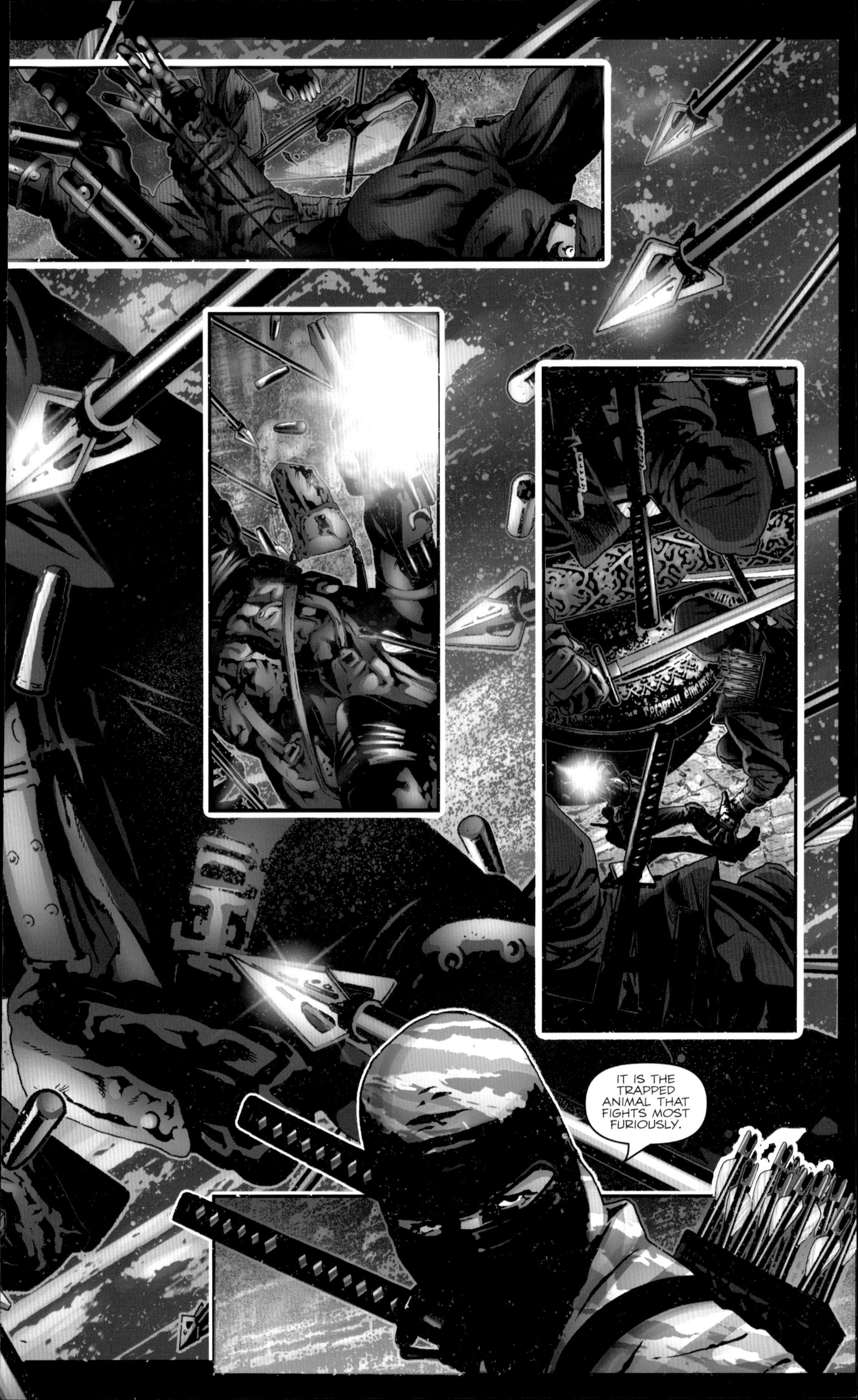
IT IS THE TRAPPED ANIMAL THAT FIGHTS MOST FURIOUSLY.

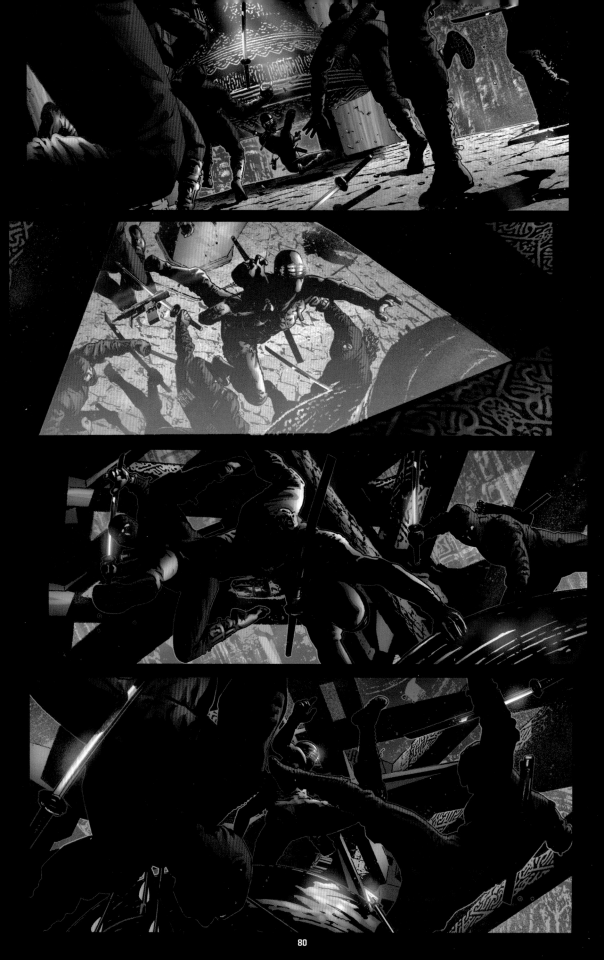

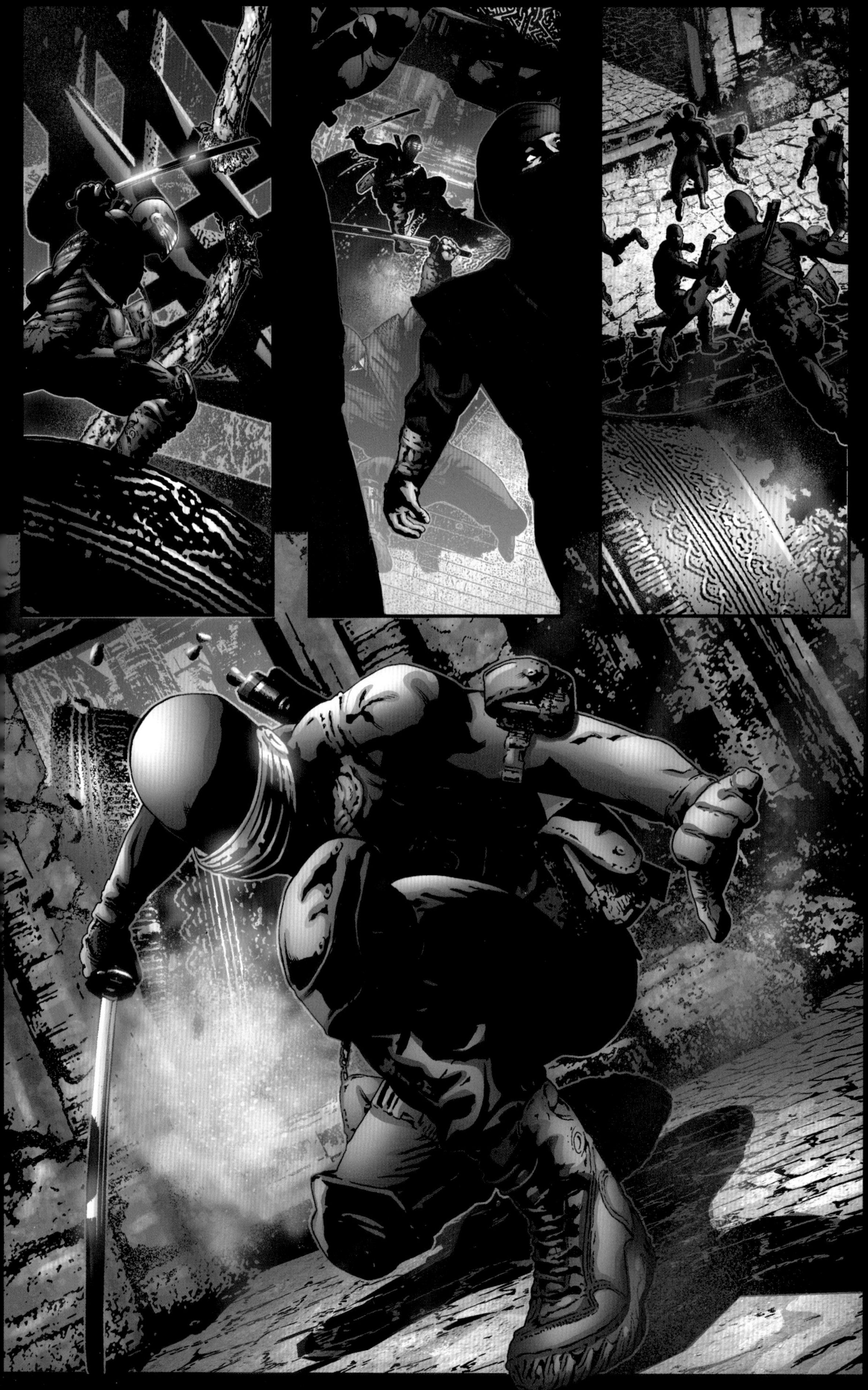

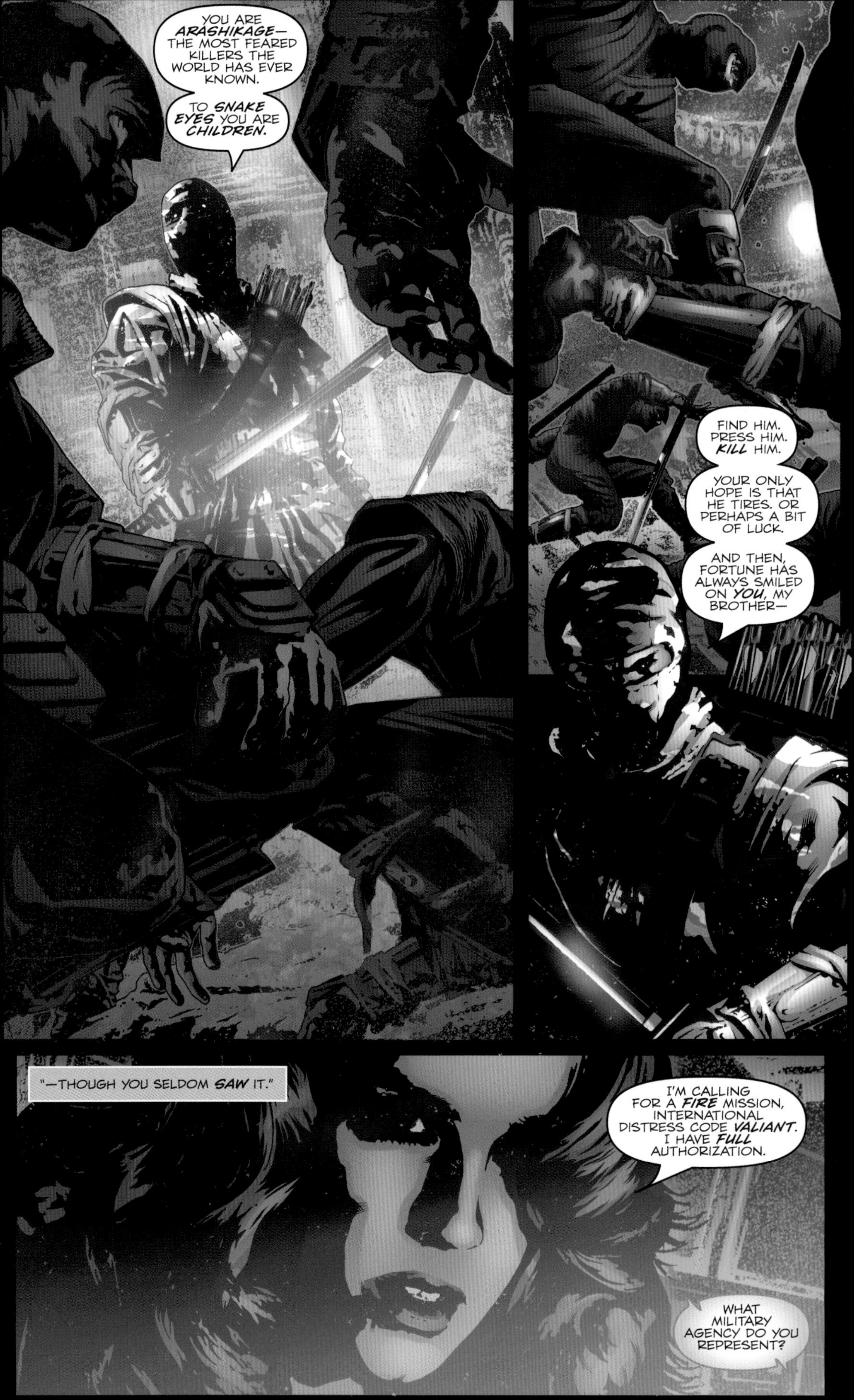
YOU ARE ARASHIKAGE— THE MOST FEARED KILLERS THE WORLD HAS EVER KNOWN.
TO SNAKE EYES YOU ARE CHILDREN.
FIND HIM. PRESS HIM. KILL HIM.
YOUR ONLY HOPE IS THAT HE TIRES. OR PERHAPS A BIT OF LUCK.
AND THEN, FORTUNE HAS ALWAYS SMILED ON YOU, MY BROTHER—
"—THOUGH YOU SELDOM SAW IT."
I'M CALLING FOR A FIRE MISSION, INTERNATIONAL DISTRESS CODE VALIANT. I HAVE FULL AUTHORIZATION.
WHAT MILITARY AGENCY DO YOU REPRESENT?

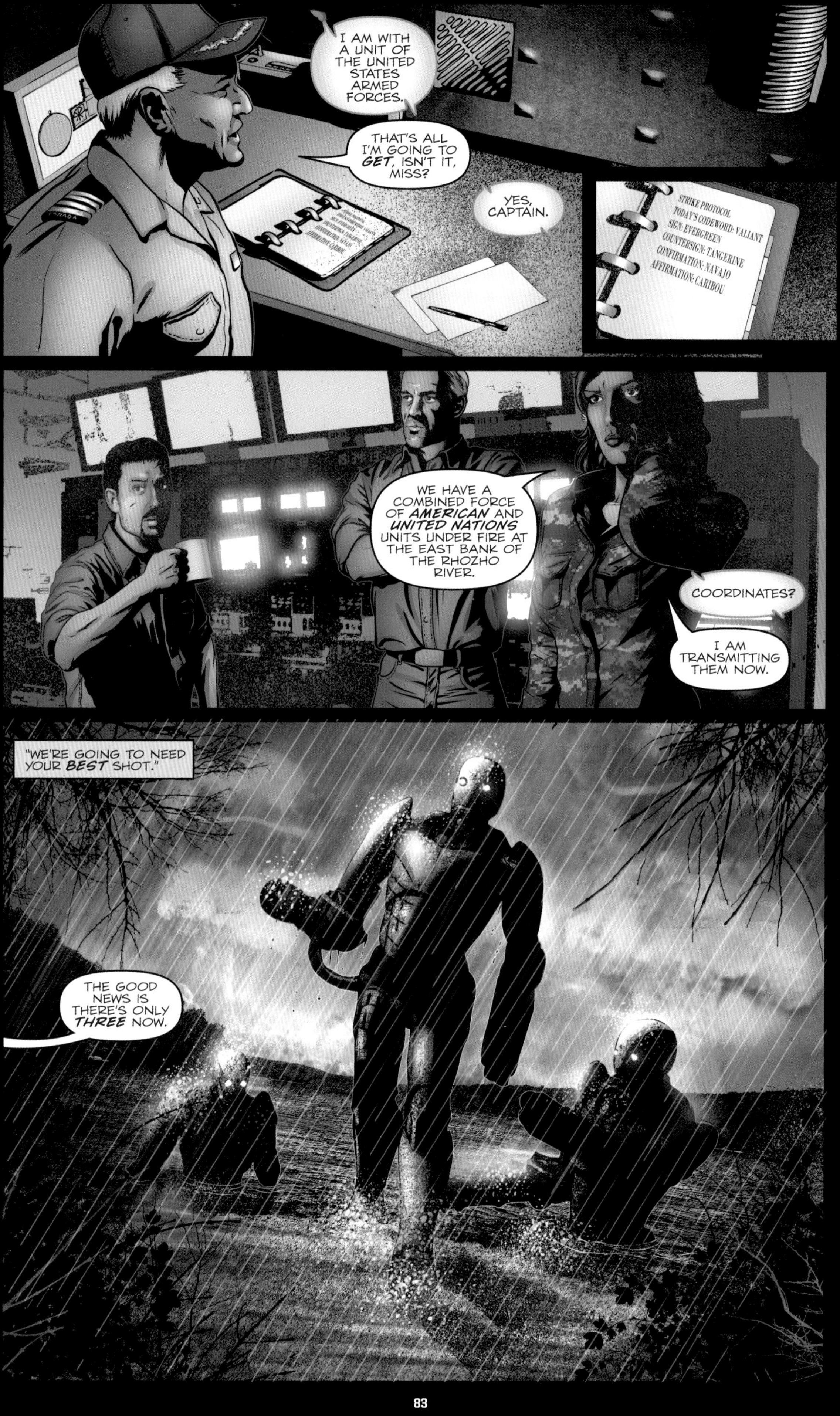
I AM WITH A UNIT OF THE UNITED STATES ARMED FORCES.
THAT'S ALL I'M GOING TO GET, ISN'T IT, MISS?
YES, CAPTAIN.
STRIKE PROTOCOL
TODAY'S CODEWORD: VALIANT
SIGN: EVERGREEN
COUNTERSIGN: TANGERINE
CONFIRMATION: NAVAJO
AFFIRMATION: CARIBOU
WE HAVE A COMBINED FORCE OF AMERICAN AND UNITED NATIONS UNITS UNDER FIRE AT THE EAST BANK OF THE RHOZHO RIVER.
COORDINATES?
I AM TRANSMITTING THEM NOW.
"WE'RE GOING TO NEED YOUR BEST SHOT."
THE GOOD NEWS IS THERE'S ONLY THREE NOW.

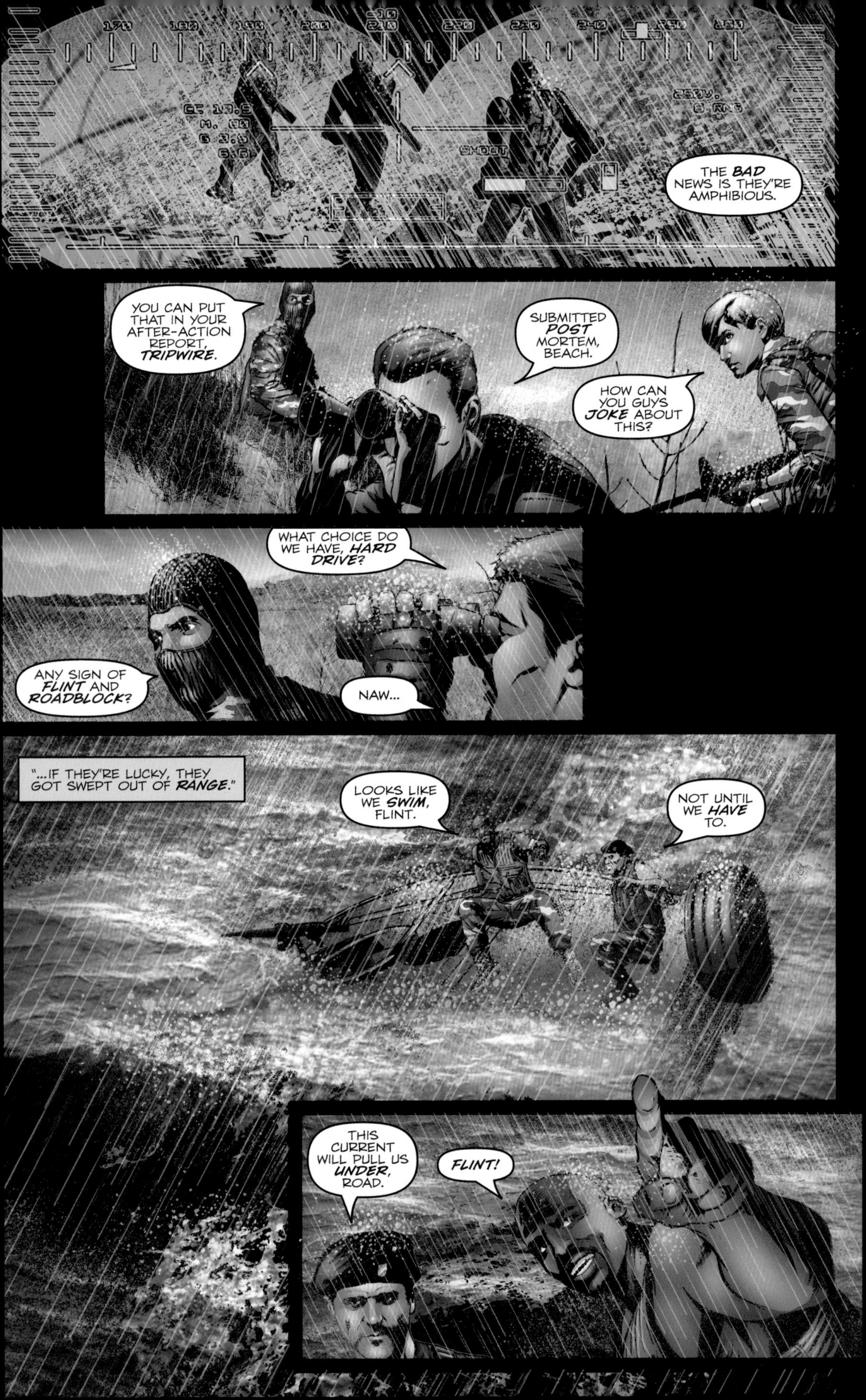
THE BAD NEWS IS THEY'RE AMPHIBIOUS.
YOU CAN PUT THAT IN YOUR AFTER-ACTION REPORT, TRIPWIRE.
SUBMITTED POST MORTEM, BEACH.
HOW CAN YOU GUYS JOKE ABOUT THIS?
WHAT CHOICE DO WE HAVE, HARD DRIVE?
ANY SIGN OF FLINT AND ROADBLOCK?
NAW...
"...IF THEY'RE LUCKY, THEY GOT SWEPT OUT OF RANGE."
LOOKS LIKE WE SWIM, FLINT.
NOT UNTIL WE HAVE TO.
THIS CURRENT WILL PULL US UNDER, ROAD.
FLINT!

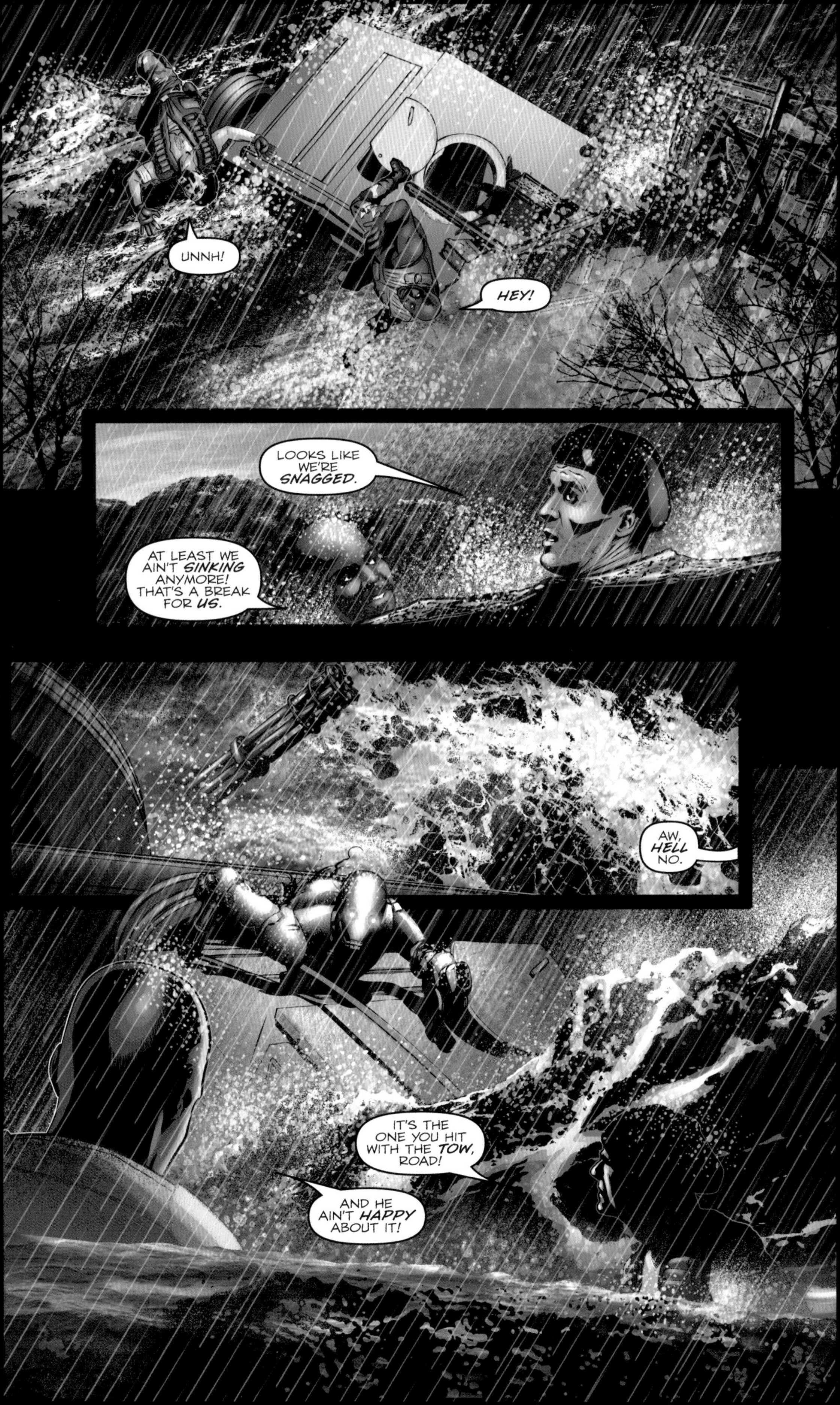
UNNH!
HEY!
LOOKS LIKE WE'RE SNAGGED.
AT LEAST WE AIN'T SINKING ANYMORE! THAT'S A BREAK FOR US.
AW, HELL NO.
IT'S THE ONE YOU HIT WITH THE TOW, ROAD!
AND HE AIN'T HAPPY ABOUT IT!

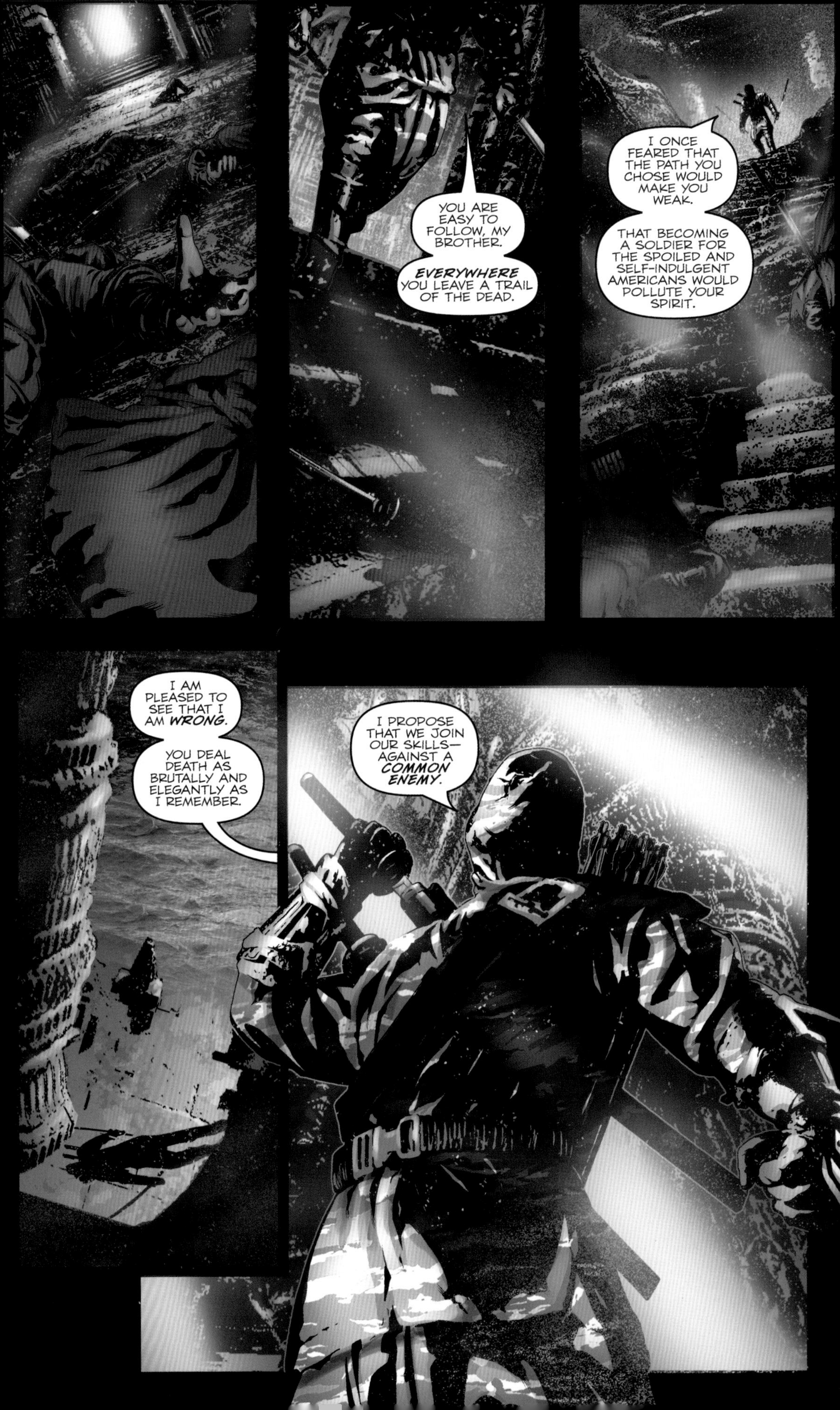
YOU ARE EASY TO FOLLOW, MY BROTHER.
EVERYWHERE YOU LEAVE A TRAIL OF THE DEAD.
I ONCE FEARED THAT THE PATH YOU CHOSE WOULD MAKE YOU WEAK.
THAT BECOMING A SOLDIER FOR THE SPOILED AND SELF-INDULGENT AMERICANS WOULD POLLUTE YOUR SPIRIT.
I AM PLEASED TO SEE THAT I AM WRONG.
YOU DEAL DEATH AS BRUTALLY AND ELEGANTLY AS I REMEMBER.
I PROPOSE THAT WE JOIN OUR SKILLS— AGAINST A COMMON ENEMY.

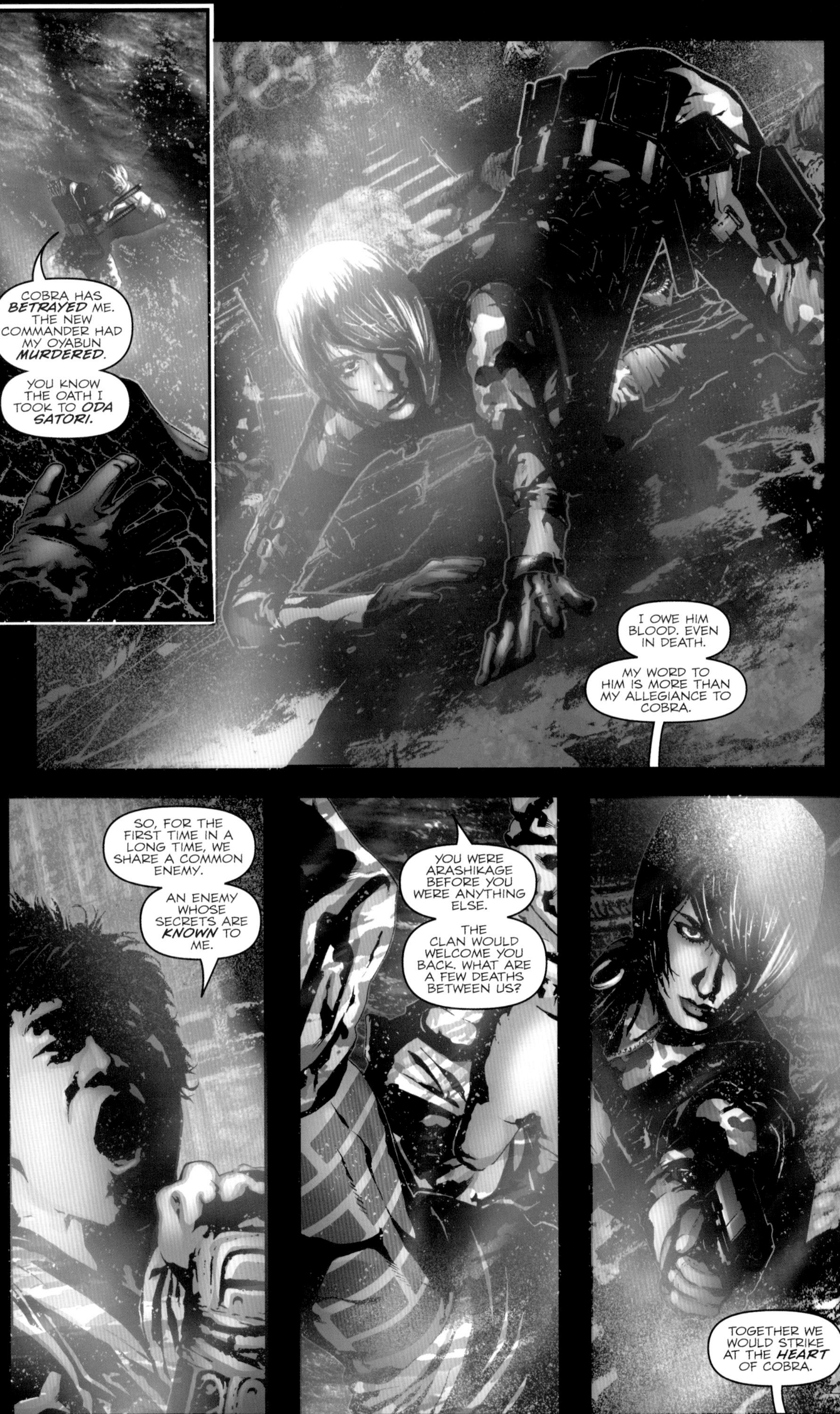

COBRA HAS **BETRAYED** ME. THE NEW COMMANDER HAD MY OYABUN **MURDERED**.
YOU KNOW THE OATH I TOOK TO **ODA SATORI**.
I OWE HIM BLOOD. EVEN IN DEATH.
MY WORD TO HIM IS MORE THAN MY ALLEGIANCE TO COBRA.
SO, FOR THE FIRST TIME IN A LONG TIME, WE SHARE A COMMON ENEMY.
AN ENEMY WHOSE SECRETS ARE **KNOWN** TO ME.
YOU WERE ARASHIKAGE BEFORE YOU WERE ANYTHING ELSE.
THE CLAN WOULD WELCOME YOU BACK. WHAT ARE A FEW DEATHS BETWEEN US?
TOGETHER WE WOULD STRIKE AT THE **HEART** OF COBRA.

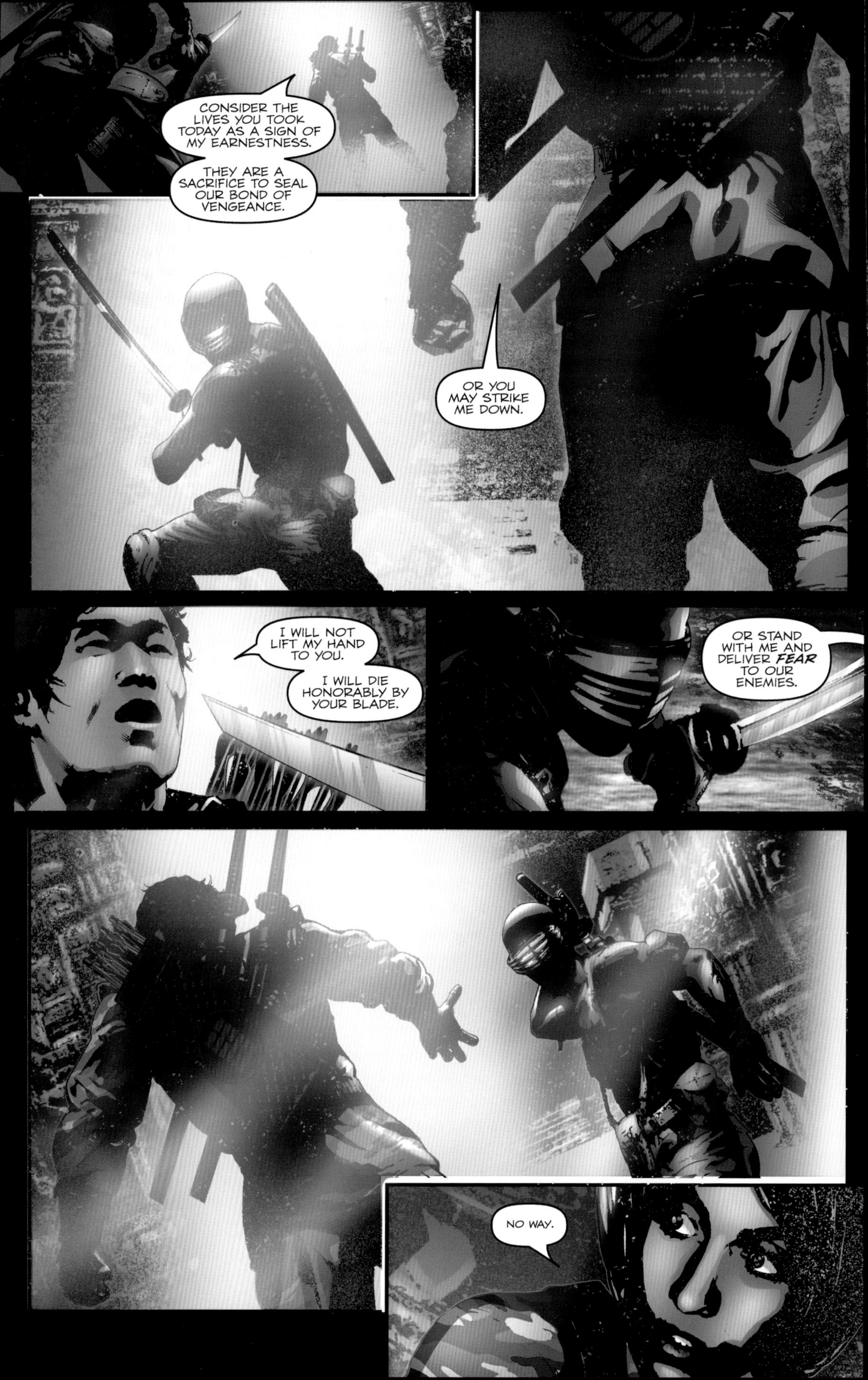
CONSIDER THE LIVES YOU TOOK TODAY AS A SIGN OF MY EARNESTNESS.
THEY ARE A SACRIFICE TO SEAL OUR BOND OF VENGEANCE.
OR YOU MAY STRIKE ME DOWN.
I WILL NOT LIFT MY HAND TO YOU.
I WILL DIE HONORABLY BY YOUR BLADE.
OR STAND WITH ME AND DELIVER FEAR TO OUR ENEMIES.
NO WAY.

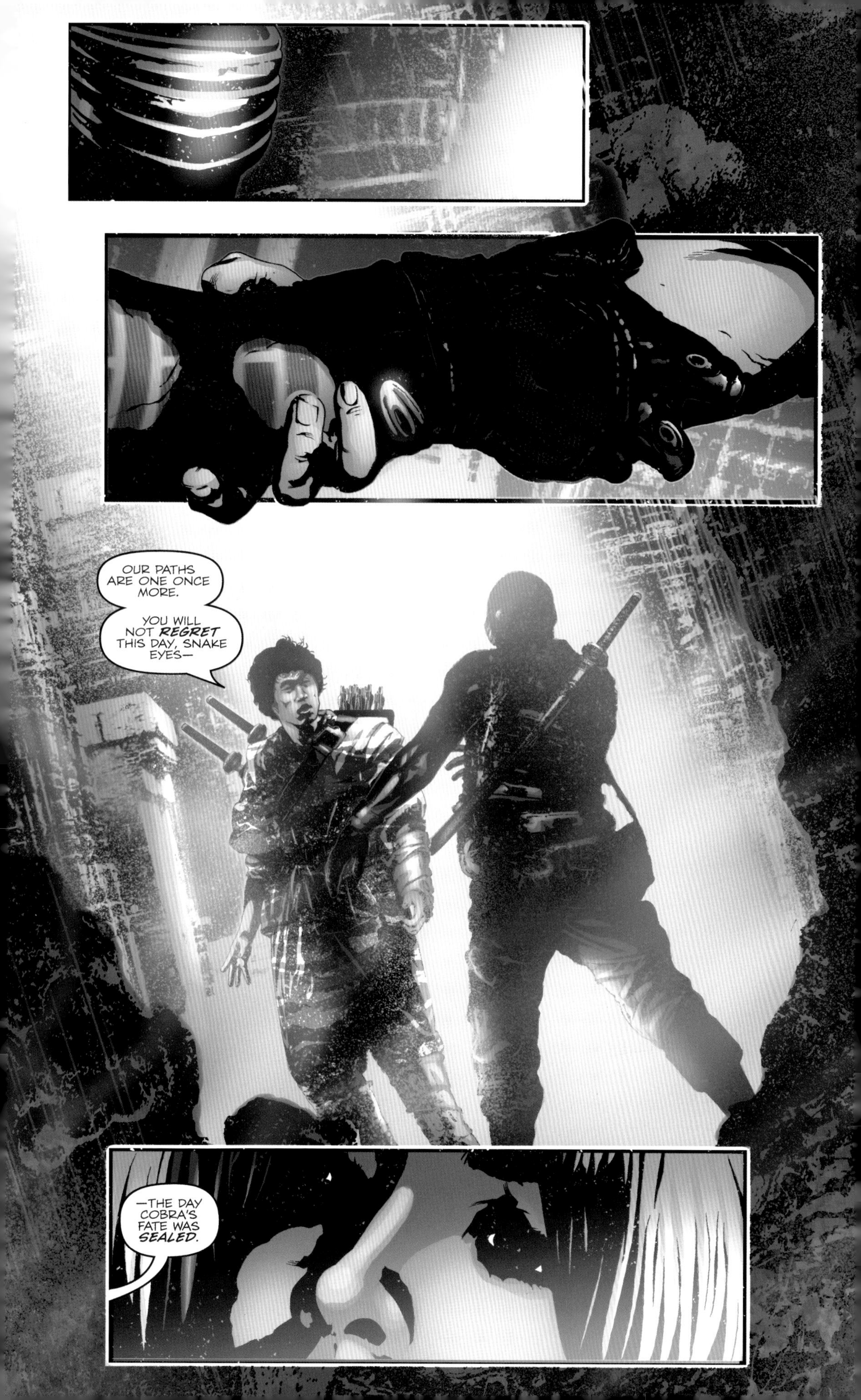
OUR PATHS ARE ONE ONCE MORE.
YOU WILL NOT REGRET THIS DAY, SNAKE EYES—
—THE DAY COBRA'S FATE WAS SEALED.

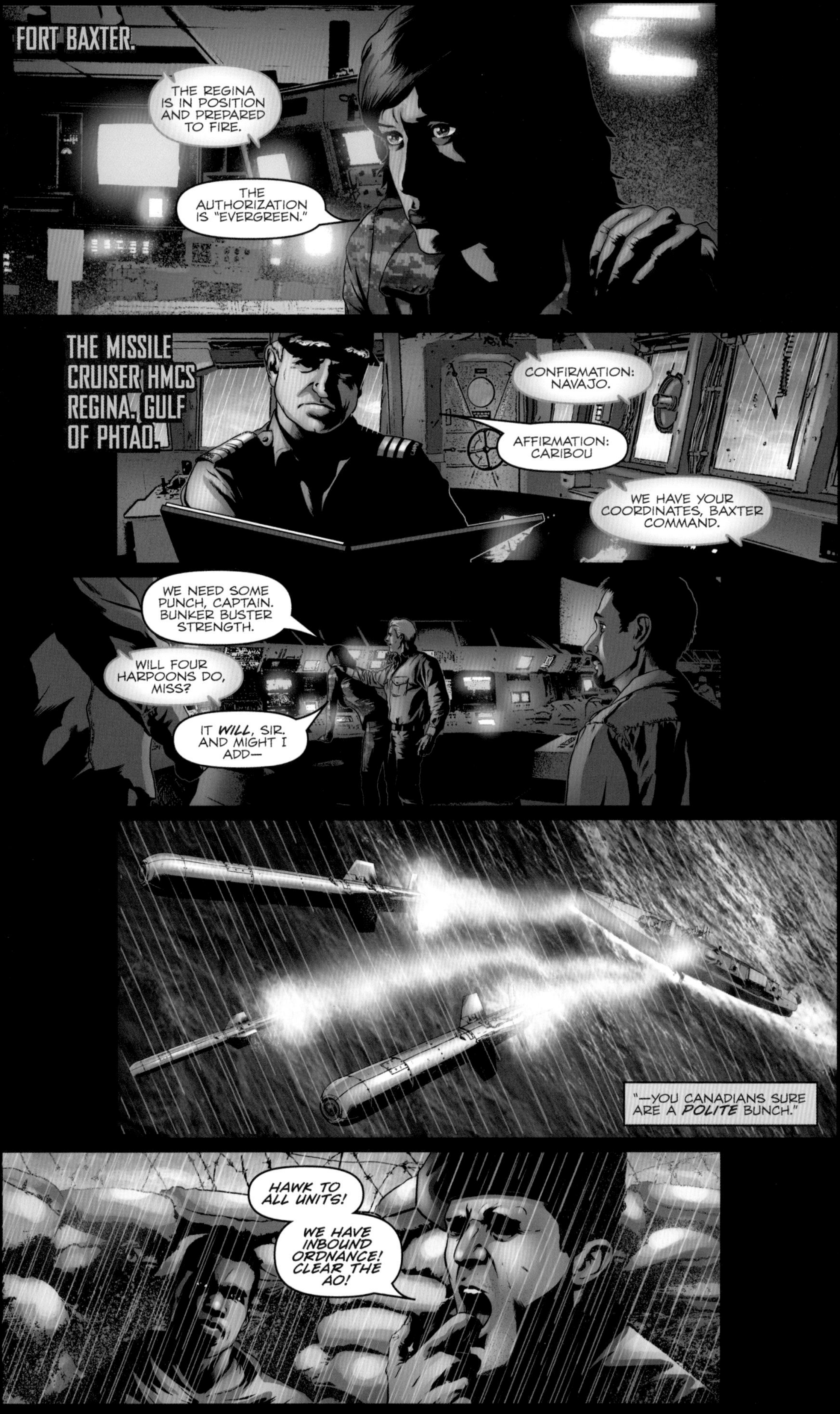
FORT BAXTER.
THE REGINA IS IN POSITION AND PREPARED TO FIRE.
THE AUTHORIZATION IS "EVERGREEN."
THE MISSILE CRUISER HMCS REGINA. GULF OF PHTAO.
CONFIRMATION: NAVAJO.
AFFIRMATION: CARIBOU
WE HAVE YOUR COORDINATES, BAXTER COMMAND.
WE NEED SOME PUNCH, CAPTAIN. BUNKER BUSTER STRENGTH.
WILL FOUR HARPOONS DO, MISS?
IT *WILL*, SIR. AND MIGHT I ADD—
"—YOU CANADIANS SURE ARE A *POLITE* BUNCH."
HAWK TO ALL UNITS!
WE HAVE INBOUND ORDNANCE! CLEAR THE AO!

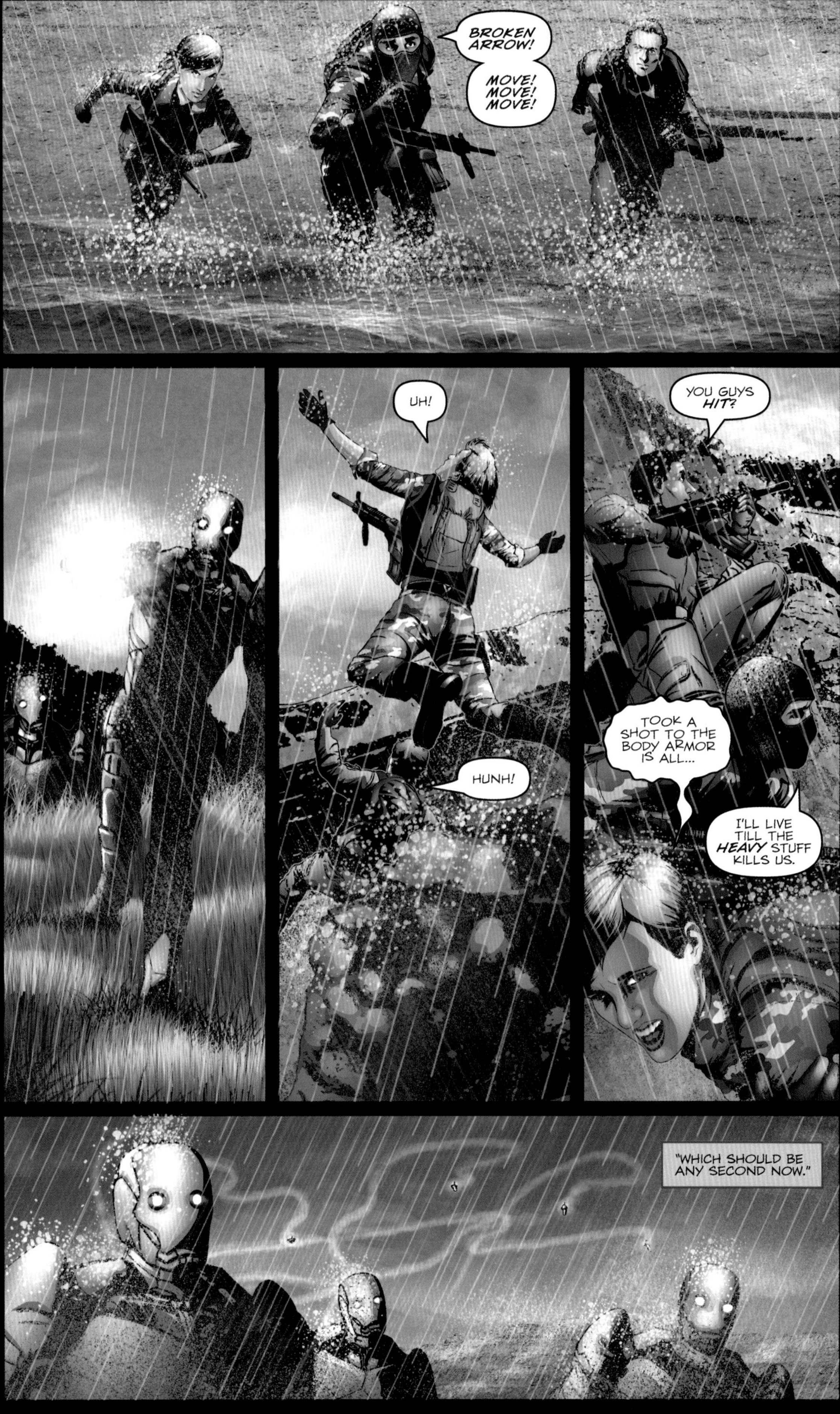
BROKEN ARROW!
MOVE! MOVE! MOVE!
UH!
HUNH!
YOU GUYS HIT?
TOOK A SHOT TO THE BODY ARMOR IS ALL...
I'LL LIVE TILL THE HEAVY STUFF KILLS US.
"WHICH SHOULD BE ANY SECOND NOW."

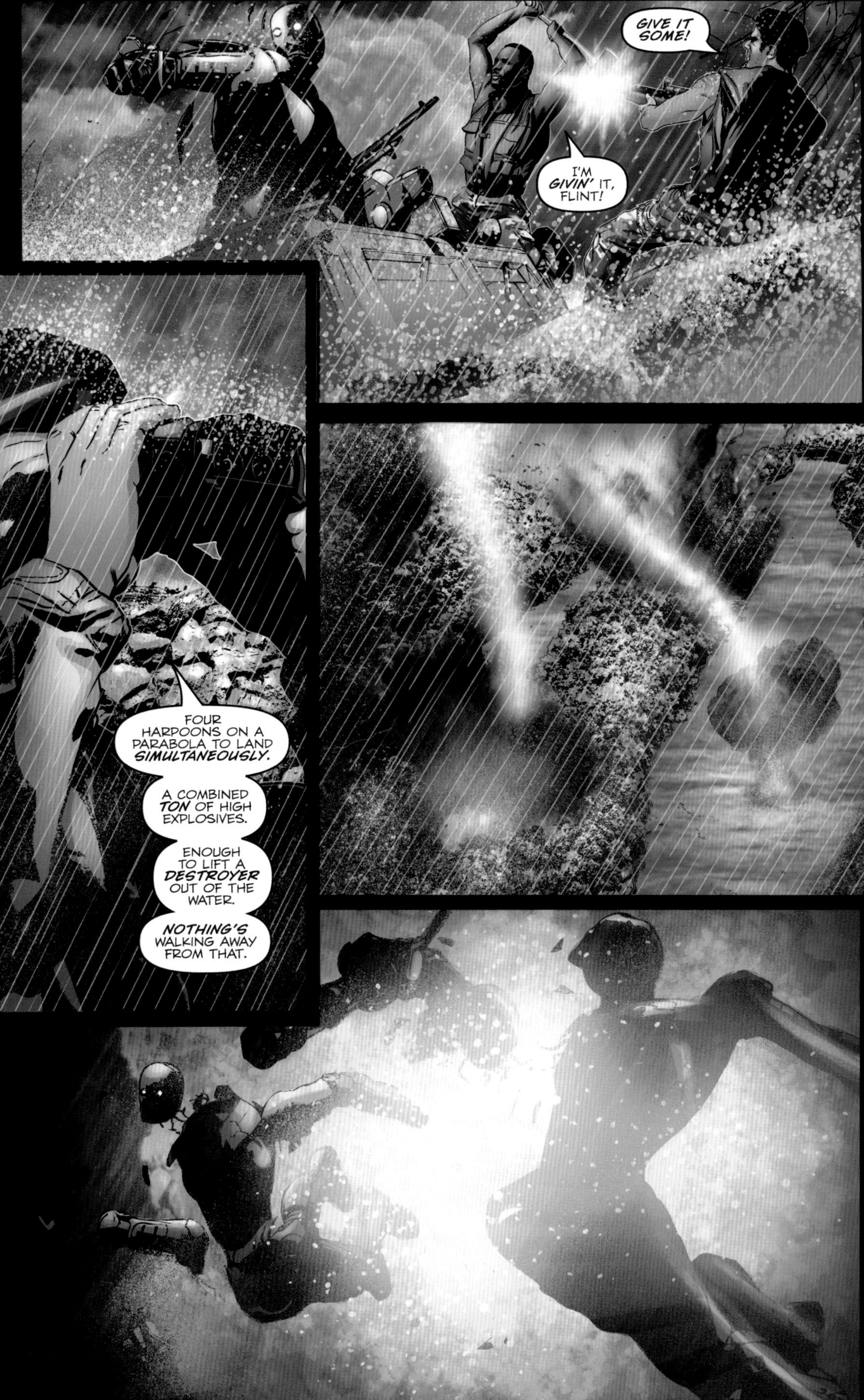
GIVE IT SOME!
I'M GIVIN' IT, FLINT!
FOUR HARPOONS ON A PARABOLA TO LAND SIMULTANEOUSLY.
A COMBINED TON OF HIGH EXPLOSIVES.
ENOUGH TO LIFT A DESTROYER OUT OF THE WATER.
NOTHING'S WALKING AWAY FROM THAT.

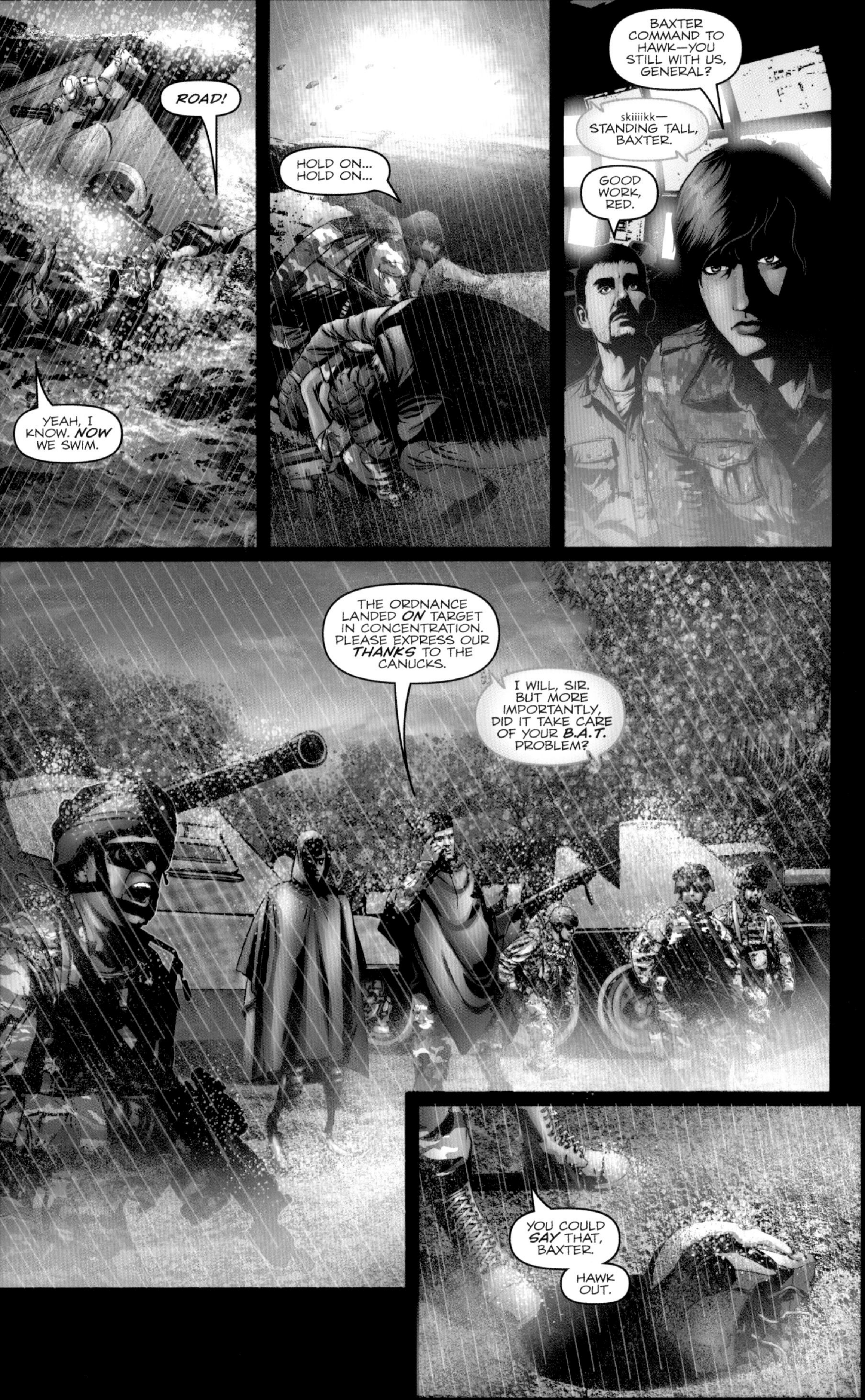
ROAD!
YEAH, I KNOW. NOW WE SWIM.
HOLD ON... HOLD ON...
BAXTER COMMAND TO HAWK—YOU STILL WITH US, GENERAL?
skiiiikk— STANDING TALL, BAXTER.
GOOD WORK, RED.
THE ORDNANCE LANDED ON TARGET IN CONCENTRATION. PLEASE EXPRESS OUR THANKS TO THE CANUCKS.
I WILL, SIR. BUT MORE IMPORTANTLY, DID IT TAKE CARE OF YOUR B.A.T. PROBLEM?
YOU COULD SAY THAT, BAXTER.
HAWK OUT.

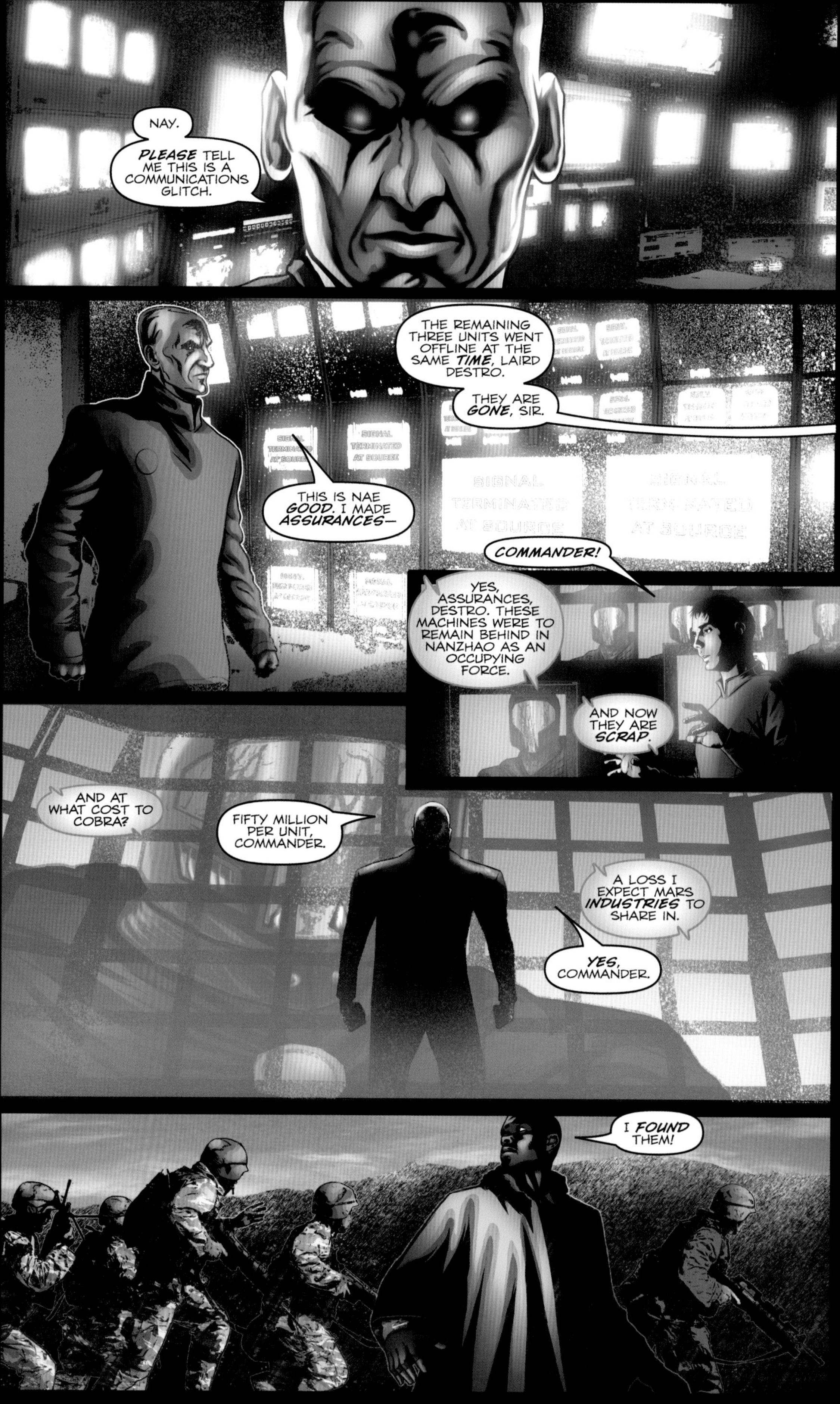
NAY.
PLEASE TELL ME THIS IS A COMMUNICATIONS GLITCH.
THE REMAINING THREE UNITS WENT OFFLINE AT THE SAME TIME, LAIRD DESTRO.
THEY ARE GONE, SIR.
THIS IS NAE GOOD. I MADE ASSURANCES—
SIGNAL TERMINATED AT SOURCE
COMMANDER!
YES, ASSURANCES, DESTRO. THESE MACHINES WERE TO REMAIN BEHIND IN NANZHAO AS AN OCCUPYING FORCE.
AND NOW THEY ARE SCRAP.
AND AT WHAT COST TO COBRA?
FIFTY MILLION PER UNIT, COMMANDER.
A LOSS I EXPECT MARS INDUSTRIES TO SHARE IN.
YES, COMMANDER.
I FOUND THEM!

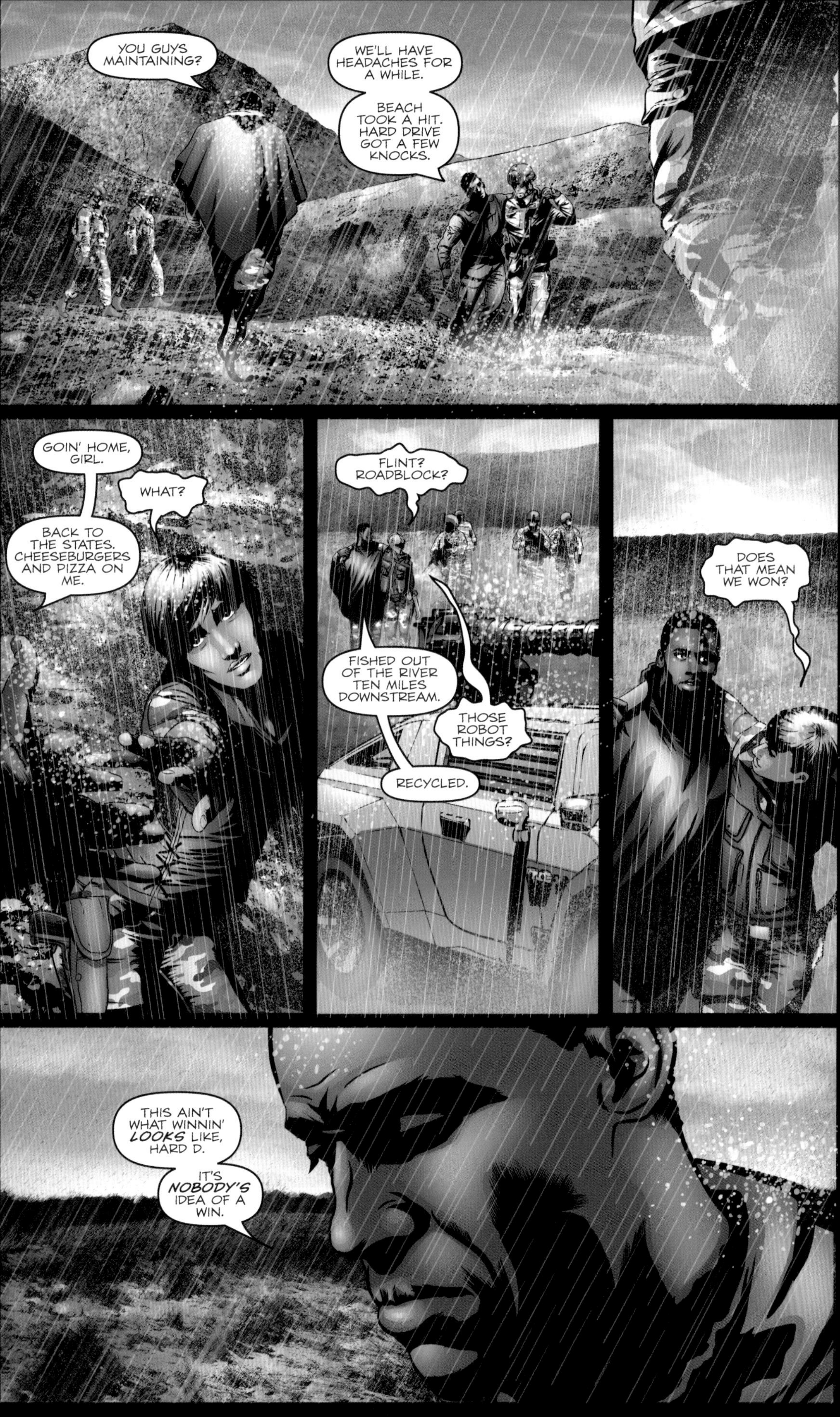

YOU GUYS MAINTAINING?
WE'LL HAVE HEADACHES FOR A WHILE.
BEACH TOOK A HIT. HARD DRIVE GOT A FEW KNOCKS.
GOIN' HOME, GIRL.
WHAT?
BACK TO THE STATES. CHEESEBURGERS AND PIZZA ON ME.
FLINT? ROADBLOCK?
FISHED OUT OF THE RIVER TEN MILES DOWNSTREAM.
THOSE ROBOT THINGS?
RECYCLED.
DOES THAT MEAN WE WON?
THIS AIN'T WHAT WINNIN' *LOOKS* LIKE, HARD D.
IT'S *NOBODY'S* IDEA OF A WIN.

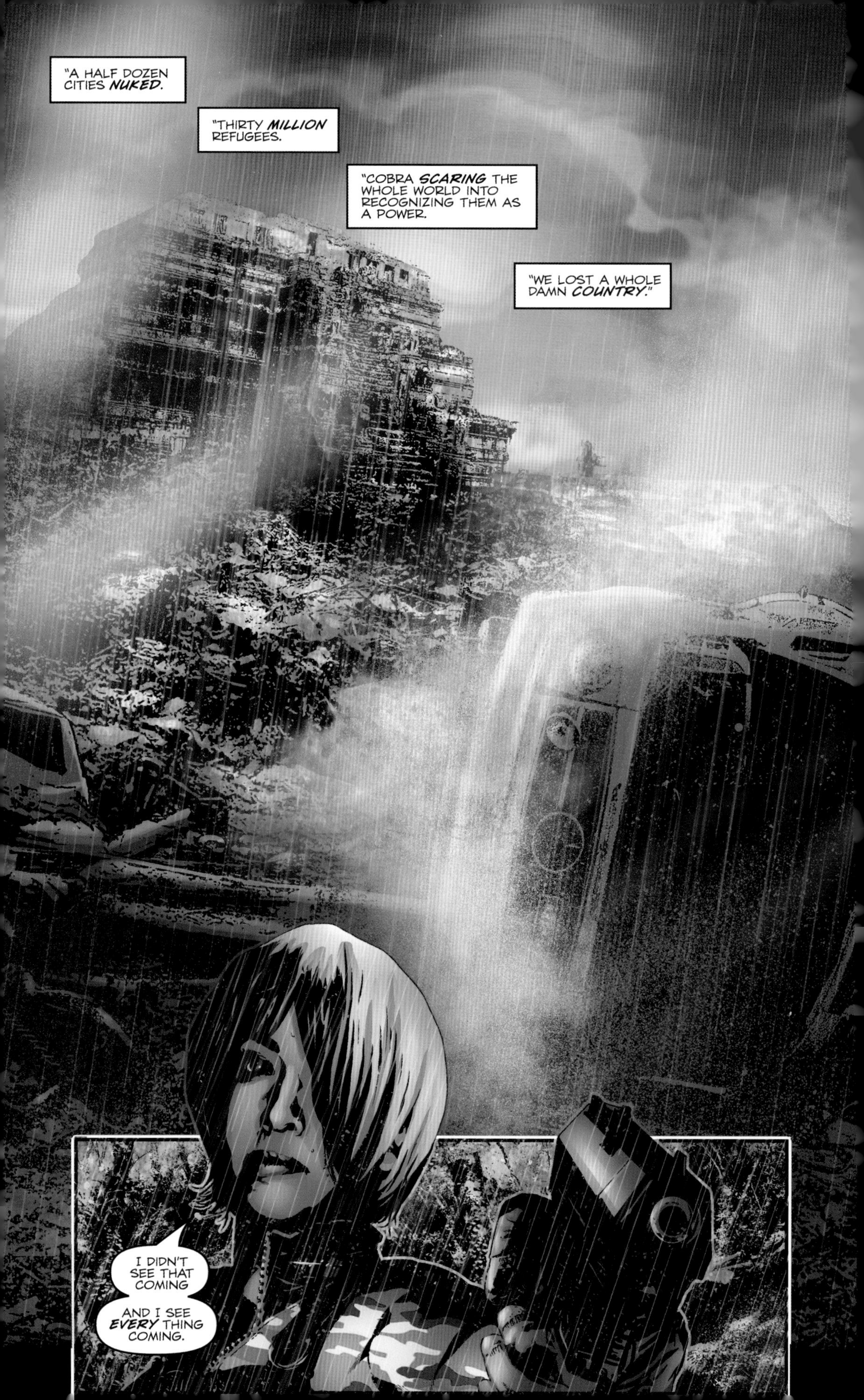
"A HALF DOZEN CITIES NUKED.
"THIRTY MILLION REFUGEES.
"COBRA SCARING THE WHOLE WORLD INTO RECOGNIZING THEM AS A POWER.
"WE LOST A WHOLE DAMN COUNTRY."
I DIDN'T SEE THAT COMING
AND I SEE EVERY THING COMING.

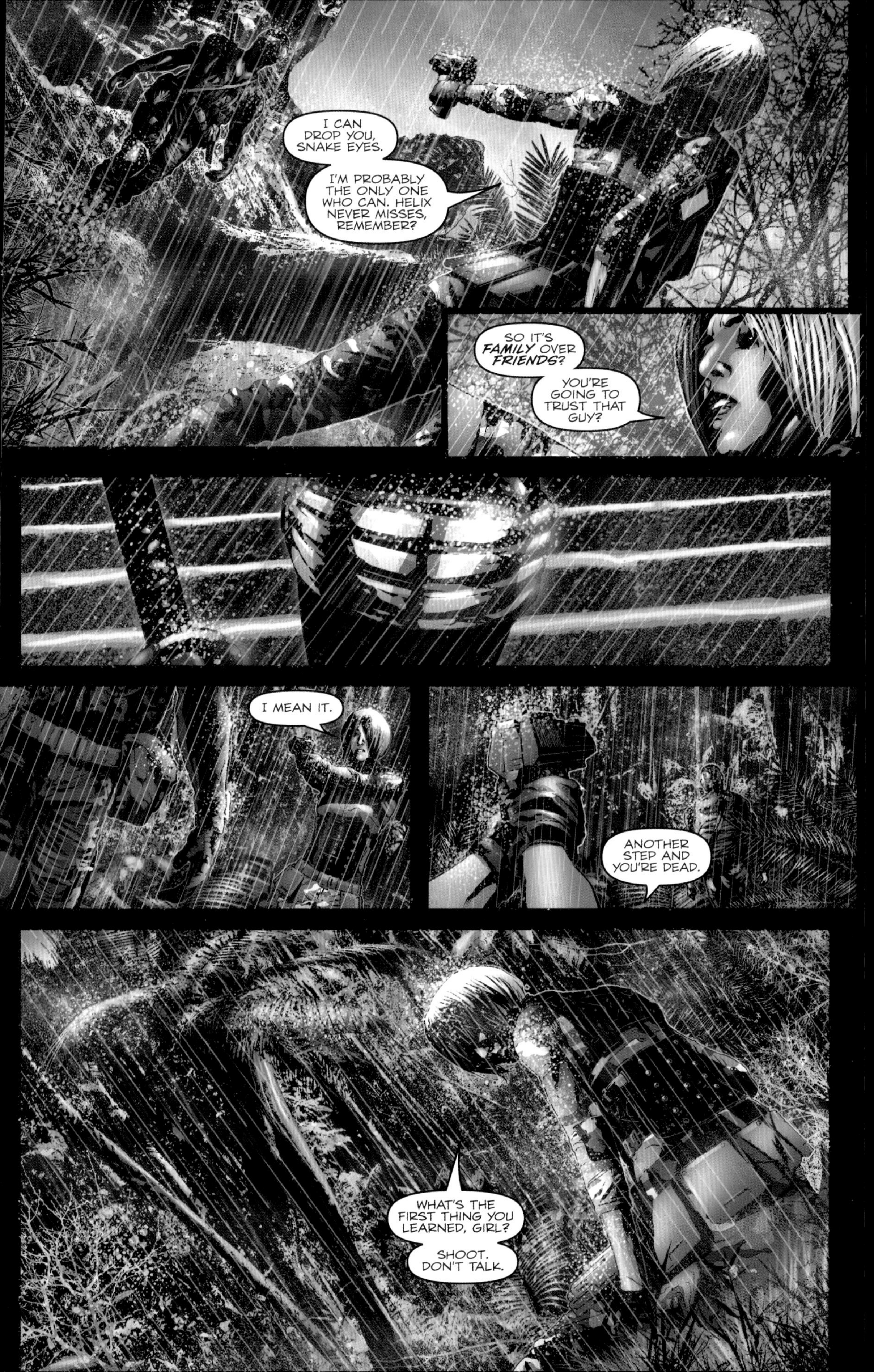
I CAN DROP YOU, SNAKE EYES.
I'M PROBABLY THE ONLY ONE WHO CAN. HELIX NEVER MISSES, REMEMBER?
SO IT'S FAMILY OVER FRIENDS?
YOU'RE GOING TO TRUST THAT GUY?
I MEAN IT.
ANOTHER STEP AND YOU'RE DEAD.
WHAT'S THE FIRST THING YOU LEARNED, GIRL?
SHOOT. DON'T TALK.

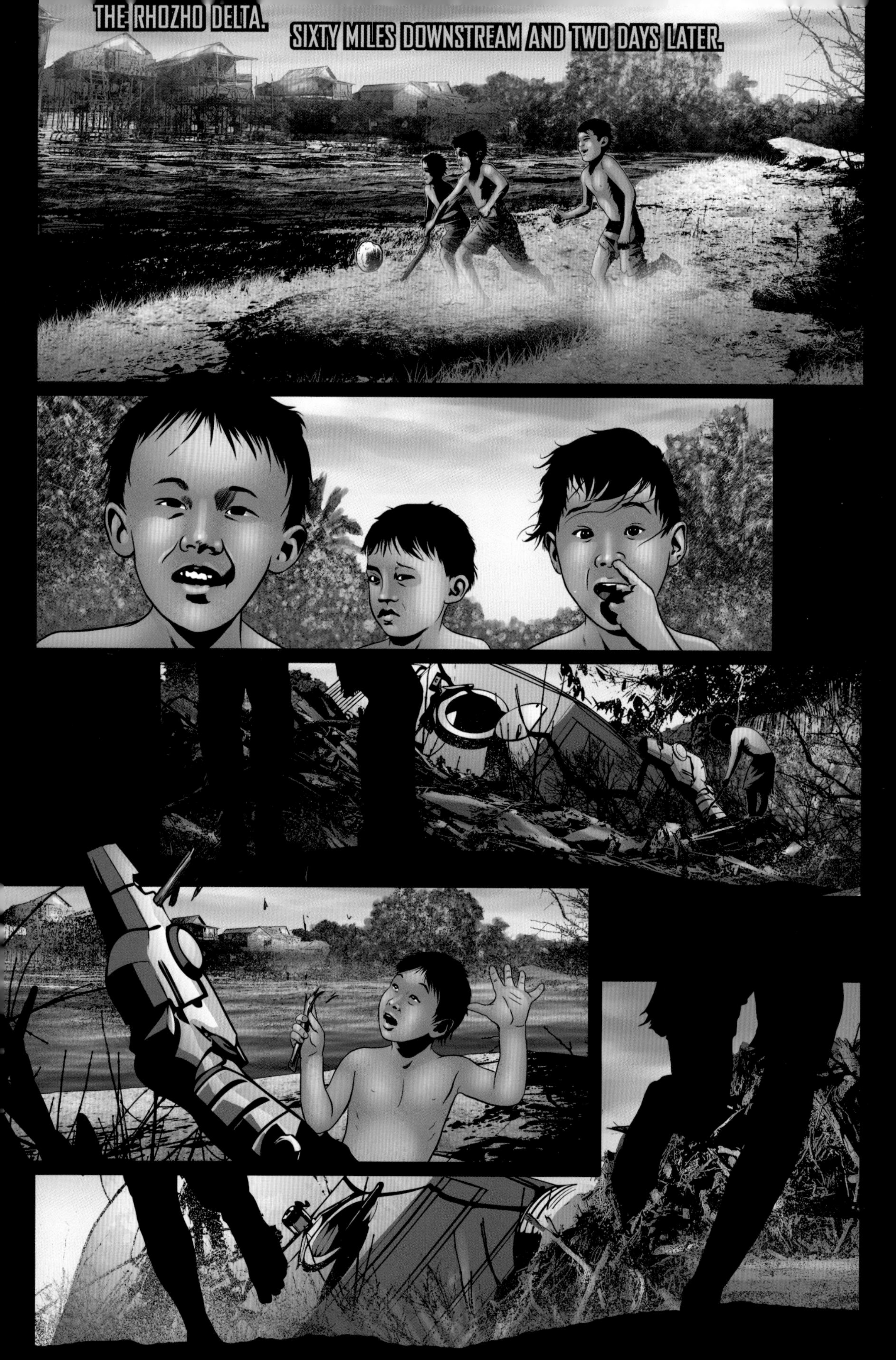
THE RHOZHO DELTA.
SIXTY MILES DOWNSTREAM AND TWO DAYS LATER.

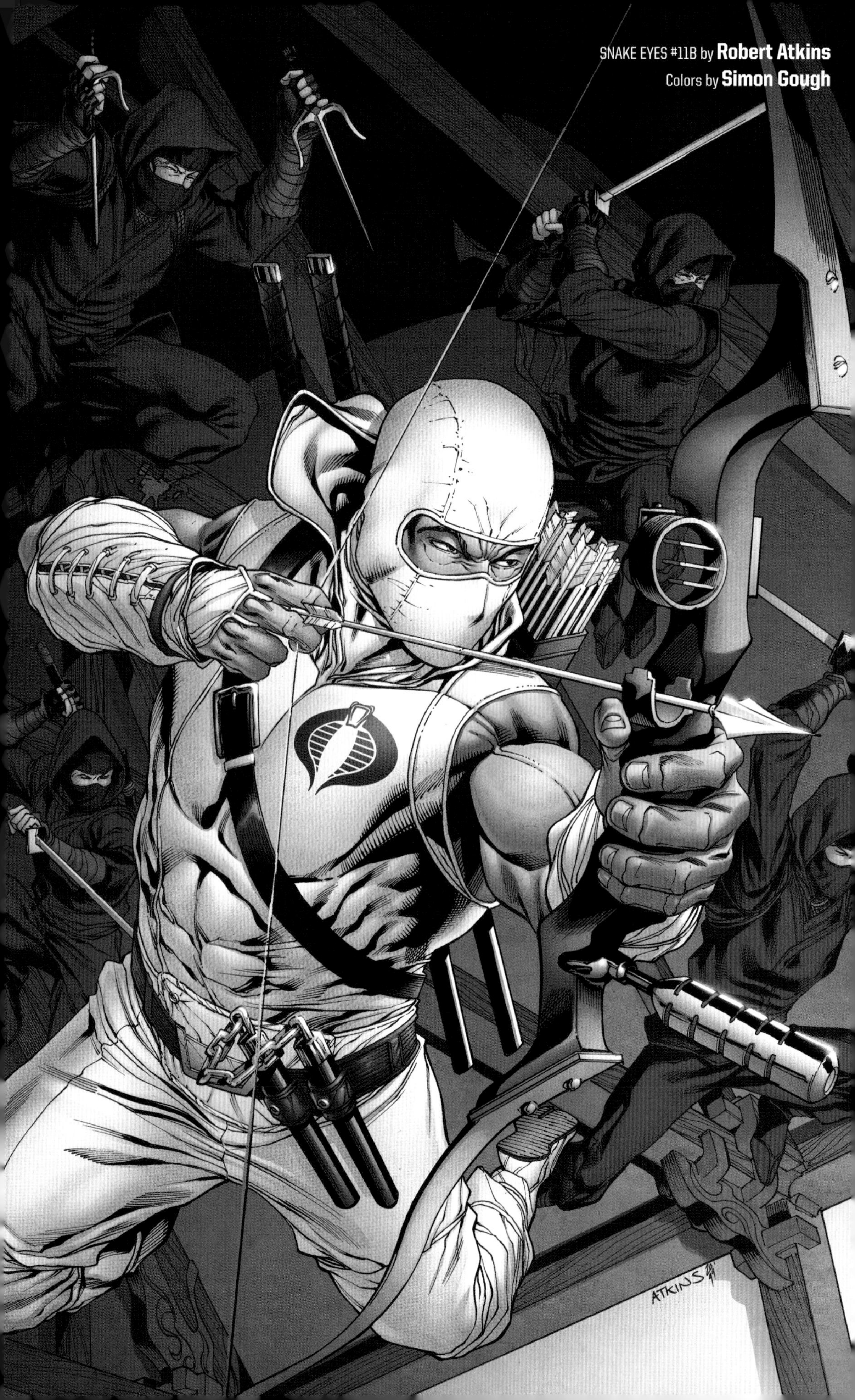
ATKINS

SNAKE EYES #11B by **Robert Atkins**

Colors by **Simon Gough**

COBRA #11A by **Dave Wilkins**

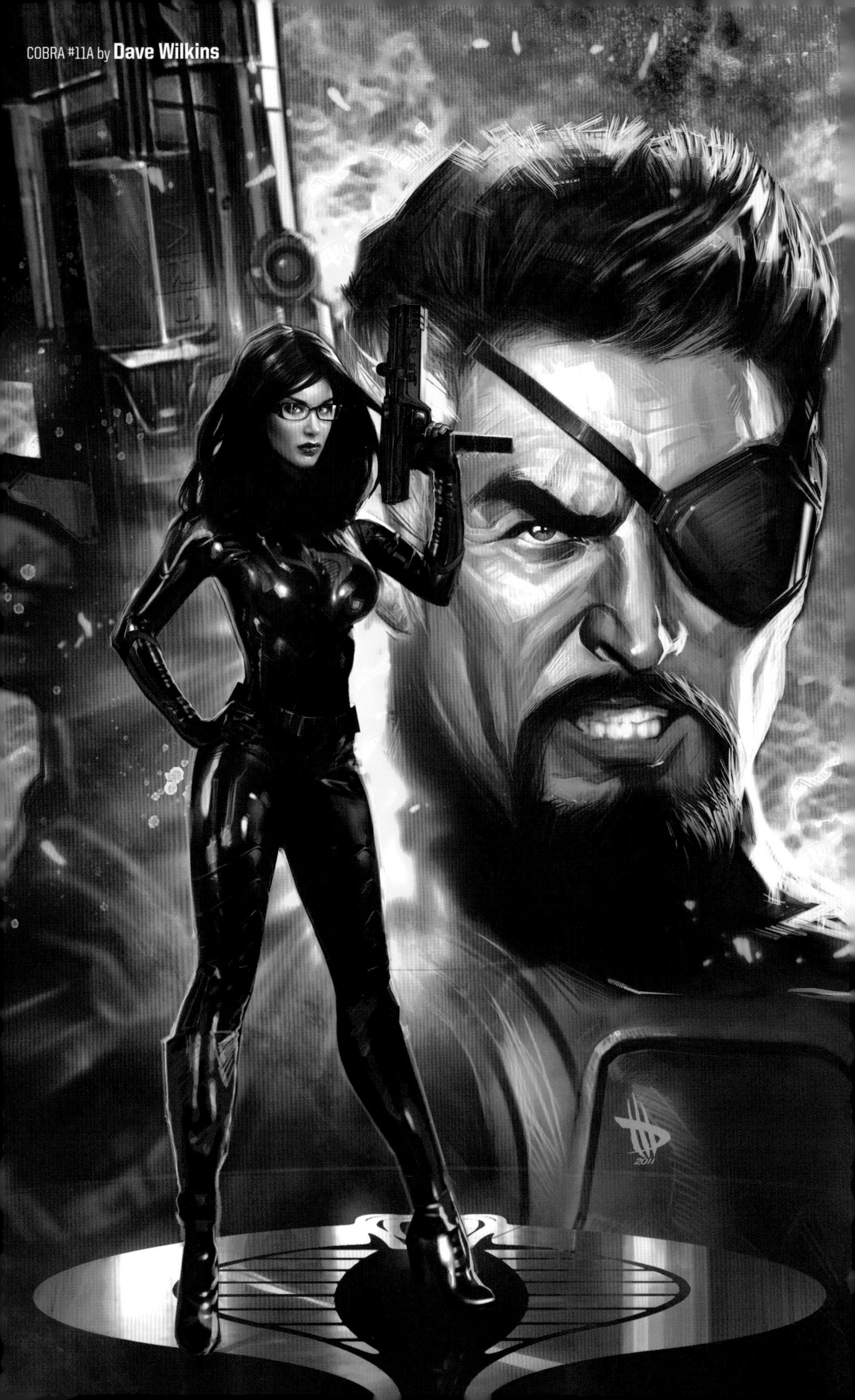

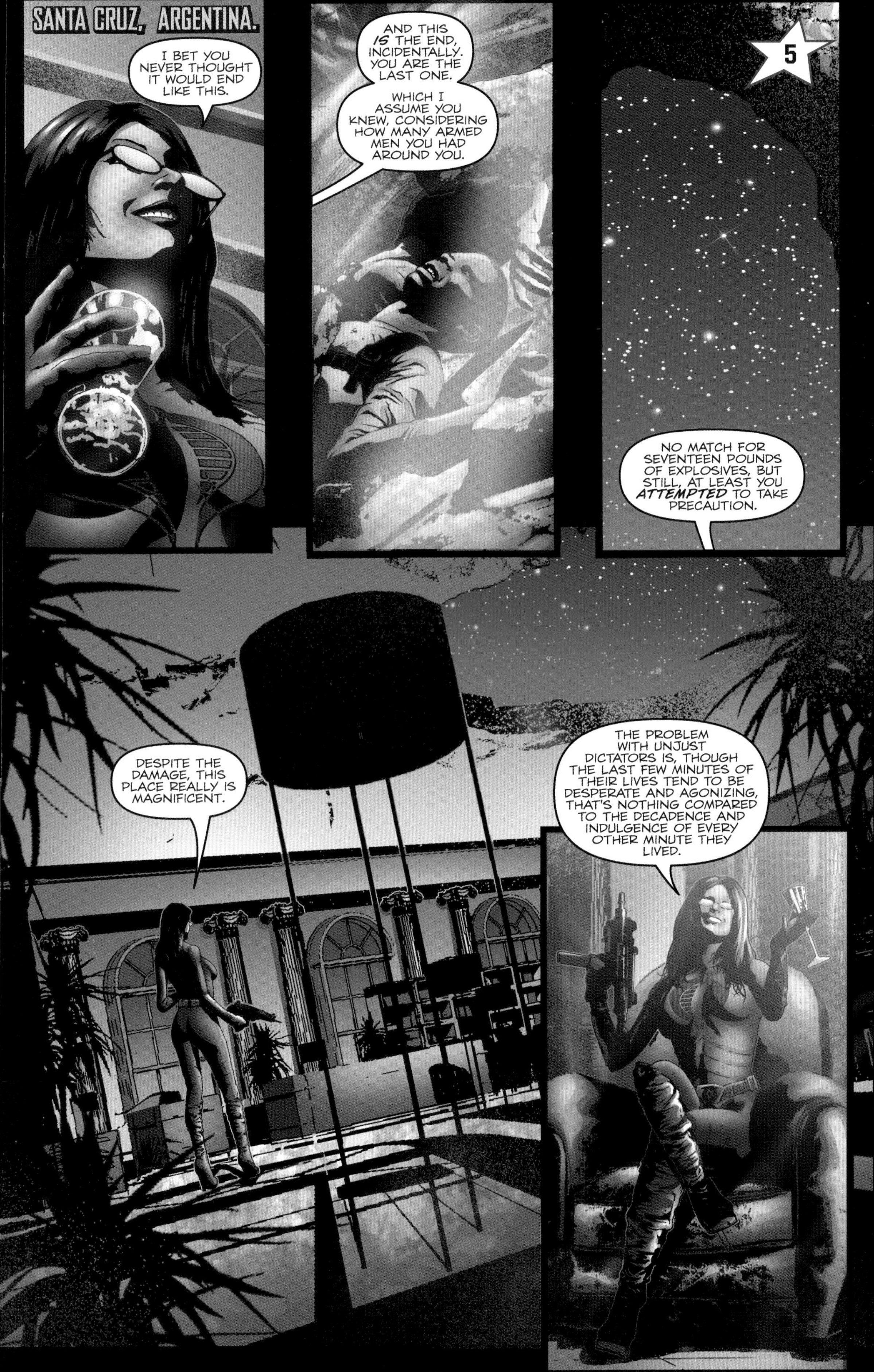
SANTA CRUZ, ARGENTINA.
I BET YOU NEVER THOUGHT IT WOULD END LIKE THIS.
AND THIS *IS* THE END, INCIDENTALLY. YOU ARE THE LAST ONE.
WHICH I ASSUME YOU KNEW, CONSIDERING HOW MANY ARMED MEN YOU HAD AROUND YOU.
5
NO MATCH FOR SEVENTEEN POUNDS OF EXPLOSIVES, BUT STILL, AT LEAST YOU ***ATTEMPTED*** TO TAKE PRECAUTION.
DESPITE THE DAMAGE, THIS PLACE REALLY IS MAGNIFICENT.
THE PROBLEM WITH UNJUST DICTATORS IS, THOUGH THE LAST FEW MINUTES OF THEIR LIVES TEND TO BE DESPERATE AND AGONIZING, THAT'S NOTHING COMPARED TO THE DECADENCE AND INDULGENCE OF EVERY OTHER MINUTE THEY LIVED.

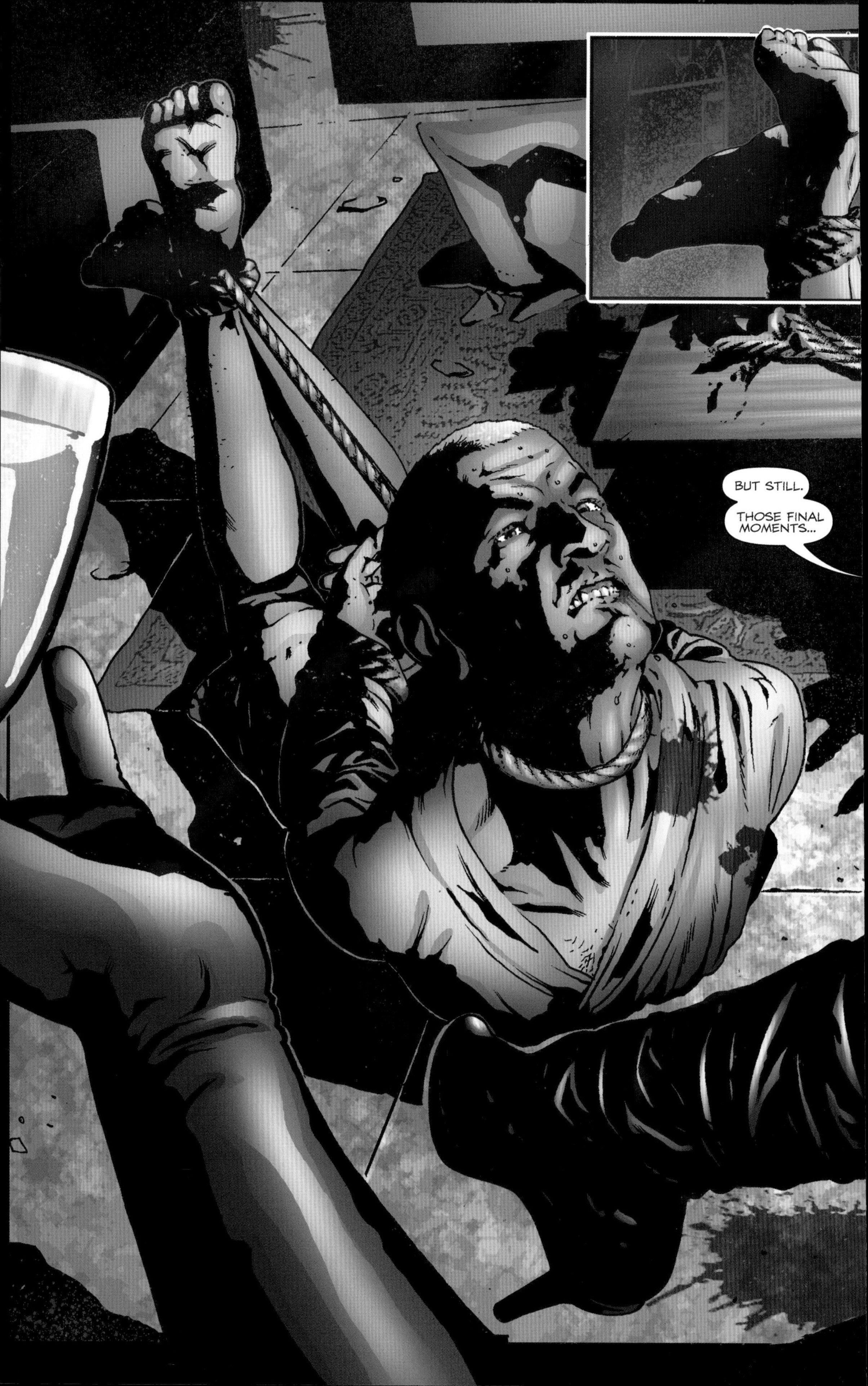
BUT STILL.
THOSE FINAL MOMENTS...

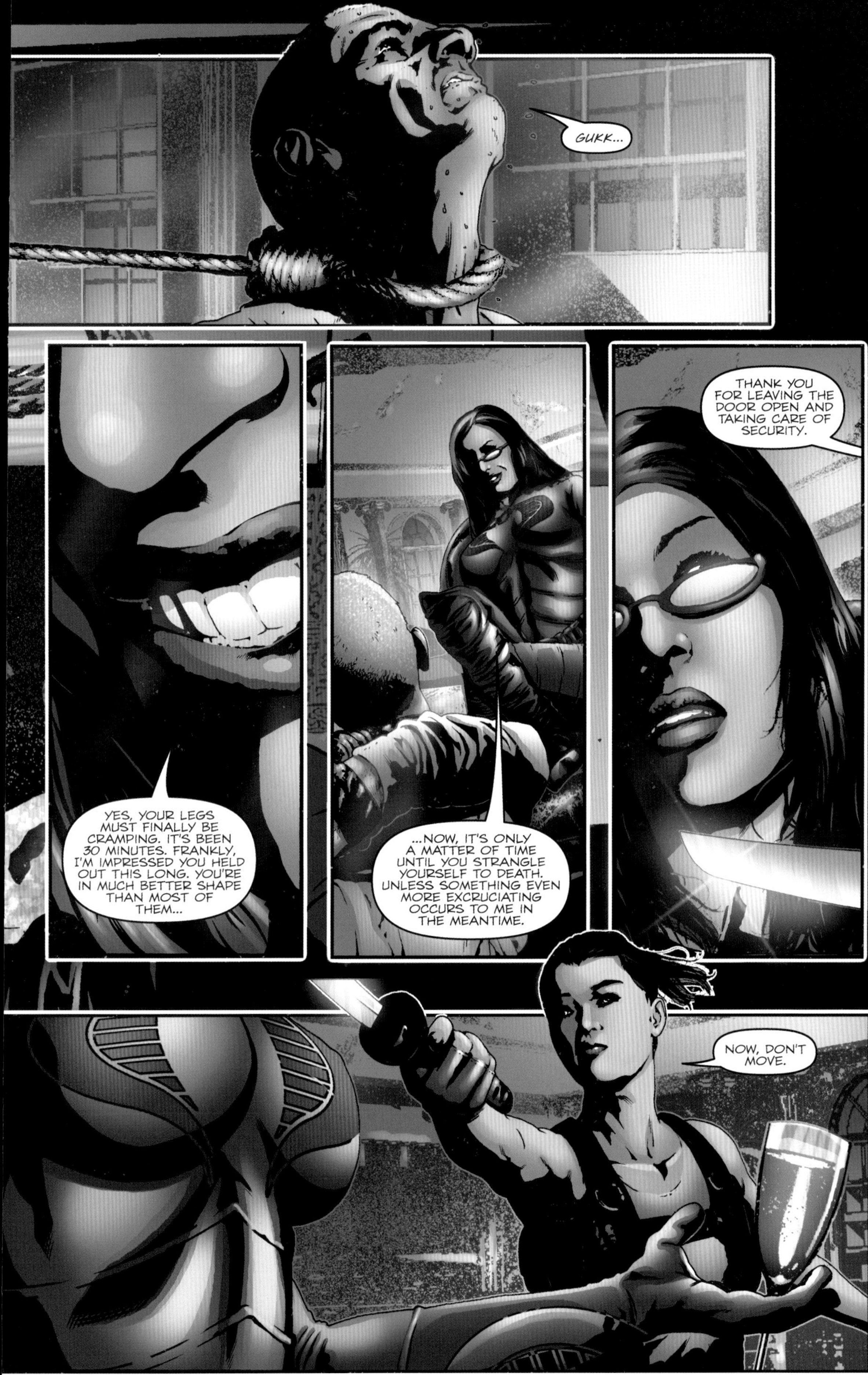
GUKK...
YES, YOUR LEGS MUST FINALLY BE CRAMPING. IT'S BEEN 30 MINUTES. FRANKLY, I'M IMPRESSED YOU HELD OUT THIS LONG. YOU'RE IN MUCH BETTER SHAPE THAN MOST OF THEM...
...NOW, IT'S ONLY A MATTER OF TIME UNTIL YOU STRANGLE YOURSELF TO DEATH. UNLESS SOMETHING EVEN MORE EXCRUCIATING OCCURS TO ME IN THE MEANTIME.
THANK YOU FOR LEAVING THE DOOR OPEN AND TAKING CARE OF SECURITY.
NOW, DON'T MOVE.

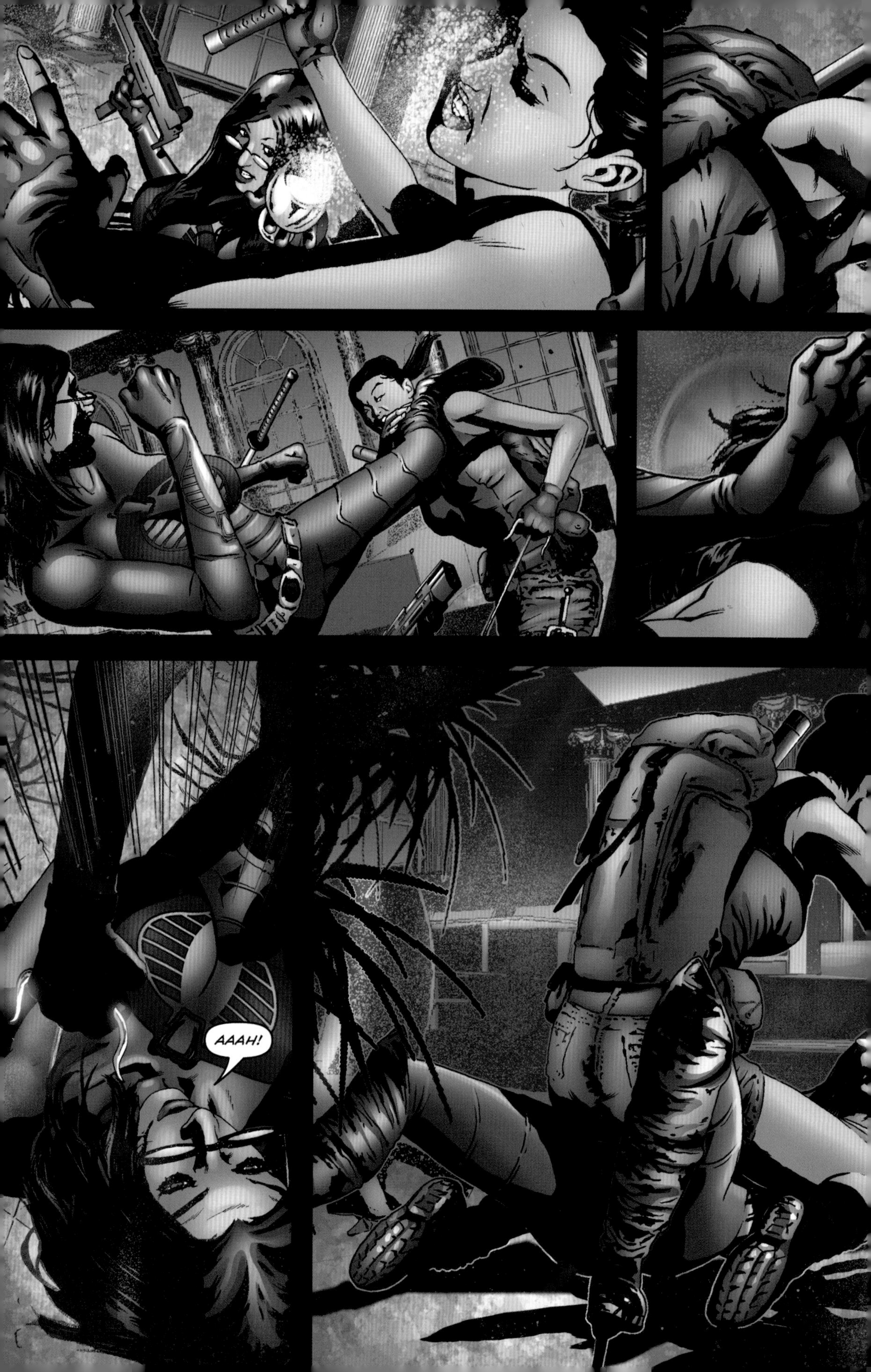
AAAH!

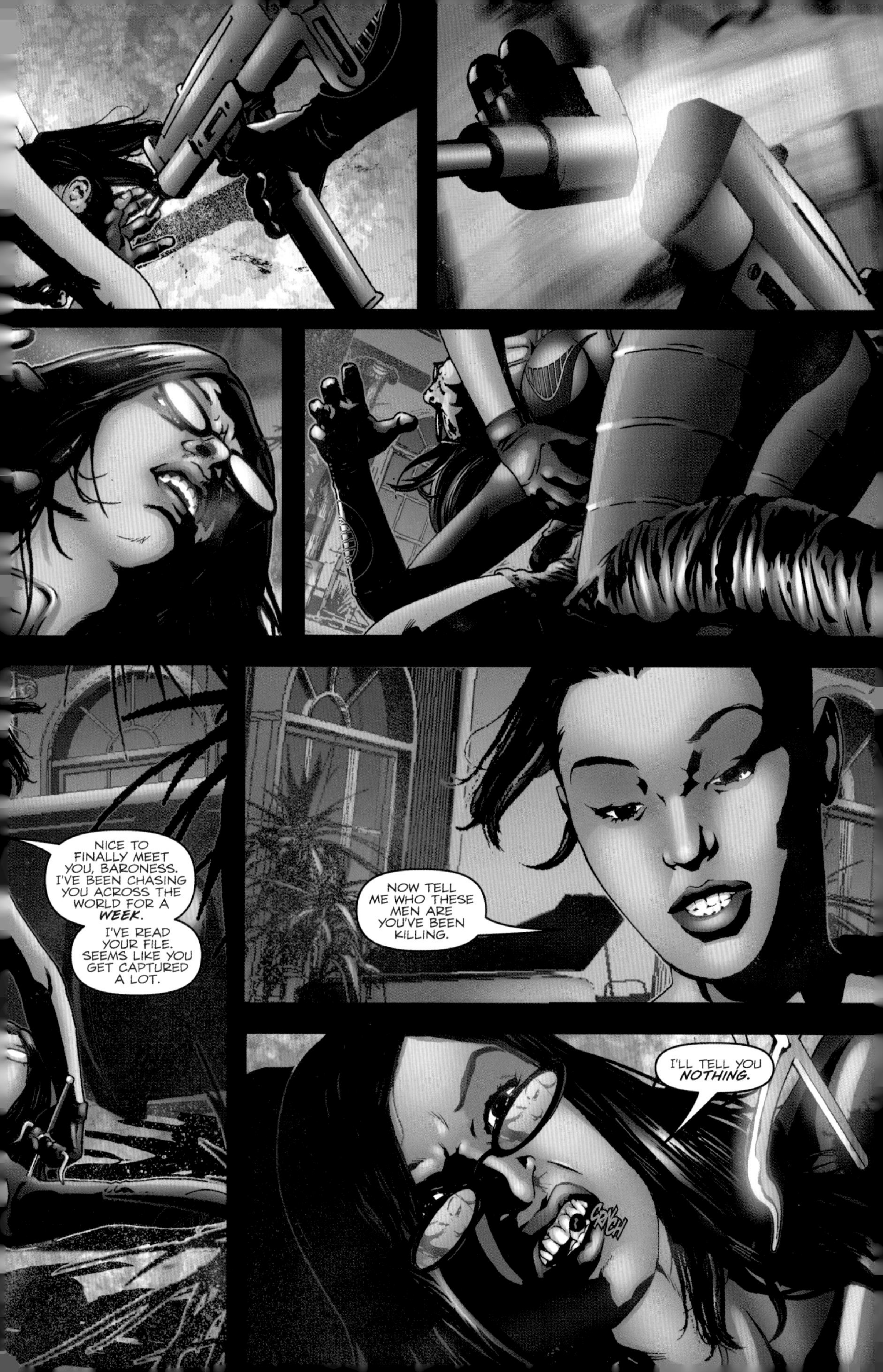
NICE TO FINALLY MEET YOU, BARONESS. I'VE BEEN CHASING YOU ACROSS THE WORLD FOR A *WEEK*.
I'VE READ YOUR FILE. SEEMS LIKE YOU GET CAPTURED A LOT.
NOW TELL ME WHO THESE MEN ARE YOU'VE BEEN KILLING.
I'LL TELL YOU *NOTHING.*

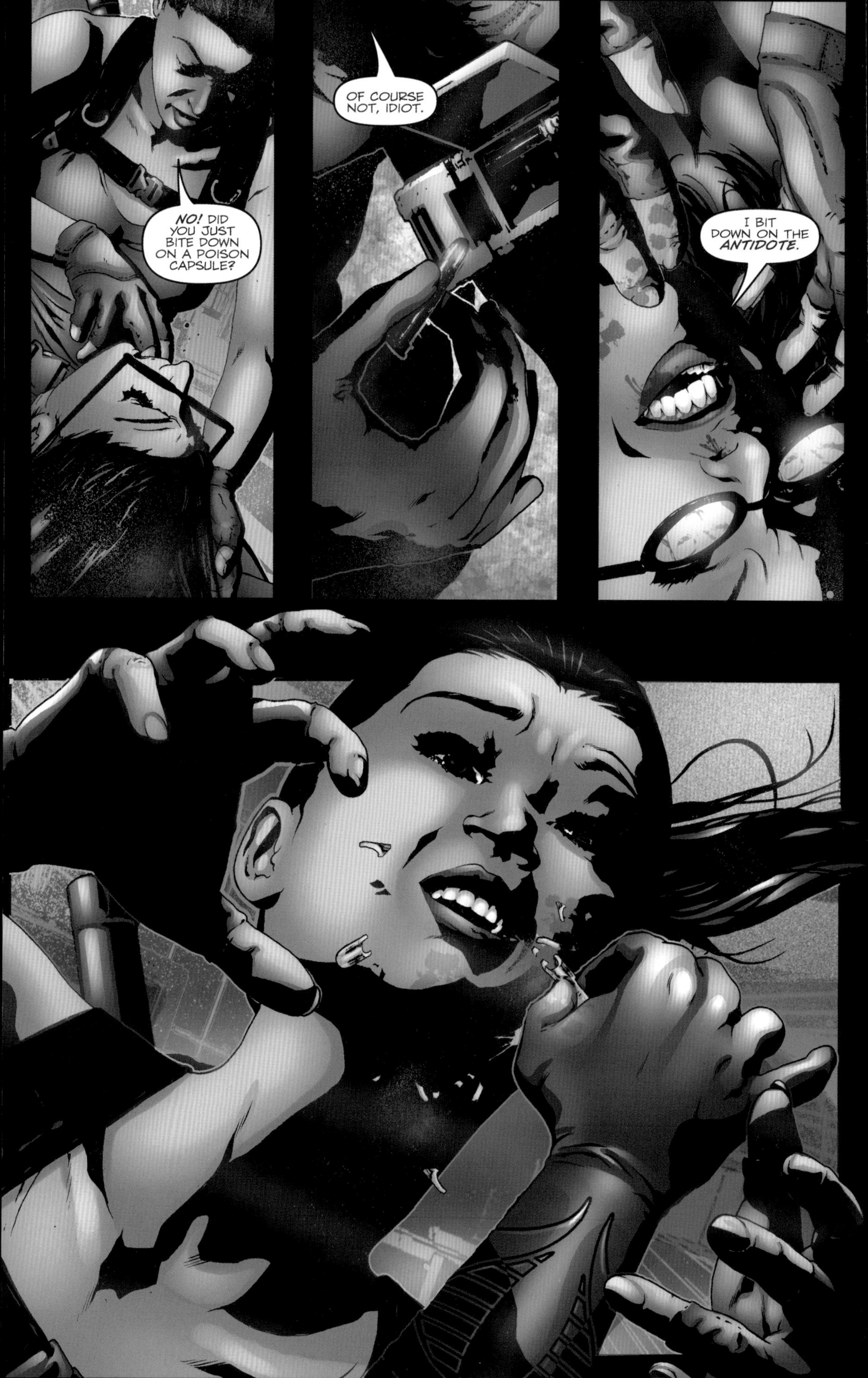
NO! DID YOU JUST BITE DOWN ON A POISON CAPSULE?
OF COURSE NOT, IDIOT.
I BIT DOWN ON THE ANTIDOTE.

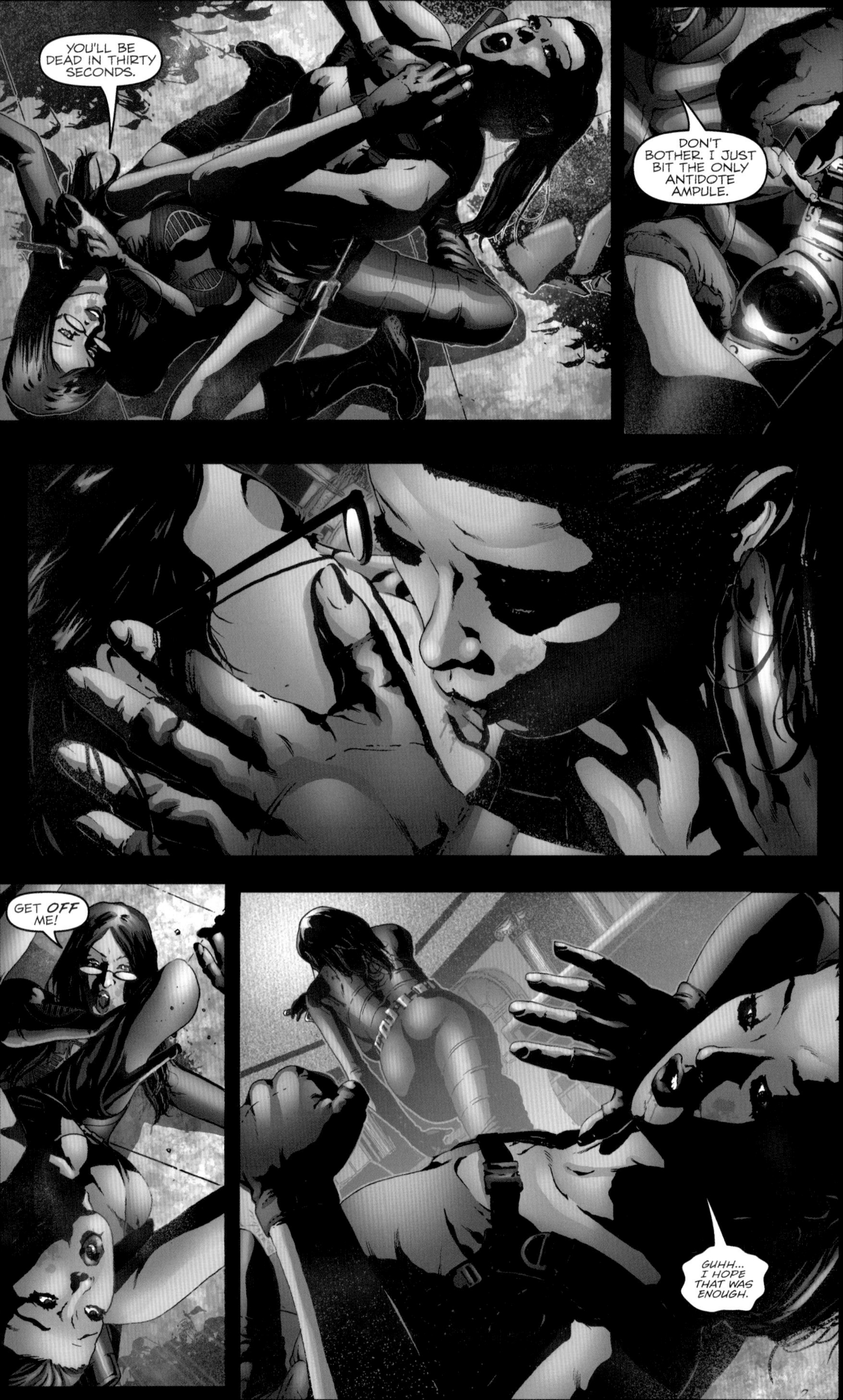
YOU'LL BE DEAD IN THIRTY SECONDS.
DON'T BOTHER. I JUST BIT THE ONLY ANTIDOTE AMPULE.
GET OFF ME!
GUHH... I HOPE THAT WAS ENOUGH.

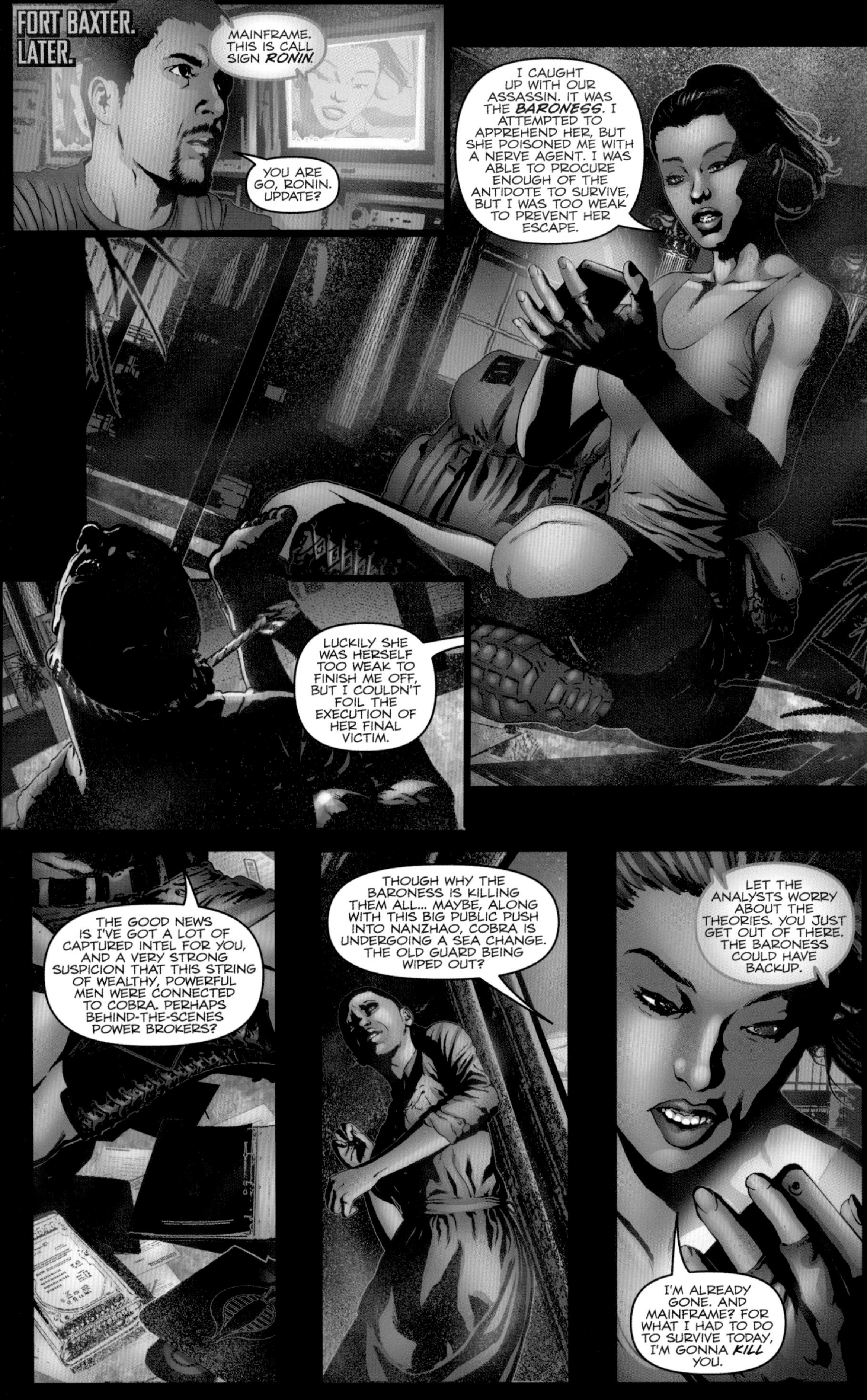
FORT BAXTER. LATER.
MAINFRAME. THIS IS CALL SIGN RONIN.
YOU ARE GO, RONIN. UPDATE?
I CAUGHT UP WITH OUR ASSASSIN. IT WAS THE BARONESS. I ATTEMPTED TO APPREHEND HER, BUT SHE POISONED ME WITH A NERVE AGENT. I WAS ABLE TO PROCURE ENOUGH OF THE ANTIDOTE TO SURVIVE, BUT I WAS TOO WEAK TO PREVENT HER ESCAPE.
LUCKILY SHE WAS HERSELF TOO WEAK TO FINISH ME OFF, BUT I COULDN'T FOIL THE EXECUTION OF HER FINAL VICTIM.
THE GOOD NEWS IS I'VE GOT A LOT OF CAPTURED INTEL FOR YOU, AND A VERY STRONG SUSPICION THAT THIS STRING OF WEALTHY, POWERFUL MEN WERE CONNECTED TO COBRA. PERHAPS BEHIND-THE-SCENES POWER BROKERS?
THOUGH WHY THE BARONESS IS KILLING THEM ALL... MAYBE, ALONG WITH THIS BIG PUBLIC PUSH INTO NANZHAO, COBRA IS UNDERGOING A SEA CHANGE. THE OLD GUARD BEING WIPED OUT?
LET THE ANALYSTS WORRY ABOUT THE THEORIES. YOU JUST GET OUT OF THERE. THE BARONESS COULD HAVE BACKUP.
I'M ALREADY GONE. AND MAINFRAME? FOR WHAT I HAD TO DO TO SURVIVE TODAY, I'M GONNA KILL YOU.

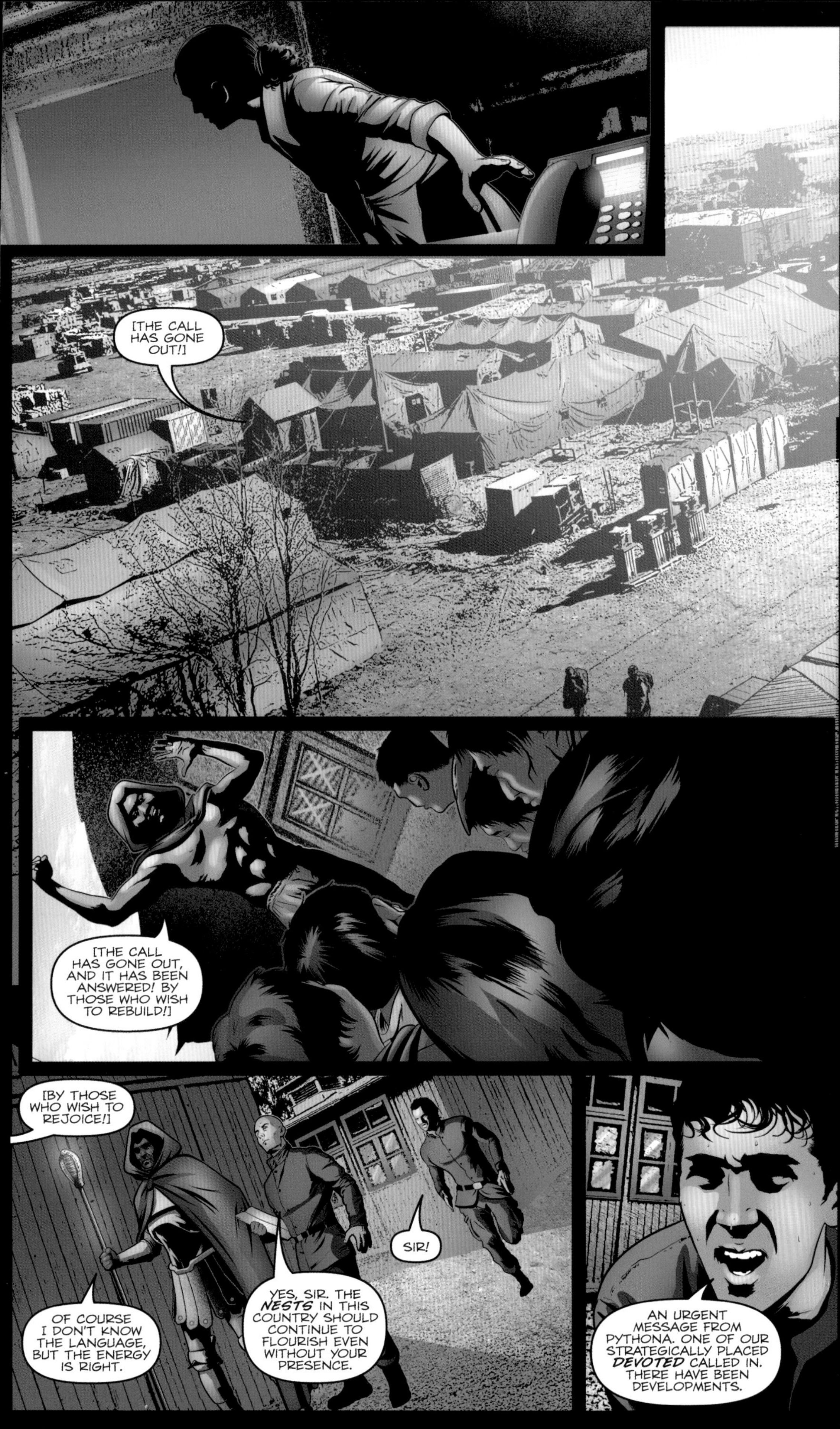

[THE CALL HAS GONE OUT!]
[THE CALL HAS GONE OUT, AND IT HAS BEEN ANSWERED! BY THOSE WHO WISH TO REBUILD!]
[BY THOSE WHO WISH TO REJOICE!]
OF COURSE I DON'T KNOW THE LANGUAGE, BUT THE ENERGY IS RIGHT.
YES, SIR. THE NESTS IN THIS COUNTRY SHOULD CONTINUE TO FLOURISH EVEN WITHOUT YOUR PRESENCE.
SIR!
AN URGENT MESSAGE FROM PYTHONA. ONE OF OUR STRATEGICALLY PLACED DEVOTED CALLED IN. THERE HAVE BEEN DEVELOPMENTS.

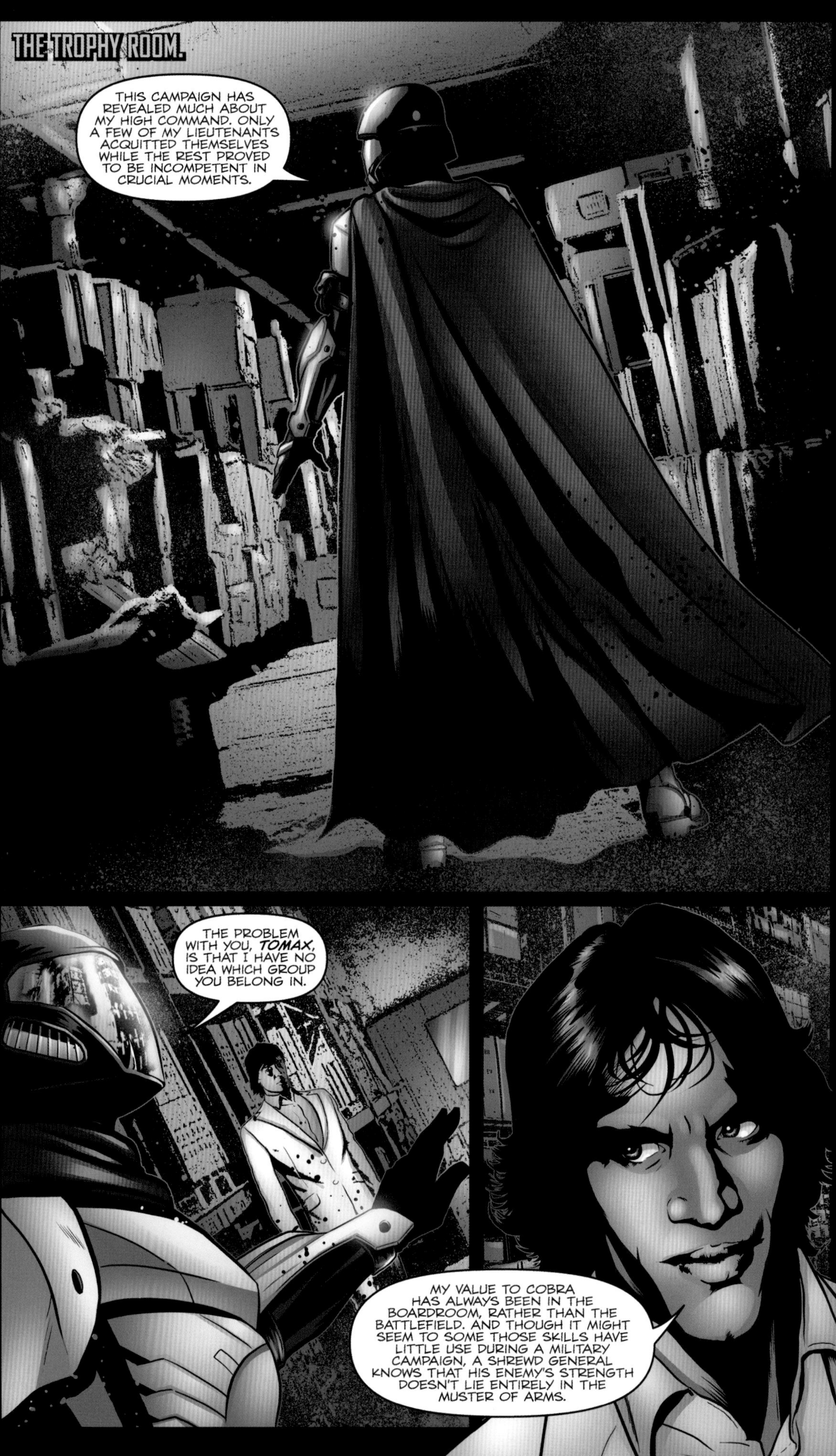
THE TROPHY ROOM.
THIS CAMPAIGN HAS REVEALED MUCH ABOUT MY HIGH COMMAND. ONLY A FEW OF MY LIEUTENANTS ACQUITTED THEMSELVES WHILE THE REST PROVED TO BE INCOMPETENT IN CRUCIAL MOMENTS.
THE PROBLEM WITH YOU, ***TOMAX***, IS THAT I HAVE NO IDEA WHICH GROUP YOU BELONG IN.
MY VALUE TO COBRA HAS ALWAYS BEEN IN THE BOARDROOM, RATHER THAN THE BATTLEFIELD. AND THOUGH IT MIGHT SEEM TO SOME THOSE SKILLS HAVE LITTLE USE DURING A MILITARY CAMPAIGN, A SHREWD GENERAL KNOWS THAT HIS ENEMY'S STRENGTH DOESN'T LIE ENTIRELY IN THE MUSTER OF ARMS.

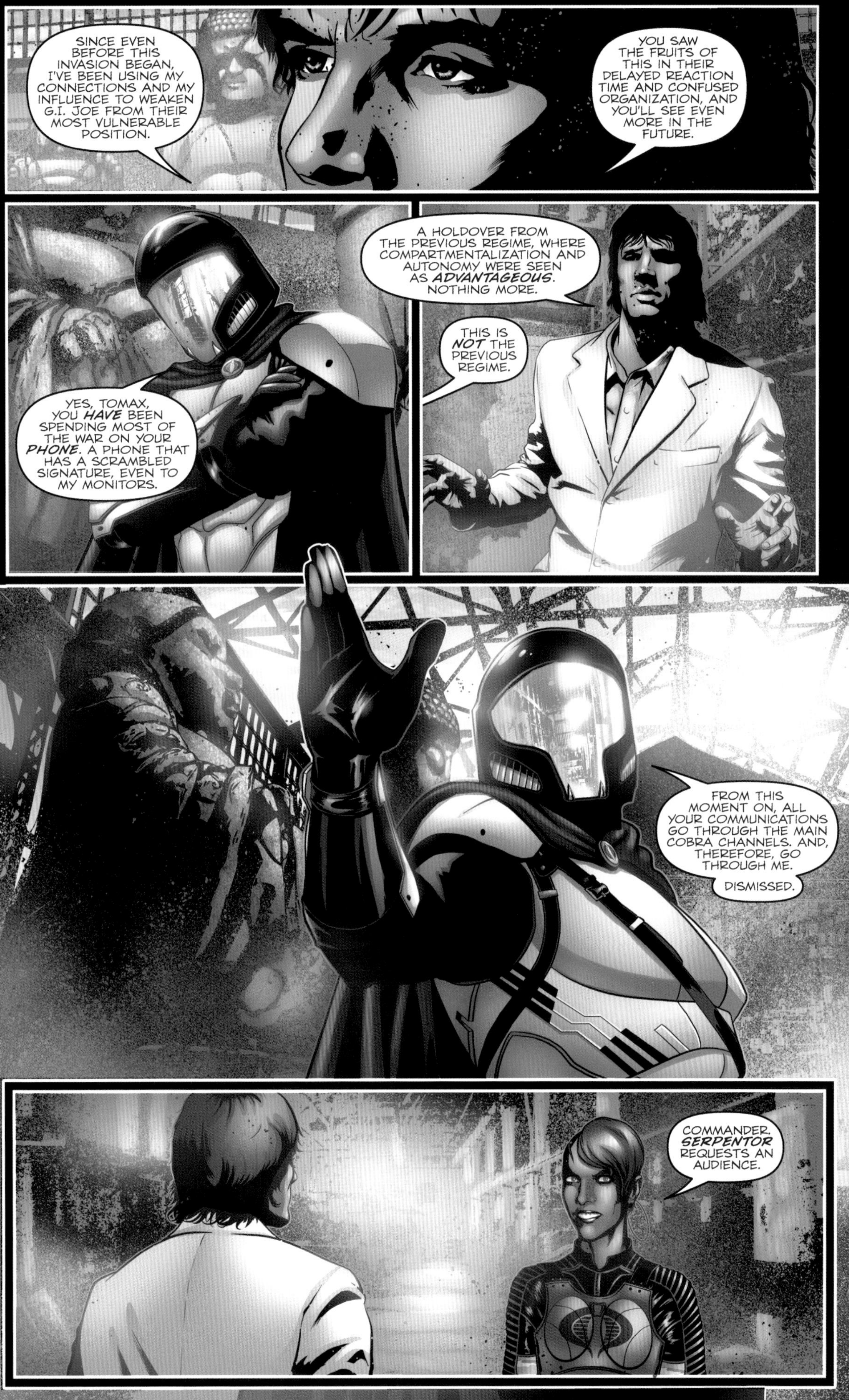
SINCE EVEN BEFORE THIS INVASION BEGAN, I'VE BEEN USING MY CONNECTIONS AND MY INFLUENCE TO WEAKEN G.I. JOE FROM THEIR MOST VULNERABLE POSITION.
YOU SAW THE FRUITS OF THIS IN THEIR DELAYED REACTION TIME AND CONFUSED ORGANIZATION, AND YOU'LL SEE EVEN MORE IN THE FUTURE.
YES, TOMAX, YOU ***HAVE*** BEEN SPENDING MOST OF THE WAR ON YOUR ***PHONE***. A PHONE THAT HAS A SCRAMBLED SIGNATURE, EVEN TO MY MONITORS.
A HOLDOVER FROM THE PREVIOUS REGIME, WHERE COMPARTMENTALIZATION AND AUTONOMY WERE SEEN AS ***ADVANTAGEOUS***. NOTHING MORE.
THIS IS ***NOT*** THE PREVIOUS REGIME.
FROM THIS MOMENT ON, ALL YOUR COMMUNICATIONS GO THROUGH THE MAIN COBRA CHANNELS. AND, THEREFORE, GO THROUGH ME.
DISMISSED.
COMMANDER. ***SERPENTOR*** REQUESTS AN AUDIENCE.

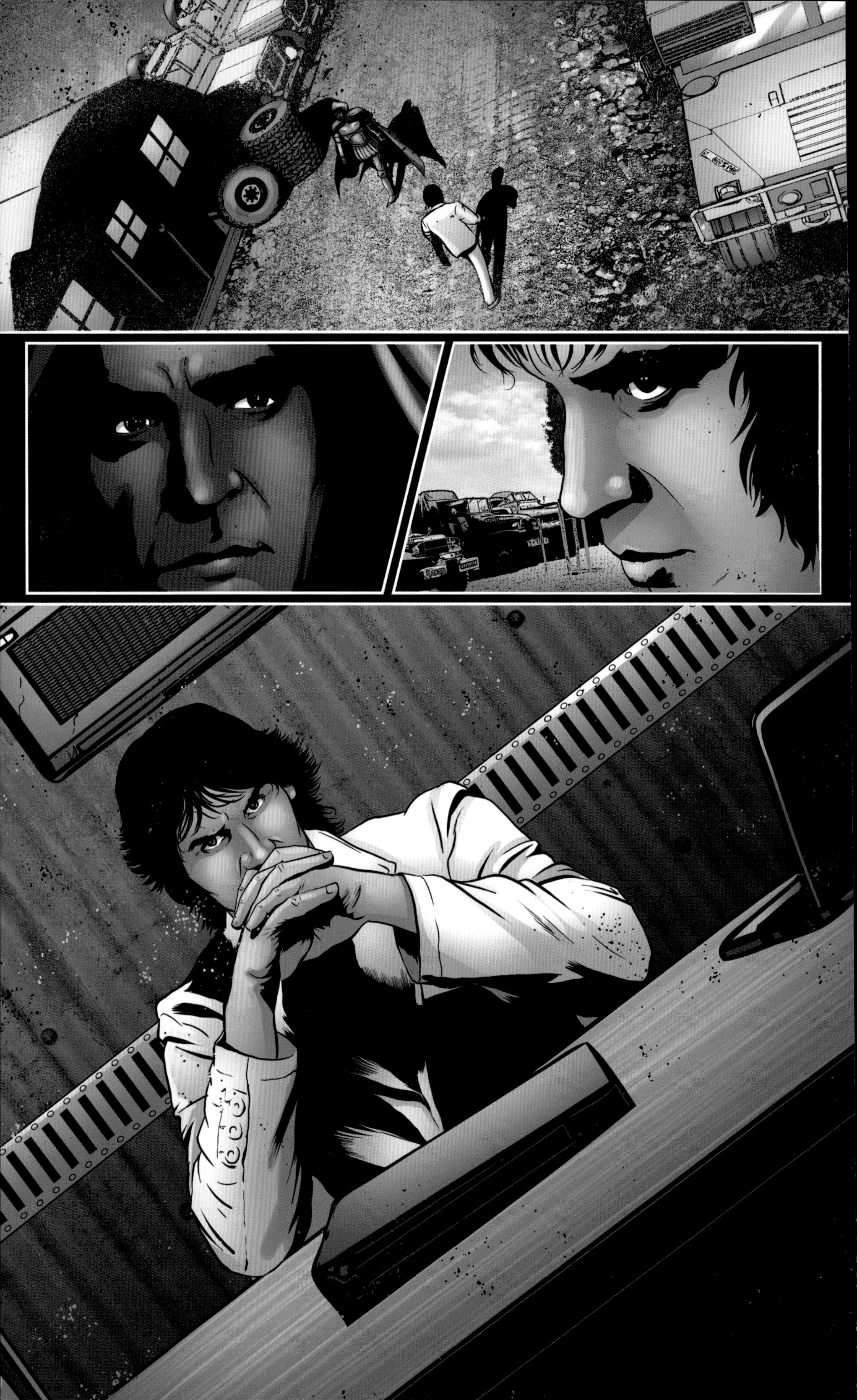

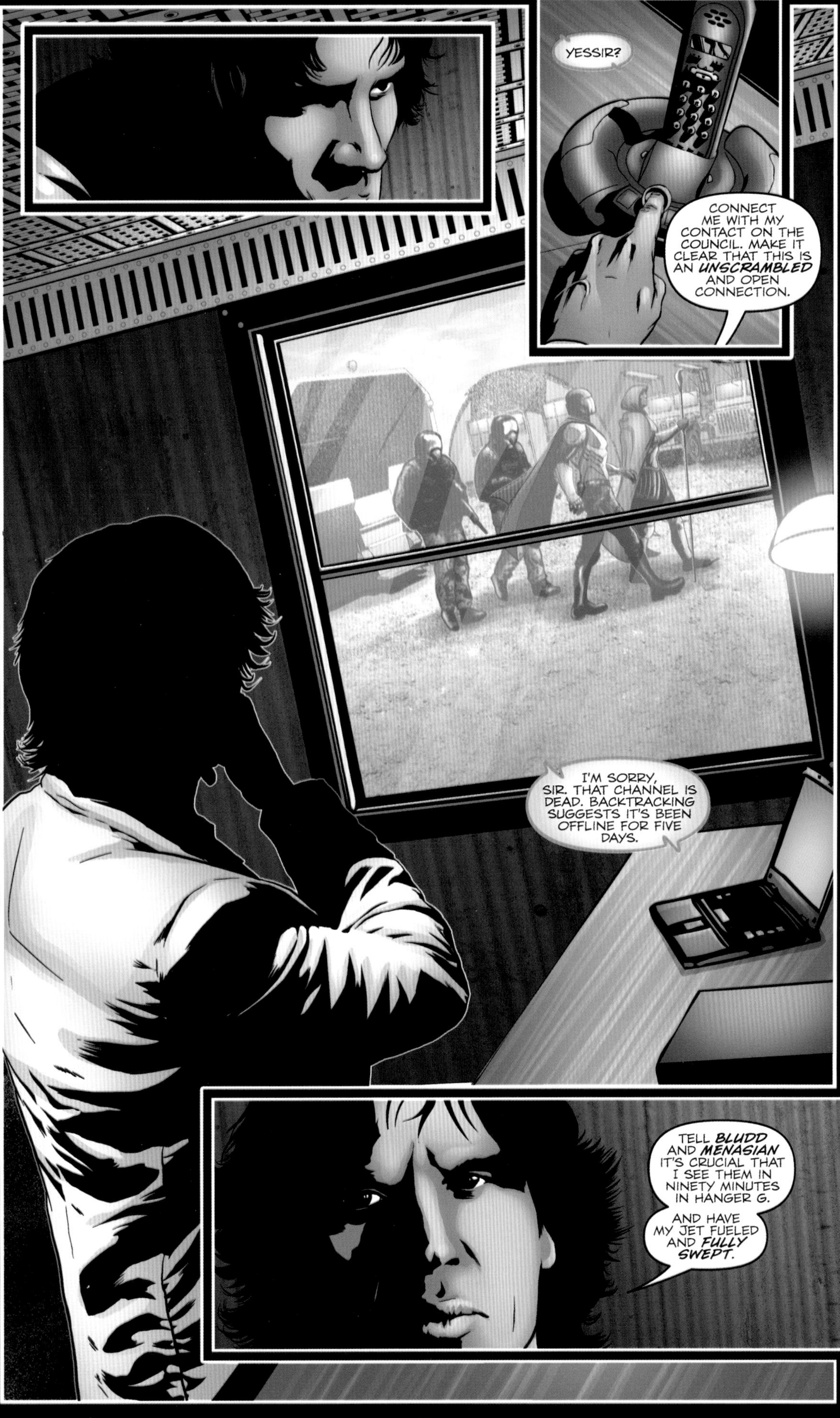
YESSIR?
CONNECT ME WITH MY CONTACT ON THE COUNCIL. MAKE IT CLEAR THAT THIS IS AN *UNSCRAMBLED* AND OPEN CONNECTION.
I'M SORRY, SIR. THAT CHANNEL IS DEAD. BACKTRACKING SUGGESTS IT'S BEEN OFFLINE FOR FIVE DAYS.
TELL *BLUDD* AND *MENASIAN* IT'S CRUCIAL THAT I SEE THEM IN NINETY MINUTES IN HANGER G.
AND HAVE MY JET FUELED AND *FULLY SWEPT*.

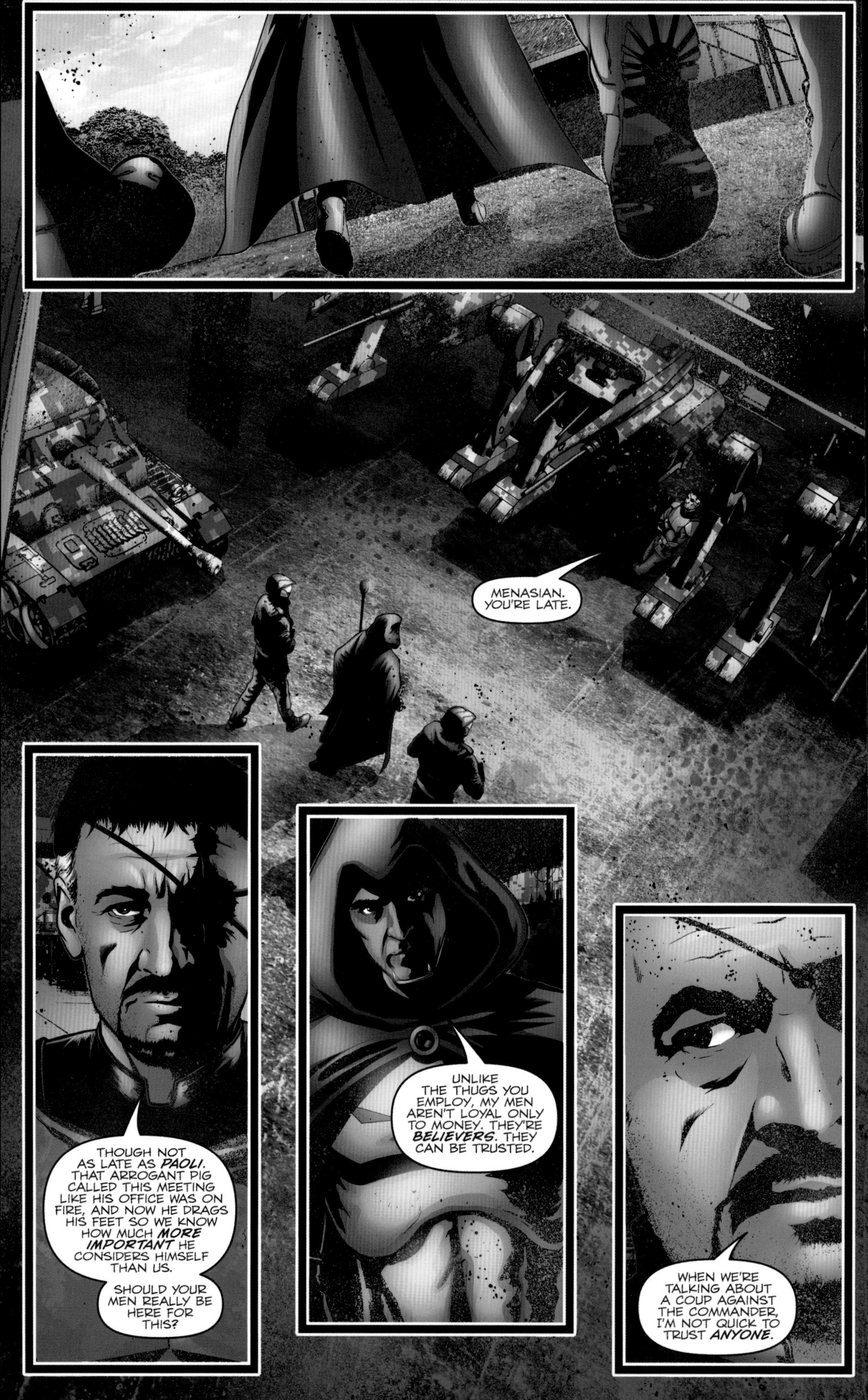
MENASIAN. YOU'RE LATE.
THOUGH NOT AS LATE AS *PAOLI*. THAT ARROGANT PIG CALLED THIS MEETING LIKE HIS OFFICE WAS ON FIRE, AND NOW HE DRAGS HIS FEET SO WE KNOW HOW MUCH *MORE IMPORTANT* HE CONSIDERS HIMSELF THAN US.
SHOULD YOUR MEN REALLY BE HERE FOR THIS?
UNLIKE THE THUGS YOU EMPLOY, MY MEN AREN'T LOYAL ONLY TO MONEY. THEY'RE *BELIEVERS*. THEY CAN BE TRUSTED.
WHEN WE'RE TALKING ABOUT A COUP AGAINST THE COMMANDER, I'M NOT QUICK TO TRUST *ANYONE*.

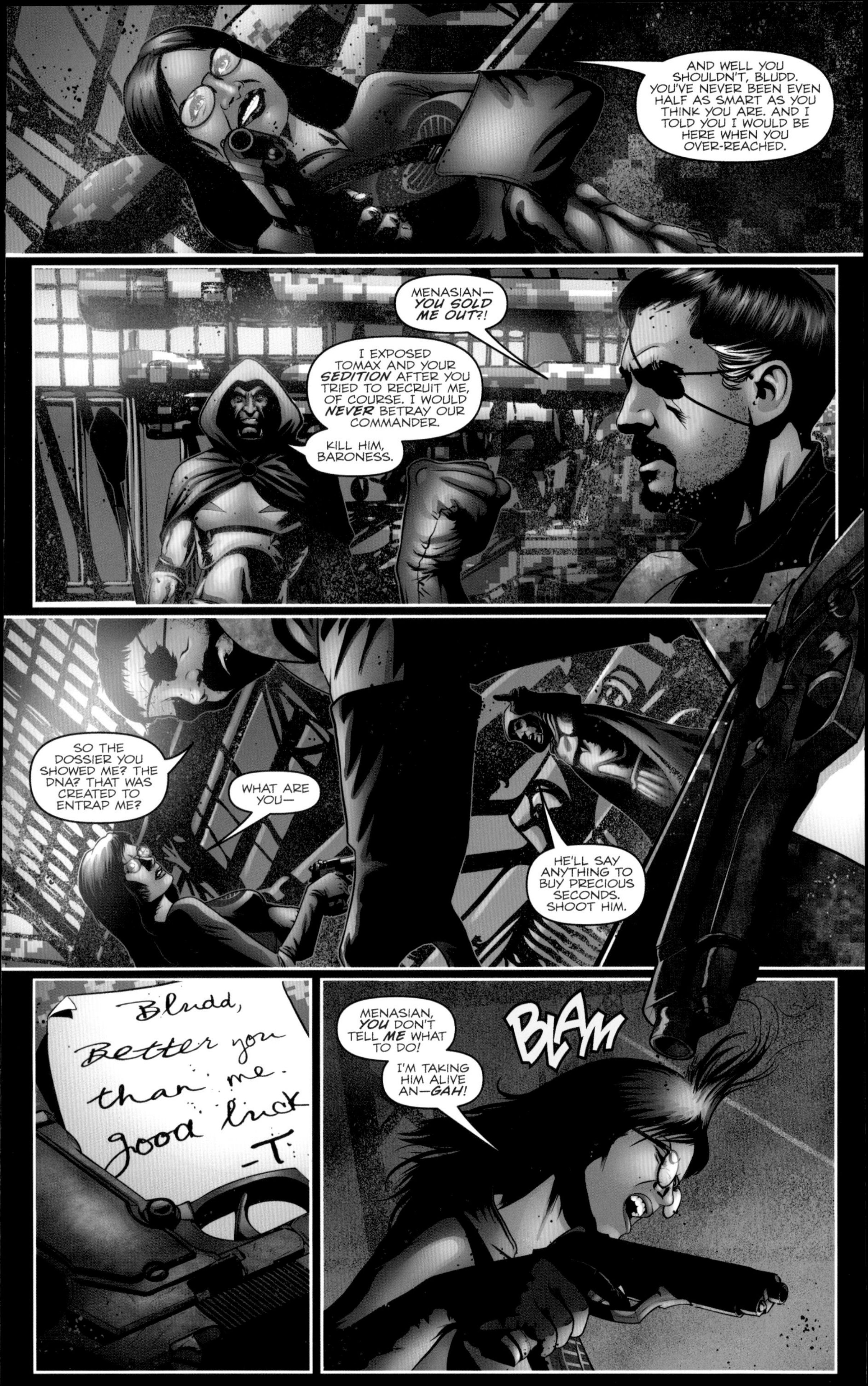

AND WELL YOU SHOULDN'T, BLUDD. YOU'VE NEVER BEEN EVEN HALF AS SMART AS YOU THINK YOU ARE. AND I TOLD YOU I WOULD BE HERE WHEN YOU OVER-REACHED.
MENASIAN— *YOU SOLD ME OUT*?!
I EXPOSED TOMAX AND YOUR *SEDITION* AFTER YOU TRIED TO RECRUIT ME, OF COURSE. I WOULD *NEVER* BETRAY OUR COMMANDER.
KILL HIM, BARONESS.
SO THE DOSSIER YOU SHOWED ME? THE DNA? THAT WAS CREATED TO ENTRAP ME?
WHAT ARE YOU—
HE'LL SAY ANYTHING TO BUY PRECIOUS SECONDS. SHOOT HIM.
Bludd, Better you than me. good luck -T.
MENASIAN, *YOU* DON'T TELL *ME* WHAT TO DO!
I'M TAKING HIM ALIVE AN—*GAH*!
BLAM

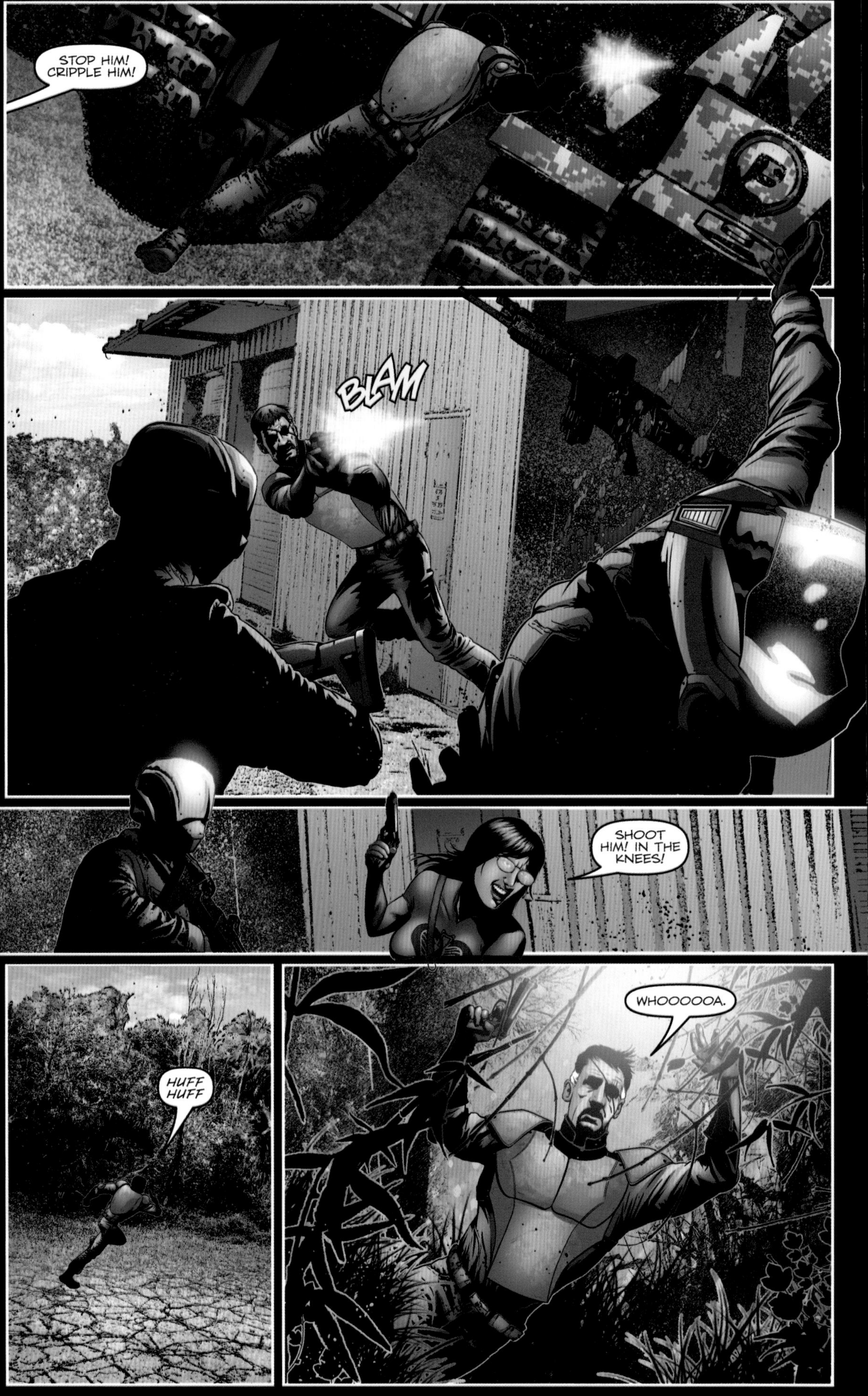
STOP HIM! CRIPPLE HIM!
BLAM
SHOOT HIM! IN THE KNEES!
HUFF HUFF
WHOOOOOA.

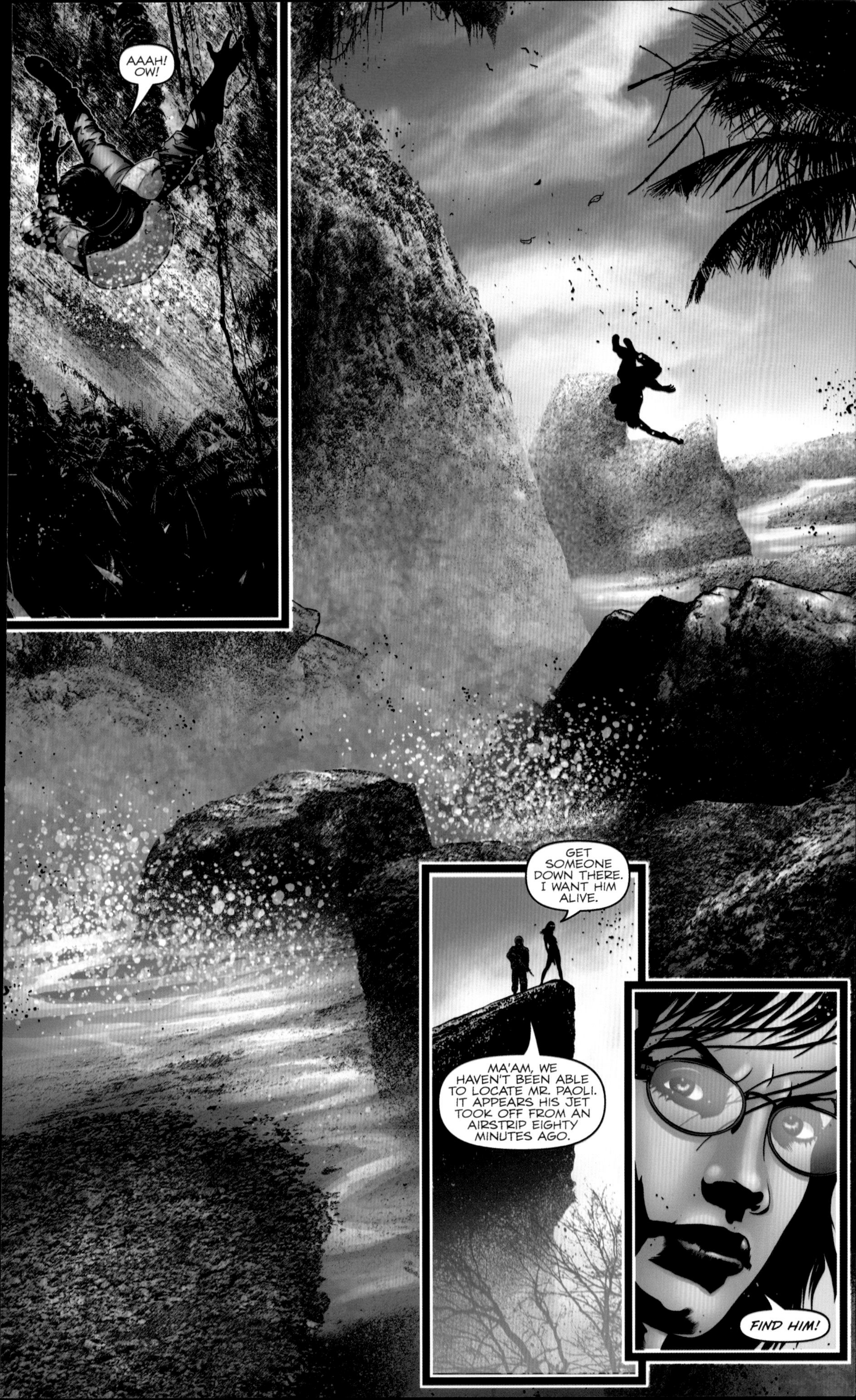
AAAH! OW!
GET SOMEONE DOWN THERE. I WANT HIM ALIVE.
MA'AM, WE HAVEN'T BEEN ABLE TO LOCATE MR. PAOLI. IT APPEARS HIS JET TOOK OFF FROM AN AIRSTRIP EIGHTY MINUTES AGO.
FIND HIM!

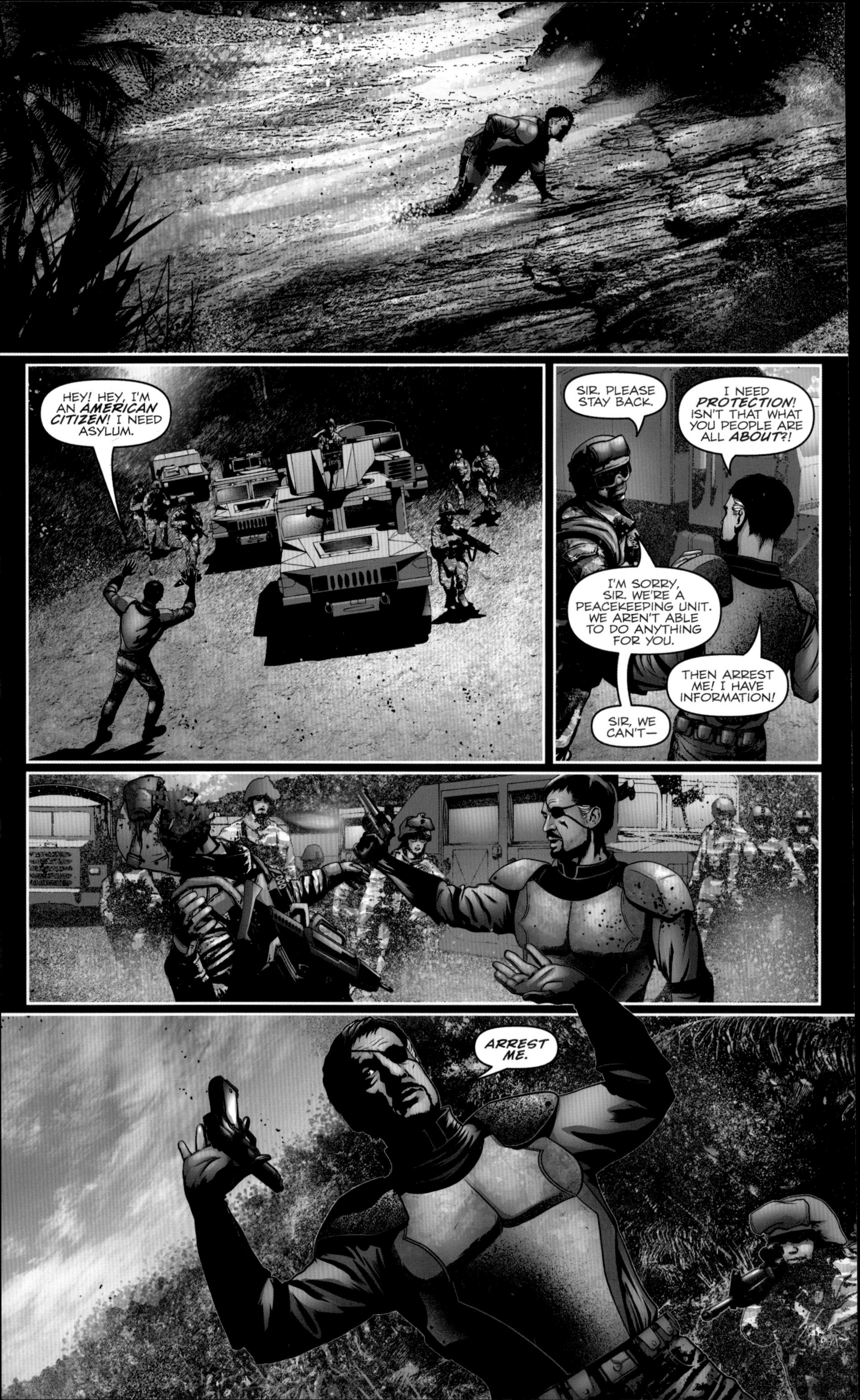
HEY! HEY, I'M AN AMERICAN CITIZEN! I NEED ASYLUM.
SIR. PLEASE STAY BACK.
I NEED PROTECTION! ISN'T THAT WHAT YOU PEOPLE ARE ALL ABOUT?!
I'M SORRY, SIR. WE'RE A PEACEKEEPING UNIT. WE AREN'T ABLE TO DO ANYTHING FOR YOU.
THEN ARREST ME! I HAVE INFORMATION!
SIR, WE CAN'T—
ARREST ME.

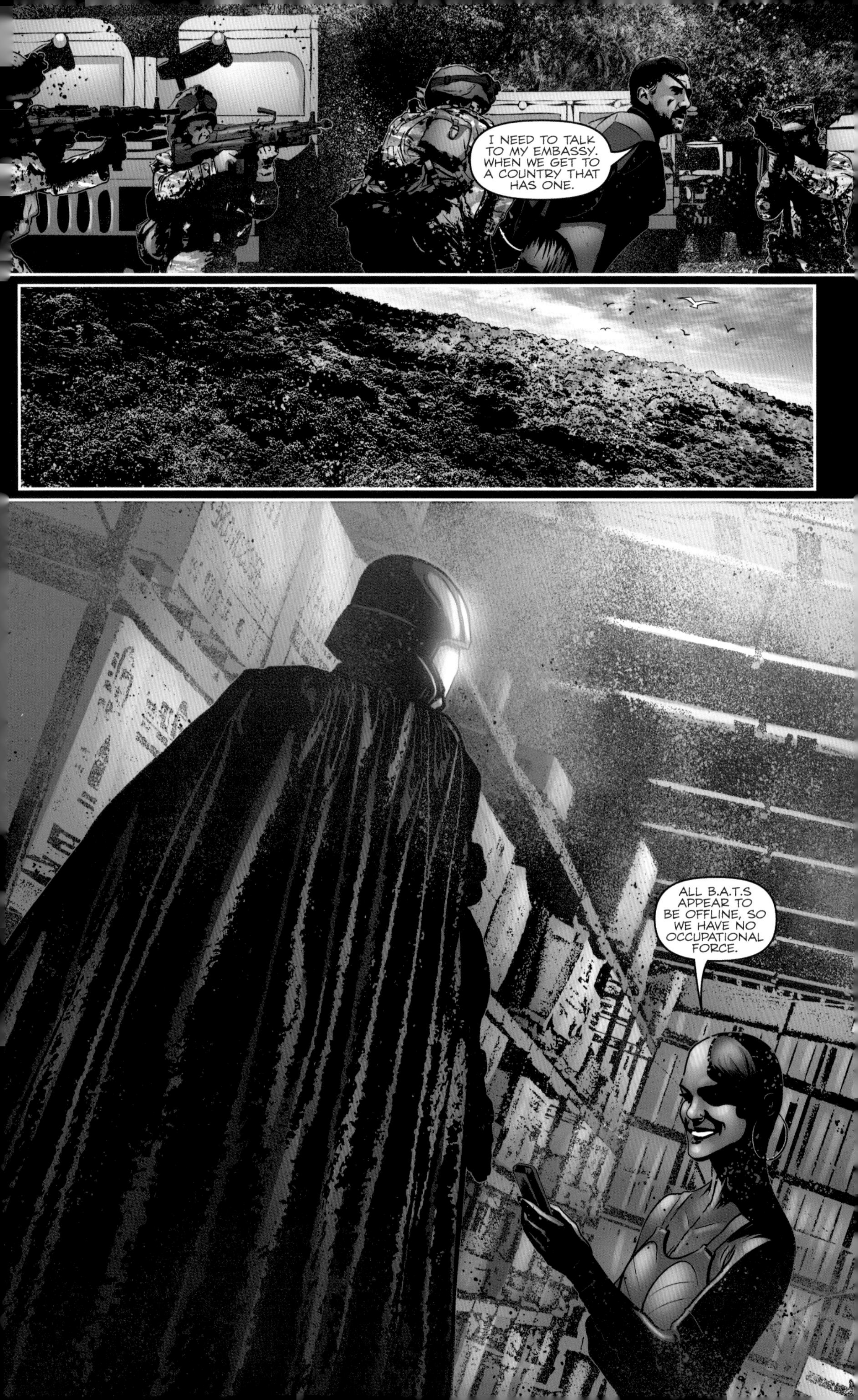
I NEED TO TALK TO MY EMBASSY. WHEN WE GET TO A COUNTRY THAT HAS ONE.
ALL B.A.T.S APPEAR TO BE OFFLINE, SO WE HAVE NO OCCUPATIONAL FORCE.

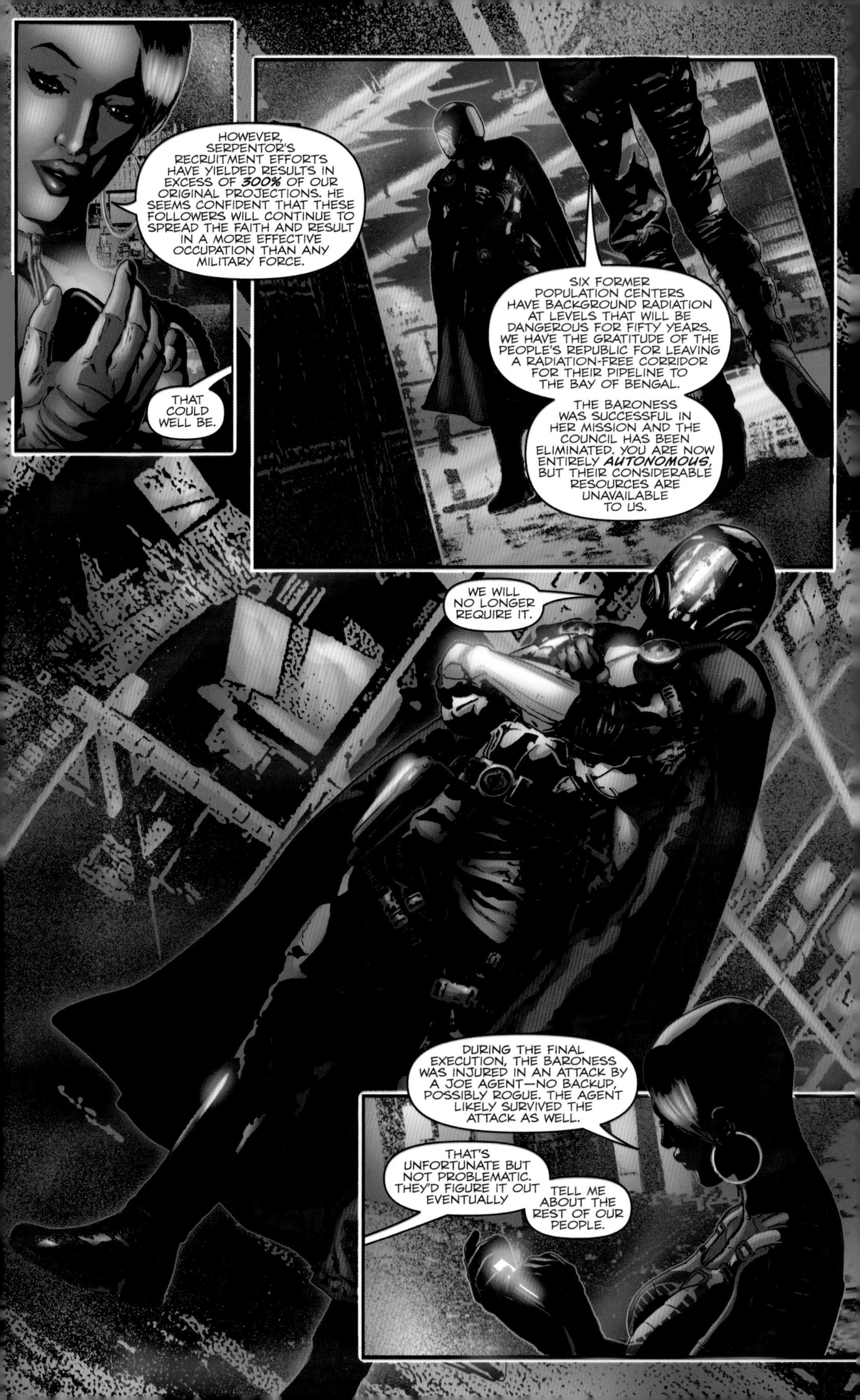

HOWEVER, SERPENTOR'S RECRUITMENT EFFORTS HAVE YIELDED RESULTS IN EXCESS OF **300%** OF OUR ORIGINAL PROJECTIONS. HE SEEMS CONFIDENT THAT THESE FOLLOWERS WILL CONTINUE TO SPREAD THE FAITH AND RESULT IN A MORE EFFECTIVE OCCUPATION THAN ANY MILITARY FORCE.
THAT COULD WELL BE.
SIX FORMER POPULATION CENTERS HAVE BACKGROUND RADIATION AT LEVELS THAT WILL BE DANGEROUS FOR FIFTY YEARS. WE HAVE THE GRATITUDE OF THE PEOPLE'S REPUBLIC FOR LEAVING A RADIATION-FREE CORRIDOR FOR THEIR PIPELINE TO THE BAY OF BENGAL.
THE BARONESS WAS SUCCESSFUL IN HER MISSION AND THE COUNCIL HAS BEEN ELIMINATED. YOU ARE NOW ENTIRELY ***AUTONOMOUS***, BUT THEIR CONSIDERABLE RESOURCES ARE UNAVAILABLE TO US.
WE WILL NO LONGER REQUIRE IT.
DURING THE FINAL EXECUTION, THE BARONESS WAS INJURED IN AN ATTACK BY A JOE AGENT—NO BACKUP, POSSIBLY ROGUE. THE AGENT LIKELY SURVIVED THE ATTACK AS WELL.
THAT'S UNFORTUNATE BUT NOT PROBLEMATIC. THEY'D FIGURE IT OUT EVENTUALLY
TELL ME ABOUT THE REST OF OUR PEOPLE.

MAJOR BLUDD FLED INTO THE JUNGLE AND DISAPPEARED. VIPERS ARE SWEEPING AND IT IS UNLIKELY HE WILL FIND SUPPORT AFTER WHAT HAPPENED TO HIS MEN, BUT HIS TRAIL HAS GONE COLD.

TOMAX PAOLI HAS DISAPPEARED ENTIRELY AND HIS ENTIRE BUSINESS INFRASTRUCTURE HAS BEEN ABANDONED. AND STORM SHADOW HAS NOT RETURNED NOR CHECKED IN IN OVER A WEEK.

HM. ACCEPTABLE.

SIR... IF I MAY...

YOU'VE BEEN SPENDING INCREASING AMOUNTS OF TIME IN HERE AMONGST THESE ITEMS. I'VE TAKEN THE LIBERTY OF INCREASING SECURITY TO EQUAL YOUR ACTUAL QUARTERS.

VERY GOOD.

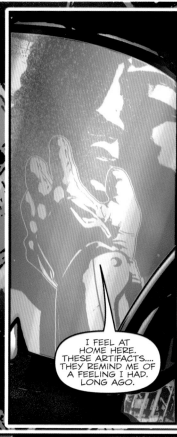

I FEEL AT HOME HERE. THESE ARTIFACTS.... THEY REMIND ME OF A FEELING I HAD. LONG AGO.

I'LL SEE TO THEIR TRANSPORT IMMEDIATELY FOR WHEN WE DEPART, AND THEIR INSTALLATION IN—

NO.

BURN IT ALL.

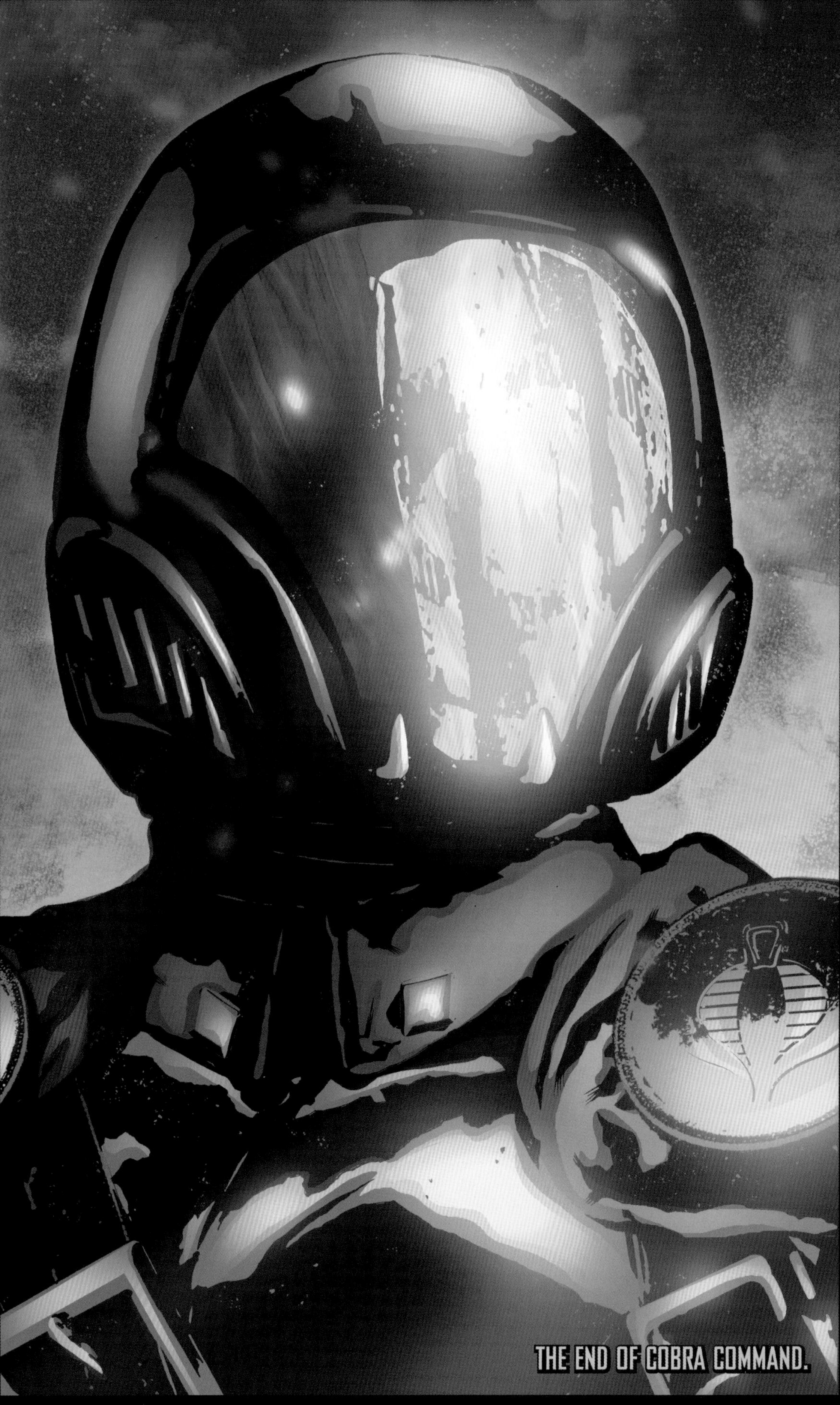
THE END OF COBRA COMMAND.

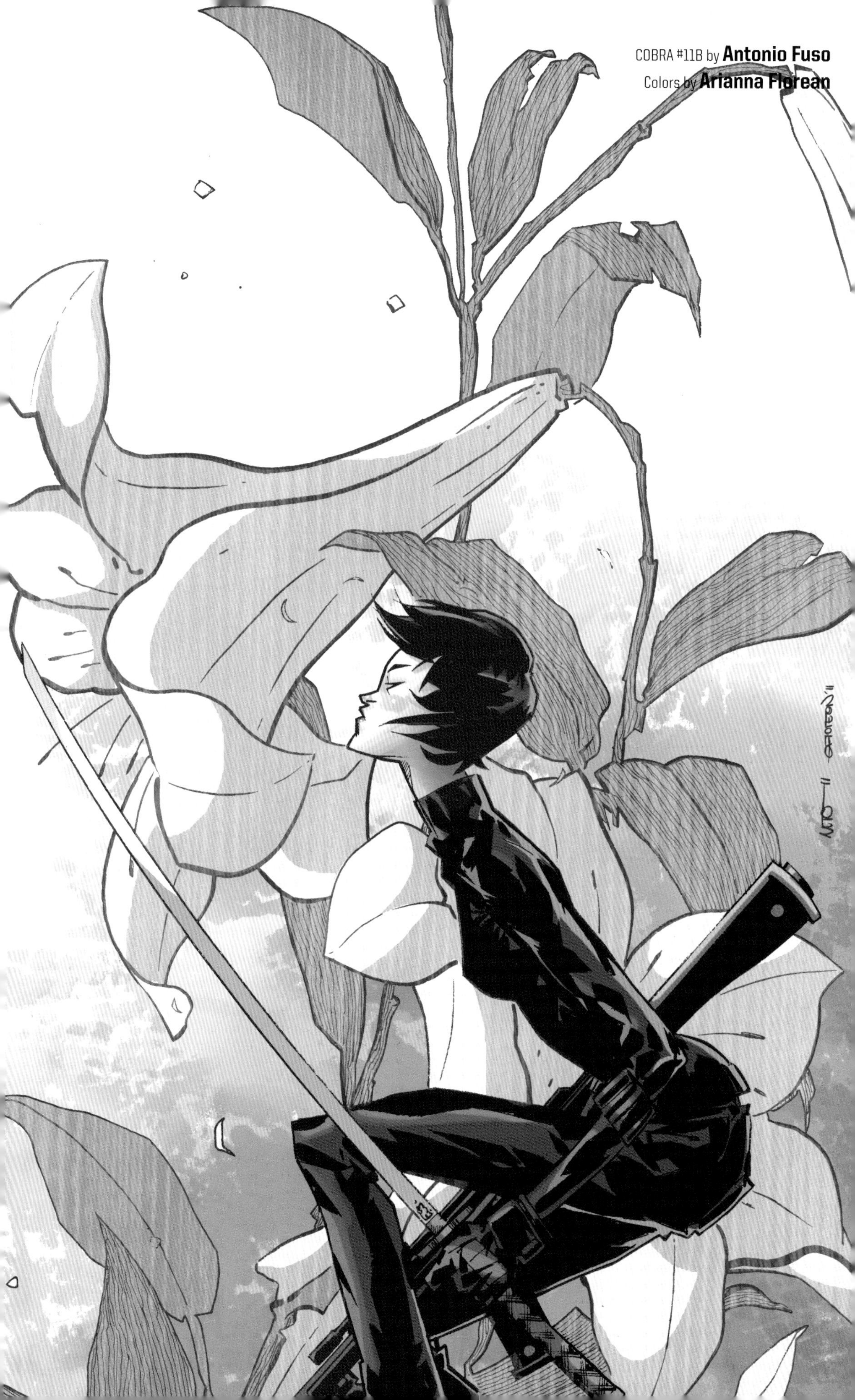

COBRA #11B by **Antonio Fuso**
Colors by **Arianna Florean**

SNAKE EYES #10RI by **Tom Whalen**

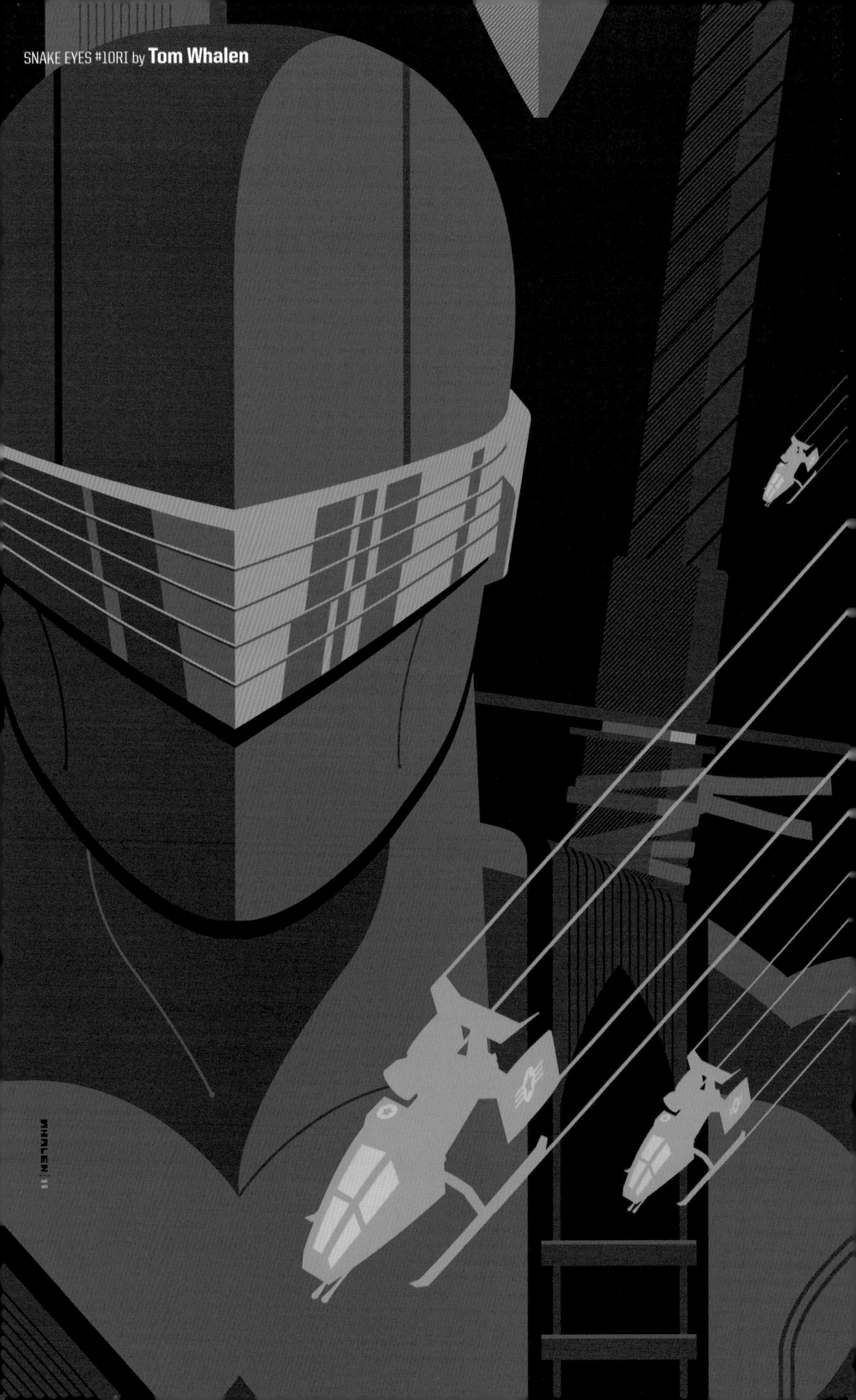

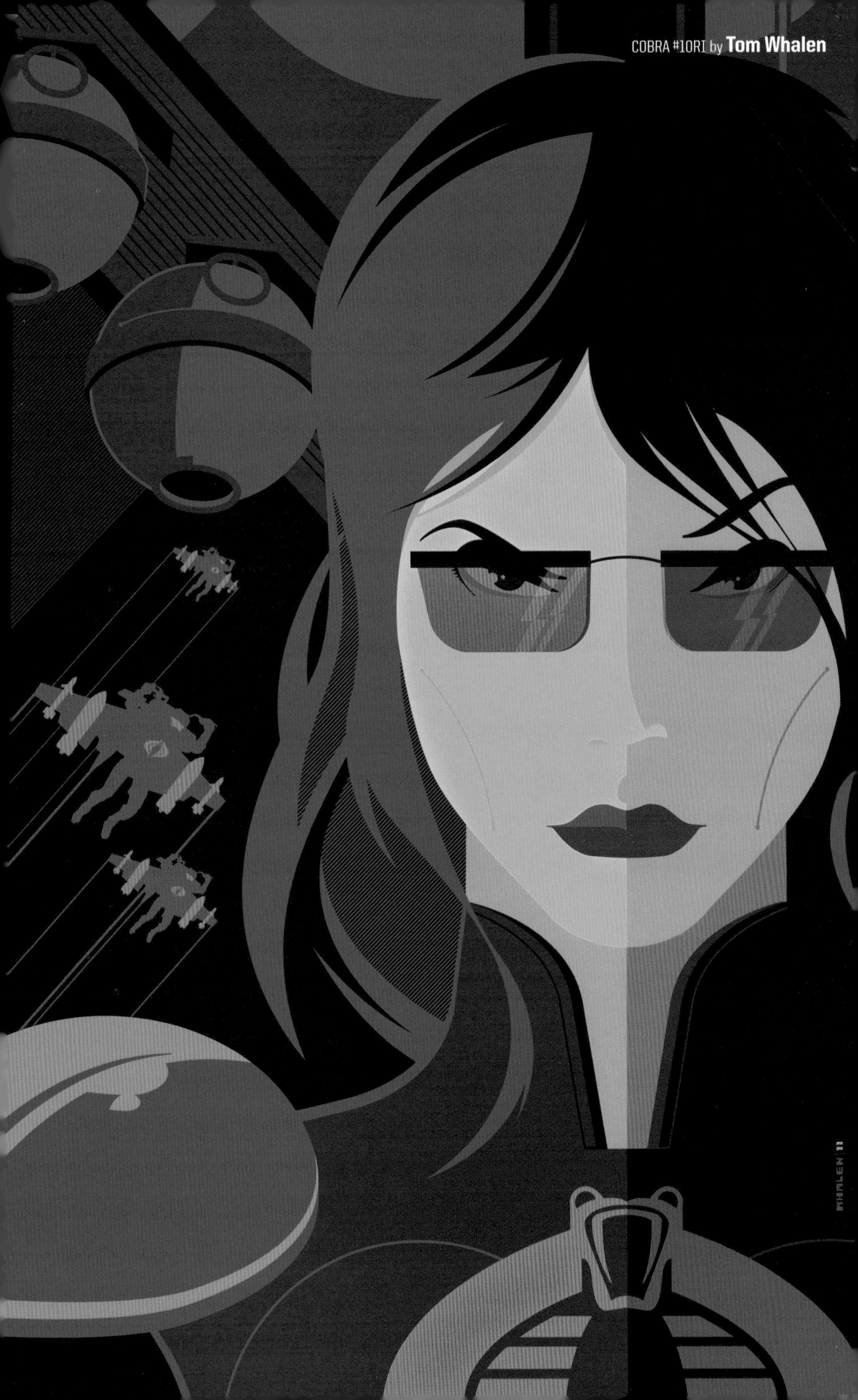

COBRA #10RI by **Tom Whalen**

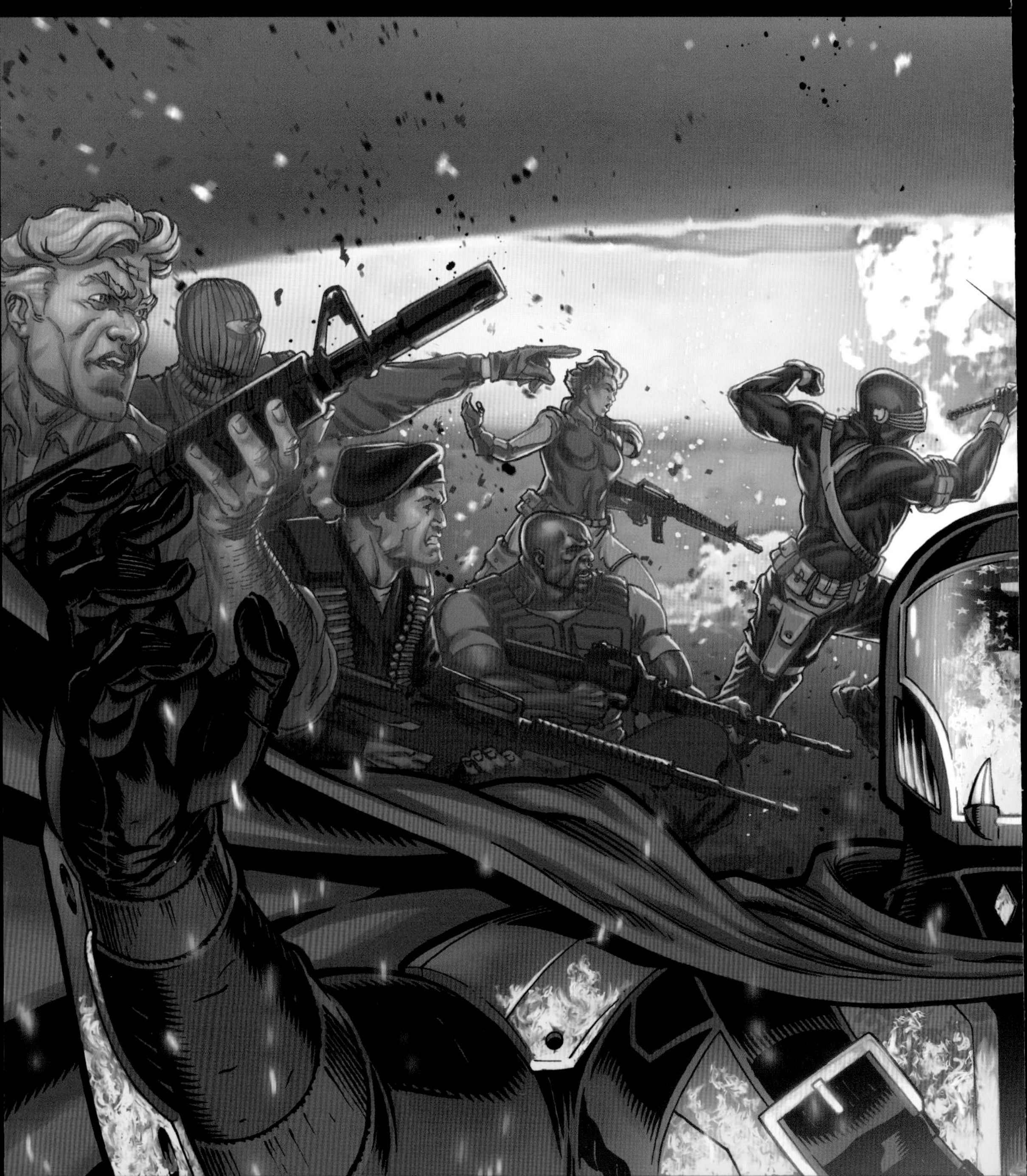

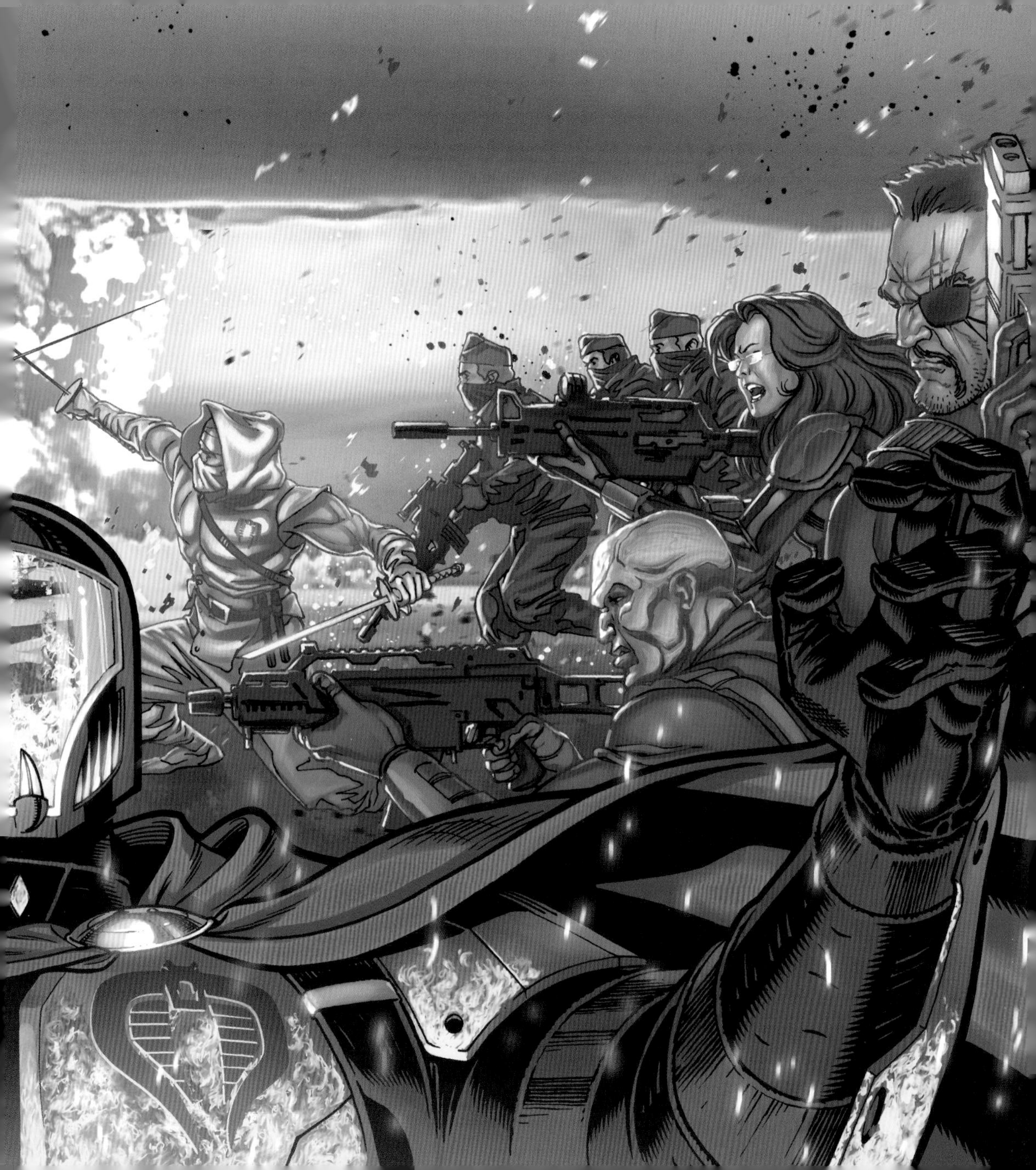

COBRA COMMAND

G.I. JOE

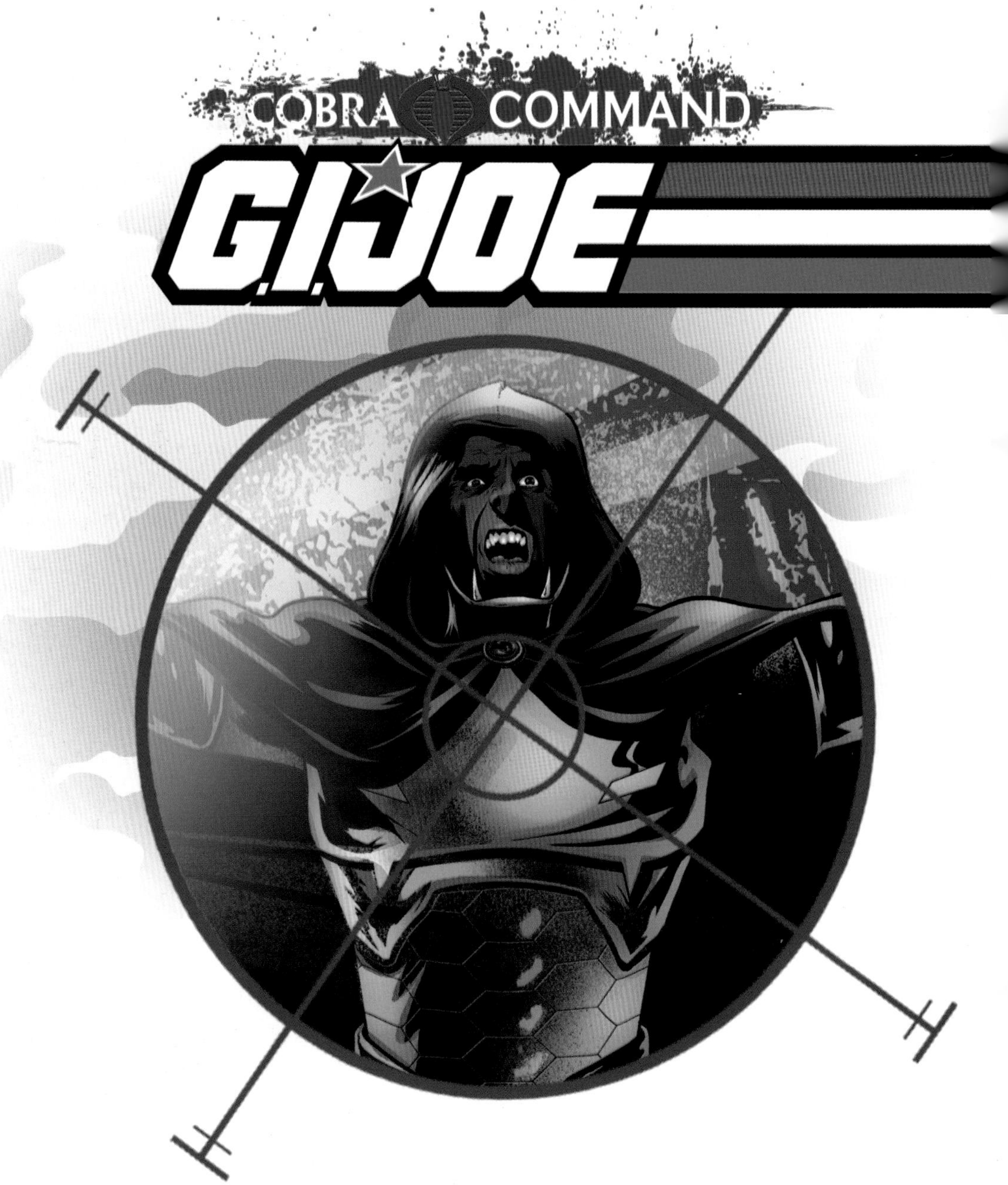